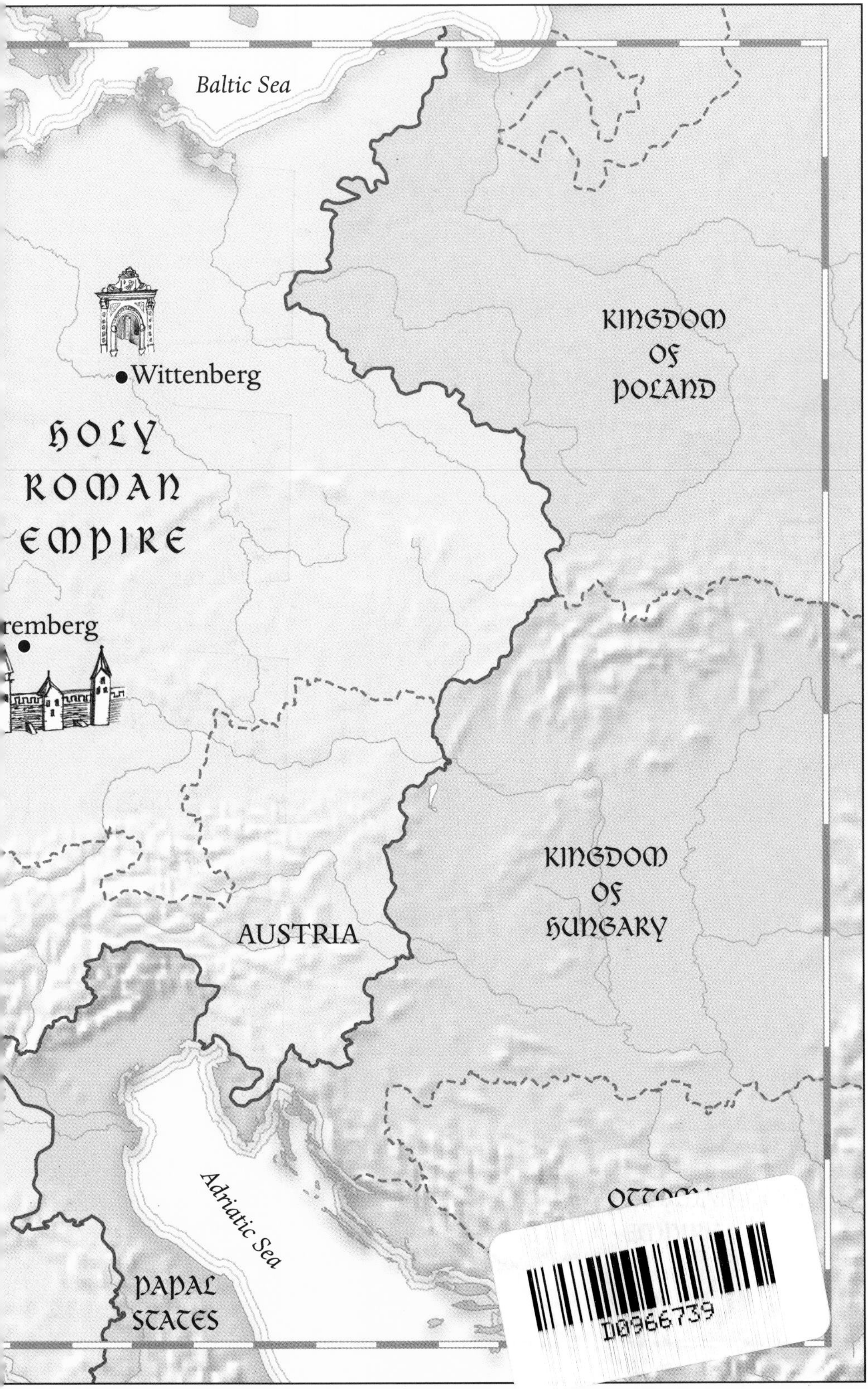

Baltic Sea
Wittenberg
HOLY ROMAN EMPIRE
KINGDOM OF POLAND
KINGDOM OF HUNGARY
AUSTRIA
Adriatic Sea
PAPAL STATES

Also by Christopher Buckley

But Enough About You

They Eat Puppies, Don't They?

Losing Mum and Pup: A Memoir

Supreme Courtship

Boomsday

Florence of Arabia

Washington Schlepped Here

No Way to Treat a First Lady

God Is My Broker (with John Tierney)

Little Green Men

Wry Martinis

Thank You for Smoking

Wet Work

Campion

The White House Mess

Steaming to Bamboola: The World of a Tramp Freighter

The Relic Master

Christopher Buckley

Simon & Schuster

New York London Toronto Sydney New Delhi

Simon & Schuster
1230 Avenue of the Americas
New York, NY 10020

First Simon & Schuster hardcover edition December 2015

Interior design by Ruth Lee-Mui
Endpaper map by Paul J. Pugliese

Manufactured in the United States of America

10 9 8 7 6 5 4 3 2 1

Library of Congress Cataloging-in-Publication Data
Buckley, Christopher, 1952–
The relic master : a novel / Christopher Buckley. — First Simon & Schuster hardcover edition.
pages ; cm
1. Antique dealers—Fiction. 2. Holy Shroud—Fiction. 3. Relics—Fiction.
I. Title.
PS3552.U3394R45 2015
813'.54—dc23 2015026355

ISBN 978-1-5011-2575-1
ISBN 978-1-5011-2578-2 (ebook)

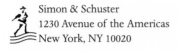

For Greg Zorthian

If even a dog's tooth is truly worshipped it glows with light. The venerated object is endowed with power . . .

—Iris Murdoch, *The Sea, the Sea*

In our corrupt times, the virtue of a Pontiff is commended when he does not surpass the wickedness of other men.

—Francesco Guicciardini, *History of Italy*, 1561

Contents

Part Two

Rome, 2017

BURIAL CLOTH FOUND IN TOMB OF 16TH-CENTURY POPE IS SAID TO BE "IDENTICAL" TO SHROUD OF TURIN

Vatican City, August 28—Workers doing repairs on the tomb of Pope Leo X in Rome's Basilica Church of Santa Maria sopra Minerva have found a cloth closely resembling the Shroud of Turin, the relic held by many to be the burial shroud of Jesus Christ.

The discovery occurred two weeks ago. Until now, the Vatican has withheld making any announcement or comment, prompting heated speculation. Word of the finding began to leak almost immediately, and the normally quiet Santa Maria has been overwhelmed by mobs of pilgrims and curiosity seekers.

According to a source within the Vatican who requested

anonymity, the discovery is "extremely problematical." In addition to the shroud's remarkable resemblance to that of Turin, the source said, "There is the question—what was it doing in Leo's tomb?"

Leo X, a member of the de' Medici family, died in 1521. He ruled as pontiff during the Protestant Reformation, and was described by one 20th-century scholar as being "as elegant and as indolent as a Persian cat." He is not held in esteem by the Church, owing to rampant corruption and decadence. His mishandling of Martin Luther's protest over the Church's sale of indulgences led to the Reformation, plunging Europe into a century and a half of religious warfare.

Pope Francis is said to have expressed "consternation" over the discovery of another shroud in his predecessor's crypt. The Church had always maintained a nuanced stance toward its most famous holy relic, neither asserting nor disclaiming its authenticity.

In 1988, after carbon-14 testing dated the Turin Shroud to between AD 1260 and 1390, the Vatican formally declared it to be a forgery. At the same time, the Church declared that the Shroud remained worthy of continued veneration "as an icon," and has certified numerous healing miracles attributed to it.

Many Christians remain convinced that the Turin Shroud is authentic, and insist that the carbon-14 testing was flawed. The discovery of what appears to be a nearly identical shroud could prove to be as problematical for them as it is for the Church.

The Vatican's Congregation for the Causes of Saints, the office within the Roman Curia responsible for the verification and preservation of holy relics, today announced that it has appointed Monsignor Silvestre Prang, S.J., to undertake "a thorough and rigorous scientific investigation" of the so-called Leo Shroud.

Prang, a Jesuit, holds a PhD in cellular and molecular physiology from Yale University. The Vatican declined to make him available for comment until his report is made public next year.

Part One

1

Basel, 1517

Dismas might have purchased the finger bone of the Apostle Thomas, but there was something not quite right about the man offering it for sale.

For one, his asking price was far too low. A relic of the finger that had probed the spear wound in Christ's side after his resurrection would fetch as much as forty or fifty gulden. And he was asking only fifteen. More troubling was the absence of fragrant odor when Dismas held it to his nostrils. A genuine relic was always pleasant to the nose. Finally, there was the variety of items the fellow had for sale: the tongue (entire) of St. Anthony of Padua; an ampulla of the Virgin's breast milk; a stone from the *scala santa*, the steps of Pilate's palace; a few pieces of straw from the *sacra incunabulum*, the holy manger in Bethlehem; and shavings from the chains of St. Peter. A suspiciously vast array of goods.

Experience inclined Dismas to trust more in dealers who concentrated in specific fields. Say, relics of the Diocletian persecution. Or *brandea*, items that had been in physical contact with the Holy Family. Relics of St. Anne, mother of the Virgin, a category at the moment in huge demand.

Most revealing of all: when Dismas thanked the man and turned to leave, he immediately lowered the price to five gulden. One saw more and more of this disgraceful behavior these days at the Basel Relic Fair.

Dismas stood in the market square in front of the new town hall with its marvelous polychrome arcades. His glance swept over the expanse, humming with commerce. There must be over three hundred exhibitors.

He noted with amusement two adjoining booths, each advertising thorns from the Crown of Thorns. Unfortunate placement. But there were so many exhibitors these days. Space was tight. Placards and banners flapped in the late afternoon breeze. One advertised a Mandylion, another a sudarium, another a foot (whole) of the Magdalene. There was always a surcharge for an entire appendage.

On the north side of the square, by the fish market, appropriately enough, was this year's most-talked-about piece: an entire boat avouched to have belonged to St. Peter in his pre-apostolic Galilean fishing days.

Owing to his status in the relic community, Dismas had been given a preview. The asking price, three thousand gulden, was preposterous, even if it were authentic, which Dismas highly doubted. To the consternation of its seller, Dismas crawled underneath with a magnifying glass. There he found wormholes of the type made by saltwater worms.

Dusting himself off, he gave the fellow a look of rebuke. Odd, wasn't it—saltwater worm damage, in a freshwater fishing vessel?

The dealer cleared his throat and said, well, see, the boat had been briefly anchored in the Mediterranean, at Joppa, before, er, being taken aboard ship for Marseille.

"Um. Well, thanks for letting me have a look."

A shame, Dismas thought, for what a splendid centerpiece it would make in the courtyard of the castle church in Wittenberg. Or the cathedral cloister at Mainz. Someone would buy it, perhaps a recently ennobled Bohemian, who'd paint it in garish colors and put it in his moat. In time he'd grow bored of it and allow his children to reenact famous sea battles in it. And finally it would rot and sink, and the nobleman would say that he'd always had his doubts about it.

More and more, these days, there was an emphasis on size. Last year, the English dealer Arnulfus of Tewksbury had brought to Basel three whole mummified camels. These, he averred, were the very ones that had carried the magi to Bethlehem, bringing gifts of gold, frankincense, and myrrh. Dismas friskily asked Arnulfus why he had not also brought with him the star in the east? Really, it was all getting a bit out of hand.

How many years now had he been coming to the relic fair? His first time was in 1508, so—nearly ten, now. Realizing this made him feel old, for embedded in the math was the alas undeniable fact that he was now past thirty years of age.

He thought back to the time he'd first stood here in the square, almost in this very spot. There'd been a quarter the number of booths and tents. Who'd have imagined such growth as this? The *annus mirabilis* was 1513. These last four years had been almost indecently profitable for Dismas, owing to the passion—lust, really—for relics on the part of his two principal clients.

He bought a grilled sausage and a mug of lager from a vendor and, finding shade, consulted his purchase lists.

Frederick's wish list had four dozen items. Albrecht's was, as usual, more extensive: nearly three hundred. Though he would never admit it—even to Dismas, his chief supplier—Albrecht was determined to catch up to Frederick, whose collection now stood at more than fifteen thousand holy relics. Dismas sighed. He was tempted to blow Albrecht's entire budget on the St. Peter's fishing boat and be done with it. Frederick's list was, no surprise, far more discerning than Albrecht's. Frederick wanted quality; Albrecht, quantity.

"Saint Bartholomew—jaw particles, teeth, skull fragments (frontal)."

Frederick was mad for St. Bartholomew. Insatiable. He owned more than forty relics of the apostle, including his entire facial skin. Bartholomew had been flayed alive by the King of Armenia for introducing Christianity. The apostolic epidermis was mounted in Wittenberg in a splendid jeweled monstrance.

There were theories about Frederick's Bartholomew obsession. One was that it was due to Bartholomew being the patron saint of bookbinders. Frederick was a great bibliophile. A more mischievous theory was that it was snobbery, Bartholomew being the only apostle born of noble blood, though Dismas could find no scriptural authority for this. Sometimes, when Frederick was in the right mood, Dismas teased him about it.

St. Afra was also on Frederick's list. Always a challenge, Afra. She reflected Frederick's current taste for German saints. She'd been a prostitute of the Roman Temple of Venus in what was now Augsburg. She converted. When she refused to renounce her new god, she was taken to an island in the river Lech, tied to a stake, and suffocated with smoke. Frederick wanted her relics because she was a martyr of the Diocletian persecution and Diocletiana had long been a theme with him.

Dismas rarely proposed a specific relic unless it was something truly unusual or spectacular. Frederick's knowledge of the field was vast and scholarly. He'd been collecting relics since 1493, when he made his pilgrimage to the Holy Land. He knew exactly what he wanted and, happily for Dismas, he wanted a lot. His collection was now second only to the Vatican's, which numbered some seventy-six thousand. But there was really no competing with Rome for relics.

And yet—Dismas suspected that Frederick *was* competing with Rome. Certainly, Albrecht was competing with Frederick. Unlike Frederick, Albrecht was suggestible, especially where vogue entered in. When fourth-century Slavic martyrs became the rage, Albrecht dispatched Dismas to comb the Adriatic coast and corner the market. Frederick was above these vicissitudes. He set the chic.

Dismas returned to his list.

St. Agatha, patroness of wet nurses. A young and beautiful Sicilian girl, virgin, lusted for by the Roman consul. (How lucky, the homely, unlusted after female Christian converts.) Agatha refused the consul's attentions and was handed over to the torturers. They sliced off her breasts, which miraculously grew back. The now livid consul ordered her to be roasted to death over coals. Frederick wanted a nipple, but any other part would do.

After months and months of inquiry, Dismas reported to Frederick that no Agathan nipples were to be had. However, he had succeeded in locating a partly melted gold ring said to have been on her finger when she met her terrible but sanctifying end on a brazier in Catania, Anno Domini 250.

As for St. Afra, another martyr requiring assiduous searching, he'd finally located a fragment of her patella. Given the time and effort that had gone into these two commissions, Dismas could have charged more than his usual commission. But he didn't. If the search had been for Albrecht, he'd have surcharged triple.

He consulted Albrecht's list. Weaponry. Albrecht had a penchant for knives, daggers, axes—anything that had been used on a saint. One of his most treasured pieces was the hammer used to drive the nails into Christ's hands and feet.

Item: "Maurice—sword." The one used to decapitate St. Maurice, Roman legionary of Thebes. During a campaign to punish the insurrectionary Helvetii, the Roman commander had ordered his men to sacrifice to the Roman gods. Maurice and other Christian converts in the ranks demurred. The commander ordered decimation, every tenth soldier killed. (Hardly morale boosting, in the middle of a campaign.) When the converts still refused, a second decimation was carried out. When they refused again, the commander ordered the entire troop slaughtered.

No easy commission, this, but Dismas had a good relationship with a dealer in St. Gallen who'd sent word that he thought he could lay his hands on at least a portion of the sword hilt.

Dismas worked his way down Albrecht's list. Not another? Yes, another St. Sebastian arrow.

Albrecht had a particular taste for apostate Roman soldiery, and in that category, St. Sebastian reigned as the beau ideal. Into the bargain, Sebastian was a member of the Emperor Diocletian's own Praetorian Guard. The irony with Sebastiana was that he survived the firing squad of archers. Perhaps they'd taken pity on him and fired into nonessential parts. When Diocletian learned that his former bodyguard was still alive (if presumably heavily bandaged) and still ministering to Christians, he furiously ordered him to be hacked into pieces until well and truly dead, then tossed into the Cloaca Maxima, the Roman sewer. Sebastian arrows were always in demand, and not just by Albrecht. Over the course of his relic-hunting career, Dismas had come across enough of them to supply the entire Roman army.

Next on Albrecht's list was another item wielded by a Roman soldier. The Holy Lance. He sighed.

Again and again—and again—Dismas had explained to the Archbishop, ever so patiently, that the "one and true" Holy Lance was simply not available. Yes, the relic marts teemed with "one and true" Holy Lances—dozens, scores. But as Dismas had pointed out, the spear tip most likely to have pierced Christ's side was in a vault in St. Peter's. In Rome. Since 1492, when Sultan Bayazid of Constantinople had gifted it to Pope Innocent VIII, by way of lessening the pontiff's inclination to crusade. Dismas had told Albrecht that it was beyond all likelihood that the present Pope Leo X would part with such a prize piece. Though Leo, being Leo, might be induced to sell. His asking price would be exorbitant. All this Dismas had explained, only to be told by Albrecht that he was not convinced that the one true Holy Lance really was in the Vatican. By which he meant: *Just bring me a lance. Any lance.*

Since arriving in Basel a week ago, Dismas had been offered no fewer than ten "one and true" Holy Lances, one for as little as twenty-five gulden. Absurd. His integrity would not allow it, even if it meant being able to scratch "Holy Lance" off Albrecht's wish list once and for all.

In all his years of relic hunting, Dismas had never wittingly purchased or sold a relic he knew to be fraudulent. To be sure, with relics it was impossible to be entirely confident of the provenance. You never really knew that it was the thumb bone of St. Contumacious of Tyre, or a bar of the iron grille on which St. Lawrence was broiled alive. All you could do was honor your profession and the relevant questions: Did the relic emit fragrance? Had there been verification by ordeal? Had it caused a miraculous healing? Finally, had the saint permitted it to be stolen from its prior shrine? The correct term was "translation." There was logic to it: Saints were living beings, even dead. No saint, or member of the Holy Family, would permit his or her relic to be translated from one owner to another unless they favored relocation.

Another test was: Had the saint exacted punishment if his relic had been disrespected? St. Appianus had famously paralyzed a young woman when she squatted to urinate beside his tomb. She remained frozen in this mortifying posture until the entire town, including the bishop, interceded with prayers for her forgiveness.

So at the end of the day, a reputable relic hunter had only his judgment—and honesty—on which to rely. Alas, of late there had been a marked increase in counterfeit and charlatanry, of hunters and dealers of the most dubious kind. Like all too many of the characters here in Basel.

Dismas had shared his chagrin with Master Schenk, chief registrar of the relic fair. Schenk said, yes, yes, indeed, it *was* unfortunate. He suggested that Dismas, so respected by his peers, should address the exhibitors himself on the subject. Schenk would arrange it. Dismas could share his misgivings with the other brokers and vendors on the final day of the relic fair, at the farewell wine and cheese reception.

Crafty Schenk. He clapped Dismas on the back and smiled. A splendid idea. He left Dismas to rebuke himself for letting himself be trapped. A speech—on standards—to this bunch? As well preach chastity in a bawdy house. Too late now. Dismas made his way to the town hall in gloom.

"Dismas?"

"Markus? Is it—you?"

They embraced with the intensity of two men who've stood side by side in battle. Their last battle together had been the disaster at Cerignola, when they'd fought on the French side. The Spaniards had inferior numbers but had brought to the field something new, terrible, and loud called gunpowder.

When it was over, Dismas and Markus were among sixteen of their unit of ninety still alive on a field sponge-soft with blood and air rank with smoke, staring at the bodies of their comrades. Their armor was strangely pocked with holes that seeped. Dismas saw it as a portent of the End of Days, gave up his career as a mercenary, and put on a monk's habit at the nearest monastery.

"What on Earth are you doing here?" Dismas said. "Not bone dealing, sure?"

Markus made a face. "God help me. I haven't sunk that low. Helping some fat-assed banker guard his gold. After this I'm finished. Going home. To the cantons. I've got money saved. I'll find myself a girl with red cheeks, big tits, and a creamy-white bottom."

Dismas laughed. "You're too old for that."

"Old? I've got a cock of iron. So what are *you* doing here?" Markus looked his old friend up and down. He said suspiciously, "You look prosperous. What crimes have you committed? God in Heaven, don't tell me you're"—he gestured over his shoulder at the mass of relic dealers—"one of *these* lowlifes?"

"I am. And I'll thank you not to call me a lowlife. I'm an honest man."

"Honest? Hawking pieces of the True Cross? Breast milk of the Virgin? How much did you get for your soul, then?"

"Listen to you. A gold sentry. I'm a respectable man."

"I thought you were going to be a monk."

"Did. Couldn't get used to the hours."

"All right," Markus said, "I'll listen to your lies, but you're buying the drinks."

"I have to give a speech. Let's meet later. And yes, I'll buy the drinks. As usual. If I'm going to listen to your lies, I'll need to be good and proper sloshed."

"Giving a speech? To this scum? What are you speeching about? How to rob tombs?"

"As it happens, about reform. Which they won't want to hear. Maybe you should come along. *I* might need guarding."

"I've got better things to do than listen to you give the Sermon on the Mount. I'll see you later. The Red Boar. Near the Saint Alban tower."

Dismas's mood was much brightened, but the cheer dissipated when he entered the great hall, noisy and sweaty and loud with hundreds of relicmongers. The event was open only to the trade. The wine and lager were flowing.

Schenk saw him and came over. His face was apple-florid from wine. He was in an excellent frame. Sales had been brisk, topping even last year's record. He banged his gavel to quiet the crowd. Told them how wonderful they were, what a success it had all been, how good it was to be among so many old friends and among new friends.

Dismas thought, *It's these new friends who are the problem.*

Schenk went on about the great responsibility of their business. Then with a snort said, "And here to tell us a bit about that is a person—no, more than a person. He is a *personage*!" Schenk chortled at his cleverness. "A personage known to us all, esteemed everywhere. Especially"—he crooked a thumb over his shoulder to the north—"up there!"

Dismas stepped forward in an effort to cut him off, but Schenk's bonhomie, fueled by the wine, was implacable. He went on about Dismas, the Personage. Dismas, the Legend. Relic Master by Appointment to His Grace Albrecht, Archbishop of Brandenburg and Mainz. Relic Master by Appointment to the Elector Frederick of Saxony, Frederick the Wise. And before that, he'd been Dismas the Soldier, the *Reiselaufer*. "So don't make him angry or he'll cut off your balls!"

Dismas said to laughter, "I'll do that to you if you don't sit down and shut up."

But Schenk went on, regaling them about Dismas's early years in the trade—in the Holy Land, how he'd been the first relic hunter to procure an entire skeleton of one of the holy innocents slaughtered by Herod's soldiers. The audience murmured and nodded. Schenk said, "It's in the collection of Frederick, in Wittenberg."

Then he was on to Dismas's years in the catacombs outside Rome.

"That cough of his? You've heard his cough?" Schenk imitated Dismas's cough. "That's from the catacombs!" Murmurs, applause.

Dismas couldn't take any more. He put his arm on Schenk's shoulder and declared, "I think our dear Schenk is the truest relic here!" Laughter.

Schenk said, "I warn you—he's going to give us a lecture, so, quick, fill your glasses—and cover your ears with your hands!"

Dismas knew there was no point in talking ethics to a boozed-up crowd with purses bulging with guldens. Better just to tell them, Well, fellows, it's been a good year, and here's to us. But let's at least *try* as we go forward to keep in mind that ours is a special calling, a sacred calling, really, and as a . . .

He looked out over the sea of glassy eyes.

He had to force the phrase from his lips . . . a confraternity of professionals, we . . . we . . .

They stared back, blearily.

"Well," Dismas said, "we have to hold ourselves to standards. That's all."

Silence. Stares. *What in God's name is he talking about?*

Dismas sucked in his breath and said, "I've seen some items this week that frankly do not represent the highest standard."

Someone in the crowd shouted, "If it's standards you give a shit about, what about your Tetzel?"

A roar of approval.

"He is not my Tetzel," Dismas said. He loathed Tetzel, but he had to be somewhat careful here. "You can have him."

Scattered laughter. But now indulgence hawking was on the table.

"He works for your Archbishop Albrecht!"

Dismas held up his hands in surrender.

"My Tetzel? My Albrecht? Friend, if the Archbishop of Mainz hires Friar Tetzel to sell indulgences for him, what would you have me do? I'm just a bone dealer, like yourself. Bones bring pilgrims. Pilgrims bring money. This is the business we have chosen."

"That's well and fine," someone shouted. "But if you're going to preach about standards, preach to Tetzel."

"Preach? To a Dominican?"

Laughter.

"Didn't he claim that his indulgences could free a man from Purgatory even if he had ravished the Virgin?"

Into the silence that fell—the topic of carnal relations with the Mother of God had a sobering effect—Dismas said, "If Tetzel said such a thing, then he should buy an indulgence for himself. As for me, I need a drink, before you bastards finish it all off yourselves."

Dismas's inquisitor sought him out. He was a Milanese named Vitranelli. His field was lapidary relics. Pieces of the Via Dolorosa, on which Jesus walked to his death; the stone he stepped on when he ascended to Heaven; rocks used to stone saints to death. His manner was courtly. He said he hadn't meant to sound flippant. But surely Master Dismas agreed that indulgence sales, especially in Brandenburg and other parts of the Empire, were a scandal.

The Milanese seemed a good fellow. Dismas said to him, as one professional to another, "Look, Tetzel makes me want to puke. But what would you have me do? He works for Albrecht. Albrecht is a client. A big client. Do you lecture your clients about their employees?"

Vitranelli shrugged in a distinctly Milanese way. "I am concerned because Tetzel will destroy it for all of us. Sooner or later, someone will say, Enough! It is time again to drive the money changers from the temple. To clean the stables. And if it should come to that, what will become of *us*?"

Dismas nodded. He understood all this very well. His other

principal client, Frederick of Saxony, was repelled by the outrageous indulgence hawking by Albrecht and Tetzel. Frederick did not permit Tetzel to ply his trade inside the borders of Saxony. So Tetzel set up shop just over the border, infuriating Frederick. But what could he do about it? So long as Tetzel remained on Brandenburg soil, he was under the protection of Albrecht.

Vitranelli insinuated that Frederick's "outrage" was really only jealousy, putting on airs. Pope Leo had issued a bull licensing Albrecht to sell indulgences (splitting the proceeds fifty-fifty with Rome). The bull had also nullified all *other* indulgence sales sold within the Holy Roman Empire, including Frederick's. Albrecht had the monopoly. If you wanted to buy yourself, or a loved one, out of Purgatory, you had to get the indulgence from Albrecht. To be sure, others continued to sell them—including Frederick—but they lacked the sanction of Rome. And could thus be considered worthless. A dizzying business, indulgences.

Dismas conceded Signore Vitranelli's point about Frederick's indulgence selling. Galling, to concede a point of ethics to a Milanese! He said to him in a just-between-us way, "Here's the situation, as you yourself know. Albrecht's family, the Brandenburgs, want power, as much as they can get. They wanted the archbishopric for their little Albrecht. But he was only twenty-three at the time, too young by canon law to be archbishop. So what did they do? Arranged for a papal dispensation."

He continued. "But a dispensation like that costs a fortune. So they went to Jacob Fugger, the banker of Augsburg. Fugger provided the money. They bought the dispensation.

"Then the Electorate of Mainz came available for purchase. And that's real power, to be one of the seven electors of the Holy Roman Empire. They who decide who's going to be emperor. Now the Brandenburgs want *that* for their young Albrecht as well. So it was back to Fugger for more gold—this time, twenty-one thousand ducats.

"Now Albrecht had to sell indulgences, a lot of indulgences, in order to pay back his loans. And so," Dismas said, "we have his Friar Tetzel and his circus. Meanwhile, Pope Leo is supposed to be using his fifty percent share of Albrecht's indulgence sales to rebuild Saint Peter's in Rome. In marble, with a great dome."

Dismas smiled. "But as you in Milan, and as we here know very well, Leo has other expenses. His pet albino elephant, Hanno. His hunting lodges. His banquets and revels and associated carnalities, which make the *Satyricon* of Petronius look like a lenten retreat. And in the end, everyone is working for Fugger."

"Who is German," Vitranelli said, with a note of triumph.

"Yes, German," Dismas said. "I don't suggest that venality is a uniquely Italian characteristic. But whether all this is what Our Lord had in mind when he said, 'Go forth and multiply,' is"—he shrugged—"well, it's a question for theologians. Not for a grubby bone dealer like myself."

Signor Vitranelli smiled and conceded that indeed, the workings of divine grace were beyond the comprehension of man.

This settled, they refilled their cups and drank.

Dismas said, "As to the venality of the Germans, sure, there's Fugger. And yes, Frederick displays his relics, and yes, people pay for the privilege of venerating them. And purchase indulgences. And convince themselves that this will lessen their time in Purgatory. But what money Frederick makes selling indulgences, he spends on building his university and Castle Church. Not on pet elephants and banquets. It's something to see, his university. And I'll tell you this, signore. He and the other German princes are less and less happy to be sending guldens and ducats over the Alps to Pope Leo in Rome. To help him to pay for all that marble."

"How many relics does Frederick have?"

"Fifteen thousand. Perhaps more."

Vitranelli made a face. "That's a good client. And you have two."

"I don't complain. They're very different people. For Albrecht, the relics are business. Frederick loves his relics for themselves. When

I'm hunting for him, it's . . . well"—he grinned—"I don't like to say 'quest.' Three years in the Holy Land will cure you of that word, sure. But I feel good when I am searching for him. With Albrecht it feels more like . . . well, I can't explain. I'm drunk, you see."

Vitranelli held up his cup. "Holy bones."

"Holy bones," Dismas said to the clunk of pewter. He left to find Markus at the Red Boar.

2

Rhine

From Basel Dismas traveled north to Mainz. He would have preferred to be going to Wittenberg, via Nuremberg, for then in Nuremberg he could visit with his friend Dürer, pass a pleasant night or two at the Edengarten, his favorite bordel, sleep in his own bed, then proceed on to Wittenberg and Frederick's court. But Albrecht was impatient and had sent word that he wanted his purchases without delay. So Mainz first it must be.

It was not an especially arduous journey by boat down the Rhine, except for the incessant self-appointed toll takers demanding money. He hired a skiff with good cargo space and four stout Swabian oarsmen. This time of year the water was low and the current less swift. Markus agreed to keep him company. Always good to have someone with his skills. If the wind held fair, and the Swabians did not malinger, as Swabians were prone to, they would make Mainz in less than a week.

Late afternoon on the first day Dismas and Markus sat on the afterdeck watching the sun bronze the trees along the eastern bank. Beyond loomed the darker evergreens of the Black Forest.

"You should have bought that Saint Peter's fishing boat for your archbishop," Markus said, oiling his crossbow with a cloth. "Then you wouldn't have had to hire this tub."

Dismas grunted. "I don't think the Archbishop would have cared about the sea worms."

Markus wound the cranequin on his crossbow, winching back the string.

"In the old days," Dismas said, "you could do that without sounding like an old man straining at a crap."

"Shut up and steer your boat. If you can manage it."

Markus cranked. The string angled until it caught in the nut. Dismas knew the crossbow well. Markus had held on to it all these years. He remembered how at Cerignola, before the Spaniard arquebusiers opened fire and everything went to hell, Markus had made a miraculous shot across the field of battle, sending a bolt through the visor of a Spaniard captain of cavalry, *as he charged*.

He was fast, too, Markus. He could get off three bolts in the time it took to count fifty. He wasn't bad with pike and halberd either. Or mace, or ax, or sword. Any weapon, really. Dismas had seen him use them all.

"I hope your eyesight's better than your failing strength," Dismas said. They had always been this way with each other, fraternally abusive.

Markus shouldered the crossbow, aiming at the eastern bank, a half furlong distant. Whatever he was aiming at was beyond range of Dismas's eyesight.

Markus squeezed the trigger lever. The string released with a snap. The bolt whistled forward, arcing toward the shore. A moment later came the smack of metal on wood. Voices. Markus lowered the crossbow and smirked. Dismas turned the rudder toward the shore, toward the shouting.

It was a small fishing village with a chapel. The voices grew louder as the boat neared. A clutch of villagers stood along the shore shaking their fists and tools. A stone's throw from the bank, Dismas turned the rudder parallel to it. No sense landing in the middle of a clutch of furious peasantry. He ordered the Swabians to stop rowing but to be ready to put their backs into it.

Now they could make out the shouts. They were being called names: devils, fiends, blasphemers, Jews.

"Markus. Look what you've done."

Markus pointed at the church. Dismas couldn't make it out at first. Then he saw.

"Markus."

The bolt protruded from the center of the wooden cross atop the church. The precise center, where the upright post and crossbeam met.

"Row," Dismas ordered the Swabians. "Quickly."

The villagers were hurling rocks, running along the shore. A priest had joined them.

Dismas steered toward the middle of the river. The shouting faded; the crepuscule descended.

"What was it you were saying about my eyesight?"

"You're a sinful man. Target practice—on a church."

"*And* from a moving vessel."

"They burn people for blasphemy. What's gotten into you?"

"Why do you care, you're such a big man in these parts."

"I'm relic master—by appointment—to the Archbishop of Mainz and Brandenburg. Do you suppose he would be pleased to hear that while transporting holy relics to him I stopped along the way to fire crossbow bolts into his churches?"

Dismas kept the Swabians at the oars until well after dark, which made them grumble and demand more money.

They anchored for the night off the western bank and ate a cold supper of cheese and sausage and bread. Dismas and Marcus lay on the deck under bearskins, passing a bottle of brandy as they looked up at the night sky.

"I'm not so religious," Markus said.

"I noticed."

"And you. You've turned into a pious old woman. You should wear a black shawl. And a rosary around your neck."

"You used to be devout. Always you crossed yourself before battle. You kept a flask with holy water. You even drank from it once."

"I was thirsty."

"Still, a sacrilege. Little wonder you've progressed to shooting at churches."

"I keep brandy in my flask now."

They watched the stars in silence.

Markus said, "Cerignola was the end of religion for me."

"Why should you give up God because of gunpowder? Since the world began, God in his wisdom has given us tools with which to slaughter each other. Jawbones of asses. Slings. Swords. Crossbows. Why shouldn't he give us gunpowder?"

"Maybe he's impatient for us to finish each other off so we can have the End of Days. It would save him the trouble of killing us."

"Have you ever read the Bible?"

"Yes, sure. I read Latin. Some, anyway."

"And what of the rest of us, who can't?"

"That's what priests are for. To tell you what's in the Bible."

"Why can't we have a Bible in German?"

"Well, Moses and Jesus and the others didn't speak German."

"What shit you talk, Dismas."

"Hell, I don't know why we're not permitted Bibles in our own language. There must be some reason. That's why we have theologians. Really, Markus. You are a good shot but you are very ignorant."

"Okay, Master of Theology, then explain indulgences to me."

"Well, it's very simple. Indulgences allow us to shorten our time in Purgatory after we die. We can buy them from the Church. One ducat for—depending on the current market value—say, fifty years' reduction of your sentence. You can purchase them for your own soul, or for the souls of your loved one. Is that so complicated?"

Markus shook his head. Dismas went on.

"As for the relics, if you venerate before a certain relic, or make a pilgrimage to a relic, then you also earn an indulgence. If you can't afford to purchase your indulgence, then you can earn it by making a pilgrimage to a shrine. Or attend, say, fifty masses. Or whatever. It's really a very clever arrangement the Church has worked out, you see."

"All right, then, Latin Bible reader, tell me: Where in the Bible is this scheme for making money off frightened believers described? Did Jesus sit down with the Apostle Peter and tell him, 'All right, here is how you will finance my Church. When people come to you and say, "I have sinned," you tell them, "Not to worry! Give me a ducat and I will take away fifty years from your time in Purgatory." ' "

Dismas thought Markus's attitude very impious. At the same time, he could not recall where, exactly, in the Gospels Jesus had outlined the particulars of the indulgence business. It must be in there somewhere.

Markus prattled on with his grievances.

"Why is it that every time someone translates the Bible into a language people like us can understand, they burn him at the stake?"

"Because people like you, Markus, would misinterpret it. Look here, I don't know. Why are you asking me all this? Do you lust to read the Bible? It would do you good, sure. I'll find you a Latin tutor when we get to Mainz. *And* a confessor. One with lots of time to hear your scarlet sins."

"I'll tell you why they burn people for translating it. They're afraid."

"Of what?"

"That if we read it for ourselves, we won't need them anymore. To intercede. Religion's a business like any other. The middlemen fatten. Why should we need middlemen between us and"—Markus pointed at the stars—"whatever the hell is up there?"

Dismas groaned. "Hell is down, Markus, not up. And you must not speak about God that way. It's not decent. Or wise. He might hear."

"Don't you see? It's about control. The priests—your Archbishop Albrecht, to say nothing of that fat, Florentine sodomite in Rome—"

"Are you making reference to the Holy Father? Sure, our boat will be destroyed by lightning."

"He's the worst of the lot. If God is the sun, they're standing between him and us. And where does that leave us? In shadow."

"What a sophisticated argument. God is the sun. Tell me, where did you get your diploma in divinity? In Heidelberg?"

"Have you heard about this Copernicus person?"

"Yes," Dismas said. "Albrecht says he is a heretic."

"Because he declares that the earth revolves around the sun? Well, he's sure to end up tied to the stake in Kraków, poor bastard."

"And how does this Polack know that the earth revolves around the sun? Tell me that."

"You're the ignorant one. He's a scientist."

"Ah? It was a scientist, sure, who came up with the gunpowder that damn near killed us at Cerignola. Was that also a wonderful new idea? Hm?"

"All right, then. You tell me this—how does the Pope know that the sun revolves around the earth?"

Dismas groaned. "How should I know such a thing? Maybe God told him. If you want to talk about revolutions, my head is making them from all this brandy and your jabber. Go to sleep, man."

They kept clear of churches the rest of the way to Mainz.

Markus didn't linger. It was getting on fall and he was anxious to be heading back to the cantons before the first snow.

"Come with me," he said.

It was a tempting thought. "Can't. I've got to get all this to Albrecht. Then it's on to Wittenberg."

"This bone dealing, Dismas. There's something not right about it."

"We used to earn our living by killing. Was that right?"

Markus grinned. "Well, that's for you and your brother theologians to decide. But if you're convinced the End of Days is coming, do you want God to find you peddling saints' testicles?"

Dismas laughed. "And where do you want God to find you, Markus?"

"In bed, screwing."

3

Albrecht

"Ah, Master *Dis-mas*."

Albrecht, twenty-eight-year-old Archbishop of Mainz and Brandenburg, greeted his relic master, gliding into the loggia, attended by his entourage.

He was a person of serious mien, with a long nose, glum, pouchy eyes, and pursed lips. Though relatively young, he was already in possession of what looked to be the first of many jowls.

Albrecht's customary tone with Dismas was the exaggerated noblesse oblige of an aristocrat at pains to be more courteous with his tradesman than necessary. Dismas was used to it by now. They'd been doing business together for half a dozen years. Albrecht was the sort of client who was always telling you how lucky you were to have him for a client. Dismas played along, though this posturing had grown tiresome. More annoying was Albrecht's continual attempts to wheedle information from him about Frederick's relics. Dismas gave elusive answers.

"Your grace."

Dismas bent to touch his lips to the quail-egg-sized sapphire on Albrecht's index finger.

Dismas gave nods to the Archbishop's attendants. Among them he recognized Pfefferkorn, Fugger's man. Word was the Brandenburgs had another benefice in mind for Albrecht—a cardinal's hat. What a fortune *that* would cost. Two archbishoprics, the Electorate of Mainz, and now a cardinalate. Well. It would make Albrecht Primate of Germany—at twenty-eight, one of the most powerful men in the Empire. Dismas reflected that only aristocrats knew their precise age. He could only guess at his own.

Here came pudding-faced Friar Tetzel, bald but for a wisp of white hair at the top of his pate, a lonely cloud hovering above a polished orb. He looked all business, eager to inspect Dismas's Basel purchases so he could decide how many days', months', or years' remittance from Purgatory each relic warranted. Markus's questions echoed. What a business!

The entourage included a flutter of monsignors, lesser clerics, and various body men. Looming above other heads was that of Drogobard, High Marshal of Mainz. He served Albrecht in a variety of offices: chief of the Cardinal's Guard, spymaster, adjutant inquisitor, superintendent of cells, high executioner. A fine collection of responsibilities. An even finer payroll.

Dismas had noticed on his way into the cathedral cloister that the square outside was freshly scorched, and that preparations for another burning were under way. He himself had no reason to fear Drogobard, but neither would he desire to come into his purview. Drogobard gave Dismas a curt nod.

What's this?

In Albrecht's train were two men immediately and unpleasantly recognizable to Dismas by dint of their flamboyant attire: full-skirted, multicolored jerkins, embroidered doublets, wide-brimmed hats with extravagant plumage. They carried halberds, razor-sharp.

Dismas suppressed a groan. Christ. Landsknechte? German mercenaries. What was this rabble doing in an archbishop's retinue?

They might dress like popinjays, but their skills were lethal. Dismas had gone up against them many times in the course of his own *Reiselaufer* soldiering days. He would never begrudge Landsknechte their ability, and thus felt free to despise them. They were barbarous, incapable of remorse for even the cruelest acts. Their only loyalty was to their purses. They'd cut the throat of the sleeping infant Jesus for a price. Herod could have employed them to murder the innocents.

They returned Dismas's icy stare with smirks. He wondered: Did they know who he was, or was it only typical Landsknechte arrogance?

The relics had been laid out for inspection on tables along the cloister loggia. Tetzel made a distasteful face as he held up an ampulla filled with crimson dust.

"What's this?"

"Blood. Saint Cyprian."

"And how much is his grace being asked to pay for *that*?" Dismas found Tetzel's haughtiness more risible than offensive.

"The purchase price was fifteen gulden. And as his grace well knows, he is under no obligation to buy it. For that matter, to buy anything here, should it not meet with his satisfaction."

"Now, now, Friar Johann," Albrecht rebuked Tetzel. "None of that, none of that. We are well pleased to welcome the martyred Bishop of Carthage into our keeping. Dismas, what of Saint Agatha and the other one, Saint . . ."

"Afra. On that table, there. Your grace."

"You see, Tetzel? Oh, well done, Dismas, well done."

Albrecht and Tetzel glided over to the table to examine and confer. Tetzel held up the two relics to the light.

"Virgins. Martyrs. And at the hands of Diocletian . . ." Albrecht nodded, impatient for Tetzel's evaluation.

Tetzel set them back on the table and rubbed his chin. "For the ring, we would offer an indulgence of ten years. Twenty, depending. For the piece of Afra . . ." He turned to Dismas and said with annoyance at having to ask for information that should have been volunteered, "And what *kind* of bone is it?"

"Patella."

"I am not an anatomist," Tetzel sniffed.

Dismas pointed to his kneecap.

"Ah. The very bone on which she knelt as she was martyred."

"Possibly," Dismas said. "We don't really know. Do we, Brother? All we know is that she was tied to a stake and suffocated."

"Yes, yes, yes," Tetzel said with a dismissive wave. He said to Albrecht, "Fifty years."

Archbishop and vendor worked their way down the tables, assigning each relic a value. Donate such and such sum to venerate such and such a relic, and so many years would be deducted from your term in Purgatory.

They lingered over the bit of hilt from the sword that had decapitated St. Maurice. Albrecht gestured to Fugger's agent Pfefferkorn to join in the evaluation.

Fugger held the monopoly on papal finances. He'd even handled the negotiation between Albrecht and Rome over how much Albrecht would share with Rome from his indulgence sales. He had handled, too, other indulgence contracts.

For instance, Pope Leo had demanded twelve thousand ducats to license Albrecht to sell indulgences for venerating relics of the twelve apostles. Outrageous! A thousand ducats *per apostle*? Albrecht counteroffered seven thousand, a sum pegged to the seven deadly sins. They compromised on ten thousand. Tongues wagged that the sum must be based on a thousand ducats per commandment.

Pricing indulgences was, to be sure, a complicated and technical business. But in its way, it was equitable. Everyone had to pay to have his sins remitted, even kings and queens. And archbishops. Those worthies were expected to give twenty-five gold florins per indulgence. Twenty for abbots, cathedral prelates, counts, barons, and other high nobles. For lesser nobility, six florins. Three for burghers, three for merchants. For those of more moderate means, one florin. Since Our Lord had decreed that the Kingdom of Heaven must also open to the poor, those wretches could earn a remittance with fasting and prayer.

Prayer cost nothing. Peasants could pray while they toiled. Fasting was hardly a privation inasmuch as peasants spent their entire lifetimes fasting, one way or another.

Albrecht and Tetzel and Pfefferkorn concluded their deliberation over the St. Maurice sword hilt. Tetzel said he would feature it in his next procession.

Dismas had no liking for Tetzel, but he recognized that he was—as Schenk would put it—a considerable "personage." A man of many hats: Grand Inquisitor of Heresy in Poland. Grand Commissioner of Indulgences in the Germanic states of the Empire. And as befitting a Dominican monk, a capable homilist.

Tetzel's protocol was to arrive at a town at the head of a solemn procession, bearing the papal bull of indulgence on an embroidered cushion. A heavy metal coffer would be set down, *thunk*, in the center of the square. And Friar Tetzel would preach to the clink of coins. Indeed, he had composed a couplet on this very aspect. It was famous.

As soon as the coin in the coffer rings,
The soul from Purgatory springs.

Dismas had witnessed this on a few occasions. What a performance. He could recall it almost word for word, with a shudder.

> Listen now, God and Saint Peter call you! Consider the salvation of your souls and those of your loved ones departed. You priest, you noble, you merchant, you virgin, you matron, you youth, you old man, enter now into your church, which is the Church of Saint Peter.
>
> Consider that all who are contrite and have confessed and made contribution will receive complete remission of all their sins.
>
> Listen to the voices of your dear dead relatives and friends, beseeching you and saying, "Pity us, pity us. We are in dire torment from which you can redeem us for a pittance."
>
> Do you not wish to? Open your ears! Hear your father saying to

> his son, the mother to her daughter, "We bore you, nourished you, brought you up, left you our fortunes, and you are so cruel and hard that now you are not willing for so little to set us free? Will you let us lie here in flames? Will you not for a quarter of a florin receive these letters of indulgence, through which you are able to lead a divine and immortal soul into the fatherland of paradise?"

In addition to his other talents, Tetzel was a supple theologian. He'd pioneered a new form of indulgence whereby you could buy full forgiveness for sins you had not *yet* committed. Even Jesus might marvel at that. It had aroused a bit of controversy, along with his sensational claim that a papal indulgence could free you from Purgatory even if you had—shudder—violated the chastity of the Mother of God.

Dismas knitted his brows trying to understand that one, at the technical level. Even assuming your villainy was so monstrous as to contemplate such a terrible thing—how exactly could a person living fifteen centuries after the time of Christ have carnal relations with the Virgin Mary? Especially when after her death, her body had been assumed whole into Heaven. He preferred not to think about this. A matter best left to the theologians.

Albrecht and Tetzel and Pfefferkorn completed their evaluations. The 296 relics Dismas had brought from Basel would provide an aggregate indulgence value of 52,206 years off time in Purgatory. And provide his grace with a tidy return on his investment.

Monsignor Henk, curator of the cathedral collection, tabulated that his grace's collection now comprised over six thousand relics, with a total value of 9,520,478 years' reduction of Purgatorial sentences.

"We are pleased, Master Dismas," Albrecht announced. "Come and take refection with us. Much do I have to discuss with you."

They sat, the two of them, in Albrecht's study, under the chandelier made from antlers.

"Your trip here from Basel went well?"

"Yes, your grace. It's easier by boat. A fine time of year. Pretty. The leaves and such."

"Yes. You stopped along the way?"

"At night, to anchor."

"No . . . incidents?"

"Our trip was without event. God be thanked."

Albrecht nodded. "Yes, God be thanked. With such cargo as you carried. We ask because we had some report. From upriver."

"Oh?"

"An attack. On a church."

"Oh. That's not good."

"No. And to think that it happened while you were on the river. What if *you* had been attacked?"

"Well"—Dismas smiled—"here I am. Safe. What manner of assault was it, might I ask?"

"It was a blasphemy. A defacement."

Dismas shook his head. "That's bad."

"Very wicked indeed. Crossbow."

"This wine is very excellent, your grace. Is it from your own vineyard?"

"We are pleased you like it. I shall give you some bottles."

"Your grace is too kind."

"You are off to Wittenberg? To see your 'uncle' Frederick?"

"As his grace can see, I came first to you."

"And we are honored, Dismas."

"The honor is mine, your grace."

"We wish you would call us Uncle."

This, again? Dismas's pulse had quickened at the mention of the church desecration. He smiled wanly. "I couldn't. Your grace is a prince of the Church."

"Not yet. Soon. God willing."

"The Elector Frederick is much older than your grace. For that matter, I am older than your grace. It would be, well, awkward to call you Uncle."

"Then call us cousin," Albrecht said with impatience. "See here, Dismas, we are trying to convey our fondness for you."

"Your grace—cousin—shames me with his benevolence."

"But do not call us cousin in front of others."

"No. Certainly."

"And what are you bringing your uncle Frederick?"

"Well, you should ask him. Cousin."

"But I am asking *you*."

"Then speaking as your cousin, I must candidly say that I would feel uncomfortable. Just as I would feel uncomfortable if the Elector Frederick asked what I was bringing to you. Professional standards. You know."

"Really, Dismas. You are being very Swiss today."

Dismas smiled thinly.

"I see my cousin employs Landsknechte?"

"Ah, of course. You were a *Reiselaufer*. One forgets about these blood feuds among mercenaries. Are Landsknechte so awful as that? They are pretty, you must admit. *How* they preen. Drogobard tells me they spend their entire wages on attire and frippery. Like the Swiss Guard in Rome."

"With respect," Dismas said, jaw muscles clenching, "the Pope's Swiss Guard descend from *Reiselaufers*. Who have nothing in common with Landsknechte. God be thanked."

"Oh, come. Landsknechte and *Reiselaufers* both enjoy reputations as the finest paid killers in Europe. You have much in common."

"If his grace insists."

"Don't *pout*, Dismas. Hatred is a mortal sin."

"Perhaps Friar Tetzel will sell me an indulgence."

"What a mood you are in today! Have some more wine. It will cool your Helvetian blood." Albrecht filled Dismas's glass. "Now, is it true what I am told, that there was in Basel a boat? A boat that belonged to the Fisherman?"

"There was a boat. But I very much doubt it ever belonged to Saint Peter. It was a disgraceful fraud. Not even a good disgraceful fraud."

Albrecht sighed. "How splendid it would have looked in our cloister courtyard. Truly, it would have been something."

"Would my cousin have me purchase frauds for him?"

"No. But admit, Dismas, it would be something."

"I give my promise—if ever I should come across the true fishing boat of Saint Peter, I will buy it for your grace, whatever price is asked."

Albrecht was looking out the window with its circular mullions.

"Never mind fishing boats. What we truly lack, Dismas, is a shroud."

Dismas stifled a groan. Another recurring theme.

"Not *a* shroud," Albrecht self-corrected. "We mean of course *the* Shroud. The true burial cloth of the Savior." Albrecht made a sign of the cross.

Dismas said, "As I have told my cousin, I have seen many—many—'true' shrouds. In Basel this year I counted fourteen."

Albrecht looked sad. "And not *one* worthy?"

Dismas shook his head. He almost felt sorry for Albrecht.

"Not to be vulgar, but truly I would not have hesitated to blow my nose on any of them. The effronteries one sees these days are beyond imagination. I regret to tell my cousin that this poses a great risk to your—and to the Elector Frederick's—commendable passion for holy relics. You have both breathed new life into an ancient commerce. But demand outstrips supply. Prices rise. Scoundrels enter. Forgers and fakers. It is sad. More, a scandal. In Basel I spoke to Master Schenk about this. I said to him, Look here, Schenk, if this continues, people will lose all confidence in the market. The bad will drive out the good. And *then* what?" Dismas spoke with such passion that he nearly said, "If your Friar Tetzel does not first ruin everything with his outrages."

Albrecht was not listening. His mind was somewhere beyond the mullions.

"The Duke of Savoy has a shroud," he said. "You know it, surely."

"In Chambéry. Yes. I saw it. Years ago."

"And?"

"Of all the so-called true burial shrouds of Our Lord, it has the best pedigree, you might say. It appeared first in Lirey. France. In I believe

1353. It was the property of the knight Geoffrey de Charny. A knight of great reputation. But a Templar, and one must always be *en garde* with relics fetched from the Holy Land by Knights Templar. As I recall, it was denounced as a forgery not long after it surfaced in Lirey. By the local bishop. One Pierre d'Arcis. But you know how it is."

"No. Tell us. *How* is it?"

"The people paid good money to see it. So despite the Bishop's denunciation, the de Charnys continued to display it. A century later, de Charny's granddaughter, Margaret, gifted it to the House of Savoy, to the Dukes. They built the Sainte-Chapelle in the castle at Chambéry as its shrine. It has remained there ever since."

Albrecht said pensively, "And what did you make of it?"

"I would call it more subtle than other 'true' shrouds I've examined. With most, the paint is practically still wet. It could be the one true shroud. Still, I have my doubts."

"Why?"

"Well, the custom in Our Lord's time was for the Jews to wrap their dead for burial in two cloths. The body in one, and the head in another. The Gospel of John makes reference to it as a 'napkin.' The Chambéry shroud is one piece. It shows the image of an entire body, head to toe."

"The Gospel of John is not definitive," Albrecht sniffed. "We think you are mistaken there, Dismas."

"Your grace's knowledge far exceeds my own. I have only my experience in the relic trade to rely on. And this." Dismas tapped his nose.

"Would the Duke of Savoy sell it?"

Dismas shook his head. "Unlikely. It's a mint. I mean," Dismas added uncomfortably, "a reliable source of revenue. Savoy is not a wealthy duchy. The duke needs the money. He displays it with regularity. Pilgrims come. Kings and queens come."

Albrecht was staring out the window again. "He is called Charles the Good. Why? we wonder. What is 'good' about him?"

"They say he's kind. He takes care of his poor, and does not oppress his subjects. He doesn't have an easy time. Always he is being invaded by the King of France."

"Then they should call him Charles the Much Invaded," Albrecht said. "They call your uncle Frederick 'The Wise.' *Is* he so wise, I wonder?"

"Well, he's learned, sure. Speaks three languages, in addition to Latin and Greek. He's building a great university. They say his Master of Theology is a scholar. An Augustinian friar. Luther. Very holy person, they say."

"I speak five languages. In addition to Latin and Greek. Frederick's grandfather was called Frederick the Meek. His brother, Johann the Constant. His nephew, Johann the Magnanimous. Who devises these names? And there was that troublesome cousin. What did they call him? George the Bearded." Albrecht smiled playfully. "And how will we be called, Dismas?"

"Albrecht Cardinal Brandenburg. Perhaps someday, His Holiness, Pope Albrecht?"

"A German pope? Judgment Day will come first. But as to the business of the shroud. If John's Gospel is correct about the Jews and their head napkins—a wonder Jews would be willing to pay for a second cloth—then the Chambéry shroud must be a fake."

"This is my thinking, yes."

"Then it follows that somewhere out there exists the true shroud."

Dismas frowned. "Well, perhaps, but . . . one might ask, is it *likely* that Our Lord would leave us such a memento of himself?"

"Yes. It would be proof that he rose from the dead. Find it for us, Dismas. Find it and we will make you rich. You know that we are your best client."

"One dreams of a client like your grace."

"You spread yourself too thin. Come to Mainz, Dismas. Work exclusively for us. For God's sake, Frederick must have enough bones by now. His castle is an ossuary. Come to Mainz. You would not regret it."

Dismas had heard this overture before. "Your grace's generosity is beyond the comprehension of such a wretch as myself."

"You try our patience, Dismas. Go to Wittenberg. Go to your *uncle* Frederick."

Albrecht rose and extended his hand to be kissed. On his way out, Dismas asked, "Who's being burned?"

Albrecht was scribbling at his desk. He didn't look up. "Um?"

"I saw them setting fresh faggots at the stake. In the square. They tell me there's been a lot of burnings."

Albrecht continued writing.

"We had another outbreak of the plague. Drogobard insists on burnings. Good for morale. We're running out of Jews, so it's been witches, mainly. Let's pray we don't run out of those. Safe travels, Dismas. Watch yourself in the Thuringian Forest. We've had reports of banditry. Give our love to Uncle Frederick. The Wise."

4

Frederick

Dismas would have preferred to travel to Wittenberg through Nuremberg so he could deposit his earnings with his banker, Master Bernhardt, change clothes, and visit with Dürer. But with All Saints fast approaching, there was no time. All Saints was the most important feast day of the year for Frederick. His relic galleries were opened for public viewing. Dismas had purchases from Basel that required mounting.

He arrived in Wittenberg on the twenty-seventh of October, eight days after leaving Mainz. When transporting gold, he posed as a monk. The disguise would not in itself stop a brigand, but his halberd would, concealed in the cart close at hand.

Frederick's majordomo Klemp greeted him with warmth and enthusiasm. The servants here always made him feel welcome and cherished. In Mainz, the best he'd get from Albrecht's staff was a grudging nod, to remind him of his social rank. On top of which, now at Mainz he must endure the smirks of Landsknechte.

"The Elector has been asking for you every hour!" Klemp said. "He asks, 'Where is my nephew Dismas?' He sent out riders. Didn't they find you?"

"I went north. To avoid Thuringia."

"Come, he's in the galleries. Did you bring wonderful things?"

"One or two. Saint Barbara. A *toe*."

"No!"

Klemp clapped his hands together. "The last of the Fourteen Holy Helpers? What joy this will bring him!"

"He's been after me for years to get it for him. Between us, Klemp, I was about to chop off one of my own toes and tell him it was hers."

Klemp giggled. Sweet old thing. They made their way to the galleries.

"Master, look who is arrived!"

Frederick's back was to them. He was bent over, peering into a case, a cane in each hand. The gout and the stones now kept him from his hunting. He'd put on great weight.

He turned slowly. Dismas's first experience of Frederick had come before even meeting him, when he saw Dürer's portrait of him as a younger man. In it, Frederick stares at the viewer with intense, bulging eyes above a broken nose and beard. If one did not know it was a portrait of Frederick "The Wise," one might think its subject was called "The Mad."

Frederick lifted his arms, summoning a hug. Dismas could barely get his arms around him. It was like embracing a bear.

He released Dismas, looked him up and down.

"Is it Brother Dismas now? Have you given up your sinful ways?"

Dismas was still wearing his monk disguise.

"Klemp, get this miserable excuse of a friar proper clothes. And bring us wine."

Klemp scurried off.

Frederick growled. "Prodigal. Do you realize there remain only four days before All Saints?"

Dismas explained about his circuitous route. The wine arrived. Frederick eased his frame into a chair. It creaked.

"You come from Mainz."

"His Grace the Archbishop commands me to convey to you his love."

"Um. Albrecht's buying himself a cardinal's hat. The Brandenburgs will have no money left at this rate."

Dismas regaled Frederick with an account of Tetzel and the indulgence-pricing session.

Frederick shook his head. "Friar Martin is exercised. Livid. Spalatin says he's about to burst on the subject of Tetzel and his indulgences. Tetzel. There's a scoundrel. Plants himself right across my borders, to taunt me. I can't stop my subjects from crossing over. If they want to drop their guldens into Albrecht's coffer, it's their business." He waved the thought away and smiled. "Now, Nephew Dismas, what have you brought your old uncle?"

Dismas presented him with St. Barbara's toe. Frederick's eyes welled. He didn't ask what Dismas had paid. He didn't care. Together, they placed it in the gallery along with bits of the other Holy Helpers. There were 117 gold and silver monstrances in Frederick's galleries. The Holy Helpers had special meaning for him, as they had lived in the Rhineland at the time of the Great Plague. Worshippers at their shrine prayed for relief from fever and sudden death, for surcease from headache, illness of the throat, tumors, tuberculosis, family discord, temptation on the deathbed, and other afflictions. And now, with Barbara's toe, the collection was at last complete. Prayers said here would have even greater power than before. And, yes, Frederick could charge more for indulgences purchased here. But it was money to buy bricks for his university.

Frederick and his relic master spent the next days mounting the other Basel purchases throughout the galleries.

There were eight galleries in all. Gallery One held relics of holy virgins; Two, female martyrs; Three, holy confessors (St. Sebald's rib was the prize here); Four and Five, devoted to holy martyrs, were stacked almost to the ceiling. In truth it did resemble an ossuary.

"It's starting to feel like a warehouse, Uncle."

The centerpiece here was the mummified holy innocent Dismas had procured in the Holy Land.

Gallery Six held relics of the holy apostles and evangelists; Seven, of patriarchs, prophets, the Holy Family, the Nativity, and the ministry of Christ. Here was the straw from the manger; a strip of swaddling cloth; a strand of Jesus's beard; the thumb of St. Anne, mother of the Virgin Mary—and the very first relic Frederick had bought, in 1493, on the island of Rhodes on his return from pilgrimage in the Holy Land.

Gallery Eight was the holy of holies: relics of Christ's passion. A length from the cord that bound his hands as he stood before the Sanhedrin and Pilate; bits of the rod he'd been given as a mock staff; a piece of the scourge that flayed his back; the sponge soaked in vinegar held up to him on the cross; bits of the nails driven into his hands and feet; and holiest of all, pieces of the cross itself. Most precious to Frederick was a thorn from the Crown of Thorns—a thorn, moreover, that had pierced Christ's forehead. It was difficult to stand in Gallery Eight without being overcome with emotion. Few among those who came to venerate here remained standing or dry-eyed.

Meals at Wittenberg were taken twice a day, in midmorning and late in the afternoon. Toward dusk on the eve of All Saints, after all the preparations had been completed, Frederick bade Dismas join him at table along with Spalatin, his secretary and confidant, and court painter Lucas Cranach.

Dismas knew both men. He enjoyed the company of Spalatin, a kind and humorous man whose conversation was scholarly but never condescending. He loved gossip. Cranach Dismas found hard going: dour, touchy, without humor, and rather full of himself. But, sure, a painter of talent and formidable industry. He seemed to own everything in Wittenberg, so perhaps he was entitled to his self-regard.

He and Dismas had gotten off to a bad start some years ago when Frederick tasked Cranach with assembling a catalog of his relic collection. At the time it comprised (a mere) five thousand relics. Dismas knew that this was not a commission Cranach rejoiced over. He would rather be painting portraits and altarpieces. But one did not refuse a request from one's patron. Cranach took out his resentment on Dismas, chafing at him endlessly over the authenticity of this or that relic, harrumphing and huffing. They'd nearly come to blows over the leaf from the Burning Bush. A tooth of St. Jerome had also been a cause of contention. In the years since, Cranach had relaxed into a sullen companionability. Dismas's friend Dürer also received Frederick's patronage, occasionally. Dürer had opinions regarding Cranach. He did not regard him highly. Dismas did not feel confident to judge Cranach's work. It seemed quite good.

It was quite possible what bothered Dürer was—money. As court painter, Cranach enjoyed not only official prestige but also a fine salary—rumored to be fifty gulden, not counting the special commissions. Dürer insisted this was more than he deserved. It amused Dismas to listen to Dürer go on about Cranach. Artists.

What a feast was laid on. Small wonder Uncle Frederick had grown so in girth. Food arrived and continued to arrive on great salvers: venison, bear, pheasant, snipe, carp, crab, pike, herring, cod. Cheeses, apples, plums. Dismas gorged, having spent the previous week eating road rations. Wine flowed in rivers. At length Dismas thought he might explode.

They were into the sweets when one of Spalatin's undersecretaries entered with an air of urgency. He bent to whisper into Spalatin's ear.

Frederick said, "Let's hear it."

"Friar Martin, your grace."

"Yes?"

"He's . . ."

"Speak, man."

"He's posted a notice, your worship. On the door of the castle church."

5

Dürer

What sort of notice?"

"It's rather lengthy, your worship. I've not had time to read it all. It's . . . well, denunciations, I suppose you'd call them. Of Friar Tetzel. Ninety-five denunciations."

Spalatin groaned, "I *knew* something like was in the offing."

"Ninety-five?" Frederick smiled. "Is our church door sufficiently commodious?"

"He might have given us notice," Spalatin said. "If your grace will excuse me."

Spalatin went off with the undersecretary, leaving Frederick, Dismas, and Cranach in silence.

Dismas having finished his recitation, Dürer said, "That must have given Frederick a proper case of indigestion." He dabbed at the canvas on his easel. "Did they have to give him a purge?"

Dismas sat by the large window in Dürer's studio.

"He seemed quite amused by it all. It was Spalatin who was perturbed."

"You say Luther posted them? I thought he nailed them to the door."

"That's what the sensation-mongers are saying. It was just pages of a pamphlet, pasted on."

"It may not be so amusing for Frederick much longer," Dürer said. "They burn people for that sort of thing."

Dismas shook his head. "Not in Wittenberg. Frederick's not a burner. Doesn't even keep a full-time executioner. They have to bring them in special."

"Well, I'm with Luther," Dürer said. "These indulgences stink to Heaven. Why should Germans have to pay for domes in Rome?"

Dismas stood and stretched. He stood behind Dürer and looked at the portrait on the easel. It was of the banker Jacob Fugger, he who'd made the loans to Albrecht.

"Is he so handsome as that? Or are you improving your price?"

"It's perfectly accurate," Dürer said. "He's a fine-looking man. I don't tart up my portraits. Like *some* in Wittenberg."

Dismas snorted. "I was wondering how long you'd go without making a sour remark about poor Cranach."

"Poor Cranach? That's good. He's so poor he clinks when he walks. What masterpiece is he working on? From what I hear, he doesn't even do his own work himself anymore. Just goes around his workshop telling the apprentices, 'More blue, there. Some yellow, here.' "

"At least he doesn't put himself in every painting, like you do. A week ago I was with Frederick in the galleries. He's got your *Martyrdom of the Ten Thousand* there."

"A masterpiece, that."

"Yes, it's lovely. And even by candlelight I can make out your face in it at ten paces. You should have titled it *Martyrdom of the Ten Thousand, Featuring Albrecht Dürer Smack-Dab in the Center.*"

It was Dürer's great painting of the gruesome and varied executions of the ten thousand Christian soldiers on Mount Ararat, at the hands of the Persian King Shapur, at the behest of the Emperor Hadrian. Or was it Diocletian? No one seemed quite certain which. Dürer had put himself in the center, along with his friend Konrad Celtis. Celtis had died some months before Dürer started painting it. Dürer claimed he included himself only as homage to his dead friend. Dismas suspected otherwise.

"Still in the relic gallery, is it?"

"Yes, Nars," Dismas said. "Still there."

It was Dismas's nickname for Dürer—after Narcissus, archetype of Vanity, owing to his friend's predilection for self-portraiture and inserting himself in his paintings.

"Don't let Cranach near it. He'll want to improve it."

Dürer applied burnt umber to Fugger's fur stole. It was a constant theme—Cranach's desecrations of his work. The grievance had its origin in an incident years ago. The Holy Roman Emperor Maximilian, Dürer's chief patron at the time, had commissioned Dürer to adorn his printed prayer book. For reasons never quite explained, Dürer had halted work on the project. Whereupon Cranach finished it. Oh, the lamentation! One might think Cranach had assaulted Dürer in the face with a bucket of paint. But that affront was nothing compared with an even more monstrous liberty. Cranach had presumed to finish a portrait of Maximilian by Dürer. This could never be forgiven. Artists.

Dürer sniffed at Dismas's taunts. "I paint beauty wherever I find it. If I find it in the mirror, so be it."

He was a handsome fellow, Nars: tall and lean, hair a cascade of ginger ringlets, a finely trimmed beard and mustache in the Italian style (naturally), the cheekbones of a knight, sensuous mouth, and drowsy lover's eyes. His gaze, when it fell on you, either in person or in the portraits, was elusive. Dismas ascribed this to his melancholia. Dürer absolutely believed that he was under the influence of Saturn. Gloomy Saturn.

"You can barely make out that it's Celtis and myself," Dürer said.

Dismas suspected he was saying this in order to prolong a conversation about himself. He smiled and thought, *All right, Nars, let's talk some more about you*. He said: "And what about your *Adoration of the Magi*? You made yourself one of the magi! Or *The Feast of the Rose Garlands*. The retablo at San Bartolomeo in Venice. There you are, in the foreground, holding a piece of paper with a Latin inscription boasting that you completed the painting in only five months. When you know very well it took you seven. You're without shame. Every time you paint Christ, he looks more and more like you."

Dismas put his cloak on over his shoulders.

"Come on. You've made Fugger handsome enough. Sure, he'll double your commission. I'm thirsty. I need a drink. And then the Edengarten. I haven't had a woman since Charlemagne was emperor."

"I'd be careful, I were you," Dürer said. "Not so long ago I did a drawing of a man with the pox." He shuddered. "Ghastly. Between the French pox and the plague, we're doomed."

Nuremberg was regularly stricken by plague. Dismas lost his wife and children to it; Dürer, his mother, on whom he doted, as she did on him. Nars was fearful to the point of hysteria about plague, and whenever there was an outbreak fled over the Alps to Italy. He did have a reason to go to Italy. He studied there. Dismas told him he shouldn't feel guilty about his mother. He couldn't very well haul an aged woman over the mountains. Still.

"The brothels are licensed," Dismas observed.

"See for yourself." Dürer went to a drawer and pulled out a sheaf of thick paper. He handed it to Dismas.

Dismas winced. "Christ."

"Still want to visit the Edengarten? I did that from life. Didn't stand too close."

It was a woodcut titled *Syphilitic Man*. Dismas was not displeased to hear that the subject was a Landsknecht. His disease was well advanced. He wore his typical fancy dress, but his face, arms, and calves were grotesquely pustular and oozing. One of Dismas's clients, a wealthy man in Geneva, was afflicted, and had begged him—on his knees—to procure for him a relic of St. Job, the Christianized patron saint of syphilitics. The Cloak of the Virgin was also considered effective.

Dismas handed the drawing back to Dürer. "I'd feel sympathy for him if he weren't a Landsknecht."

Dürer stared at his work. "He was an arrogant prick, even in this state." He put the drawing back. He said in a conspiratorial tone, "You know who's got it?"

"The Pope?"

"No. *He's* got a nasty fistula. I don't have to tell you how he got it."

Dismas made a face. "I don't want to know. How would you know such a thing?"

"Raphael told me."

"Who?"

"Dis. Your ignorance is truly superb. Raphael the painter."

"One of your Italians, is he?"

"As for the pox—the Emperor. He's dying of it."

"Everyone knows that," Dismas said. "Did you hear the latest? He went to a monastery in Füssen. Apparently it wasn't pleasant. Sores all over his mouth. Kept dipping his cup into the communal bowl with all the monks. So they had to dip theirs. Nice for them, eh? But no surprise. Maximilian's more debauched than Tiberius."

"Some respect. Please. He is my patron."

"Then you should get a new patron. Neither of *my* patrons is covered with revolting sores." Dismas sighed. "Well, now I don't want to go to the Edengarten. I may never again after this conversation. But I do need a drink. Come on."

Dürer's house was in the Tiergärtnertor, in the shadow of the castle. They went to their usual tavern, the Corpulent Duke, and sat at a quiet table in the corner.

Dürer was moody. Dismas drank beer; Dürer brandy, one after another.

Abruptly he said, "The thing is, if the Emperor *is* dying, as they say he is, I'm going to need a new patron."

"Always you're worried about money," Dismas said. "You're Albrecht Dürer, for God's sake. You're not going to starve."

"Do you know how many mouths I feed? I don't have kids, but there's my brother, Hans, and his family. Big eaters, all. And Agnes's family. And the servants, and the assistants. Materials to buy. Believe me, I depend on Maximilian's stipend. And my hands." He held them out, as if for inspection. "They feel stiff all the time. And my eyes. What happens when they go? Eh?"

"In that case, maybe you should embellish the portrait of Fugger. You can use me for a model."

"How much does that hack Cranach earn a year as court painter?"

"Frederick doesn't tell me these things. Nars, why do you obsess about Cranach?"

"I hear he gets two hundred gulden. Two hundred! That was Agnes's entire dowry."

"I doubt he gets that much. But sure, he makes a decent living. I'll tell you this—sup at Frederick's table and you don't starve."

"That's the life. To think that Cranach is living it. There's no justice in this life. We'll have to wait for the next."

"I wish you would listen to me about Master Bernhardt."

"That banker of yours?"

"The man is a genius. Give him guldens, he turns them into ducats, and the ducats into diamonds. He has quadrupled my money."

Dürer shrugged. "I'll mention it to Agnes. She handles the money. What money there is."

"Well," Dismas said. "This is a marvelous talk we are having. Syphilis. Papal fistulas. A debauched and moribund emperor. And now poverty and starvation. What else shall we talk about? Have you been to any good public executions lately? You could come with me to Mainz. Every day they have burnings."

Eventually Dismas succeeded in making Dürer smile—at the story of Albrecht's disappointment that Dismas failed to buy him the fake St. Peter's fishing boat.

"What he really wants is a shroud."

"Shroud? I could make him a shroud."

Dürer's tongue was getting furry from brandy. "A shroud so . . . beautiful Christ would want to come back down from Heaven and curl up inside it."

"Nars. Don't talk so."

Dürer thumped his mug on the table. "Hey there, Magnus! Move your fat bottom and bring me more brandy. And more of your horse piss for my friend Dishmus."

"Albrecht doesn't want a shroud made by you," Dismas said. "He wants the one in Chambéry."

Magnus the tavern keeper, an immense fellow and thank Heavens tolerant of gibes about his posterior, came and poured more brandy into Dürer's mug.

"You know," Dürer said, leaning across the table toward Dismas, "together we could make some good money, you and me."

"I don't think I want to hear this."

"Well, listen anyway. I will make the shroud. And you will sell it to that excuse for an archbishop. I'll give you twenty-five percent."

"So generous. How is Agnes?"

"Screw Agnes."

"I would only she's your wife. I am trying to change the subject, Nars."

"Why not do it? You despise Albrecht."

"I have never said to you the words 'I despise Albrecht.' "

"Oh, pah. You've said as much to me a hundred times. He's a pig. Not a pig on the scale of the Pope, but a pig nonetheless. And Tetzel. There's scum. Tetzel they should burn."

Dürer drained his cup and banged it up and down on the table. The tavern quieted. He climbed onto the table on unsteady legs.

"Nars. Sit down."

Dürer raised his cup. "To Friar Martin Looter. Looth . . ."

People stared.

"Come on, you people. Drink! To Friar Martin *Loo-ther*! Yes, that's it. Death to the sodomite Pope in Rome!"

"Hey!" someone said. "You shouldn't say such things!"

Magnus lumbered over. "Master Dürer. Please. No trouble."

Dismas tugged at Dürer's leg. "Come down from there, Nars."

"Magnus! More brandy! For everyone, brandy!" He raised his cup. "Drink, everybody! Drink to Albrecht Dürer!"

"Who?" someone said.

"To Albrecht Dürer! Who wipes his ass with the paintings of Lucas Cranach!"

Dismas and Magnus got Dürer off the table and carried him to the door.

"You are a great man, Magnus," Dürer said, slumping against him. "The greatest I have ever known. The greatest in all the . . . Empire."

Dismas said to Magnus, "I'll get him home."

The cool night air felt good.

"Let's hope no one calls the guard," Dismas said.

"Screw the guard. What are they going to do?"

"Nars. You can't stand up in a tavern and shout that the Pope is a sodomite."

"Well he is. Luthh . . . Why cannot I say his name? Looo . . ."

"Because you are drunk, Nars."

"Shh. Listen. I will say it. Loo-terr. Looter is the new Pope now. Dismas?"

"Yes, Nars."

"I love Looter."

"Yes. That's good. Now come."

"Take me to him. I will make my confession to *him*."

"Friar Luther is in Wittenberg, Nars. We are in Nuremberg."

"I want to paint him. I will make him immortal."

"I think he's already taken care of that. Anyway, Cranach beat you to it."

"Cranach? Cranach? Cranach is . . . a cunt."

"Shh, Nars. For God's sake."

"He even looks like a cunt."

"If you keep up like this, I'm going to take you to the jail myself."

"I will fight the guard," Dürer said, collapsing against a wall.

Dismas picked his friend up by the arm.

"When Agnes sees you in this state, you may wish the guard had got you first."

6

Boat of the Fisherman

The following spring Dismas returned to Mainz.

He had spent the winter hunting in warmer regions, in search of relics for Albrecht. The latest vogue was Italian martyrs of the sixth century. He also found some other rare pieces: a rib of St. Chrysogonus and a nice fragment of St. Speciosa's coccyx, avouched to have worked some brilliant healings. Normally he'd have given Frederick first refusal, but Frederick was so long on Speciosa he could reassemble his entire skeleton.

He made his way into the cathedral as he usually did, by the side street that led to the cloister. Turning the corner, he was surprised to find a crowd of pilgrims, among the usual penitents and supplicants.

It wasn't a feast day. Why then were they here? The shirts of the penitents were ripped and stained red from self-flagellation, a devotional practice that Dismas found distasteful. Others, lacking limbs, dragged or pushed themselves forward over the cobble. Faces showed ravages of smallpox and starvation. The crowd pressed toward the cloister door, where Dismas saw the two Landsknechte he'd encountered here the previous autumn.

"What's going on?" Dismas asked someone in the crowd.

"It's the Apostle Peter's fishing boat. Two hundred years' indulgence!"

Christ, Dismas thought. He pushed his way through the crowd to the entrance. One of the Landsknechte blocked his way with his halberd.

"Where do you think you're going, pilgrim?"

"I'm not a pilgrim. Stand aside."

"It's ten kreuzer to get in." He took in Dismas's cloak and boots, which marked him as a person of means. "For you, fifty."

"I'm here on archbishop's business. And if you don't stand aside, I'll shove that halberd so far up your bunghole it'll come out the top of your head and knock off your helmet."

The other Landsknecht moved toward Dismas. Dismas drew his dagger from beneath his cloak put the blade under the man's jaw.

"Steady, Landsknecht."

They made no further move against him. They weren't stupid. A man who would accost Landsknechte with such belligerency would have authority behind him, unless he was a fool or suicidal. A cleric inside saw what was happening and rushed out, scolding like a schoolmaster.

"What's the meaning of this? Master Dismas!" He barked at the Landsknechte. "You, and you, stand down. Now! Come in, Master Dismas."

Dismas sheathed his dagger and entered the cloister, Landsknechte glaring after him with bemused hatred.

"Why does his grace employ such scum?" Dismas said.

The cleric shrugged. "I don't care for them, myself."

In the middle of the cloister courtyard Dismas saw a boat. Not the boat he had seen in Basel. This one was high in the bow and stern, single-masted. Its sail was raised and hung limp in the windless interior of the courtyard. It was surrounded by kneeling pilgrims, hands touching its hull as they murmured their prayers. Nearby was the indulgence coffer box. And there was Tetzel, doing brisk business.

"Pray, what is *that*?" Dismas asked.

The cleric seemed surprised. "Your boat."

Dismas stared. "What can you mean?"

"The boat of the Apostle Peter. The one you bought for his grace in Basel last autumn. Very popular with the pilgrims. You saw the crowd outside. Been like this since it arrived. His grace is very pleased."

Albrecht received Dismas alone, in his study.

"Cousin. We have missed you. You wintered well?"

"Yes," Dismas said, straining to control his emotions. "I have pieces I think your grace will approve."

"You have never disappointed us, Dismas."

Albrecht was in a jolly mood. Doubtless the continual clinking in the courtyard jollied his temper. A sound sweeter even than wind chimes.

Dismas cleared his throat. "Might I ask your grace—what is that nautical object in the courtyard?"

Albrecht smiled. "A great success. You saw the crowds? Day and night, they come. We have had no peace."

"So I saw. But with respect, I ask again—*what* is it?"

Albrecht sighed. "Now, Dismas, we're not going to have a scene, are we? It's too boring. Come, have some wine."

He poured from a silver ewer.

"It's modeled on the boat in the wall painting by Giotto. You know it, perhaps?"

"No."

"Such a face, Dismas. It's very well done."

"Forgive me, but I was surprised when Father Nebler informed me that I purchased it for your grace. In Basel."

"Ah, therefore the sour face. Well, you are our official relic master.

Why should you not have found it for us? Be proud, Dismas. It does you honor."

Dismas stared.

Albrecht said, "If it's your commission that concerns you, you needn't worry. You will be well compensated. As always."

"With respect, your grace, it has nothing to do with that. Under no circumstances would I accept compensation for that . . ."

"Dismas. If it makes the people pious, what matter if it's . . ."

"A fake?"

"Improvised."

"Your grace, *as* your official relic master, I take pains to—"

"Yes, yes. We are well acquainted with your vaunted integrity. Why? Because we hear you proclaim it on every occasion. Are we now to be subjected to yet another avowal?"

Dismas squeezed his fists under the table in silent rage. What iniquity. And now to be lectured for protesting. Albrecht launched into a jeremiad on another theme.

"This has been a most difficult season for us, Dismas. Most difficult. And we must say, your uncle Frederick has done nothing to help. No, I must say—we are aggrieved. Much aggrieved."

The Luther affair, surely. Dismas had been away from the Empire, but even in Venice and Genoa and Naples news reached him of what was happening in the north. Dürer was correct that Frederick's amusement over Luther's protest would be short-lived. His Master of Theology was the talk of all Europe.

Albrecht warmed to his subject.

"This obstreperous friar had the temerity to send me his odious theses. Theses! There's a dignified term for the rantings of a drunken monk. He enclosed a groveling letter, addressing me as 'Your Illustrious Sublimity.' And calling himself '*fex hominum*'—a shit among men! That's nothing but the truth. And then presumed to lecture us—we, who hold three archbishoprics—on church doctrine pertaining to indulgences. Gall. The Dominicans issued a pamphlet defending their brother Tetzel and his legitimate practices. And what did the students in Wittenberg do? Your uncle Frederick's students? Burned them! Eight hundred pamphlets! Did your uncle do anything to punish this gross impudence? He did—nothing."

Albrecht worked himself into a fine lather.

"Then, when his holiness demanded that your uncle give Luther over to the Dominicans for examination, what does he do? Again nothing! Refuses. Refuses the Holy Father in Rome!"

Albrecht crossed himself.

"When his holiness demanded of Frederick that at the very least he banish Luther from Saxony, *again* he refused! And now? Now Frederick says he will banish Luther, or hand him over to proper authority in Rome, only if he is convicted of heresy. But Frederick will not hand him over for judgment. It is"—Albrecht held up his hands in an attitude of martyrdom—"unconscionable."

Dismas said, "These are matters above my station."

"*So* modest, Cousin."

"I'm a bone dealer, your grace. Not a theologian—like yourself."

"Yes. Well, bone dealer, do you know what's going to happen to your trade if these heresies promulgated by your uncle's precious monk take hold? If indulgences are swept away, do you suppose the people still will clamor for a rib of Saint Sebald or a lock of Saint Apollonia's? Do you suppose you will have any patrons *then*?"

This was something Dismas had, indeed, considered. As Frederick had, sure. By protecting Luther, Frederick was undermining the very foundation of belief in relics. Wagering the value of his own vast collection. Many indulgences were earned by venerating relics. If indulgences were abolished, who would come to venerate the holy bones?

Luther's indignation and attacks had increased pari passu with Rome's denunciations of him. Now he indicted not only indulgences, but also the papacy itself. And in such language! His most recent pamphlet called St. Peter's "that insatiable basilica." He wrote, "Let the Pope build it with his own money! He is richer than Croesus!"

He was issuing pamphlets at a furious pace. The presses could hardly keep up. He'd denounced the validity of the sacrament of penance. Denied the very existence of Purgatory. Denied the authority of Rome. The ground shook beneath his slippers.

It was—unthinkable: three of the most powerful men in Europe—the world—the Pope, the Emperor Maximilian, and Albrecht—all wanted Luther tied to a stake and burned. Yet each time they reached out to light the fire, Luther snatched the torch from their hands and set fire to their own robes. How was a mere monk able to do this? Because he was protected by the Elector Frederick, who declined to hand over one of his Saxon subjects to other authority. What did Frederick have to gain by shielding Luther? Only the ill will of this troika. And here, perhaps, was the greatest irony of all: Frederick himself remained devoutly Catholic. So far as anyone could make out, he didn't agree with Luther on a single point of his heretical doctrines.

Albrecht's fury now ventilated, he spoke in a gentler tone. "You go to Wittenberg?"

"By way of Nuremberg. I've not been home in many months."

"Assure our brother in Christ Frederick of our"—he sighed—"continuing love. How goes it with his collection? *Still* larger than our own?"

"In numbers, yes," Dismas said evenly. "But he has nothing so dazzling as your grace's fishing boat."

"Then he will be jealous."

"Doubtless."

Albrecht extended his ring to be kissed.

"Fare you well, Dismas. Return to us soon. Bring us wonderful things. You know how we depend on you. And, Dismas?"

"Your grace?"

"Emphasize to your uncle that his collection, being larger than our own, will suffer more than ours should Luther's apostasies take root. All those galleries of his, suddenly"—Albrecht leaned and blew out the large candle on his desk—"emptied of meaning. Tell him."

7

Disaster

The trip to Nuremberg seemed to take forever. Dismas was thoroughly dejected by Albrecht's flagrant trumpery. He felt a heavy foreboding about things to come. He couldn't predict the future, but it seemed unlikely Luther would survive, even with Frederick's protection.

Frederick was powerful, sure. He was ruler of Saxony and an elector of the Holy Roman Empire. But only one of seven electors. Albrecht was another. If the Emperor Maximilian was dying of the pox, as seemed certain, would his successor continue to countenance Frederick's shielding of Luther? Rumors were that Maximilian would be succeeded on the throne by his grandson Charles, King of Spain, a more resolute, indeed adamant, champion of Catholic doctrine. Charles might well declare "Enough!" and brush Frederick aside to seize Luther. What then? Internecine war within the Empire? Could Frederick withstand that? Surely not. Thinking about this, Dismas felt a great weariness descend on him. He felt old.

Finally his journey ended. Early one morning he saw through the mists the walls of the free imperial city looming ahead. Nuremberg presented itself grandly, with its walls and battlements and towers. But now it came to Dismas that he yearned for a different landscape.

It was time to go home, like Markus. To the mountains. To Mürren, his first home, the little village atop the great cliffs. The realization, which struck him almost physically, gave him a jab of happiness. He found himself grinning. Yes, it was time. He spurred his horse to a trot.

He would call on his friend Dürer. No, first he would visit the bathhouse and soak in hot water. Then put on fresh clothing. Then Dürer. They would dine splendidly, get a bit drunk, but not so drunk this time that Dürer would climb onto the table and shout insults at the Pope. Then a good sleep in clean linen in his own bed. And in the morning, he would go to Master Bernhardt and collect his savings.

He calculated what it would amount to. Master Bernhardt's last accounting came to over two thousand gold florins. A tidy sum. More than enough to last him out his lifetime. He'd need a cart to carry it. He felt like laughing. Yes. He would go home, find a sweet and pretty girl and fill her belly with babies. He would build his home above the town, and every morning look out at the mountains, at the Eiger and the Jungfrau. It was a view to take your breath away, no matter how many times you'd seen it. No more sniffing about for bones and truckling to venal archbishops. He couldn't remember when he'd felt such peace of mind. Not since Hildegard and the children were alive.

He found Dürer in good form. He had spent his winter in Venice. He talked with excitement about some new technique Dismas only vaguely comprehended, called *chiaro-oscuro*. Something to do with the contrast of light and dark. He proudly showed Dismas some new woodcuts, which were indeed exemplary. And he announced that he was writing a book on mathematics, a subject on which he was deeply knowledgeable.

Italy always seemed to refresh Dürer, even though he deplored Italian morals. He was full of gossip, much of it about Pope Leo's extravagances and strange inclinations. These lurid details reinforced his increasing regard for Luther. He told Dismas that Leo had recently financed a war—at astronomical cost, eight hundred thousand gold ducats—in order to obtain for his nephew Lorenzo the Duchy of Urbino. In consequence, some cardinals had plotted to poison Leo.

"Pity they didn't succeed," Dürer said. The cardinals were dealt with gruesomely.

Talk of Leo led to talk of Luther's latest philippic against Rome. He was now denouncing the Pope as "the Antichrist." And oh, dear, as "a great, raging Babylonian whore." Dismas made Dürer promise there would be no drunken profanations tonight at the Corpulent Duke.

Dürer winced at the memory. His hangover the next day had been Homeric, Agnes's wrath Medean. Tonight, they agreed, would be jolly, but a night of Socratic moderation.

Over dinner, Dismas told Dürer about Albrecht and his St. Peter's fishing boat fraud. He told him, too, of his epiphany that morning on the road to Nuremberg, of his plan to give up relics and go home. He said that this prospect made him happy, but also sad, because it meant they would see less of each other. Dismas said when he built his cabin, he would make a room in it with big windows so that Dürer could paint when he came to visit. Dürer said there was nothing of interest to paint in the cantons.

"What would you have me paint? Cows?"

Dismas said in that case, he would buy an enormous mirror, so Dürer could paint his favorite subject.

Dürer laughed. It was a pleasant meal.

Then Dürer said, "Thank God Agnes didn't follow your advice and give our money to that bounder Master Bernhardt. Sounds like you got your money out before the calamity befell."

"What do you mean?" Dismas said.

"Dismas—you *did* get your money out?"

"He still has my money."

A look of horror came over Dürer.

"I only assumed because you seem so happy that . . . you'd withdrawn your funds."

"I've been away, Nars. I returned only this morning."

Dürer now looked stricken.

"Nars, what's happened?"

"Christ in Heaven."

"Just tell me. What's happened?"

Dürer signaled the tavern keeper. "Brandy. Two great brandies." Magnus lumbered off.

Dürer said to Dismas, "Bernhardt is in the jail."

"Jail? Why?"

"Well, I suppose it's called stealing."

"Stealing? Stealing from . . . who?"

Dürer shrugged. "Well, everyone. From everyone who gave him their money to invest. It's quite a list. You're in fine company, at least. Ernest, Duke of Brunswick. Gerlacht of Isenburg-Neumagen. Bruno of Isenburg-Büdingen. Many Isenburgs. Many Schwarzenbergs. George, Duke of Hohenfels. A number of Hohenzollerns—Freinar, Heinrich. Franz."

Seeing the look on Dismas's face, Dürer said in an effort to cheer him:

"Maybe Albrecht of Mainz had some money with him. The disgrace isn't that he swindled the nobles. Screw the nobles. They'll just squeeze more money out of their peasants and go on drinking the best wines and putting up tapestries. But it seems a number of monasteries and convents also gave him money. Listen to this. The foundation that supports the Neustadt Almshouse? He took *them*, too. What a bastard, eh? Also the Furth Benevolent Society for the Blind. It's one thing to rob rich assholes. But stealing from the blind? That takes balls. Sure, there's a hot place in Hell for him . . ."

Dürer's voice trailed off. He put his hand on Dismas's shoulder.

"Was *all* your money with him?"

The execution of Master Bernhardt two weeks later was well attended. The consensus was that beheading by sword was a far too benevolent way of delivering the despicable embezzler to Satan. There were appeals for a more protracted death. It was proposed that Nuremberg invite the executioner of Mainz to carry out the sentence. Mainz was a center of invention, and not just of moveable type. Its executioner had recently introduced a protocol called "The Grand Marionette." The condemned was impaled ear, hand, and foot with large fishhooks tied to rope strings, and made to dance his way to death, feet not touching the ground. (A lesser variant, designed as mere torture, was called "The Petit Marionette," in which the feet did touch.) But alas, the city council of Nuremberg felt that to execute Bernhardt in this way would only showcase the innovation of a rival city.

The Duke of Hohenfels, who had lost a grievous sum, volunteered the use of his bear pit and his champion, Siegfried. Others wanted Bernhardt burned slowly, over low heat. One recent burning—of a witch—had lasted the better part of an afternoon, owing to a combination of a stiff breeze and wet faggots.

Finally the high justice of Nuremberg, rising above the clamor for lurid retribution, ordered beheading, amidst heavy protest. At least when spectators saw Master Bernhardt being led to the Raven Stone, it was apparent his sojourn in the Nuremberg dungeon had not been a pleasant one. But this was small consolation.

Dismas did not attend, having succumbed to a black depression. He took to his bed. For a fortnight he barely moved. Hardly ate or drank. Faithful Dürer came every day, sometimes more than once, to pound on his door, but Dismas would not open it.

Finally, on the day after Bernhardt was beheaded and his body quartered and left for the carrion birds, Dismas was summoned from his evil sleep by the sound of a violent banging on his door.

Dürer had come with an ax. He shouted through the door. Unless Dismas opened it he would chop his way in.

Dismas got up and shuffled to the door.

"Christ. Stinks in here."

"I didn't ask you in. Go away."

Dürer opened the windows, and fanned the fetid air. He gathered up clothing and made Dismas dress.

"I've got very good news. But if I stay in here another moment I will puke. Come on."

Dismas could barely walk. Dürer half carried him to the bathhouse, then to the barber to be shaved and deloused, then took him home. Agnes greeted Dismas with a severe look.

"And you wanted us to give our money to that beast!"

"Not *now*, Agnes," Dürer said. "Go and make a meal. Look at him. He's starving."

"Serves him right."

"Agnes!"

Agnes went off in a huff. Dürer led Dismas to his studio, where they could not hear Agnes's grumbling.

"Look at you," Dürer said. "I could have used you as the model for my *Melancholia*." The copperplate engraving was celebrated as one of his finest works. The remark did not cheer Dismas.

"Well, do you want to hear my good news? Or would you prefer to leap out the window and kill yourself?"

Dismas sighed. "Tell me your wonderful news."

"It's not going to make you as rich as you were before that swine stole your money. But rich enough to go home to your boring cantons. And more than enough for some farmer's daughter to marry you. Dismas. Are you listening?"

"To every word," Dismas said unconvincingly.

"I'm going to make a shroud."

Dismas stared. "This is your news?"

"And you're going to sell it to that pimp, Albrecht." While Dismas was absorbing this, Dürer added, "We'll have to decide how to divide the money. But don't worry about that. There will be a lot of money. Because it will be a masterpiece."

Dismas tucked into Agnes's rabbit stew. She was not an easy woman, but she was a splendid cook.

"Slow down," Dürer said. "You'll choke."

He ladled a fourth serving into Dismas's bowl.

"Your color's returning. So, do you want to hear about Bernhardt's execution? Everyone came. I might do an engraving. It would sell like pancakes, sure."

"No," Dismas said.

"Why?"

"Because you might tell me that before they chopped off his head, he asked God's forgiveness of the priest. I don't want to contemplate the possibility that God might forgive him."

Dismas wiped his mouth, gulped down an entire glass of wine, and leaned back in his chair.

"This scheme of yours. You do understand there are many shrouds out there. I've seen—I can't even remember—hundreds, anyway."

Nars sniffed that while this might be the case, none of them had been made by Albrecht Dürer. He'd painted tempera on linen some years ago, with splendid result. He spoke in a mathematical vocabulary about bodily proportions. He prattled endlessly but learnedly about a Franciscan monk he'd met in Bologna who'd written a great treatise on measurements and perspectives.

Dismas pretended to listen. His mind was on more practical aspects. The linen. He knew a merchant in Augsburg who sold linen from Palestine to shroud forgers. The linen was usually the best part of them. It had a distinctive weave named after the bones of herring. Dismas wanted to inform Dürer of this, but Dürer was now banging on with intensity about "treble dimensionality." Finally he saw an opening and waded into Dürer's wordstream.

"What will you use for paint?"

Dürer looked as if it was a stupid question. "What do you think? Blood."

"Human blood?"

Dürer considered. "Well, I've yet to paint in the medium. It would require dilution, for the aging effect. I might add particles of rust. Oxide . . . Ground-up iron filings . . ." He was talking to himself now.

"Too bad we can't use Master Bernhardt's blood."

"Fresh blood won't be a problem. There's always a beheading. We'll pay some kid to hold a bucket under the scaffold. I would have to work quickly, mind, before the congealing. The linen would be essential."

"Yes. I've been thinking of that."

Dürer said gravely, "You understand, this won't be one of your everyday shrouds."

"Yes, Nars. You have already said it will be a masterpiece."

"I'm not talking about that. I mean, we'll need a story. Where it came from. Where you found it."

"It's called provenance."

"I *know* that, Dismas."

Dismas said, "The Chambéry shroud that Albrecht is obsessed with . . . It first appeared in the 1350s. So in theory, ours would have to have appeared sometime before that. Can you forge documents?"

"Of course," Dürer said, insulted.

"Don't play the orchid. Then once I've worked out the details of the provenance, you would have to devise the appropriate documentation."

"I must say, it seems that I will be doing most of the work."

Dismas stared. "First the orchid, now the martyr? Who will be taking all the risk? Tell you what. I'll paint the shroud and forge the documents and you go to Mainz and lay your neck on the block."

Dürer snorted. "If Albrecht is putting on displays of Saint Peter's fishing boats, I doubt he will be particular about a shroud. Especially one so exquisite. So I see no risk on your part. And enormous labor on mine."

"Fifty-fifty."

"Seventy-thirty."

"Then forget it. If I'm going to sell my soul to the devil, I won't sell it cheap."

Nars groaned histrionically. "All right. Fine. We will put such a price on it Albrecht will have to take out another loan from the Fugger. Let's drink to it."

Dürer filled their cups with wine. "How shall we toast?"

"Well," Dismas said, "we might start by begging God's forgiveness."

"That's a depressing toast, I must say."

"How do you suppose God will look on what we're doing? It's blasphemy and thievery."

"Who can know the mind of God? Maybe this is part of his plan."

Dismas stared. "Cheating an archbishop with a forged shroud of Christ? God's plan?"

"Why not? He's a rotten man and a rotten archbishop. Him with his Saint Peter's fishing boat. It's quite clear to me. We are God's agents."

"I feel exalted. What shit you talk, Nars. We do this for the worst of reasons—money."

"Very well, if you feel so guilty, then donate your fifty percent to the poor. I'm keeping mine. It may be God's work, but I'm not doing it for free."

Dismas raised his glass. "To God's mercy. May it be boundless."

They drank.

Dismas said, "No self-portraits."

Dürer rolled his eyes.

"Oh, no," Dismas said. "Don't make faces. If your shroud has your image on it anywhere, I won't peddle it to the Archbishop of Mainz."

"What do you take me for?"

"A genius of the first order. And a narcissist of even higher order."

"There is no such thing as higher than the first order. You know nothing of mathematics. But fine, yes, anything to please the relic master of Wittenberg and Mainz."

"Done. Now let's get drunk. There won't be much booze in the days ahead."

8

The Shroud of Mainz

Esteemed and Most Beloved Uncle, It is with an enormity of incitement that I write your Wholesomeness to inform you that I have come into possession of a marvelous indeed mirakulous Item . . .

Dismas put down the quill and cursed. Sure, he was no writer. Worse, he felt dirty—filthy-rotten dirty—addressing this sham to his uncle Frederick. Several times he came close to tearing it up. But he reminded himself that if Dürer was correct, Frederick would never see it.

Again he took up his pen and continued.

Long have you exprest a most reverent desir to possess ~~a~~ THE True Burial Shroud of the Savior. Most long have I ~~belabored~~ labored . . . to obtain for your Excellence this beforesaid most Holy Relick. Truth, sure, it is that you have heard me most numerously ~~declaim against~~ . . .

Dismas groaned. Really, he should hire someone to write the bloody thing for him. But that was out of the question.

. . . denunciate such Shrouds as I have seen. But now I believe that I have beheld THE One and True Cloth in which Our Savior was lained in His Tombe.

How should this great thing have eventuated, your worship may ask? Verily, do you. Now I shall relate How this was come into being. Certainly my most Knowledgefull Uncle is aware of One Boniface of Montferrat, he of ~~Notoreitty . . .~~ he of most Greate Infamy of the Forth Crusade in the earliest years of the Thirteenthe Century past? Certainly, lo. That Accursed Enterprize, in which Italliann Christian Crusaders most foully and cruelly and abomminabley assaulted their bretherne Christian brothers and sisters, and children—oh, crimson infamy!—of the City of Constantinopple. Theyr sanguinarious outrages being perpetratted until theyre bloodlust were sated, they fell to lootinge this most Holy City of its Relicks. Blasfemy, sure thy name is, suredly, the Forth Crusade!

One such relick, untowhich now had been unknown, was, it mirakulously seems, the True Burial Cloth of Our Lord Jesus Christ. Since thatt hateful Event in Anno Dominni 1204, by which again I reference the Forth Crusade, this MOST Holy Cloth has been in the possession of the heirs of the beforenamed Dastard Boniface who thank Holy God and all the Saints met his own much deserved Extinction at the hand of the also sanguinnary Bulgarian Tzsar Kaloyan soon thereafter. What joy.

The Shroud then having passed to his daughter Beatrice, Marqueza of Savvona, it then descented in a most matrilinear fashion until such time as . . .

Dismas scribbled on into the night.

Having made peace with his deplorable illiteracy, he became rather swept up in his faux provenance. Reaching the conclusion, he warned Uncle Frederick that he had paid a "Most Blushfull Sum" to the abbot of the Cappadocian monastery where Dismas had purportedly found this Holiest of Holy Relics.

In a postscript, he wrote that he would depart Nuremberg for Wittenberg with this precious cargo one week after the date on his letter.

Finally he apologized for sending such a sensitive document by post, via the Taxis courier, but explained that he desired that his message reach Frederick without delay. He signed it "Your Devoted Nephew," which gave his conscience a final prick.

On rereading his tissue—tapestry—of mendacity, Dismas felt even worse shame. Again he reminded himself that Uncle Frederick would never see the letter, as it was intended for the eyes of his other patron, Albrecht of Mainz.

Dismas rolled it into a tight scroll. Instead of sealing it with wax, he tied it with string. He wrote on the outside STRICKTLY AND MOST URGENTLY CONFIDENTIAL FOR HIS HIGHNESS BY THE GRACE OF GOD FREDERICK III ELECTOR OF SAXONY.

This ostentatious labeling would ensure that the dispatcher of the Taxis imperial post, who received a handsome stipend from Albrecht's spymaster, would open it, copy it word for word, and send the copy by his speediest courier to Mainz. The original he would hold and delay sending to Wittenberg. Thus would the bait be dangled before Albrecht. They reckoned it would whet Albrecht's appetite more than if Dismas simply arrived in Mainz with Nars's shroud for sale.

As for the original letter: by the time it arrived in Wittenberg, the ink—mixed by Dürer—would have disappeared. They contemplated the scene with amusement: the Taxis courier arriving in Wittenberg, announcing that he had a most urgent communication for the Elector. Then reaching into his dispatch case and handing Frederick's chamberlain a document completely blank, inside and out.

Dismas took the draft of the letter to Dürer's house. He'd gone there several times in the last fortnight, but each time Dürer refused to open the door to his studio. Dismas had to converse with him through the closed door, which he found tiresome.

More vexing was why it was taking Dürer so long. Dismas was

anxious. Every day brought more gossip about Albrecht's negotiations with Rome for his cardinalate. His last archbishopric had cost him ten thousand gold ducats. Now word was Pope Leo was demanding three or four times that for the cardinal's hat. Albrecht would have to go to Fugger again for another loan. How much would he have left with which to purchase a shroud?

Dismas was met at the front door by the ever dour and unwelcoming Agnes. She remonstrated. Her husband was behaving in a most peculiar manner, even by his standards. He barely emerged for meals. And he refused her entrance to his studio. She demanded to know what nefariousness was going on. Nothing good, sure.

Dismas tried to jolly her. Artists were different from normal folk. Clearly her husband was in the throes of a creative fever, at work on something magnificent. He added, "And profitable."

Agnes was not humored by these rhapsodies, and went off in a *swush* of petticoat to sulk in her own part of the house.

Dismas banged on the studio door. Hissed: "Nars. Let me in."

"Go away."

"Cranach could have done it in half the time."

The door opened. Dürer shut and rebolted it as soon as he was inside.

"It's not finished," he said.

Dismas beheld the linen tacked on the easel. It was unlike anything of Dürer's he'd seen before. The detail was extraordinary. You could make out individual eyelashes and strands of beard. It looked like a pentimento of a lustrous oil painting of great complexity that had been left out to bleach in the sun for fifteen centuries.

The face was arresting. Here was a man who had suffered unspeakable agonies but whose expression in repose of death conveyed eternal serenity. It did somewhat resemble its creator, but stopped short of outright self-portraiture. What restraint *that* must have required.

"Well?"

"It's good, Nars. Very good."

"One or two more touches. I'll fold it octavo. Easier to transport that way. I'm going to singe the corners."

"Burn it?"

"For verisimilitude."

"Why?"

"You're the relic master. If it's supposed to have been around since 33 AD, shouldn't it have got a bit scorched at some point?"

"All right. But don't let it all go up in smoke."

Dürer took a corner of it between thumb and forefinger and caressed it gently. "No. It will be perfect. So, how much are we asking for it?"

Dismas looked at it with an appraising eye. "Two hundred ducats."

"Two *hundred*? For this?"

"It's a good price, Nars."

"Why not just give it to him? I put my soul into this."

"It's a beautiful soul, sure." Dismas looked at the shroud. "All right. I'll try for three. But that's no guarantee we'll get it."

Dürer folded his arms over his chest.

"You will not sell it for one pfennig less than five hundred ducats."

"For that kind of money, he'll want Jesus's body, too."

"Pah. He'll amortize it in a month. The true burial shroud of Christ. People will come from everywhere. Magellan will sail back from the Indies to view it."

"I'll ask for five. But that doesn't mean we'll get it."

"Not a ducat less." Dürer looked admiringly at his creation. "What about Frederick?"

"What do you mean?"

"What would he pay for it?"

"Absolutely not! And shame on you even for thinking such a thing. I feel rotten enough addressing this, this . . . lie to him." Dismas thrust his letter at Dürer. "And you'd better be right about your disappearing ink, or I'll . . ."

"Stop fretting, man. You're worse than Agnes."

Dürer took the letter and read. He shook his head. "Christ in Heaven. Your writing truly stinks. The grammar, the spelling . . . All those years hanging about Frederick's university, and still you write like a peasant."

"I regret that it is not up to your standard," Dismas sniffed.

"The drift's serviceable enough." He chortled. "Albrecht will shit his cassock when he reads this."

"Let's hope his purse strings will be as loose as his bowels."

9

Render unto Caesar

Five days after handing the letter to the Taxis dispatcher in Nuremberg, Dismas set off at a casual pace for Wittenberg, bearing with him the true burial shroud of Christ, folded octavo.

On the second day of his journey, as he approached Bayreuth, he heard from behind a commotion of hooves. Six riders—at the head of them, Vitz, Drogobard's lieutenant. Dismas gladly noted the absence of Landsknechte. A favorable sign. Albrecht would know how distasteful Dismas would regard the inclusion of Landsknechte in a party to intercept him.

Dismas affected surprise at being accosted. Vitz was courtly, but insisted, as gently as a man of arms could, that the Archbishop required his presence. Most urgently.

Why? Dismas asked.

Vitz could not say. A matter of state.

Dismas feigned reluctance. He was on his way to Wittenberg, also on "state business."

Vitz remained firm. Pretense having gone on long enough, Dismas said very well, if it was truly that urgent, naturally he would accompany them to see his esteemed patron, the Archbishop.

Two days' hard riding and he was on a ferry across the Rhine to the city of Mainz, spires lambent in the glow of the dying day.

Dismas speculated what pretext Albrecht would adduce for summoning him in such an imperious way. He couldn't very well just greet him with his usual airy "Ah, Dismas," followed by "My spy network intercepted your letter to Frederick about this shroud."

He arrived at the Archbishop's palace. Servants scurried to unpack his cart. Dismas held on to the leather case containing the shroud, about the size of a large Bible.

"Dis-mas! Dearest cousin! How good of you to come! Your journey was not too taxing, we trust?"

Dismas knelt to buss the episcopal ring.

"Come, come, no need for that," Albrecht said, lifting Dismas from his obeisant posture.

"Is everything well with my cousin? The lieutenant was unable to explain why I am so urgently required here."

"Sit. Sit. You must be exhausted from your journey. Wine for Master Dismas," he ordered a servant. Wine—rather good wine—was brought and poured, the servant dismissed.

"Dismas. It has come to our attention that a certain item has surfaced."

"Oh?"

"Um. A shroud."

"Ah?"

Albrecht smiled. "Of quite extraordinary provenance."

"That does sound interesting."

"A provenance antedating the Shroud of Chambéry."

Dismas squirmed in his seat, feigning discomfort, though some of his discomfort was genuine enough.

"Well, such a find would indeed be something. Might I ask how my cousin came to hear of such a thing?"

"Dismas." Albrecht smiled indulgently. "We are Archbishop of Brandenburg, Magdeburg, *and* Halberstadt. Do you not suppose that we are well informed concerning matters within our lands?"

Dismas smiled. "I suppose a diligent shepherd must, sure, keep watch over his flocks. Must be tiring. So much territory to watch over. So many lambs."

Albrecht frowned. "But are you not excited by this news? The discovery of such a sacred relic—the true burial shroud of Our Lord?" Albrecht made a sign of the cross. Dismas made one, too.

"Indeed, I would be." Dismas nodded.

They stared at each other.

Dismas said, "I feel pity for the Duke of Savoy."

"Why?"

"When this shroud is shown to the world, his shroud will be seen for what it is. Irrelevant. Who will make pilgrimage to Chambéry to venerate a mere piece of cloth? No more pilgrims. Poor Duke."

"Ah, so my cousin *is* aware of this new shroud?"

Dismas adopted the expression of a man at pains not to divulge a great secret.

"Cousin," he said, "I find myself in a most awkward position."

Albrecht nodded sympathetically. "How so, my son? You know that our love for you is without bounds. How can we help? Unburden your soul to us."

"The item of which you speak . . . is . . . well, it is in my possession."

"Mirabile!"

"But with regret, I must inform my cousin that it is promised."

"In what way, promised?"

"To the Elector Frederick."

Albrecht's eyes had fixed on the leather case at Dismas's side.

"We must behold it, Dismas."

"Perhaps it would be better not to look upon it, cousin. Seeing it would only . . ."

"What?"

"I fear it might arouse in my cousin the desire to . . ."

"Speak plainly, man!"

"To possess it. It has great power."

"We insist, Dismas."

Dismas sighed. "As my cousin commands."

A long refectory table stood against the wall. Dismas cleared it of objects. He placed the leather case atop, unfastened the straps, and made a sign of the cross. Albrecht, too, crossed himself. Dismas unfolded the shroud with reverence and stood back.

"Ecce homo."

Albrecht gasped.

They met again later in Albrecht's study for the evening meal.

After displaying the shroud for Albrecht, Dismas had feigned exhaustion and the need of a bath. This would leave Albrecht alone in his study with the shroud, his avidity intensifying.

The meal was sumptuous, delicacy upon delicacy, accompanied by the finest wines from the palace cellars. Albrecht kept filling Dismas's cup to the brim. Dismas had prepared for this by drinking beforehand a cup of olive oil, to coat his stomach against inebriation. He pretended to be tipsy.

"Now, Dismas, you say the shroud is 'promised' to Frederick."

"Yes, and no. Yes. No. But, well, yes. I *suppose*, promised."

"Is it? Or is it not?"

"My dear uncle Frederick . . . let us toast him!"

Dismas raised his cup. "To Frederick the Wise, Elector of Saxony. Long health to him. And life."

Albrecht glumly raised his cup. "Frederick. The shroud. *Why* is it promised to Frederick? If indeed it is promised? We do not understand you, Dismas."

Dismas stood wobbily and held up his cup in the direction of the shroud. "Let us toast the shroud." He looked confused. "Is it appropriate, Cousin, to toast the shroud of our Lord Christ? Sure, this wine is worthy . . ."

"Sit *down*, Dismas," Albrecht said with mounting impatience. "But yes, it is appropriate. To the shroud. Now—"

"Y'know, Cousin," Dismas interrupted. "All my life as a relic hunter, I've dreamed of finding the shroud. And now it has pleased God to deliver it into my hands." Dismas crossed himself. "I propose a toast. To God. Er, is that appropriate?"

"*Yes*. We are certain God is well pleased. But tell me, what claim does Frederick have to it?"

Dismas shrugged. "He's always wanted one. And now"—Dismas thumped the table—"he shall have one. This is excellent good wine, cousin."

"I'm glad you like it. Have some more. But, Dismas, we, too, have always wanted a shroud. Long have you known this. Only recently we asked you to explore acquiring the Shroud of Chambéry for us."

"You did. You did. Yes. I remember. Yes." Dismas leaned on the table. "Tell you what, cousin . . ."

"Yes?"

"After I deliver the real shroud to Uncle Frederick, if you like, I'll go to Chambéry and see if the Duke of Savoy will sell us his." Dismas belched. "Whoops. I reckon once the real shroud goes on display in Wittenberg, the Duke of Savoy may decide, what the hell, and sell us his." Dismas waggled his finger. "I wager I could get it for a good price. I'll tell him, Look here, your ducalship, now the whole world knows that shroud of yours is just a rag, a piece of linen. The real one's in Wittenberg. Splendid wine, this."

"Dismas," Albrecht said. "Listen to us. We do not *want* the Duke of Savoy's shroud." He pointed. "We want that shroud there." Albrecht pointed to the table.

Dismas sighed sympathetically. "I know. I know. I wish I hadn't promised it to Uncle Frederick. But . . . there it is."

"How much is he offering?"

"It's not a question of money. Is it?"

"Dismas. I ask—*how much*?"

"Well, since you ask, six hundred."

Albrecht looked aghast. "Six hundred?"

"Um. Ducats."

Albrecht threw his napkin onto the table. "Frederick agreed to pay this enormity of a sum?"

Dismas nodded. "Um. Plus expenses."

"What expenses?"

"Going to Cappadocia and back is an undertaking. Do you know what those extortionate Venetians are charging these days for ship's passage to Anatolia? Then there's the caravan. And the guides. And you have to hire a bodyguard of Mameluks. And another bodyguard to protect you from the first bodyguard. What a country! Then you have to pay all the local sultans along the way for permission to—"

"Yes, yes, we are sure it was a laborious undertaking."

Albrecht dabbed at his perspiring forehead with his napkin. He rose and went over to look at the shroud.

"Cousin?" Dismas said diffidently.

"Yes?"

"Forgive me, but you're perspiring."

"What of it?"

"If you don't mind . . . perhaps not on the holy shroud?"

"Oh." Albrecht stepped away from the table. "All right. Five hundred. Plus another fifty for your expenses."

Dismas gestured helplessly. "But, Cousin. It's promised. To Frederick."

Albrecht looked at Dismas gravely.

"Are you aware, Dismas, of what is going on in Wittenberg?"

"Well, I've been away. Cappadocia."

"I much regret to inform you that Wittenberg has become a hive of heresy."

"Oh? Um. Hm. That's not good."

"It is monstrous. And I much regret to say that your uncle is harboring a diabolical enemy of Holy Mother Church. I speak of the foul Augustinian friar Luther, may God have mercy on his leprous soul."

"I had heard something . . ."

"Are you aware, Dismas, that your uncle Frederick has refused to deliver Luther for examination by the Dominican *inquisitores*?"

"Oh, dear."

"Further, that he refuses not only our request to hand him over, but the repeated requests of his holiness himself? What do you say to that?"

"Well, I'm no theologian. But it sounds . . . naughty."

"And now, Dismas, you propose to take this . . ." Albrecht looked reverentially upon the shroud. He made a sign of the cross. ". . . most sacred of all relics into the very den of this iniquity."

Dismas frowned. He looked perplexed. Then brightened. "Perhaps it might help to purify the den of iniquity."

"How?"

"Perhaps when Luther sees it he will repent. Or maybe when Uncle Frederick sees it, he will realize his error and hand Luther over to your good Dominicans."

"We dare not take that risk, Dismas. We speak now not as your cousin, but *ex cathedra*."

"Who?"

"Officially, Dismas. That is, in our capacity as Archbishop. We speak with the full authority of Mother Church."

"Oh. Should I kneel?"

"That won't be necessary. Look here, Dismas. We cannot in good conscience allow you to take the burial cloth of Our Blessed Lord into Sodom and Gomorrah. We cannot. Therefore, on behalf of Holy Mother Church, we, her humble servant, will take possession of it. Fear not. You will be paid. Yes. Even though we must declare that five hundred ducats *is* a most staggering sum."

"Five-fifty. Expenses."

"As you say. Done."

Dismas nodded gravely. "Well. I cannot disobey my Archbishop. That would be a sin. Would it not?"

Albrecht nodded. "A grave sin."

"Then it appears that I have no choice. But what am I to tell my uncle Frederick?"

"Leave Frederick to God's just and good judgment. We shall endeavor to bring him back into obedience to Holy Church."

"Dear Uncle Frederick," Dismas said.

Albrecht put a hand on his shoulder.

"Be content, Dismas. The shroud belongs here. God is well pleased with you. Does the Bible not tell us, 'Render unto Caesar that which *is* Caesar's. And unto God, that which *is* God's'?"

Dismas nodded. "If you say."

10

To Hell with Purgatory

Back in Nuremberg, Dismas went directly to inform his fellow conspirator of his success. They celebrated in the time-honored fashion of conspirators—by getting well and truly drunk.

"Then he says to me, 'Render unto Caesar that which is Caesar's.' "

Harghhh!

It was lively at the corner table at the Corpulent Duke.

"We should have asked for more," Dürer said, shaking his head. "I knew it."

"Five hundred and fifty is a good day's work. So, listen. Listen. Are you listening?"

"Yes."

"The next morning, I pretended to have a really bad head. And he tried to convince me that I had agreed to four hundred."

"What an asshole! You didn't let him—"

"Oh, no."

Dismas dug into his pocket and pulled out a fistful of gold ducats. He dropped them one by one onto the table, making a clinky waterfall.

"How are you going to explain all your ducats to Agnes?"

Dürer frowned. "Hadn't thought of that."

"Buy her something nice."

"A flying stick!"

Harrgh!

"Necklace, better. See? I think of everything."

"Screw the necklace. I'll tell her the Emperor finally paid me for the Aachen altarpiece."

"*You* did the Aachen altarpiece? I thought it was whatsisname."

"It was. But she won't know that."

Harrghh!

"Very humorous, Nars. Everything is humorous. Even I am humorous. And I am from the cantons, where no one is humorous. Here, have some more brandy." Dismas poured onto the table, entirely missing Dürer's cup.

"Look, what a mess," Dürer said. He dipped his forefinger into the puddle and began to paint on the table. "A new medium. God, I'm versatile."

"What are you painting? Wait, I know. A self-portrait! Yes. Looks just like you. The eyes so limpid."

"You have no aesthetic sensibility. But what else can one expect from a Switzer peasant. Look. Can't you see? It's a portrait of Albrecht! He's crying!"

Harghhh!

Dürer belched. "It shows him after he has found out that his shroud, for which he paid the sum of five hundred and fifty ducats, is fake. Look how he cries! To hell with him. Now he has a Dürer, which is better than any true shroud."

Dürer leaned over the puddle and addressed it. "Are you happy now, stupid Archbishop?"

Dismas said, "Why would he find out that it's a fake?"

"I am making a joke. You are not understanding it. One of us needs to be more drunk. I think it's you. Or me."

Dürer reached into his pocket and pulled out a fistful of ducats. He arranged them into neat piles.

"Mine are neater than yours. But I am an artist. Look how they glisten in the candlelight. There is true beauty. Are you listening? Or are you dreaming about cows in the Alps? What a philistine you are, Dismas. But a good philistine." He turned back to the ducats. "I will paint them. I will call it *Still Life with Albrecht's Ducats*!"

Harrrrghhh!

"Wait. I know," Dismas said. "You can put your self-portrait on the coins. That way you can have *many* self-portraits!"

"Tell me again what he said, about the cost."

Dismas imitated Albrecht's voice. *"We must declare, Dismas, it is a most* staggering sum."

Harggghhh!

Dürer said, "Do you know what I learned? After you left for Mainz? Albrecht is taking bribes. From the Emperor."

"Bribes? For what?"

"Maximilian is dying. He wants to put his grandson Charles, the King of Spain, on the throne. So with his last ducats, he's bribing the electors to vote for him. If only I knew this before you left. We could have asked for—a thousand. Two thousand . . ."

"Be content, man. We got five hundred and fifty."

"It's all rotten," Dürer announced with sudden gloom. "It's all corruption and rot. We live in a time of rottenness."

"Before you mount the pulpit, consider. We have just swindled the most powerful archbishop in Germany out of five hundred and fifty ducats. *Now* you may declaim about how evil are the times."

"Well . . ."

"Not everything is rotten. Frederick is not rotten. A toast—to Frederick of Saxony. Do you know, I made Albrecht toast him."

Harggh!

"You should have seen his face. I thought he'd—shit. *Spalatin.*"

Frederick's secretary was standing by the door. He looked about, spotted Dismas, and came over to their table.

"Well!" Spalatin said heartily, smiling and taking in the scene of the two lubricated friends and their piles of gleaming ducats. "I see we are celebrating."

"Yes," Dismas said, suddenly sober. "We are . . . I . . . I lost my money to that scoundrel Bernhardt."

Spalatin nodded sympathetically. "Yes. I was sorry to hear it."

Dismas gestured at the coins. "Well, I hired a lawyer. A clever fellow. And . . . he got it back for me. Some of it. Expensive, lawyers. But worth it. As you can see."

"I'm glad. Your uncle's been asking for you."

"We were just toasting him. I'm coming to see him."

"Something rather strange happened," Spalatin said. "Last week."

"Oh?"

"A courier arrived at the castle. He said he had an urgent message from Master Dismas of Nuremberg. But when it was opened, it was blank. Empty. Nothing. Was it from you?"

"I . . . no. No. I would remember, sure. Well, that is strange. Will you drink with us?"

"Thank you, no. I'm meeting Henlein, the clockmaker. He's over there. Your uncle wants a fancy clock for the lecture hall. Let's hope it's less expensive than your lawyer. Best not let him see this pile of ducats or he'll try to sell *you* a clock."

Spalatin went off to sit with the clockmaker.

"Do you think he believed me, about the letter?"

"He didn't seem to care. Why'd you tell him that, about the lawyer?"

"It was all I could think to say. Should I have told him it was the ducats the Emperor paid you for the Aachen altarpiece? One of us had to say something. There's enough money here to—"

"Buy another drink. And another after that."

It was well after midnight when they left the Corpulent Duke.

"Don't fall into the moat," Dürer cautioned.

Dismas said, "I shouldn't have lied to Master Spalatin. He's a good man."

"Yes. You should have told him the truth. That you sent your uncle a big lie written in vanishing ink as part of a scheme to swindle the Archbishop of Mainz. Ye shall know the truth, and the truth shall set ye"—Nars belched—"free. Come on, let's go to Wittenberg right now so you tell him yourself."

"If you are trying to console me, you are not."

"I'm only saying—"

"Well, don't say anything more."

"Stop tormenting yourself. We've done a great service. Maybe now Albrecht won't be able to afford his cardinal's hat."

Dismas pulled a ducat from his pocket and held it up to the moonlight.

"Where do you suppose this came from, Nars?"

"From where all ducats come. Jacob Fugger."

"More like, from some poor bastard who dropped it into Albrecht's indulgence coffer to free a loved one from Purgatory."

"If he dropped that into the coffer, he may have been a bastard, but sure, he wasn't poor. And if he was so stupid as to believe you can buy your way out of Purgatory by giving gold to an overfed friar, I say too bad for him. I'm with Luther. He says there is no Purgatory. It's all a lot of hoo-ha to scare us into believing. I say to hell with Purgatory. Hey. That's good. To hell. With Purgatory? Do you see?"

"Yes, Nars. Very amusing. Make sure to tell it to Agnes."

11

On My Honor

A few days later, Dismas was on horseback approaching Wittenberg on the Leipzig road.

He had no great affection for Wittenberg as a place. It was a small, flat town on the northern bank of the Elbe, surrounded by nothing in particular. Amusingly, various artists, Cranach among them, added to their landscapes of Wittenberg a backdrop of majestic mountains, making it look Bavarian. Yet for its drabness, you had to admire what Frederick had wrought here: a university that would someday rival even Paris.

As his horse clopped across the wooden bridge Dismas saw the great tower of the castle church rise on his left; on his right, the twin towers of the cathedral. On the far eastern edge of town was the Augustinian monastery where Friar Luther was probably at this very moment scribbling another scalding diatribe against the Holy Father in Rome. Yet another headache for Uncle Frederick.

The guards at the city gates waved him through. Soon he arrived in the courtyard of the castle church. He dismounted and stood awhile looking up at the edifice. It saddened him to think that he would never see it again, this place where he'd spent so much time over the years, filling Frederick's galleries. He was sadder, still, to think he'd never again see his great patron.

Chamberlain Klemp told him the Elector was in the long gallery. Master Cranach was painting another portrait.

Dismas went first to Spalatin's study. He was a bit anxious about the chance encounter at the tavern in Nuremberg.

"Ah, the prodigal nephew," Spalatin greeted him with a smile.

What did he mean by that? Or was it just his wonted jocundity? After a few pleasantries, Dismas asked casually, "By the way, did you ever find out more about that strange business of the courier?"

"No. Probably just a stupidity by the Taxis. Not the first, by any means. So, have you brought something wonderful for your uncle's galleries? There's not much room left. We did an inventory last month. Care to guess?"

"Over seventeen thousand, I should think."

"Seventeen thousand four hundred and forty-three. I don't think the Archbishop of Mainz will ever catch up, at this rate. Speaking of whom, we hear from Mainz that he's got himself a shroud."

"Ah? Well." Dismas laughed uncomfortably. "There are an awful lot of shrouds out there."

"This one's said to be quite something." Spalatin looked. "Have *you* not heard of it?"

"I? I've been traveling, you know. And I've seen too many shrouds in my day to get excited. How's my uncle?"

"Fair. Gout. Stones. As you know, he loves to eat."

"Ah, yes." Dismas patted his belly.

"He misses the hunt. It was such a part of his life. But that's all in the past now. Luther continues taxing."

"What's the latest?"

"We're hearing of plots against his life. We've posted guards all about."

"Would they dare try to kill him here?"

Spalatin shrugged. "He's made enemies of powerful people. The Emperor, the Pope, and our beloved soon-to-be Cardinal of Mainz. If it weren't for your uncle, Friar Luther would be a pile of ash and bone by now."

"Well, thank God for Uncle Frederick."

"Difficult to predict how it will go. One hopes that in addition to writing pamphlets denouncing Rome, Friar Luther is finding time to pray God to grant long life to the Elector. Your uncle will be glad to see you. He talks of you all the time. He's so fond of you, Dismas. You *are* a nephew to him."

"Yes. Did you get a good price on the clock?"

Spalatin laughed. "I'm no match for a Nuremberg clockmaker. We may have to borrow some of those ducats of yours. I'm glad you got them back. What a scoundrel, Bernhardt."

Dismas made his way to the long gallery. He entered at the far end. Frederick was in a great chair by the window. His eyes looked closed. Was he slumbering? Posing for portraits bored him.

Dismas approached softly. The floor creaked. Cranach turned and put a forefinger to his lips. Dismas peered at the easel. A miniature. The brushes were tiny, some had only one or two hairs. They spoke in a whisper.

"How is he?"

"Asleep."

"So I see." Dismas examined the tiny painting. "It's good."

"What have you been up to? Digging up graves?"

"No. I'm done with all that."

"What's this about Albrecht's shroud?"

Dismas shrugged. "Spalatin mentioned something."

"Shouldn't you know?" Cranach said. "It is your business."

"I've seen more shrouds than you have canvas, Master Cranach."

Frederick's eyes opened. In his youth, they bulged, giving his gaze an intense, manic aspect. Dürer's portrait had caught it. Now in old age—and great weight—they'd receded and fixed you sideways. The jowls softened what might otherwise have been a severe, even malign countenance.

"Nephew. Are you advising Master Cranach?"

Dismas smiled. "Trying to get him to add a halo, but he refuses until you are canonized."

"Little chance of that, now. Come." Frederick beckoned for a hug. "Lucas."

"Yes, your worship?"

"Enough for today."

"As you wish, my lord."

Cranach gave Dismas an annoyed glance as he wiped his brushes. A man of many parts, Cranach: court painter, burgomaster, owner of the largest publishing house in Wittenberg, owner of its pharmacy, owner and builder of properties. He and Luther were close.

Dismas thought: Dürer and Cranach, two great artists. Dürer melancholic, yet you can have a laugh with him if he's in the right mood. In all the years Dismas had known Cranach, he had never had one laugh with him, or even seen him laugh. Dismas thought Cranach's painting reflected this. No felicity.

"What have you brought your aged uncle?" Frederick asked.

"I fear I've come with empty hands. I've . . ." The words caught in his throat.

"What is it?"

"I've come to say good-bye, Uncle. I'm going home. It's time."

Frederick frowned heavily. His ears moistened.

"This is very sudden. We've work to do yet on the collection."

Dismas smiled. "You've the greatest collection in the world, Uncle. Well, after the Vatican's. Master Spalatin tells there's hardly any room left."

"And how will you make your way?"

"I'll be all right. Your generosity all these years has made me prosperous. Don't worry on that account."

"I thought you lost all your money. To that devil Bernhardt."

So. He knew. Spalatin.

"I"—he cleared his throat, evicting the lie—"I was able to recoup some of what was lost."

Frederick stared. Dismas's insides shriveled.

"I shall miss you, Dismas."

"And I shall miss you, Uncle."

Frederick twisted a ring from a finger and held it out.

"A token of my love."

"I . . . no." Dismas held up his palms in refusal.

"It belonged to my uncle. Stop dithering. Take it."

It was a signet ring engraved with the Wettin coat of arms and the crossed red swords of the Arch-Marshal of the Holy Roman Empire.

"It's too much, Uncle."

"God keep you safe, Dismas."

They embraced. Dismas walked to the door, eyes welling.

"Dismas."

"Yes, Uncle?"

"You heard. Albrecht and his shroud?"

Dismas winced.

"Yes, Uncle. I heard."

"It sounds marvelous, does it not?"

"Well, as you know, Uncle, shrouds are the most problematic of relics. How many have you and I been offered and declined?"

"Sixteen."

"There."

"Yet there seems to be great excitement over this one. Its provenance is said to predate that of the Duke of Savoy's."

"Well, still . . ."

"Dismas."

"Yes, Uncle?"

"How long have we known each other?"

Dismas's insides were on fire. "Very long, Uncle."

"I should hate to think that anything was left unsaid between us at our last meeting."

"I, too."

"Why did you not offer it to us?"

Dismas's heart beat like a cantering horse.

"I . . . was not altogether confident of the provenance, Uncle."

"Yet you were confident enough to offer it to the Archbishop."

"His grace has never been fastidious with regard to provenance. Recently, he built himself Saint Peter's Galilean fishing boat. I thought it unlikely he would cavil at this item."

"In other words, you sold him a forgery."

"Well . . ."

Frederick shook his head.

"I am disappointed in you, Dismas. I have no fondness or regard for Albrecht." His voice rose to a growl. "But he is about to become a prince of the Holy Roman Church."

Dismas wanted to melt into the cracks in the parquet.

"How much?"

"Five hundred and fifty, Uncle."

Frederick gave an impressed grunt. "I suppose I should count myself fortunate to have been spared *that* expense."

"Oh, Uncle. I would never have . . . never. On my honor."

"You speak of honor?"

"Until this occasion, Uncle, I never sold anyone a piece, to you or to anyone, that I knew to be false."

Frederick nodded sadly. "So you were virtuous. Almost to the end."

Dismas's cheeks burned with shame.

"Still I shall miss you. Now go, and tell Master Cranach to come and finish me off."

12

A Great Day

Dürer insisted on being present at the grand unveiling of the Shroud of Mainz, despite Dismas's insistence that he not attend.

"Frederick *knows*, Nars. He's not going to say anything. But Spalatin knows . . . look, if it gets out, and we're seen together here . . ."

But Dürer was obdurate. Not for anything could he be dissuaded. He seemed to regard the unveiling as just another art opening. Dismas relented in the end, but insisted that Dürer wear a monk's habit as a disguise.

"If someone shouts out, 'My God, it's a Dürer!' sure, I don't want to be found sitting there next to Dürer."

Albrecht—now officially Albrecht Cardinal Brandenburg—staged the occasion with elaboration worthy of the Second Coming.

As they made their way into the cathedral, they saw Friar Tetzel, very much open for business with his indulgence coffer.

"Swine," Dürer loudly muttered.

"Quiet, for God's sake," Dismas hissed. "What did you expect? That Tetzel wouldn't be here? Why do you think Albrecht bought the shroud? For decoration?"

They took their seats, which Dismas had made sure were not up front. From outside the cathedral, they heard a tremendous blast of trumpet.

"*Just* as Our Lord would have wanted," Dürer said.

Dismas counted 250 in the procession. Albrecht, now thirty, looked splendid in his new scarlet galero and vestments. In his lengthy homily, he paid homage to St. Boniface, martyr and patron saint of Mainz and Germany, he who had established Christianity among the heathen Franks. Albrecht referred to him several times as "our most beloved forefather in Christ," slyly insinuating direct lineal descent.

Dürer groaned and muttered throughout. Albrecht concluded by calling for all good German Christians to join in Christ and heal the recent divisions by burning Martin Luther at the stake.

"Yes, that will bring us all together," Dürer said. "Nothing so healing as a good *burning*."

It was time for the main event. On a signal, two thin golden ropes threaded through pulleys high in the ceiling lifted the shroud from its bejeweled silver and gold reliquary case, suspending it in midair above the altar.

There it wafted among clouds of incense and chords of plainchant. Many gasped, just as Albrecht had on first seeing it on the table in his study. There were moans and cries of religious extremis. Even Dürer conceded that as stagecraft, it was "Not bad."

Dismas had predicted at least one spontaneous miraculous "healing" at the unveiling. As it turned out, there were two: a blind man saw, and a lame woman walked. Both miracles courtesy of Tetzel.

When the woman, second to be healed, cried out, Dürer whispered, "I had no idea it was that good."

After the ceremony, there was a wine and cheese reception for major donors in the cloister courtyard. Dismas forbade Dürer to attend and went alone.

It was a warm day. He was thirsty, and still in a turmoil of emotions over Uncle Frederick's disappointment. He drank several cups of wine in rapid succession.

Albrecht stood at the head of the receiving line, in excelsis, beaming as he received compliments on the marvelous thing he had done for Mainz. Dismas joined the line.

Albrecht's smile tightened when he saw Dismas. He had deemphasized Dismas's role in obtaining the shroud, preferring to create the impression that its appearance was somehow miraculously coterminous with his elevation to the College of Cardinals. He extended his hand and bulbous cardinal's ring.

"Ah, Dismas. A great day."

"Indeed, Eminence."

"Bless you," Albrecht said by way of dismissal.

Dismas, emboldened by wine, stood his ground.

"How wonderful," he said to Albrecht, "such a spontaneous validation."

"Eh?"

"The healings. Two!"

"Yes. As you say, wonderful. Good to see you."

"I expect his eminence will amortize his investment in no time at all."

Albrecht's smile tightened into a rictus.

"Good day to you, Dismas."

"Actually, it's good-bye, Eminence. I'm leaving. Going home."

"Ah?" Albrecht did not look displeased.

"Retiring. How could I ever hope to top this?"

"Yes, well, bless you. Now move along, there's a good fellow. Kaspar. Countess. How splendid to see you both."

13

Not a Great Day

It would have been easier to travel south by river, even against the current, but the numerous toll stations on the Rhine between Mainz and Basel were full of nosy tax inspectors. With all those lovely ducats he was carrying, Dismas thought it more prudent to take the road, in his monk's-habit disguise.

A journey of one month, perhaps: Strasbourg, Basel, bypassing Berne to Thun, down into the Lauterbrunnental, and then the steep climb up to Mürren. He wished he were there already. But he was grateful to have the hard riding ahead to distract him from his shame over Frederick's admonition. It gnawed at his heart like a rat. He had given serious thought to donating his ill-gotten ducats to the first monastery he came across. But then what? Again take up the life of relic hunter? He could never show his face again in Frederick's court. And the thought of further dealings with Albrecht was—unthinkable. Start all over again, hawking relics in the fairs? No.

So, he resolved to push on, pray for forgiveness, or at least forgetfulness, and concentrate on home. On the bracing mountain air, the deep pine smell, meadows that burst into color in the spring, the roar of glacial rivers, the full moon on snow, and the night-shriek of owl and hawk. These would heal his soul.

Toward nightfall of the fourth day he heard hooves approaching from behind and his name being shouted and the harsh command to halt.

Lieutenant Vitz rode at the head of a dozen men. There were no courtesies or explanations. One of Vitz's men seized the reins of Dismas's horse. Swords were drawn. What was this?

He was to accompany them back to Mainz. No reason was given. On the ride back, which was briskly paced and ominously devoid of conversation, Dismas racked his brain to think what could have occasioned such a brusque recall.

They reached Mainz in the middle of the night. Despite the hour, Dismas was escorted directly to Albrecht's formal reception room. Here he found himself face-to-face with the grim-faced Cardinal, a frowning monsignor, several fretful priests, and a stone-faced Drogobard. Spread before them on a long table was the shroud. Not a good sign.

Albrecht did not extend his ring to be kissed. He pointed to the shroud and said, "Pray, explain *that*."

Dismas glanced at the shroud, then at Albrecht. "I do not understand, Eminence."

He walked to the table and examined the shroud. Nothing appeared awry. It was just as he had last seen it.

"Was it the custom of Our Lord to wear jewelry?"

"I . . . cannot think so, Eminence."

"Specifically, rings?"

Dismas peered at the image's hands. He saw it—there, on the right hand. He stared. Surrounding details swam into focus: the ring was in the mouth of a winged, crowned serpent.

He recognized it. His chest tightened. Cranach's signature: a detail from the coat of arms bestowed on him by Frederick on the occasion of being appointed court painter.

His mind reeled. What in God's name was it doing on the shroud?

Dürer!

But how had he not seen it before? He'd examined every stitch, every fiber of Dürer's shroud.

Dismas looked up at Albrecht.

"I fear that I . . . still do not comprehend. This . . . was not there before."

Albrecht motioned to the monsignor. The monsignor spoke:

"There was a fire in the chapel where the shroud is kept. There was intense heat. The emblem appeared *then*."

Dismas's mind raced. Albrecht wasn't above parading fake relics like a St. Peter fishing boat. But the Cardinal of Mainz was not one to tolerate being made a fool of in front of his own people.

Apart from a fierce desire to murder Dürer, Dismas couldn't think what to say, other than: "Could it be *another* miracle?"

"Seize him," Albrecht ordered Drogobard.

Drogobard's hand clamped tightly around Dismas's arm.

"Wait, Eminence," Dismas said. "At the unveiling, did we not all witness two miracles?"

Albrecht glared.

"And that being the case"—Dismas forged ahead—"how could the shroud be a fake?"

Albrecht was in a cold rage. But he could hardly admit to *those* frauds in front of his monsignor and the priests and Drogobard. Luther had stirred things up too much. Faked miracles were not only out of fashion but frowned upon. These people in the room might be his servants, but servants gossiped. It would get out. He was Cardinal now. Dismas had him, for the moment.

"Leave us."

The monsignor, priests, and Drogobard withdrew.

Albrecht rose from his throne and descended the steps of the throne platform. He circled Dismas.

His tone was wounded rather than censorious. "What did we do to deserve such perfidy?"

"In sincerity, Eminence, I am every bit as astonished at this as yourself." The statement was truthful at the technical level.

"No, no," Albrecht said. "None of that." He made another slow circle. "Master Cranach's signature was not supposed to reveal itself until you were safely back in your cantons. Your neutral cantons, where you are beyond our reach. But for the accident of the fire, you would have made your escape."

"Eminence—"

"One more word and I'll summon Drogobard to remove your tongue. Now, who contrived this pretty little plot? Yourself? We think not. For you are not that clever, are you, Dismas? No. You're just a dirty Switzer bone dealer, wearing fine boots bought with thievery. No. Such a witty piece of treachery would have been devised by Uncle Frederick. Frederick. The Wise."

The full horror now dawned on Dismas. Albrecht thought this was Frederick's doing, a plot to humiliate him.

"May I speak?"

"Oh, yes. Please."

"It was me. Not Frederick. It was my doing."

Albrecht scoffed. "You thought this up? You painted this?"

"Yes."

"Such talent, Master Dismas! We had no idea you were such an artist. And why did you adorn this masterpiece with Cranach's signature, pray?"

"I believe the explanation must be that . . . it is a pentimento."

"Pentimento?"

"Yes," Dismas went on. "Yes. I recall, now. I had the linen for some time. Some years ago, I remember painting Cranach's signature on it. In tempera. I put it away and forgot all about it. Tempera fades over time, you see. Especially on linen. So what had been there before must have . . . vanished. When I set about to make the shroud . . . I had forgotten about it. Careless of me," Dismas said with a nervous laugh. "So your eminence is right. I am not so clever, after all. And now I am at your mercy."

"Mercy? Is that what you expect?"

"Well, it is a virtue commended by Our Lord."

"Do not speak to us of Our Lord." Albrecht pointed at the shroud. "You have profaned his very image."

"If I might propose, respectfully—your eminence was not quite so fastidious in the matter of Saint Peter's boat."

"Guard!"

Dismas was taken away.

14

Cardinal Sin

"A message for the Elector, Master Spalatin. From Mainz. The Cardinal."

Spalatin took the letter from his servant with a certain weariness. *Another* letter of complaint from Albrecht about Luther? There had been dozens, ranging from pleading to sputtering outrage at Frederick's refusal to hand him over.

He reached for his knife to cut the seal. This one, he thought, must be some complaint to Frederick's not having attended Albrecht's installation as cardinal. Which had nothing to do with Luther. A simple matter of Frederick's health.

Spalatin read.

"Christ."

He rushed to Frederick's quarters. He gave the letter to the Elector. Frederick read, brows furrowing.

Your odious and contemptible plot has been discovered. Do you truly suppose that this shall divert us from our efforts to carry out the will of the Holy See of Rome and bring your heretical monk Luther to judgment? If so, then you err as well as contravene.

Frederick looked up at Spalatin. "What in God's name is he talking about?"

"Read on."

Your agent in this disgraceful and deceitful affair, Relick Master Dismas, is my prisoner. Pray take me at my word that he is undergoing most rigorous examination. Pray also believe that his confession, fully describing the foul details of your blasphemous machinations, will shortly be published throughout the Empire, bringing shame upon Saxony and the House of Wettin.

Signed this day by your brother in Christ, whose Holy Name you mock by your patronage of the heretic Luther, and now by sacrilege most heinous.

ALBERTUS CARINA MAGVN.

Frederick shook his head. "Has he gone utterly mad?"

"I infer," Spalatin said, "that Master Dismas's shroud forgery has been discovered. That would explain the business of blasphemy and sacrilege. Why he implicates yourself in the matter is far from clear."

Frederick stared at the letter. "It's some trick. To create advantage in the Luther business."

"Possibly. But its logic is opaque, at least to myself."

Frederick sighed. "Whatever the case, he's got Dismas."

"Yes. I fear so."

"Didn't you tell me about some new technique of their employ?"

Spalatin nodded.

"Well?"

"It's called, I believe, the Marionette. There are . . . two manners of application."

"Just tell me, Georg."

"Hooks are driven into the ears, hands, and feet. The victim is suspended, the ropes manipulated. Thus the name. There were those who desired that Bernhardt, the Nuremberg swindler, should be dealt with in this fashion. It is popular with the spectators, as it can last for days."

A look of contempt came over Frederick. "This letter. When was it sent?"

"Five days ago."

"Christ."

"He's sturdy, Dismas. He was a *Reiselaufer*, remember."

"Dangling from hooks is different from soldiering, Georg. What he did was wrong. But I won't leave him to the mercy of Albrecht's inquisitors. You'll have to ride hard. Are you up to that?"

Spalatin nodded.

"Make whatever offer is necessary. Find out why he thinks we're behind this . . . calamity."

Spalatin bowed and made to withdraw.

"Georg."

"Yes, your worship?"

"Get him back. If only so I might wring his rascal neck myself."

Spalatin was ushered into the Cardinal's reception room at the palace in Mainz. He was in such crippling pain from his journey he had to grit his teeth as he limped across the stone floor. He rebuked himself for revealing his discomfort, and forced himself upright when he entered the chamber. Bowing to kiss Albrecht's outstretched ring sent a hot spike into his spine.

"*Em* . . . inence."

"You are unwell, Master Spalatin?"

"Well, Eminence. No longer young."

"Do we gather that your journey was not leisurely?"

"I am commanded by the Elector to convey his fraternal love. He is most aggrieved and anxious to know the reason for your—if you will permit me—astonishing allegations."

"If you will permit us, we are gravely disappointed in our once beloved brother."

"That much was clear from your missive. I am charged by my master with ascertaining why your eminence holds the Elector responsible for whatever offense is alleged."

Albrecht scoffed. "Master Spalatin. Let us not play at innocence."

The Cardinal gestured to a monsignor, who took from a box a folded piece of linen. He laid it on a long table and unfolded it, in a rather less than reverential way, like a hurried shopkeeper displaying third-best goods.

Res ipsa, Spalatin thought. The thing itself. He made a sign of the cross.

"No, no, no," Albrecht said. "We both know there is no need for that."

Spalatin's gaze fell on the shroud. It was quite marvelous. He felt Albrecht's eyes boring into the back of his skull like corkscrews.

"It's magnificent," Spalatin said. "I congratulate your eminence."

"How gratified we are that you approve. Tell us, do you think the right hand of Our Lord especially magnificent."

Spalatin looked. He didn't see it at first. Then there it was—a ruby ring in the mouth of . . . Good God, *Cranach's* signature? What on earth . . . ?

He looked up at Albrecht.

"I confess I am at a loss, Eminence."

"You do not recognize the signature of your own court painter, Master Cranach?"

"I do, yes. Even so."

Albrecht tapped his forefinger on the arm of his throne chair.

"Do not trifle with us, Master Spalatin. And take care, lest the ground beneath your feet open and you find yourself in our dungeon, dangling alongside your fellow conspirator."

Spalatin tried to assemble the pieces. Was *Cranach* the author of the shroud? It was, sure, Cranach's signature. But why would Cranach . . . ?

More to the point, why would Albrecht purchase a shroud so obviously signed?

"Your eminence must believe me when I say that this is all mystery. As indeed it would be to the Elector, were he here."

"So. You simply deny everything. Shame, Master Spalatin. You, esteemed for your scholarship and intellect. Is that all you have to offer us? A shrug? Perhaps you should join your friend, below."

Threats?

"Might your eminence answer one question before making more insults?"

"Go on."

"I acknowledge it to be Cranach's signature. Or a clever imitation. Why did your eminence purchase this object in the first place?"

"The signature did not reveal itself until later. There was a fire in the sanctuary. Your court painter's signature was precipitated by the intense heat. Thus was revealed your plot. The forgery was to become evident at some later time. Perhaps when the shroud was on display. Causing us grievous humiliation. So as to blunt our efforts to bring the heretic Luther to justice." Albrecht leaned back in his chair. "The fire surely was wrought by God, to protect us from your scheme."

Stark nonsense, Spalatin thought. Raving. Yet there was Cranach's mark. He wondered: had Albrecht had put Cranach's signature there, so he could level this accusation and put Frederick on the defensive to undermine his protection of Luther? Such scurrility was not beyond Albrecht. But the impasse had been reached.

"I shall return to Wittenberg and make my report to the Elector."

"What," Albrecht said silkily. "Leave us, so soon? Stay. Be our guest. We have ample room. Master Dismas will be glad of company."

"Does your eminence threaten?"

"No, Master Spalatin. I offer hospitality."

Spalatin drew from inside his cloak a paper, folded quarto. He handed it to Albrecht.

"The Elector had desired that our negotiation be conducted with cordiality and mutual respect. But as you now threaten, I am charged to inform your eminence that one thousand of this pamphlet are printed and in readiness for distribution throughout the Empire."

Albrecht read.

CARDINAL SIN
SHAME OF MAINZ
ALBRECHT
PURCHASES HIS CARDINAL'S HAT
WITH FUGGER DUCATS,
A FALSE RELIC OF ST. PETER
AND NOW, BRIBES
FOR HIS ELECTOR'S VOTE
JESU WEEPS
AS SAINTS CRY OUT FOR JUSTICE

He looked up from it at Spalatin, cheeks flushed.

"This is villainy."

"I agree, Eminence. I can think of no better word to describe such conduct. Bad enough to deceive the faithful with a boat purporting to be that of the Fisherman. But to be a custodian of the throne of Charlemagne who takes bribes for his vote? Villainy indeed."

Albrecht's face empurpled. He rose in fury from his throne. For a moment, Spalatin thought Albrecht might order him taken to the dungeon and strung up with hooks beside Dismas.

Then all defiance went out of him, like air from a cushion. He slumped back onto his throne.

"Very well, Master Spalatin. How shall we proceed?"

15

Is Something Amiss?

Spalatin was back in Wittenberg a week later, his negotiation with Albrecht having afforded a return at a less punishing pace.

A cessation of hostilities was in place. Dismas's "examination" was suspended, and himself unsuspended from the Petit Marionette. He would remain Albrecht's "guest" pending resolution of the matter. It was agreed that his wounds would be looked after by Albrecht's own surgeon. Spalatin put Albrecht on notice that if Dismas died—that he had not already was nearly miraculous—the pamphlet would be immediately distributed. Dismas's release, however, was far from certain, and Albrecht was far from pacified. He remained convinced Frederick was the architect of the shroud fraud. Spalatin departed Mainz with Albrecht's vow ringing in his ears: if Frederick released the pamphlet, Dismas would be re-hung from hooks and danced to death. Further, Albrecht would publish his own pamphlet, accusing Frederick of confecting the shroud scheme as a means to frustrate Albrecht's valiant attempts to bring Luther to justice.

So strained were relations between Brandenburg and Saxony that publication of either pamphlet might precipitate war. Much therefore was at stake.

To mitigate the sting in Albrecht's pride at having been duped, Spalatin had devised an arrangement: Albrecht would magnanimously "loan" the shroud to Frederick, ostensibly for display in his relic gallery at Wittenberg. The shroud would never be displayed, but would disappear forever, burned to cinders in a freak fire. Frederick would compensate Albrecht for his loss with a donation of five hundred and fifty ducats to the Mainz Almshouse.

The negotiations for Dismas's release were nearly complete when Albrecht added a final condition: a meeting with Frederick, on neutral ground. Spalatin pressed: To what end? What could such a meeting accomplish? Albrecht said he wanted to look Frederick in the eye to satisfy himself that he was innocent of the scheme. Spalatin and Frederick were suspicious, but Albrecht remained adamant. Dismas would not be released absent such a meeting. So it was arranged, to be held in Würzburg.

Concealing the movement of two electors, one the Primate of Germany, another the ruler of Saxony, was difficult if not impossible, considering the size of their respective retinues. A cover story was put out that this Würzburg Diet was an effort to reach a solution in the Luther affair.

"You're certain it was Dürer?" Frederick said.

"I have little doubt. They looked a perfect pair of rascals when I chanced on them that night at the Nuremberg tavern. Drunk as soldiers. Making little castles with their ducats." He smiled. "The very tableau of venality."

"And Dürer embedded Cranach's signature in it? Why?"

Spalatin shrugged. "Artists."

"How did he do it?"

"It's child's play. Milk. The juice of a lemon. An onion. Other techniques involve bodily fluids. Urine or . . ." Spalatin cleared his throat.

"Oh, go *on*, Georg."

"Ejaculate."

Frederick grimaced. "Let's hope it wasn't that. On a shroud? God save us."

"Master Cranach approached me earlier today. Indeed, my ears are still warm from his expostulations." Spalatin could not help but smile. "He's in a proper state."

"He knows?"

"No. But he had a commission from Albrecht to undertake a great altarpiece for the cathedral at Koblenz. Yesterday he received word from Mainz canceling the commission. No explanation given. He wanted my opinion as to whether he should pursue legal action for breach of contract. I advised against."

Frederick began to laugh. Slowly at first, until his great frame was heaving like a house in an earthquake.

Spalatin, too, laughed. "It does have a mirthful aspect. His umbrage would appear to eliminate him as a conspirator. If he were complicit, I doubt he'd be snorting like a mad bull and threatening to sue."

Frederick wiped the tears from his cheeks.

"I should like to have an interview with Master Dürer," he said.

"I, too. Very much."

Frederick considered. "Nuremberg is a free imperial city. We have no juridical rights there." He looked at Spalatin. "So we cannot compel him to come to Wittenberg."

"No." Spalatin smiled. "But it would be impolite of him to decline an invitation."

Frederick considered. "I should decline, were I he."

"Let me concern myself with the particulars," Spalatin suggested.

Dürer was in his studio putting the final touches on his portrait of Jacob Fugger when Agnes entered to say that three gentlemen had arrived. Imperial emissaries, they said they were.

Normally, Dürer found interruptions while working intolerable. But one must make allowances for imperial emissaries. Especially when the Emperor Maximilian still owed him the balance for two family portraits. Perhaps these gentlemen had come with his remuneration.

"Don't dawdle, woman," he said, wiping his hands with a terebinth-soaked rag. "Show them in. And bring refreshment. The *good* ale, Agnes."

Frau Dürerin muttered that she had seen better-dressed imperial emissaries in her day, and huffed off.

Presently the door to the studio opened and the three gentlemen entered. A glance was enough to incline Dürer to agree with Agnes about their attire. The trio was devoid of plumage, silk, or medallions. Into the bargain, they were unshaven, indeed, filthy.

Dürer had vast experience of dignitaries and servants in lordly employ. These chaps looked more the kind one might encounter lurking about a riverfront or city gate. At night.

The fellow who addressed him, with courtesy and deference, looked vaguely familiar, though Dürer could not place him. Portraitists recall faces. Where *had* he seen him before?

"We are commanded by his imperial highness, the Emperor, to escort you to him. Without delay."

Dürer wondered hopefully: *Could it be a summons to the imperial deathbed?*

"Is the Emperor . . . not well?"

"His highness ails. And for this reason is desirous of your presence. Time presses."

"I'm grieved to hear it," Dürer said. Something off, here.

"Might I ask, do you bear a written order from his highness?"

"No."

A rather cavalier answer, Dürer thought. He took a fortifying breath.

"With all respect to his imperial highness, you will allow this is a bit irregular. Numerously have I been summoned to court, and always there was something signed."

The leader—where *had* Dürer seen him before?—shrugged.

"Well, your honor, I'm sure that's the case. Still, here we are, and go we must. Now, why don't you gather up your things and we'll be on our way? Yes?"

The door opened. Frau Dürerin entered with a tray of ale mugs and sweetmeats whiffing of staleness.

"What's all this, then?" she said, setting down her tray and looking the trio over with a prunish air. "Payment for past work owed is my hope."

"Thank you, Agnes," Dürer said. "You may leave us."

"I'm only saying—"

"I'm to accompany these gentlemen to court. I am summoned. By the Emperor."

"Oh? Is the Emperor wanting to pay you himself, in person?"

"Agnes."

"It's all well and fine for you, gadding off to court, while I'm left to cope with the creditors. Don't suppose there's any point asking if *I'm* 'summoned to court'?"

"With regret, Frau Dürerin, it is Master Dürer who is asked for. Urgently."

"Mm," Agnes said. "Urgently. With emperors and cardinals and electors and what such, it's always *urgently*, isn't it? Unless it's about paying what's owed. Then it's *eventually*. Urgent is as urgent does, I say."

"Agnes."

"Don't mind me. I'm only a serving wench here. Scullion. While everyone else in the house is summoned to court. Shall I pack your kit? Will his honor be requiring his sable-lined doublet? Or will the sateen do? Don't ask me what's the fashion these days at court. It's been so long since I was asked."

Agnes left them, grumbling.

"Fine lady, your missus. Time to go, your worship."

Dürer now remembered where he had seen him. In Wittenberg. He was one of Spalatin's men.

"Is your name perchance Theobald?" Dürer asked.

"Theobald. Well, it's a good enough name that I wouldn't mind having it. But there's no time for chin-wagging, your honor. Never mind the packing. You'll have all the necessities when we arrive. At court."

"Now hold on," Dürer said. "Hold on one whisker. Your name's Theobald or mine's not Dürer. And your master isn't the Emperor Maximilian. It's Georg Spalatin, who serves the Elector Frederick. What's all this about? What's going on here?"

"No time for banter. Come along, now."

Dürer's face flushed red.

"I'm not going anywhere until you explain the meaning of this—this outrage!"

Theobald said in a tone gentle and firm, "Now then, your honor, we can do this two ways. There's easy. And there's not so easy. Easy's easier all round, for you, ourselves, and the lovely frau. No need to alarm her. No one wants that, I'll reckon. With all respect, she seems armful enough as is. Wouldn't care to see her in a pet. No."

"But I don't *understand*," Dürer stammered. "If Master Spalatin desires to see me, there's no call for chicanery. We have an excellent relationship. I *demand* to know the reason for this!"

The door opened. Agnes entered with a bag of husbandly necessities.

Dürer opened his mouth to cry alarm. As he did, he felt the sharp tip of a dagger pressing into the small of his back.

"Let me take that from you, Frau Dürerin," Theobald said pleasantly. "And may I say what a pleasure it's been to make your acquaintance. We'll take good care of his honor here, and hurry him back to you."

"Don't on my account," Agnes said, turning to go. "And if it's another portrait that's wanted, I'll thank you to make sure he's paid up front, in ready money. *And* for the two what's owed."

"Be assured," Theobald said gallantly, "I'll see to it, personal, like."

There was little conversation on the three-day ride to Wittenberg.

On arrival, Dürer was taken immediately to Frederick's reception room. There he found waiting the Elector and Secretary Spalatin. Their expressions conveyed neither welcome nor warmth.

"Master Dürer," Frederick said in a sepulchral tone. "How good of you to come."

"My lord. With respect, I protest most vehemently. Why have I been abducted in this manner? If you desired my presence, I would gladly have—"

Frederick held up a silencing hand.

"Master Dürer, are you aware of what has befallen my nephew Dismas?"

Dürer stared. "He went home. To Murrim or whatever he calls it. In the cantons. Why? Is something . . . amiss?"

Frederick regarded Dürer stonily.

"It is well you seem unawares, Master Dürer. If I thought you were awares, I should be displeased. Hard displeased."

Dürer looked from Frederick to Spalatin.

"What's happened? Is Dismas unwell?"

"He was hung from hooks in the dungeon of Mainz," Spalatin said. "For near on a week. I leave to you to construe if that constitutes unwell."

Dürer felt his chest constricting.

"Be assured, Master Dürer," Frederick said, his voice rising, "if I am not satisfied by the answers you give, you shall experience *my* dungeon."

The blood drained from Dürer's face.

When their interview concluded, Frederick rose from his chair on two canes.

"We depart for Würzburg tomorrow. You shall remain here, Master Dürer. It is not for me to dictate the prayers of another man. But I urge you to pray for my success there. Should I return without my nephew, then your prayers must need be most fervent, and for your own behalf. I bid you good night."

16

Penance

The Diet of Würzburg took place in the great hall of the Bishop's palace.

By prearrangement, the two doors at either end of the hall opened. Albrecht and Frederick entered and walked toward each other, Frederick on two canes, Albrecht with a sprightly, officious step. Frederick inclined with difficulty to kiss Albrecht's ring. Surprised by the gesture, Albrecht intercepted the Elector as he bowed and embraced him. An unwitting observer would have thought it a meeting of two old and cherished friends. They sat in facing chairs. Albrecht spoke first.

"How is our dear brother?"

"Old and fat. Scarlet becomes my dear brother. I regret I was unable to attend your installation. I hear it was a glorious occasion. As you see, my health is not robust. I am grateful to be able to extend personally my most cordial congratulations."

"We thank you most humbly. To be sure, it is humbling."

"I have no doubt you will discharge your office with the humility for which you are known. Now, to the substance of our meeting. I ask that you produce my errant nephew, that I may be satisfied that he has survived his ordeal. For without him, we can have no purpose here."

"Errant?" Albrecht clucked. " 'Errant' is inadequate to describe his wickedness."

"Let us not quibble over words. Produce him."

Albrecht said nothing. Spalatin thought, *Dismas is dead*. But then Albrecht raised a finger. A monsignor opened a door. Moments later Dismas entered, shuffling, supported on each arm by a Landsknecht.

His ears were mutilated where the hooks had torn out. His bandaged hands dangled limply before him. He seemed only dimly aware. He looked about the large room. When his eyes located Frederick and Spalatin, he smiled wanly and collapsed, supported by the two Landsknechte.

Frederick's tone was glacial. "Is *this* the justice of Mainz?"

"We burn blasphemers. So as you see, the justice of Mainz has been mild."

All cordiality gone, Elector and Cardinal glared at each other, hatred radiating off them in nearly visible waves. Looking on, Spalatin thought: If they were younger, they'd be at each other's throats, swords drawn. The meeting was over, surely. Albrecht had only insisted on the meeting in order to have the satisfaction of seeing Frederick's heart crack.

It was Frederick who broke the silence.

"What are your terms?"

"Luther for Dismas."

"No."

"Then we see nothing further to discuss." Albrecht gestured to Dismas's guards to take him away.

"Master Spalatin," Frederick said in a commanding voice.

"My lord?"

"Send word to Wittenberg. Commence distribution of the pamphlets. Then print another thousand and distribute them. Let all the world know what corruption has befallen the See of Mainz. Let all the world know that the Cardinal of Mainz sells his vote, along with his soul."

Frederick now rounded on Albrecht directly.

"You know me, Albrecht. I *will* do this. And neither you, nor Rome, will ever lay hand on Luther. Your name will echo in infamy down the ages. And when the next Dante writes his *Inferno*, there you shall be with the other simoniacs who sell absolution and heavenly favor for gold and silver. There you shall be, buried upside down in your own hole the size of a baptismal font, your wretched feet protruding to be licked by eternal flames. Think hard on that, brother. And consider—hard—if this man's death is worth all *that* to you."

Spalatin walked purposefully to the door. He'd reached it when Albrecht called out, "Wait."

The Diet of Würzburg did not end, but continued for some hours, tempers flaring, cooling, flaring anew, cooling again. Both men pressed every advantage. Spalatin could barely believe what he heard. What—after all—did Albrecht want? Frederick's relics.

Frederick consented to part with some of his rarest pieces: three thorns from the Crown of Thorns; the loincloth of St. John the Baptist; and dearest of all, the Holy Prepuce, one of the twelve of its kind averred to be the circumcised foreskin of the infant Jesus. Handing that over to Albrecht was hard sacrifice. Then when all seemed done and done, Albrecht said, "One more thing."

"No," Frederick said. "Enough."

"Dismas must make his confession."

Frederick and Spalatin looked at each other.

"You want him to *confess*?" Frederick said.

"He has sinned. Grievously. He must be shriven. It is for his own good."

"Look at him. Has he not done penance enough? Your concern for his immortal soul is touching. Rest assured I will see he is attended by a confessor. If he lives."

"We prefer to hear his confession here and now."

"For pity's sake, Albrecht."

"What if he should perish on the road to Wittenberg? Do you want him to go to judgment with the odious sin of blasphemy on his soul?"

Frederick sighed and gave a curt nod.

Albrecht motioned the two Landsknechte. They dragged Dismas over to him. He'd gone unconscious again. One of the Landsknechte slapped him sharply on the face to wake him. Spalatin saw Frederick's knuckles whiten around his cane handles.

Albrecht blessed Dismas with a sign of the cross.

"Do you wish to make confession?"

Dismas managed a nod.

"Do you confess that you committed sacrilege by contriving a shroud purporting to be that of our Blessed Savior?"

Dismas nodded.

"And are you sorry for your sin?"

Again Dismas nodded.

"We will grant you absolution for your sin. On condition that you undertake penance. Do you agree to do such penance as we give you?"

Dismas gave another nod, head sagging.

Albrecht looked at Frederick. A smirk.

"Your penance is to translate from Chambéry to Mainz the true burial shroud of Our Lord Jesus Christ."

17

Dismissal

There was no rejoicing or triumph on the way back to Wittenberg, only numb relief at Dismas's rescue. Frederick was in a black mood over Albrecht's trickery. He retired to his chambers and left them only to prowl his plundered relic galleries in the small hours of the night.

Spalatin devoted his hours to searching for a canonical loophole that might nullify the penance Albrecht had meted out to Dismas. He consulted with a number of divines. Naturally, he turned first to Wittenberg's own resident theologian, Friar Luther.

Luther ruled that Albrecht's penance was invalid, on the grounds that a penance mandating a crime, in this case, stealing the Shroud of Chambéry, was *eo ipso, contra lex naturalis*. That is to say, in itself an act contrary to natural law and therefore, canonically speaking, without basis or authority.

Tempted as Spalatin and Frederick were to accept this ruling, they thought it best to get other opinions. Luther's authority with respect to canon law was by this point somewhat shaky. Luther might still be a monk of the Roman Catholic Church, but he was a monk who almost daily denounced the Pope as "Antichrist" and Rome as "Babylon." His most recent pamphlets had gone so far as to nullify several of the holy sacraments themselves, on the grounds that they were nowhere specified in the New Testament. Luther's new doctrine desacralized confirmation, marriage, priestly ordination, and extreme unction. Even Erasmus of Rotterdam, himself sympathetic to reform, was appalled. Luther upheld the validity of baptism, Holy Communion, and an attenuated form of penance, while stoutly insisting that salvation came from faith alone, not priests. And certainly not from popes. Rumors were that Luther was revising the Ten Commandments themselves. Where would it end? Friar Martin was upending a millennium and a half of church doctrine. All of which made Frederick and Spalatin dubious as to the validity of his ruling as to Dismas's penance.

Spalatin consulted other church doctors, among them Melanchthon and even the great Erasmus. (For obvious reasons, he did not identify Dismas or reveal that the penance had specified the Shroud of Chambéry.) These grandees of the Roman Church ruled that, unusual as such a penance might be, it was valid on the grounds that relic translation was not in itself a crime. Church doctrine, after all, held that a relic could not be translated unless the saint—or member of the Holy Family—consented to it. The test of the penance's validity lay in whether the translation was effected. If Spalatin's unnamed penitent succeeded, this must be construed as divine approval of the penance and translation. This was not the ruling Frederick and Spalatin had hoped for. Spalatin conveyed the bitter news to Dismas.

His recovery proceeded. He was attended by Frederick's own surgeon, a chatty little Italian who referred to his wounds as his "stigmata." It was a jocose, if impious, reference to the five bleeding wounds miraculously received by St. Francis of Assisi, symbolic of Christ's. Dismas was recovered enough to be mildly amused by the little doctor's levity. His chief source of amusement on his sickbed derived from fantasizing exotic torments for Dürer.

There was little enough cheer in contemplating what lay ahead of him: a surely doomed journey of six hundred miles to steal the most closely guarded relic in Christendom. No joy there.

Spalatin tried to lift his spirits by telling him that one of the theologians with whom he'd consulted was certain that if Dismas was killed in the course of performing his penance, he would be spared the fires of Hell and that his sentence in Purgatory would not exceed seven centuries.

Dismas's misery was made more acute when Spalatin informed him that he was to be accompanied on his mission by three of Albrecht's Landsknechte, to ensure that Dismas did not make a run for the cantons. Albrecht insisted. The Confederation had declared itself neutral territory only a few years earlier, in 1515. If Dismas crossed over, he would be beyond the pale of Albrecht's authority, or anyone's.

Dismas guessed that the Landsknechte had orders to kill him even if he did not try to escape. But so dismal were all his prospects that he did not care. He was a dead man either way. The best he could hope for was a quick death while doing his penance. Time in Purgatory was said to pass quickly enough. Seven hundred years wasn't so bad, really. Maybe he could purchase an indulgence along the way to Chambéry.

Dürer, meanwhile, languished in another part of the castle, under house arrest, biding his time with mounting anxiety. Word was conveyed to Frau Dürerin that her husband was in good health, indeed prospering, having been commissioned by the Emperor to paint a great altarpiece. Alas this would prolong his return to Nuremberg, for some time yet.

A month passed. The talkative little Italian surgeon pronounced Dismas's wounds healed. The scars of the stigmata remained, a permanent disfigurement. His hands and feet were holed through. His ears, torn in two, now had a tendency to flap when he moved briskly, imparting an elfin aspect. Dismas concealed them by growing his hair long. He found himself praying to St. Francis of Assisi, his fellow stigmata-bearer, while acutely conscious of the difference between St. Francis's wounds and his own deserved ones. Dismas had no illusions of innocence. He had done something wicked. He had earned his wounds. He was resigned to whatever lay ahead.

But he wanted to meet it head-on, and so set about preparing himself physically for the ordeal. He put in hours in the castle courtyard with Frederick's fencing masters and armorers, polishing old skills and learning new ones. He had put aside weaponry after Cerignola, vowing never again to take up arms, except to protect himself.

Finally one day in early March, the summons came. Dismas made his way to Frederick's reception hall. Waiting for him were Frederick, Spalatin, and Dürer, who for once in his life looked sheepish. Dismas bowed to Frederick, nodded to Spalatin, and ignored Dürer.

"Nephew. You look much improved."

"I owe my uncle everything."

Frederick took in a deep breath, swelling the bellows of his chest.

"As you are aware, Master Spalatin has conferred with numerous authorities on the matter of the penance. Were it for myself to pronounce, I should dismiss it. But it is not. And this, Dismas, I regret. To the innermost chamber of my soul, I regret it."

It pained Dismas to see Frederick in such distress.

"Uncle. I understand."

Frederick nodded at Spalatin. Spalatin spoke.

"The Duke of Savoy displays the Shroud in Chambéry this fourth day of May, in two months' time."

Dismas calculated. Ten miles a day.

"The Cardinal requires that you be accompanied by three of his men. For our part, we have insisted to the Cardinal that they conduct themselves as men under your command. You are their captain. Their orders are to assist you in the translation. I am aware of your disinclination toward Landsknechte. Bear in mind that above all else, the Cardinal desires the success of your mission. It seems therefore reasonable to suppose they *will* assist you."

Frederick gave Dürer a withering sidelong look. "It is my order that you will also be accompanied by Master Dürer. You have your penance to discharge. Master Dürer has his."

"With respect, Uncle, Master Dürer can mine salt in Silesia for his penance. I decline his company."

"I am not sending him for the purpose of disconcerting you. He disposes of skills that could prove useful in such an undertaking as this."

"I am well acquainted with the skills of Master Dürer. I want no part of them."

"I do this for *your* benefit, Dismas."

Dürer spoke.

"With respect, your worship, Dismas surely has enough to concern him without having to—"

"Master Dürer. Here is your choice. You will accompany Dismas to Chambéry, subject to his command and rendering him every assistance. Or you will remain here. You are a painter. We can always use painters. Can we not, Master Spalatin?"

"Yes, your grace. The superintendent informs me that the cellar walls are in need of lime-washing."

"Which cellar walls?"

"All, your grace."

"How long do you reckon it would take one painter to accomplish this task?"

"A long time, I should think. And once it were finished, it would be necessary to begin again, at the beginning."

"Well, Master Dürer. How do you choose?"

Dürer said nothing.

"Then it's arranged. Georg, Master Dürer, leave us."

When the others had gone, Frederick said to Dismas, "Come, let me give you my blessing." He pressed something into Dismas's hand.

Dismas looked. It was a fragment of bone, edged in gold and attached to a gold chain. Dismas recognized it and smiled.

"The knuckle of Saint Christopher. Protector of travelers."

"I paid you twelve gulden for that. I'm not sure you deserve such an expensive gift."

"No. Sure, I don't."

"For that money, it had better be genuine, or you'll . . ." The words caught in his throat. The old man was fighting tears. ". . . have even more to answer for. But if it is genuine, it will keep you safe. God go with you, Dismas."

"And with you, Uncle."

Part Two

18

Cunrat, Nutker, Unks

It was an unusual company of pilgrims that crossed the Elbe River headed south on the feast day of St. Joseph of Arimathea, Year of Our Lord 1519: five monks, consisting of a Swiss mercenary-turned-relic-dealer, three German mercenaries, and a melancholic Nuremberg painter.

Dismas drove the horse cart, sitting in mute proximity to Dürer. The Landsknechte rode one in front, two behind. Their names were Cunrat, Nutker, and Unks. Dismas made no effort to converse with them. Like all their kind, they prided themselves on their flamboyant attire, similar to the papal Swiss guard. It pleased Dismas to discomfit them by making them don rough woolen monk habits. They chafed at this but, being under Dismas's command, had no choice in the matter.

Their retaliation, pyrrhic given the unseasonably warm weather, was to wear their own dandified outfits beneath their monk robes and cowls. This gave Dismas the added satisfaction of observing them itch and sweat.

True to Landsknecht ethos, Cunrat and Nutker and Unks were haughty, arrogant, and brutish. Their humor was base and cruel, triggered by a flatulent horse or some remembered gruesome incident. They spoke aloud about Dismas in the third person in a coarse persiflage of sniggers, taunts, and derision.

One day their theme of conversation was Dismas's mutilated ears. They carried on a protracted dialogue trying to settle which type of goblin he most resembled. The next day their topic was bovine sodomy, a familiar trope among Landsknechte, who taunted Swiss *Reiselaufers* by calling them "cow buggerers." So amusing.

Dismas ignored this simian babble and prayed to St. Francis for patience. When he grew weary of prayer, he fell to calculating how many of them he could kill before being killed himself. He thought one, sure, possibly two, but not the third. They were superb fighters. Dismas shut his ears to their japery and tried to focus on the hopeless task before him.

It was Dürer who rose to their bait, though Dismas suspected this was his way of attempting a peace offering.

"Hey, you girls," Dürer said, "don't you have more intelligent conversation than idiot jokes about buggering cows?"

Nutker laughed. "Cunrat, did you hear? Painter just called us girls?"

"Well, if we're girls, he should come back here and give us a good fucking."

"Hey, Painter," said Unks, "come give this girl a kiss."

"Fuck yourselves," Dürer said.

Dismas groaned. Six hundred miles of this?

St. Francis, gentlest of the saints, grant in thy benevolence—this once, only—that my companions should every one of them be smitten with plague. Or pox. Or, if it please you, struck by lightning.

Dürer muttered companionably, "Well, this is marvelous."

"Do not speak to me."

"Look, Dis, I'm sorry if things—"

"I said do not speak. Not one word more."

"It wasn't my fault."

"Not your fault? How was it not your fault? You put Cranach's signature on it. With your *sperm*."

"How was I to know they were going to put the thing in an oven?"

"It wasn't an oven. It was a fire, in the sacristy. Now shut your mouth. Or I'll carve Cranach's signature on you with this." Dismas produced his dagger.

Some hours later, Dürer tried again.

"You're not the only one who's suffered, you know."

This was too much. Dismas reined the horses to a halt.

"Did you just tell me you're not the only one who's suffered? Did you actually tell me that?"

"I'd call *this* suffering. One moment I'm in my own house, in my own studio, and next I'm being abducted by thugs."

"That's your definition of suffering, is it? Being interrupted at painting, in your studio? Care to hear mine?"

"I'm not saying you, too, haven't suffered."

"Out."

"What?"

"Out. Get out of the cart."

"Gladly."

Dürer stepped down. "Good-bye to you and good luck." He turned and started to walk off.

"Oh, no. Not 'good-bye.' You're coming with us, sure. You can walk to Chambéry. It's only six hundred miles. The exercise will do you good. Then you'll have some actual suffering to snivel about."

Dismas turned to the Landsknechte.

"Painter will walk to Chambéry. If he tries to run away, shoot him. Aim for his head. You can't miss. It is the largest part of him."

Off to a fine start.

Some miles later Dismas found himself musing on the irony of ordering Landsknechte to threaten Dürer with the same weapons they had used against him and Markus at Cerignola.

The horse cart had a concealed compartment. In it the Landsknechte had stashed a veritable armory—arquebuses, pikes, halberds, axes, swords, even a brace of handheld shooting weapons called *pistalas*, along with several kegs of the hated gunpowder. If this arsenal were to be discovered, it would belie their imposture as mendicant monks. To minimize the risk, they would avoid large towns, and make camp at night in woods, away from the road.

One night, a week into the journey as they sat by the fire under the stars, Dürer took out his sketchpad. He and Dismas had not exchanged a word since their altercation. Dürer's feet were bare, warming by the fire.

Dismas said, "What are you drawing, then?"

"None of your damn business."

Dismas looked at the drawing on Dürer's lap.

"Your feet? Another self-portrait. That'll fetch a fortune."

Without looking up, Dürer said, "What would you know about art? You're a philistine Swiss. Did I say 'philistine Swiss'? I repeat myself."

"Hey, Painter," Unks said. "Why don't you paint my cock?"

Dismas had concluded from a week of listening to their inane banter that of the three Landsknechte, Unks was the most stupid. He was also the most physically imposing.

"I don't do miniatures," Dürer said.

Unks rose and stood over Dürer. He drew his sword and pointed the tip at Dürer's chest.

"Call this small?"

Dürer flicked his forefinger against the blade, making a *tingg*.

"It's hard. I'll give you that much."

Unks's pride assuaged, he sat back down. Dürer continued to sketch his blistered feet, lambent in the firelight.

Dismas watched as the drawing took shape. It was good, though he could not imagine who would buy a picture of blistered feet. In Dürer's studio he'd seen a drawing of two hands clasped in prayer. Dürer made it into an engraving that sold many copies. But hands in prayer were one thing, blistered feet, another.

"You could call it *Pilgrim's Feet*," Dismas said. "Maybe that will help you sell it."

He made a pillow with some folded burlap and laid his head on it.

"Don't forget to put Cranach's signature," he said sleepily. "With your man-jam."

Dürer said, "I thought it an apt medium for a Cranach signature. More fitting than honey or caramel. Or onion juice. Or vinegar."

"You're Narcissus, sure. And we shall both die because of it."

Dürer stopped sketching. "Do you think we will die?"

"Yes."

Dürer stared into the fire. He pulled a fresh sheet from his sketchbook. "Then I will make your portrait. At least there'll be something left of you to remember."

"I don't want to be remembered."

"Don't be blithe. I'm offering immortality."

"You sound like Satan. What company I keep these days."

"Why do you think people pay me to make their portraits? To cover their walls? It's fear of being forgotten. Everyone wants immortality."

"Vanity of vanities, sayeth the preacher. All is vanity. God knows you know about that."

"Listen to Dismas the theologian."

"I'm not a theologian. I'm going to be killed on this mission because of your vanity. But at least I'll die doing my penance. One of Spalatin's theologians says I won't have to spend more than seven centuries in Purgatory. How many will you spend there, I wonder, for your part in this catastrophe? Or maybe it won't be Purgatory for you. Someplace warmer, perhaps."

Dürer put down his sketchpad. "That was cruel, Dis."

"Did I hurt your feelings? Shame on me."

"You know I'm a melancholic. Why would you tell me I'm going to Hell?"

"I didn't say I want you to spend eternity in Hell. Though I admit that I have wished for just that many times these last months."

"Luther says that penance meted out by priests is bullshit," Dürer said. "He says we don't need priests for that. We can deal directly with God."

"Then you'd best start dealing directly soon."

"Why should priests—or cardinals—have the power to condemn us or absolve our sins? I'm with Luther. Salvation comes from faith. Faith alone."

"If you want to wager your immortal soul on it, go ahead. Myself, I'll do my penance."

"So this is your revenge? To torment me for six hundred miles with visions of Hell?"

"It wasn't my plan," Dismas said. "But it's not a bad one. Good night."

19

Count Lothar

They skirted Karlsruhe and instead of taking the Rhine road, went southeast into the Black Forest. It was a more arduous way, but the main roads were full of imperial busybodies. Land without a ruler is unpredictable.

The Emperor Maximilian had died. The throne of Charlemagne was vacant. The election to fill it approached. Spalatin had confided to Dismas that Frederick himself had declined the crown, having been urged to seek it by—of all people—Pope Leo. Another irony: Frederick had decided to cast his vote with Albrecht for Maximilian's grandson King Charles of Spain. To provide a counterweight to the growing power of France. Pope Leo, too, wanted Charles as a check against King François.

Dismas understood little of high politics. But perhaps it was to the good that Albrecht and Frederick and Pope Leo should ally themselves in this, despite their bitter differences over Luther.

What would happen now to Luther? Charles of Spain was

strenuously—fanatically, they said—Catholic, a champion of the Inquisition. And Frederick was not a healthy man. He'd declined the Holy Roman throne, Spalatin had told Dismas, because he felt his life ebbing. What would happen to Luther then? Such were the morbid thoughts that weighed on Dismas as they made their way along the rough and rutted paths of the Schwarzwald.

His gloom became even more acute when, one night after they'd made camp on high ground in the forest, the moon came up, revealing in the south the snow-frosted peaks of the Alps.

"What's wrong with you tonight?" Dürer said, noticing Dismas staring so mournfully at the mountains. "Ah, sick for home."

"I'd be there now but for you."

"Can we not have one night without you moaning that I've ruined your life?"

"Sorry. Thoughtless of me."

Cunrat, Nutker, and Unks stood watching them at a distance, around their own campfire. They'd been keeping an even more vigilant eye on Dismas since entering the forest, being close to the border with the cantons.

Dürer said, "They think you're going to bolt now that you can smell the snow. Snow. Swiss aphrodisiac. I'll distract them for you so you can make a run for it. Hey there, Landsknechte. I heard a marmot squeak. Why don't you go shoot it for our supper?"

Nutker replied with an obscene gesture.

Dürer sighed. "So, it's to be another mouthwatering supper of salt beef and millet. It's playing hell on my bowels. Haven't had a decent crap in days. I've got a bolus inside me the size of a—"

"Nars. I don't want to hear about your bowels."

"That's how I'm going to die on this death march. Of cemented intestines. What a glorious death."

"Shh."

"Don't tell me to—"

Dismas grabbed Dürer's arm.

"Quiet."

Through the trees appeared a flicker of torches. Then came the rumble of hooves. Voices.

The Landsknechte were already on their feet, arming. At night they removed their arsenal from the cart to have it handy.

Nutker and Unks lit the arquebus fuses. Cunrat sprinted toward a rock outcrop at the edge of the campfire, cranking his crossbow as he went.

"Look smart," Dismas said. "I'll do the talking."

Five men on horseback, each with torch, stepped forward out of the trees. Dismas raised his hand in a greeting.

"Peace to you."

The men took stock of the scene before them: two monks sitting by one fire, two other monks by a second fire, armed with arquebuses with lit fuses.

The leader, a stout man with severe, unpleasant features, was expensively attired and mounted on a caparisoned horse. He spurred forward toward Dismas. His tone was arrogant, commanding.

"Identify yourselves."

"Who asks?" Dismas said.

"Lothar of Schramberg. These are my woods. I say again, identify yourselves."

"As you see, my lord, we are monks," Dismas said.

Lothar stared at Nutker and Unks.

"Monks, bearing arms?"

"The woods are dangerous, as his lordship knows, the woods being his."

"What I know, *surely*, is my woods are full of poachers who kill my game."

Dismas thought: *So you are out here in the middle of the night in the forest hunting for poachers?*

"We have no ill designs on your woods, your worship. We wish only to pass through, in peace."

"I am Count Lothar. Godson to the new Emperor, Charles."

Dismas bowed. "We are honored. Has the election been decided, then?"

"It will be, soon enough. Hand over your weapons."

This brought sniggering from Cunrat and Nutker.

"Forgive them, my lord," Dismas interjected. "We have been much accosted on our journey by footpads and highwaymen."

"That's no excuse for insolence."

"I will deal with them. Might I ask your lordship, with respect, why you are abroad at such an hour? Sure, it cannot be for poachers."

"We hunt a witch."

"A witch. Ah, well, that *is* a grave business. Then sure, your lordship will agree best we keep our weapons. For protection."

Lothar scowled, trying to determine if this was impudence or fear.

Dismas considered. A noble, witch-hunting, at this hour? Witch-fever in the southern part of the Empire ran high. Whenever there was an outbreak of plague, witches and Jews were in for it. Other times, witchery was a pretext for getting rid of a troublesome or inconvenient woman. Impotence was often ascribed to the evil influence of a witch.

Dismas had a repugnance of witch-hunting. As a boy, he'd witnessed a terrible and prolonged burning of three girls. Their torment went on for hours. But witch-fear was everywhere. Even Luther, now making a career of not believing, professed it. Yet none of this explained why an overfed, name-dropping count was out prowling the forest at night instead of rogering his countess or servant girls in a warm bed at his schloss.

"She's a bad one," Lothar said. "Greaser."

It was believed that witches smeared evil potions on things, to make spells.

Dismas made a sign of the cross.

"Pray, my lord, what did this creature infect with her satanic balm?"

"My barn."

Nutker and Unks burst out laughing. Dismas himself also thought Lothar's lament anticlimactic, but kept silent.

Fuming with indignation, Lothar said, "I'll have those two whipped for insolence."

"Pay them no heed, your lordship. They are novices. I will chastise them myself. Was your barn much harmed?"

"All my livestock, dead."

"Villainy," Dismas said, crossing himself again. "I shall pray to Saint Hubert for your success."

"Who?"

"Saint Hubert, your worship. Patron saint of hunters."

"She also greased the door of the church."

"God have mercy on us," Dismas said, crossing himself a third time. "And you seek this succubus hereabouts?"

"She was to be burned, but escaped. Well, monk, have you seen a woman?"

"No. But pray describe her, in case we encounter this fiend, that we may better gird our loins against her."

"She's comely."

"In that case, she can grease this!" Nutker announced, rubbing his crotch expressively.

"Pray keep quiet, Brother," Dismas rebuked him. "Praise God, your worship, we have not encountered any women."

"Name's Magda. Ginger hair. Lots of it. Curly, like that one's, there." Lothar pointed at Dürer.

"Red hair." Dismas crossed himself a fourth time. "Sure, a sign of the Cloven-Hoofed One."

"If you come across her, bring her to me at Schramberg. You'll be well compensated."

"If I come across her," Nutker said, "I will come *in* her!"

He and Cunrat guffawed.

This was too much for Count Lothar, who was accustomed, as most nobles, to obsequiousness in the lower orders.

"Take care for your tongue, monk, or I'll have it out!"

"Come and take it." Nutker stuck his tongue out at the Count and wiggled it obscenely.

"Brother," Dismas said through gritted teeth. "Respect for his lordship, if you please."

"Seize him!" Lothar ordered his men.

Nutker and Unks took aim with their arquebuses, fuses sizzling. Lothar's men remained in their saddles.

Lothar angrily wheeled his horse and galloped away back into the woods, his men following.

"Fools," Dismas said to Nutker and Unks.

"We don't lick Habsburg arse, like you."

Cunrat emerged from behind the rock. He walked up to Nutker and cuffed him across the face with the back of his hand.

Dismas and Dürer sat by the fire, too unsettled to sleep. Dismas watched sparks from the fire waft upward into the night, joining the stars, dancing above the moonlit Alps.

20

Magda

Dismas awoke at first light to sounds.

It was biting cold. The fire was out and his blanket was stiff with frost. Was that Nutker's voice? He peered out from under his blanket to locate the source of the noise and saw Nutker struggling, pulling something from the hidden compartment in the horse cart. Was it a leg? Yes, a leg. A woman's bare leg, kicking violently.

Nutker called out. "Unks! Look what I've caught! It's alive! Oof! A big one! Get over here, you lazy bastard, and give me a hand!"

Unks went to join in the strange melee. Each had a leg now and was pulling. The legs kicked mightily.

Dismas's gelid brain tried to make sense of the scene. Then through the rime he remembered the events of last night.

"Together—one! Two! Three!"

The Landsknechte braced their feet against the cartwheels and gave a yank. Out came their prize, landing on the ground with a thud, wriggling like a fresh-caught salmon.

"Hey, hey! Steady! Steady!" Cunrat grappled with his catch, now flailing at him with its arms. "Oh, it's alive! Ow! Damnit! It bit me!"

He gave her a sharp kick. "Stop! Or I'll give you a thrashing!"

The girl lay on the ground, breathing hard, fists up, cocked.

Dismas shouldered his way into the melee.

A woman. Young, pretty with—damn—ginger-colored hair and yes, lots of it. She looked up at her captors with frightened but defiant eyes.

"Are you . . . Magda?"

The girl said nothing.

Cunrat joined them.

"Sure, it's her," he said. He spat onto the ground and drew his sword.

Dismas stayed Cunrat's arm.

"I will deal with this. Nutker, Unks, get the fire going. Load the cart. Go on, now. There's good fellows."

Dismas looked at the girl on the ground. A looker, all right, beneath all the grime. Her hair did resemble Dürer's. Ringlets matted with pine sap. She had the look of the hunted—haggard, desperate.

"What were you doing in the cart?" Dismas asked.

"Hiding, what do think?" A somewhat impudent response, Dismas thought, considering.

He extended his hand and pulled her to her feet.

"You *are* Magda?"

"Yes."

Cunrat recoiled, sword out and ready to strike. Evidently Cunrat believed in witches.

"Off with you, then," Dismas said. "Go."

She stood her ground.

Cunrat said, "You're not letting her go?"

"*Away*, girl," Dismas said. Still she didn't move.

"What about the reward?" Cunrat said. "He said we'd be compensated."

"We have a long way to go. Our mission is not to stop and collect witch bounties."

"We can't just let her go."

"She doesn't seem to be going anywhere. Look here, girl, didn't you hear? I said off with you."

Still she didn't move.

Dismas whispered in her ear, "These men will kill you if you stay."

She stared, hollow-eyed, trembling.

"When did you eat last?" Dismas said.

The girl shook her head.

"We'll give you some breakfast. But then you go."

The three Landsknechte now all had swords drawn.

"Bad business, witches," Cunrat said.

"I'll deal with it, Cunrat. We'll give her some food. Then she can fly off on her stick." Dismas turned to her. "Girl. If we feed you, do you promise not to turn these three fellows into spiders or whatever it is you turn men into?" He turned to the Landsknechte and said with contempt, "There. Satisfied?"

Cunrat conferred with Nutker and Unks.

Dürer was blowing on the embers. Soon the fire was going.

"Sit, girl," Dismas said.

He poured the remains of the good *Spätburgunder* wine they'd bought in Dasenstein for the larcenous price of half a gulden a quart. She downed it in three gulps. Dürer ladled her out a bowl of gruel. She made quick work of it.

"You have beautiful hair," Dürer said.

Dismas groaned.

"But what a mess it is." Dürer reached and plucked a leaf from the tangle of ringlets.

The girl spoke.

"They were close. I saw your fire. I could not go more. I hid in the cart. I heard everything. What he told you was lies. He is not a good man. I was going to leave. But I was so tired from running I fell asleep. I don't mean you trouble. Let me stay by the fire until you go."

Dismas left her with Dürer and went over to the Landsknechte campfire. Nutker and Unks were staring warily at the girl, as if at any moment snakes would slither from her nostrils and ears.

"We can't just leave her," Dismas said.

Nutker said with alarm, "You're not proposing we *take* her?"

"A short way. Beyond the reach of that asshole count."

"She's a witch. You heard him."

"Nutker," Dismas said patiently. "Last night you had such a low opinion of him that you put out your tongue to provoke him into a fight so that you could kill him. Now you are saying you believed him?"

Unks said, "He's a prick noble. But that doesn't mean she's not a witch. They're everywhere in these parts."

Nutker nodded.

Dismas considered. He looked back at the girl.

"Well, there's one way to find out."

Unks nodded. "Yes. Tie her up and throw her into a lake. If she sinks, she's not a witch."

"No, no," Nutker said. "Fire is best. If they don't burn, they're a witch."

Dismas nodded, as if giving serious thought to these scientific protocols.

He said, "There's a newer test. Completely reliable, according to Kramer and Sprenger. And who knows more about witches than them? They wrote the book, didn't they?"

The Landsknechte stared.

"Kramer and Sprenger?" Dismas reiterated. "The greatest of witch-hunters? The greatest ever?"

Still they stared.

"Lads," he said companionably, "sure, you've read their *Malleus Maleficarum*. It's the definitive tract on witch-hunting."

"Yes." Cunrat bluffed. "I know this book."

"Of course you do. Everyone knows it. Then you know that the only truly reliable proof is the test of Saint Boniface."

"Saint Boniface . . ."

"Who's Saint Boniface? And what's his test?" Unks said.

"Well, Unks, it's not only the most reliable, but also the simplest. There's the beauty of it. You take a crucifix. Any crucifix will do. Except . . . what kind was it, Cunrat? Ivory?"

Cunrat frowned. "Yes. Ivory."

"Yes. Any crucifix except ivory. You press the crucifix to the forehead. For the count of twenty. If she shrieks and the crucifix scorches her flesh, there's your witch, sure. Witches cannot bear the touch of the crucified Jesus. Thank God for science."

The Landsknechte looked at each other.

"Right, then," Dismas said. "Who's got a crucifix?"

No one, as it turned out.

Dismas groaned. "Fine monks we are. Not one crucifix between us."

Unks said, "I could whittle one."

"Bravo, Unks," Dismas said, giving him a clap on the back. "Thank God at least one of us is thinking this morning."

Dismas returned to the other campfire. He whispered to the girl, "Play along. Your life depends on it."

Presently Unks finished his crucifix.

"Very good, Unks. This will do nicely."

Dismas held it up to the heavens. He cleared his throat.

"Woman, you cannot deceive Saint Boniface. Let us pray—for your sake—that you are no witch. For if you are, sure, you will be discovered. And into our fire you will go. And from there, to the fires of Hell. Whence you came. Prepare."

The girl stared.

"I said, are you *ready*?"

Magda nodded.

"By the power of the living God, and Saint Boniface, I apply the test."

Dismas held the crucifix against her forehead. The Landsknechte watched intently.

"Well?" Cunrat said.

"Patience, Cunrat." Dismas counted: ". . . eighteen, nineteen, twenty."

Dismas removed the crucifix.

"Behold. She did not shriek, and her flesh is unburned. She is no witch, God be thanked. All right, girl, onto the cart. We'll take you as far as we can. Come on, everyone. Let's get moving."

Dürer helped Magda up onto the seat beside them. She gave Dismas a sly smile. Dismas went to the back of the cart to make sure everything was loaded. There he found the Landsknechte conferring.

"Come on, fellows," Dismas said. "Time to mount up."

Cunrat said, "We were talking, the lads and I."

"Yes?"

"If she's not a witch, why not have a bit of sport? She's a tasty one."

Dismas sighed. "Cunrat."

"Where's the harm?"

"Is that our mission, then? To outrage young women?"

"I wouldn't call it a mission."

Dismas calculated. Better to buy a postponement rather than assert uncertain authority.

"There's no time, Cunrat. The Count may return, with a troop."

Cunrat waved the thought away. "Then we'll have sport with him."

"Yes, but I don't fancy getting myself killed just for sport. Tell you what. When we get to Basel, I'll treat the lot of you to a night at the Purring Pussy. You can fornicate until your lances droop."

Cunrat considered. "All night?"

"Until the cocks crow."

So it was agreed. Dismas climbed up onto the cart and took the reins.

"What was that about?" Dürer said.

"A discussion of the sleeping arrangements in Basel."

They rode as fast as the cart would allow and at night they camped in a meadow at the foot of a cliff. It was a pleasant place. A small waterfall streamed into a pond full of trout. The Landsknechte amused themselves trying to catch them with crossbow bolts, with amusing lack of result. Dürer, never one to volunteer for camp chores, sat and sketched. Dismas bathed under the waterfall.

Magda disappeared into the forest and returned holding up a fold of her skirt filled with mushrooms of the type called *Pfifferling*. She deposited them by the campfire, then circled the pond, stooping to pick plants. She returned, again holding a fold of her skirt, now filled with watercress and wild mint. Dismas finished washing and stood by the fire to dry. He saw the mushrooms and cress and mint.

"Well, a feast."

"It would be if we had fish," Magda said.

"Our sharpshooters are working on it," Dürer said, not looking up from his sketch.

Nutker and Unks finally despaired of catching trout. They rummaged in the compartment of the horse cart, extracting one of the small kegs of gunpowder. They poured some into an empty wine bottle. Unks cut a length of arquebus fuse. Dismas looked on warily.

"What are you doing?"

"Fishing," Unks grinned.

They walked to the edge of the pond. Cunrat was in the pond up to his thighs, his back to them, aiming at trout. Nutker and Unks giggled like boys. They lit the fuse, waited, and tossed the bottle into the pond.

"Christ!" Dismas muttered. He shouted, "Everyone—down!"

Cunrat heard the splash of the bottle behind him and turned, just in time to face the explosion. An enormous geyser of pond water rose into the air. The shock wave hurled Cunrat backward into the water.

Nutker and Unks bent over double, roaring with laughter.

Cunrat emerged from the pond, covered with muck and weed, face crimson with rage. He waded toward them like an ungainly, vengeful sea god and hurled himself at them, fists flying. The three of them rolled about, grappling, cursing, laughing. Dismas and Dürer and Magda looked on.

"Iron discipline, Landsknechte," Dürer observed, continuing to sketch.

Dismas's ears were ringing from the explosion. He rubbed them and, so doing, revealed to Magda their mutilation. She stared, then looked away, as if conscious of having trespassed. She pointed to the pond.

"Our feast arrives."

Dozens of trout floated on the surface. The Landsknechte ceased their Greco-Roman wrestling and with triumphant halloos waded in after the fish.

Dürer went over to observe the haul of fish, leaving Magda and Dismas alone.

"Your ears," Magda said.

"I hear fine," Dismas said.

"There is an ointment."

"Best be careful, talking about ointments. They'll think you are a witch after all."

"Thank you. For this morning."

"I don't believe in witches."

"I know that book. The *Malleus*."

"You can read?"

"Yes, I can read. And I don't remember any test of Saint Boniface."

Dismas looked at the Landsknechte, wading among floating trout.

"It's good they can't read," he said. "He was a brave fellow, Boniface. A monk. Like us. English, of the Benedictine order. He came here to convert the Franks. Not an easy mission. There was an oak tree that the Franks worshipped. Sacred to Thor, their god. To show them that he did not fear the wrath of Thor, Boniface took an ax and chopped it down. Very brave, to do that. He used the wood to build a chapel."

"I will say a prayer to him tonight."

"In the end, they cut him into pieces. But now no one here worships Thor. Once I sold one of Boniface's ribs to a—" He caught himself. "So, how will you cook your mushrooms?"

"With herbs." Magda was looking at him. "What were you doing selling Saint Boniface's rib?"

Dismas shrugged. "Well, relics are common enough, in our world."

"What is your world, Dismas?"

"As you can see, we're monks."

She smiled. "I have known many monks. But never have I met monks who stick their tongues out at noblemen. Or hold weapons like soldiers. Or fish with gunpowder. Or want to 'outrage women.' And do not have even one little crucifix between them."

"Well, you see, those three are novices. They are in training. They lack discipline."

"And what is your order?"

"It's a new one."

"What do you call yourselves?"

"Bonifacians."

Magda laughed. "I have not heard of this order."

"Well, you wouldn't have. Like I said, it's new."

"And what is your calling? I don't think you are shepherds. Or makers of jam."

"We move about. We are mendicant."

"Mendicant. Beggars, with weapons?"

Dismas shrugged. "You get more donations."

She giggled. It was a sound sweet as wind chimes.

"Why do you ask so many questions?" Dismas said, feigning impatience.

"I'm interested."

"In monks?"

"In you, Dismas."

Dismas felt his cheeks burn. "I am not interesting."

"So, tell me. What do the Bonifacians do? Other than beg with guns and crossbows?"

"Well, we translate."

"You don't look like scholars."

"Relics. We translate holy relics."

"Into what?"

"No. Translation means relocating them. It's called translation, you see. When a relic—the bone of a saint, a piece of straw from the holy manger, whatever—desires to go to a new place, say from one shrine to another, we Bonifacians perform the translating."

Magda giggled again.

"This is amusing?"

"And how do you know when a relic wants to go from one place to another? Does it say, 'I am tired of being in Lyon. I want to go to Milan'?"

"Don't be impious, girl. It's a serious business."

"I'm only asking how the relic lets you know it wants a change of scenery."

Dismas sighed. "It's complex. Takes years to learn. Anyway, this is why we must carry weapons. To protect the relics in our care."

"What holy company I am in."

"I did not say that we are holy."

"If you say."

"I do say."

"Still I'm glad to be in your company."

He blushed again. "I'm a sinful man."

"Why do you tell me this?"

"That's my business."

"You saved my life. And stopped your *novices* from taking what remains to me of my dignity. Was this sinful?"

"That was only . . ."

"Bonifacian?"

Dismas smiled. "If you like."

She smiled, looking at him in a way that made him uneasy and happy at the same time. "I do."

That night they gorged on trout and mushrooms. For the first time since leaving Wittenberg, they camped around a single fire.

Cunrat pretended still to be furious at Nutker and Unks, but was thwarted by his relish at the abundance of trout and the mushroom fricassee. They ate and ate. She was a good cook, this Magda girl.

When they had eaten their fill, she poured them cups of the tea she'd brewed with the wild mint. It was an unusual, bracing taste that made their mouths tingle and imparted a mood of contentment and serenity.

Cunrat said, "So you're not a witch. Who are you, then?"

Magda stared at the embers. Her ginger ringlets glowed in the light of the campfire. Dürer had given her some of his terebinth to remove the sap, before she bathed in the waterfall. Dismas realized that he was staring at her. But he couldn't take his eyes off her.

"My father, he was the apothecary of Schramberg. A respected man. He was a friend of Paracelsus."

"Who?"

"Shut *up*, Unks," Cunrat said. "Let her speak."

"A physician and botanist. A very great man. He travels all over the world to find new medicines. He lives at Basel. I have met him, twice. When I was little, my father took me there.

"He died from the plague. Also my mother and my sister and the two brothers. I did not die because Papa had sent me to the convent in Heidelberg, to learn apothecary.

"I returned to Schramberg. I got work in a tavern. It was there he saw me. Lothar, he who you saw last night.

"He desired me. One night when I was leaving the tavern after finishing work, his men came for me.

"I was kept in his castle. For I don't know how long. Months. There was nothing I could do. Always the doors were locked. I tried to kill myself."

Magda held out a wrist. Scars.

"Soon after, one night one of the servant women, she took pity and helped me to escape. I went to the marshal in Schramberg and told what happened. He said he was sorry for what happened, but could not do anything. Lothar is Count of Schramberg. And also he is godson to the King of Spain, who will become Emperor.

"I hid with a friend, a girl who worked with me at the tavern. She told me, 'They are saying you are a witch.' Perhaps Lothar did this to protect himself. So I could not accuse him.

"I left Schramberg. I thought to go to Basel, beyond the Empire. Perhaps find work in apothecary. There are many in Basel. But someone saw me and told. There is always a fear of witches. For days I was running. Until I saw your fire."

21

Attack

Dismas was awakened by a hand shaking his shoulder. He opened his eyes. Cunrat.

"They come."

Dismas stood. He heard. Horses, numerous. Worse was the other sound. Dogs. Not search hounds, but the local type, of Rottweil, bred for one purpose. He felt his bowels loosen and cursed his stupidity for lingering here instead of pushing on.

The Landsknechte were lighting their fuses and loading arquebuses and cranking crossbows. The horse cart was parallel to the cliff face behind them.

"Give a hand," Cunrat commanded. Together they heaved it over onto its side, making a cover.

"Can you handle one of these?" Dismas asked Magda. Without answering, she took the crossbow from him and began to load. Capable, this girl.

Dürer, always the last to wake, rubbed his eyes.

"What's happening?"

"It's an attack, Nars. They have dogs."

"*Christ*, Dis."

Dürer had a horror of dogs, even tame lap creatures. He'd been bitten as a child.

"Can you shoot?" Dismas asked him, holding out a crossbow.

"No!" he said in a tone of helpless panic.

Dismas grabbed a halberd, a long lancelike spear, razor-sharp at the tip.

"Can you handle *this*?"

Dürer's face had gone the color of porridge.

"I . . ."

"Nars. They have *dogs*." He thrust the halberd at him.

Dürer took it, looking stricken.

Cunrat was looking up at the cliff behind them. The far edge was some twenty-five yards from where they stood.

"Nutker." Cunrat made hand gestures, pointing at the cliff. Nutker nodded, grabbed a sack, and threw into it one of the small kegs, along with fuses, flints, matchbox, and bottles.

"Quick," Cunrat said, "before they clear the woods."

Nutker gathered up his bundle and ran, hunching low, to the edge of the cliff and disappeared.

The sounds were close, now.

Cunrat said, "Dogs first. Don't waste your shot. Wait till you can smell them."

The riders burst out of the wood into the meadow, dogs bounding ahead of them.

Dismas counted ten riders, four dogs. Seeing the overturned horse cart, the riders reined to a halt. The dogs continued.

"Steady," Cunrat said. "Unks, left. Dismas, right. I'll take the middle. Steady, now. Steady . . ."

The dogs were ten yards off, coming straight for them. Dismas saw their spiked collars.

"For the love of Christ, *shoot*!" Dürer moaned.

"Easy, Painter. Steady. Steady. *Now*."

The blasts from the three arquebuses were nearly simultaneous. Thunder, billows of acrid white smoke.

They heard yelps but could not see through the smoke.

Then came snarling.

Dismas felt something strike him midsection, knocking him over. The dog was on him, trying to get at his throat. He could smell its breath. He got his hands around its neck, trying to avoid the snapping teeth. The collar spikes embedded in his hands. It was a powerful dog. Its jaws snapped, straining at Dismas's throat. He couldn't control it. Then it gave a squeal and fell away.

Dismas looked up. Dürer was holding the shaft of the halberd, wriggling with the dog's death throes. Dismas rolled over and plunged his dagger into its heart.

Another dog had Unks by the shin. Unks cursed and brought his sword down onto its spine, severing it. Even dead, its jaws remained clamped around Unks's shin. He pulled his dagger, inserted the blade between his leg and the mandible, and twisted it loose. His leg was drenched with blood.

The smoke had cleared. The two other dogs lay dead, one with a bolt from Magda's crossbow protruding from its forehead. Already she was reloading.

"All right," Cunrat said. "Now for those *other* dogs. Make your shots count." Cunrat paused, grinned, and said to Dismas, "Hey, did you hear? I made a jest. I said make your shots count. And he *is* a count!"

Dismas's heart was trying to hammer its way out of his rib cage. It had been a long time since he had last been in combat. And here was Cunrat, amidst smoke and blood, making jokes. They were cool ones, sure, Landsknechte.

Furious at the slaughter of his dogs, Lothar was barking commands at his men. Half dismounted and took cover.

The first volley splintered the horse cart and pocked the cliff face behind them. A crossbow bolt brought down one of their horses. It thrashed in agony. Unks crawled over to it, exposing himself, to end its misery.

Volleys continued without cease, each increasingly accurate, until it was too perilous to attempt to return fire.

"So, it's to be a siege," Cunrat grunted. "Not so good for us. We've got to draw them closer. For Nutker." He pointed at the top of the cliff. He sighed. "But how to do this, I don't know."

The firing paused. Cunrat thrust his head above the wagon and shouted. "Hey, you girls. If you want a fight, stop hiding like cunts and come and give us one!"

The answer came in a vicious volley of lead and bolts.

"It appears they prefer to siege," Cunrat observed. "I think we will be here for"—he laughed—"ever!" He was on his back, looking up at the cliff. "But not a bad place to die."

Magda stood.

"Get down, girl," Cunrat said.

She walked out from behind the horse cart.

A shot hit the cliff behind, missing her narrowly.

Lothar shouted, "Fool! Hold your fire!"

"*Girl,*" Cunrat hissed. "What are you *doing*?"

Dismas murmured, "She's giving herself up. To spare us."

Dismas stood. He raised his hands in surrender and walked out from the behind the wagon. If he could reach Magda, he might be able to pull her back to safety.

"Christ," Cunrat muttered. "They're both mad. Painter, talk sense into them."

Magda continued to walk toward the attackers.

"Unks, Painter. Do what I do," Cunrat said.

He stood up, arms held high, and stepped out from behind the horse cart. Unks did the same. Dürer made a sign of the cross and stood.

Cunrat whispered, "Don't advance. Hold your ground."

Magda's back was to them. She didn't see what was happening.

Dismas kept walking toward her. He hissed, *"Magda."*

She stopped, turned, and saw them all with hands raised. She shook her head. *No.*

Lothar was waving his men forward, spurring his horse.

Magda turned to face Lothar. He walked his horse toward her, men following.

In the next instant Nutker's bomb landed, fuse hissing.

"Down!" Cunrat bellowed.

Dismas blinked open his eyes. His ears screamed. He lay still, not daring to move, afraid to discover a limb gone, or his insides piled on the ground beside him in a steaming mound.

Despite the din in his head he could make out other sounds—familiar, urgent, steel on steel. He gasped for air and forced himself upright. He put his hands to his ears to stop the sound. They came away wet with blood.

The pretty little meadow was now scorched ground strewn with men and horses, dead and dying. The wounded animals made pitiable sounds; men cursed and cried in agony. Amidst it all, fighting continued. Cunrat engaged two attackers. Unks grappled with another, using a rock for a weapon. Dismas looked. Where was Magda?

He found her on the ground, still, limbs twisted. Blood flowed from her mouth, nose, and ears.

Rage rose within him.

Lothar. Dismas prayed he was still alive so that he could kill him.

Through the din in his ears he heard something. He turned. A man came at him from the side, swinging a nail-studded mace. He heard the whoosh as it passed within inches of his skull.

Dismas rolled. The attacker turned to strike again. Dismas lurched to his feet and sidestepped. As the man went by him, Dismas sank his dagger into the back of his neck.

Dürer? Where was Dürer?

By the cart, flat on his back, covered with debris. Dismas staggered to him, knelt, and shook him. Dürer's eyes opened. He looked up at Dismas uncomprehendingly.

Alive, God be thanked.

Dismas stood and turned back to fight. Cunrat had dropped one of his attackers. Unks was on his feet, holding a rock slimy with brain matter. He tossed it away and picked up a sword and walked through the bodies of men and horses, plunging it into them, finishing those still alive.

It was a scene Dismas had seen many times on a far vaster scale. Cunrat decapitated his remaining attacker and let out a great roar. It was over.

Lothar? Where was Lothar?

Dismas snatched a halberd from the ground. It felt familiar in his hand. This had been his principal weapon in his *Reiselaufer* days. He waded through the carnage, searching.

He heard a sound from behind. He swung, nearly impaling Nutker. Nutker was breathing hard from running down from his perch atop the cliff.

"The girl?" Nutker said.

"Dead."

Nutker's face crumpled. "No."

"Over here!"

It was Unks. Dismas, Nutker, and Cunrat converged. There at Unks's feet lay Count Lothar of Schramberg. Alive, just.

His right arm was gone at the elbow. His face was shredded and blackened. Amidst the mask of gore, a single lidless eye looked up at them in horror and fear. His jaw moved. He tried to speak but there came only a gurgle of blood and lung froth.

Unks looked at Cunrat. Finish him?

Cunrat was breathing hard. He shook his head. It didn't need saying. *Let him linger in agony*. Unks shrugged.

The Landsknechte set about their looting.

Dismas stood to savor Lothar's death throes. He knelt on one knee beside him. His hand went into the fold of his monk's habit, to reach for his dagger. He had never tortured a man before, much less a dying man.

"Fray . . ."

What was he saying?

"Fray . . ."

Dismas realized. He was saying *friar*.

"Con . . ." With tremendous exertion, Lothar got out the word: *"Confess . . ."*

Dismas recoiled. Christ in Heaven. Lothar thought he was a monk. He was asking him to hear his dying confession.

Lothar's jaw stopped working. The only trace of life was in the unblinking eye. It fixed on Dismas, desperate, pleading.

The dagger dropped from Dismas's hand. He stared. Then, without knowing why, he made a sign of the cross over the dying man and leaned into his ear and whispered, "Are you sorry for your sins?"

The eye stared. The death rattle began.

Dismas pronounced the words. *"Ego te absolvo a peccatis tuis, in nomine Patris, Filii, et Spiritu Sancti. Amen."*

A surge of foamy blood rose from Lothar's mouth and he went still.

Dismas stood. Then bent over and retched. The hissing in his ears became intolerable. He put his hands to them, staggered a few paces, and collapsed.

When he opened his eyes, Cunrat and Nutker were kneeling beside him.

"Dismas?"

Cunrat shook him by the shoulder gently.

"Dismas. She's alive."

With great effort, they righted the horse cart. They made bedding and lifted Magda onto it.

Her bleeding had stopped. She could speak but her words were slurred and incoherent. She asked for her father and mother.

Dürer spooned some of her mint tea into her mouth, which

seemed to refresh her. She asked why it was so dark, though it was daylight. She said the bread must be ready now, and to take it from the oven. Presently she fell into a sleep from which they could not waken her.

Cunrat and Nutker and Unks went about their spoils-taking methodically, without the usual whoop and halloo that usually accompanied Landsknecht looting. Then Nutker let out a yelp of delight. He'd found Lothar's severed arm in the pond, being nibbled at by trout.

He waded in after it and threw it on the ground.

Dismas watched all this from the cart, where he sat, cradling Magda's head, soothing her forehead with a cold cloth and praying.

There were rings on the pudgy, bloody hand. Count Lothar was one for ornamentation. Dismas thought of Albrecht, whose own ten fingers were similarly festooned with fourteen rings, the largest being the one requiring the kiss of obeisance.

Unks hacked the fingers off the hand, the more easily to remove the rings. Dismas looked away.

There was other loot: a gold dagger; a sword of exquisite Toledo steel, hilt ornately engraved with an inscription from Lothar's godfather, Charles, King of Spain, future Holy Roman Emperor. Medallions; buckles; pins; insigniae; and a soft leather purse embroidered with an *L* and a coronet. Nutker examined this and said it was made from the scrotum of a boar, and a jolly big boar, from the size of it. It jingled deliciously, with ducats. A fine haul.

Spoils tallied, now came the business of the bodies.

Grim: ten men, half as many horses, four dogs. Should they make a bonfire?

Dismas said no. The smoke might draw others. And anyway the fire would leave too obvious a trace. Sure, searchers would come, Lothar being Lothar. Yet the prospect of getting all this meat into the ground was daunting.

Unks—lazy fellow—proposed stripping them of clothes, boots,

equipage, everything, burying that and leaving the corpses for the bears, boars, wolves, and carrion birds. A feast.

Nutker pronounced this an inspired solution. But Dismas and Cunrat knew must be done. They had just killed the godson of one of the most powerful rulers on earth. It would not be prudent to leave his mortal remains as carrion.

"But the horses," Unks protested. "We'll be here all day!"

"And night," Nutker added.

A compromise was reached. They would hitch the dead horses to the live ones and drag them a distance into the forest, in various directions. The bears and wolves would take of those corpses.

This done, they set to work to bury the dead. And, sure, it was a long day.

To conceal the smell from search dogs, they burned pine branches over the bodies in the pit before filling in the earth. They covered the ground as best they could. At length the meadow was restored to some semblance of its former appearance. But it felt an evil place now, from which they were eager to be gone.

They rested a spell before departing. Dürer sat beside Dismas on the cart seat, sketching while the Landsknechte packed up their weaponry.

Dismas looked over at what he was drawing.

It was the landscape he'd done the day before. Now he had drawn a clump of grave markers, crosses, where the bodies were buried. Ten.

"*Christ*, Nars."

"They were bastards. And I rejoice that they're dead. But they were Christian bastards. There should be something to mark their graves."

"Why don't you put in a fucking *chapel*, then?" Dismas said.

Without looking up from his sketch, Dürer said, "Was that the sign of the cross you made over Lothar? Or were you swatting flies?"

"I sent him to Hell."

"With a blessing. You should have stayed a monk."

"Planning to show that in Basel, are you?" Dismas said. "Why don't you make an engraving and sell copies?"

Dürer tore the page from the sketchpad, crumpled it, and tossed it from the cart.

The Landsknechte mounted. They set off for Basel.

It was hard going in the dark. Magda remained unconscious. Dismas let Dürer take the reins and cradled her head in his lap. Several times he put his ear to her chest to see if she was still alive. He put a flask of water to her lips but it trickled down her chin.

Nutker rode over. He looked stricken.

"Is she . . . ?"

Dismas shook his head.

Nutker's voice was plaintive. "I didn't *see* her. I was making the bombs and putting in the powder and the fuses. I didn't *see* her."

"It's all right, Nutker. It wasn't your fault. It wasn't anyone's fault but mine."

"What was she doing, walking to them?"

"Trying to save us."

Nutker looked at her. He reached over from his saddle and brushed her cheek tenderly with his hand.

"Don't die, Little Sister."

Noon the following day found them on the downslope out of the Black Forest, where the path improved.

They moved as fast as they could without overly jostling her. With the mounts they'd taken from Lothar, they could spell the cart horses and keep going without rest. By late afternoon they saw the twin spires of the cathedral. At sundown they crossed the bridge over the Rhine into the city. At the gate, they were challenged by guards.

"What's in the cart?"

"A dying girl. Who'll be dead if we don't make haste."

The guards recoiled, suspecting plague.

"She fell. We seek Paracelsus, the surgeon. Do you know him?"

"Why should I?"

Dismas dug into his purse and tossed the captain a gulden, enough to buy drinks for the whole guard.

"Paracelsus. Name's familiar . . ."

Dismas dug another gulden from his purse and tossed it to him.

"Street behind the college. Before you come to the armory."

"Bless you, my son."

Dismas spurred the horses. The Landsknechte charged ahead.

When Dismas turned the cart down the street behind the college, he saw the Landsknechte dismounted, going door to door, accosting people on the street. Nutker had one man up against the wall and was shaking him, demanding to know where Paracelsus lurked.

The surgery was through an alley that led into a courtyard. The alley was not wide enough to accommodate the cart, so they carried Magda on a stretcher improvised from blankets, Nutker going ahead of them bellowing, "Paracelsus! Paracelsus! Show yourself, Paracelsus!"

A stout, florid-faced man of grave mien presented himself in the doorway, the image of affronted dignity. He had enough chins for three men. His cheeks matched his cherry-red cap. Here was Philippus Aureolus Theophrastus Bombastus von Hohenheim, called Paracelsus.

"What's the meaning of this? Cease that noise or I'll have out the guard!"

Dismas spoke. "She's dying, your honor. You knew her father. The apothecary at Schramberg. Her name is Magda."

Paracelsus bent and opened her eyelids.

"Bring her in. Quickly, now."

They laid her on a table. Paracelsus ordered, "All of you, out." He said to Dismas, "You, stay."

An assistant in a bloodstained apron appeared. He and Paracelsus spoke in Latin. Dismas knew enough to make out their talk.

Paracelsus put his ear to her chest, then pressed two fingertips to the edge of her wrist. He seemed to be counting silently. He lifted her eyelids again, concentrating this time on one eye. He opened her mouth and peered in while the assistant held an apparatus that reflected and magnified candlelight. He looked into her nose and ears. He picked at some of the encrusted blood in her ear and put it to his tongue.

"Gunpowder."

Dismas nodded.

"Well? Must I drag it out of you? What happened?"

"It was a bomb, your honor. It—"

"When?"

"Yesterday."

"*When*, yesterday?"

"Morning."

Paracelsus fired questions: Had she been conscious at any point? Vomited? Had she raved in delirium? Convulsed? He probed her scalp with his fingertips. His fingers were fat as sausages, but moved with the nimbleness of a lutist's. He conversed with the assistant. He said the word *aemidus*.

"She's bleeding, inside her head. The blood swells and presses on the brain. I must relieve the pressure." He regarded Dismas's monk habit. "I take it she is not your wife?"

"No, your honor. We found her. In the forest."

Paracelsus grabbed Dismas's sleeve, lifted it to his nose, sniffed.

"Gunpowder. What's your order, then?"

Dismas saw this was a man to whom it was useless to lie.

"Does it matter, your honor?"

Paracelsus gave commands to the assistant, who disappeared into the next room. He took a small razor and shaved Magda's scalp above the ear on the side opposite the eye he had concentrated on. He dabbed at the exposed flesh with a small sponge redolent of spirits.

He told the assistant to hurry. He looked on his patient with a tenderness Dismas thought paternal.

"She was a sweet little thing. Does Franz know?"

"Dead. Whole family."

"Then we must save her. Sure, God wills it."

The assistant returned with a tray of instruments. The largest was a device with a small knob-handle of ivory. The shaft curved to a U, then continued straight, tapering to a fine silver point in the shape of a miniature broadhead arrow. Dismas recognized it as a trepan. He'd seen cruder versions in the army.

"If you're going to be sick, get out."

Dismas remained. The assistant put Magda's head in a padded wooden vise, and Paracelsus commenced to drill into Magda's skull. Dismas winced at the sound. A squirt of blood shot across the room. Paracelsus let the gushing subside. After some minutes, he lifted her eyelid. He grunted and held a bandage tightly against the hole he'd drilled.

The assistant wiped Magda's wounds with more of the pungent fluid and bandaged her head.

"If she makes it through the night, she'll live. Stay with her. If she revives, her pain will be great."

He reached for a small blue vial on a shelf.

"Give her this. Two drops in water. No more than two drops. One drop more than two and she'll stop breathing. Do you understand?"

"Yes, your honor. Thank you. Bless you."

Paracelsus looked at Dismas. "Is that the blessing of a monk?"

"No."

"Who are you?"

"My name is Dismas."

"The Good Thief. Did you steal the getup you're all wearing?"

Paracelsus looked at the window into the courtyard. Pressed against it were the faces of Dürer and the Landsknechte.

"Your fellow monks look like murderers and cutpurses. We're not fools on this side of the Rhine, you know. What's your game, then? Why is Franz's daughter lying on my table, near death and reeking of gunpowder?"

"If she dies, does it matter? If she lives, I'll explain. You have my word."

Paracelsus scoffed. "How do you know I won't call out the constable? They keep a busy executioner here. Suits me, as it keeps me well supplied with fresh bodies. Well, Good Thief? How do you know I won't hand you all over?"

"I don't. My life is in your hands. As much as hers is."

Paracelsus stared. His countenance softened.

"You're a Swiss. You can always tell. Those others there—Germans. I'll be back in the morning. Remember—no more than two drops. So now her life is in *your* hands, Good Thief."

22

Paracelsus

Magda opened her eyes early the next morning.

The Landsknechte and Dürer had kept their vigil in the courtyard outside. When Dismas told them she would live, they dropped to their knees and prayed. Nutker blubbered. Dismas was astonished. Never had he seen a Landsknecht pray, or weep.

She had no memory of what had happened in the meadow, but strangely, immediately recognized Paracelsus, even though she had not seen him in years. His gruffness of the day before was gone. He was all tenderness. She could stay here until she was recovered. Sisters from a nearby convent would attend her, day and night. He held her hand and kissed her forehead.

Dismas found lodging for himself and the others in an inn grandiosely named Edenhaus, in the southeast quarter of the city near the paper mill. The mill's stink of rotten egg and sulfur made the air rather less than edenic, but its location near the St. Alban's gate to the south would make for a hasty departure should need arise.

Dismas made good on his promise to treat the lads to a night of pudendal merriment at the Purring Pussy. They invited Dismas and Dürer to accompany them, but they declined. Dismas was in no mood for bawds; for his part, Dürer was a faithful husband, and morbidly fearful of pox.

"They'll come back with a dose," he said. "Mark my word. One night in Venus, the rest of your life on Mercury."

Paracelsus had devised a treatment for the pox consisting of minute doses of mercury. It had a slightly better effect than the reigning "cure"—guaiacum. Like the pox itself, guaiacum came from the New World, distilled from the hardwood tree *Lignum vitae*. The immensely profitable trade in guaiacum was a Fugger monopoly. Wherever you looked, there was Jacob Fugger—lending ducats to Albrecht to buy his cardinal's hat; to Pope Leo, to cover expenses sacred and profane.

Paracelsus scoffed at guaiacum, viewing it as no more than a self-dealing arrangement between Fugger and Rome. What's more, he said so, and loudly, though such accusations could lead a man to a dungeon or the gallows. His majestic contempt for authority reminded Dismas of Luther. And come to think of it, they were both incendiaries as well. Luther had torched one of the papal bulls denouncing him. Paracelsus had set fire to a great pile of volumes of the great Arab doctor Avicenna and those by the Greek physician Galen, to show what he thought of *them*.

"So, do we continue on?" Dürer asked Dismas.

"To Chambéry? What choice do I have? I don't want to spend eternity in Hell."

"But Luther says—"

"Nars. Luther has been declared a heretic. I won't risk my immortal soul on his . . . *theories*. Go home. I release you."

"This was my fault."

"Yes, Nars, it was. And you'll have to live with that. But you might as well live. You've a wife and your painting. Anyway, my life's done. Albrecht's penance was only a way to get me killed without starting a war with Frederick."

"What about the girl?"

"She'll make a good life here. Paracelsus treats her like his daughter."

Dürer said, "What if I could make a copy of it?"

"Of the Shroud?" Dismas grunted. "Yes, we know you can do that."

"I'm trying to help."

"I can get myself killed without your help, thank you."

"If I could make a copy—an exact copy—maybe . . . we could switch them."

"Yes. Good. Knock on the Duke's door. Tell him, 'I am Dürer, the painter. I am here to make an exact copy of your shroud. Then we will switch it with the real one. May I have the keys, please? There are four, so I'll need all of them.' "

"Why do you mock me?"

"Because you are mockable."

"It's going to be displayed, isn't it?"

"On the castle wall. Can you make an exact copy from such a distance? Standing in the crowd? You must have the eyes of a hawk."

"Perhaps with a star glass . . ."

Dismas chuckled. "Yes. Set your easel in the square, in the middle of the crowd, and stare through a star glass. Brilliant."

"You're not very encouraging."

Dismas threw up his hands.

"Very well. For the sake of encouragement—let's imagine that you somehow make your exact copy. How then do you propose to switch it with the real one?"

"Well, we won't know until we get there. Will we?"

Dismas looked at Dürer.

"What are you telling me, Nars? That you're coming with me to Chambéry?"

"I don't want to spend eternity in Hell, either."

"I thought you'd gone over to Luther."

"I don't know. Maybe Luther isn't right. Anyway, I'm not going to spend the rest of my life being haunted by your fucking ghost. I'm doing it for me. Not you."

Dismas smiled. "Ah. Well, then, now I understand."

It was almost dawn when the Landsknechte returned from their brothel, making a drunken clatter that woke the proprietress, an ill-tempered crone like all the rest of her kind.

Dismas was already up, getting ready to go visit Magda.

"How was Venus? Did you leave the girls limp?"

Cunrat and Nutker were holding each other up, wobbling. Unks looked strangely sober and glum.

"What's the matter with him?"

Cunrat, weaving on his feet, held up a rigid finger and curled it. *"Pffft!"*

"Fuck you," Unks said morosely.

"Ah, don't be so hard on yourself," Cunrat said. "Hey, Nutker. Did you hear? I told him don't be so *hard* on himself."

Their roar of laughter brought a remonstration from upstairs.

Dismas saw that Unks's fists were clenching.

"Cunrat, Nutker," Dismas scolded. "Don't be unkind. It happens to everyone."

"Never to me," Cunrat said.

"Or to me," Nutker said.

God hates me, sure, Dismas thought. On top of everything, now he must keep peace among whoring Landsknechte because one of them could not perform.

He put a hand on Unks's shoulder to steer him away from the others.

"Never before has this happened," Unks moaned. "Never."

"Don't worry, man. To me, it happens all the time. You're tired, that's all. Go to bed. Get some sleep. Tomorrow eat raw meat and drink springwater, then go back to the bawdy house and you will be a Minotaur."

Unks shook his head and said no, he was finished—forever—with whores. They could go to Hell, along with the rest of the world.

Dismas entertained Magda with the story, sitting on her bed in Paracelsus's surgery.

She was better, though her eyes were glassy. She said this was from the drops Paracelsus gave her for the pain. A tincture he called *ladanum*, a marvelous thing he had brought back from Arabia Deserta. From a gum that wept from a flower called *Papaver*. Paracelsus distilled it, adding this and that. It greatly helped with the pain, but made you feel warm and sleepy, "like in a dream."

Magda listened to the account of Unks's disgrace at the bordello.

"Ah. There is something for this," she said. "My father used to make it for his customers. A tea, brewed from the bark of a tree from Africa. What's it called? Yohimbe. Yes. Paracelsus knows it, sure."

Dismas smiled. What things Magda knew. She blushed, suddenly embarrassed.

"Paracelsus does not believe you are a monk," she said. "He asked me many questions. He likes you." She whispered, "He thinks the others are murderers."

Dismas smiled. "Nars wouldn't like to hear that. He's a snob."

"Nars . . . ?"

"Painter. With the hair like yours."

"Yes." She nodded. "He is different from the novices. Well, we must do something for poor Unks. Give me some paper."

She wrote down the name of the African bark and instructions.

"Give this to the apothecary in the Saint Andreas district."

Dismas took the paper from her. What a business.

"What's wrong?" Magda said.

"Nothing. Well . . . no. A lot."

She took his hand. "What troubles you, Dismas?"

"Better that you don't know."

She looked so pretty with her head against the clean white pillow. Like one of the women in the painting by the Italian, what was his name—Botticelli?—that he had seen in the villa of one of his clients. He wanted to tell her everything. But, no. What purpose, involving her in his calamity?

He smiled. "Rest. We'll talk later."

She squeezed his hand. "You will come? Promise?"

"Yes." He stood, looked at the paper in his hand, and rolled his eyes in dismay.

She smiled. "You must take care of your novices. But don't let him take too much. It's strong."

Dismas went to the apothecary in the St. Andreas district and presented the paper, thoroughly embarrassed to be asking for such a thing. He emphasized to the apothecary that it was not for himself. For five gulden, a damnable price, he left with a small bottle of brown liquid.

He presented it to Unks, telling him that it was from Magda and that he must not take more than three sips before setting off for the bordel. So of course Unks drank the entire vial.

The next morning, again just as dawn was breaking, the three Landsknechte returned to the Edenhaus, making a terrible ruckus. As before, Cunrat and Nutker were inebriated to the point of barely being able to stand.

As for Unks, Dismas had never seen such a look of triumph. He walked with a peculiar gait, like someone who had just ridden a great distance on horseback. He held his hat over his groin. When he saw Dismas, he removed the hat with a courtier-like flourish.

"Look!"

"God in Heaven," Dismas said. "Cover yourself, man!"

"It won't go down."

Dismas shrugged. "Well, it's a better problem than before."

23

The Dance of Death

One afternoon some days later, Dismas and Dürer went to see a cloth merchant Dismas knew from his visits to Basel.

The merchant rummaged amidst his catacomb of supplies and emerged sneezing with a roll of linen under his arm. Spread out, it measured fifteen by four feet. Dismas thought these dimensions roughly correct. The weave pattern, alternately inverted *V*'s, indicated that it came from Palestine or Judea—possibly Galilee, but probably not. The merchant guaranteed it was "at least" two centuries old. Dismas knew very well this was just an excuse for charging more.

Dürer examined it minutely, rubbing it between his fingers, examining the threads with a magnifying glass. From his satchel he took a small box of paints and dabbed at a corner. He nodded approval.

The haggling went on for an hour, Dismas and the merchant accusing each other of larceny and bad faith. The usual ritual of purchase. Dürer looked on with amusement, never before having seen the business side of his friend.

Finally the sale was consummated for eighteen gulden. Dismas grumbled that this meant he could not afford meat for a month. The merchant pretended to believe him.

When the coin and cloth had exchanged hands, the merchant smiled greasily and said, "Making a shroud, eh? I thought Dismas the Relic Master didn't go in for that?"

Mortifying, to be chid by such a person. Dismas knew that indignation would be misplaced. But at the practical level, no good could result from a chatty merchant bruiting it about the marketplace that Dismas the Relic Master had purchased material for a Jesus shroud.

He could send Cunrat and the lads around to pay the fellow a visit. But no. Low as he may have fallen, Dismas was not one for thuggery and threats.

"It's to be a surprise. For someone of importance. And power. Should the surprise be spoiled"—Dismas lowered his voice to a whisper—"I tell you, out of friendship, you wouldn't want to experience his displeasure."

Dismas slid two more guldens across the table at him.

"For your discretion."

The shop was in the north end of town, in the St. John district. It was a pleasant day, so on their way back to the Edenhaus, Dismas and Nars took the road near the river. Presently, on their right, they saw it, painted on the wall of the Preacher Cloister.

Dismas had seen it many times; oddly, Dürer had not, though of course he knew of it. Everyone did. It was celebrated.

The mural had been there almost eighty years now, a thanks-offering after an outbreak of plague. An admonition that Death comes for everyone, no matter their rank: Emperor, Pope, Cardinal, Knight, Merchant, Mother and Child, Peddler, Beggar, Turk and Jew. Thirty-nine types were here represented, dancing—grappling—with the skeletal figure of Death.

Dürer sniffed and pronounced it appallingly bad art. Dismas had no opinion as to its aesthetic value. He pointed out to Dürer that at least it was a more humane response than what Basel had done a century earlier, after another outbreak. Six hundred Jews were rounded up, shackled inside a barn on an island in the Rhine, and burned alive. Everyone agreed that this offering had pleased God, for the plague did not return to Basel for some many years.

Dismas had never given the Dance of Death mural more than passing thought. Now, suddenly, strangely, he began to feel queer inside, sick-like, as if a pestilence were roiling within his bowels.

"You all right?" Dürer said. "You look peculiar."

Dismas turned away from the mural, reeling. His breathing quickened. His chest tightened. He began to sweat. His heart beat a staccato rhythm. His head spun. His face and hands were clammy hot. He pulled off his gloves.

"Dis—what is it?"

"I . . ."

Dürer supported him. "Sit."

Dismas slumped to the ground. He put his head between his knees and tried to slow his breathing. After some minutes the sickness subsided. His heart ceased its drumbeat. He rose slowly, leaning against the mural. Then it came to him that the mural had triggered the memory of his own dance with death in Albrecht's dungeon.

"All right?" Dürer asked.

Dismas nodded. "Give me a moment."

While Dismas composed himself, Dürer read aloud from the inscription beneath the image nearest them, of the Count being led away by Death.

"In this world I was well known,
and also called a noble Count.
Now I'm felled by Death,
and placed here in this dance."

Dürer snorted. "Not *quite* the way it happened. Ah. Look who else is here."

The Cardinal. Dürer read:

"I was by papal choice
cardinal in the holy church.
The world honored me greatly.
Now I cannot ward off Death from me."

Dürer reached into his satchel and took out his paint box. Dismas looked on.

"What are you doing? We'll be arrested."

Dürer continued, working briskly. Done, he stood back a few paces to admire his work.

"There!"

The Cardinal in the mural now bore an unmistakable resemblance to Albrecht Cardinal Brandenburg, Primate of Germany.

"Christ, Nars. Let's go, before they throw us in jail."

"I want to make one of Luther."

"I thought you admired Luther."

"An homage—Luther with his boot up Death's arse!"

"I'm sure he'd be honored. Come on."

When they were a safe distance, Dürer said, "What was all that about, back there?"

"Explain later. First, a drink."

They reached the cathedral square, on the city's high ground. They bought beers and sat on the terrace in the shade of linden trees. It was a fine day, and the view to the east was splendid. They could see all the way to the Black Forest. The beer calmed Dismas's jangled nerves. Dürer discoursed on religious art.

"What shit, that mural," Dürer said. "There's plenty of money in Basel. They could have afforded something better than *that*."

"Cranach?"

Dürer snorted. "But the point isn't to make good art, is it? No. It's to loosen the bowels of the faithful so they'll loosen the strings on their purses. No coincidence it's painted on the wall of the Preacher Cloister."

"You're the one preaching."

"Know who they should have got? Bosch."

"Who's Bosch?" Dismas said. "Beer's good. Should be, at this price."

"Who is Bosch?" Dürer shook his head. "Sometimes I forget what an ignorant Swiss peasant you are."

"Illuminate me."

"Jeronimous Bosch. Netherlander. He's dead now maybe three years. He did this triptych. A triptych is a three—"

"I know what a triptych is."

"It's called *The Garden of Earthly Delights*. When I saw it, I almost shat myself. Took my breath away. One of the panels is Hell. Didn't sleep for a week. Next to Bosch's Hell, Dante's Inferno is a summer field. I tell you, if the town fathers of Basel had got Bosch to paint their mural? Basel today would be known as the Holy City. A city of angels. Why? Because no one would dare to commit the littlest sin, for fear of ending up in Bosch's Hell. You could—"

"Dismas?"

Schenk, the director of the relic fair. Christ.

"Franz. Well. Hello."

Dismas stood and greeted him. He introduced Dürer. "Here is my friend . . . Heinrich."

Schenk plumped himself down without being invited.

He said with his wonted tone of mischief, "What are you doing here? You're out of season."

"Neither buying nor selling. Passing through."

"Passing through. Hm, but to where? Come on. Out with it."

"Milan."

"Ah." Schenk's eyes twinkled with conspiracy. "And what's in *Milan*?"

Dismas glanced over both his shoulders and said in a whisper, "The True Cross. The whole thing. One piece."

Schenk roared with laughter.

"Then your pockets are full and you can afford to buy me a drink."

Dismas ordered a round of the indecently expensive Torgau beer.

They chatted pleasantly about nothing in particular until Dismas noticed that Schenk was staring wide-eyed at his hands. Hell. He'd pulled his gloves off at the mural and forgot to put them back on.

"In God's name, man, what *happened*?"

"This? Oh. A stupid thing. Accident."

Schenk's gaze remained fixed on the strangely symmetrical holes in the skin between Dismas's thumbs and forefingers. What kind of accident could cause such parallel wounds?

Dismas's mind, still unsettled from the episode at the mural, went blank. Schenk waited for an answer.

Dürer interjected. "He's being polite. It was my fault."

"*Your* fault? How . . . ,"

"We were hunting. It was cold. Very cold. Yes. Dismas was holding his hands together so, you know, blowing into them to get them warm. Blowing. I was loading my crossbow, and clumsy fool that I am, it discharged. Bolt went clean through both his hands. Another inch and he'd have holes in his cheeks. Just as well he doesn't, what this beer costs."

"Merciful God. How dreadful."

"Um," Dismas said. "Hurt like a bastard." He held out his hands and grinned. "But now—I have the stigmata. Which is only proof of what everyone already knew—that I'm a living saint."

Schenk laughed.

"But enough of me," Dismas said. "What's the gossip?"

"Well, let's see. Otto Henger was through, week before last. On his way to Dalmatia in hot pursuit of a mandible of Saint Jerome. Seven teeth intact, Henger claimed." Schenk shook his head gloomily. "The Luther business is starting to have a depressing effect on prices. People are more skeptical now about relics and indulgences. Damn Luther. Listen to this. A skull of Saint Diomeda—an exquisite piece—that should have fetched a hundred gulden in Antwerp went begging. Finally someone snapped it up for twenty-five."

"Twenty-*five*?" Dismas said. "That's terrible."

Schenk shook his head. "Why not just give it away? Bad sign."

Schenk said that he had the greatest respect for Dismas's client Frederick, but he simply could not understand—for the life of him—why he was protecting the very man whose heretical promulgations were undermining the relic business. Frederick, whose collection was rivaled only by the Vatican's! Personally, Schenk said, he admired many things about Luther. Yes, he agreed with a lot of what he had to say. And, yes, he admired the Elector for his principled stand, what with everyone howling to burn Luther at the stake. Still . . .

Schenk shrugged off these melancholy thoughts and predicted that the market would stabilize and rebound. These theological scraps always affected prices. Sure, the fellow who'd bought St. Diomeda's skull would probably sell it next year for two hundred gulden. More.

He wiped his lips. What else? Let's see. Erasmus of Rotterdam had taken up residence in Basel, adding great luster. It was said Erasmus was sympathetic to some of the reforms Luther advocated. But he absolutely rejected Luther's insistence that faith alone was necessary for salvation. As for Luther calling the Pope—Schenk lowered his voice—a raging whore of Babylon? Erasmus was *appalled*. What had gotten into Luther? Rumor was it was something to do with his bowels. He was all blocked up, they said.

What else? The new city hall was being hailed throughout Europe as a marvel. Remember all that complaining about how much it was going to cost! Ha. Oh, and the council had worked out an agreement with the Confederation: if Basel is attacked, the cantons will provide military assistance. In return, Basel will mediate disputes among the cantons.

There was something else. What? Oh, yes, some German noble had gone missing in the Black Forest.

Dismas and Dürer had been half listening to Schenk prattle. Now they perked, careful not to show too much interest.

"A missing noble," Dismas ventured. "Did he get himself lost?"

"Lothar. Count of Schramberg, in the Rottweil. Met him once or twice. Came to the fair, looking for bargains. I was not impressed, to be honest. You know the kind. Arrogant. Reminding you every five minutes how important he was, not only being a count, but nephew of the Spanish King, him who's about to be emperor."

"Godson, not nephew," Dürer corrected.

Dismas stifled a groan.

"Ah? You know him?"

"Only by . . . reputation," Dürer said. "What did you mean he's gone missing? How does a count do that?"

"It's a mystery. Damned strange. Went out hunting with a dozen of his people and never came back. Vanished. *Pfft*. Well, wouldn't be the first time the Black Forest has swallowed someone up. Some say it was witchcraft."

"Oh, come."

"Ah, he's probably off whoring," Schenk said. "They say he's a bit of a beast with the womenfolk. They've got searchers out looking. Being as he's the Emperor's godson, like you say, they're wanting to find him."

Schenk pointed to the east.

"Think of it—all that ruled by a Spanisher now."

"Burgundian," Dürer corrected. "Ghent-born."

"Well, he is King of Spain. Might as well be a Spanisher. Seen his portrait? A Habsburg, sure. You could plow a field with his jaw. And more Catholic than the Pope. He'll be giving Leo lessons! *And* bringing his Dominicans and the Inquisition with him. Your uncle Frederick's going to have a time of it protecting Luther now. Mark you, there'll be war between France and Spain. Thank God for the Confederation. Enough of fighting in other people's wars, I say. Bad for business."

They finished their beers. Schenk wished Dismas good hunting in Milan. He teased Dismas that his intact true cross was sure to be the talk of the fair.

He left. Dismas and Dürer made their way toward the Edenhaus, both preoccupied with the same thought.

"Do you think they'd look for him here?" Dürer asked nervously.

"There's no reason to. But I think time to move on. That was clever, Nars, that business about shooting me with the crossbow. Mind you, it's just the sort of thing you *would* do."

As he put on his gloves, Dismas again felt the queasiness rising within him that had knocked him to the ground in front of the mural. He shuddered and walked on.

Dismas didn't want to make a show of hasty departure. There was no need for one. Schenk had only passed along a bit of local news. Basel was not in an uproar over a dissolute German count gone missing. He told Dürer to be ready to leave in the morning—assuming he was still resolved to continue on to Chambéry. Yes, Dürer said. He would accompany Dismas to Chambéry.

Dismas alerted Cunrat, telling him to be ready to leave at first light. He suggested to him that he and the other lads might want to get a decent night's sleep tonight instead of conducting another marathon of venery at the bawdy house.

Cunrat said he would consider it. He and the lads had scoured the apothecaries of Basel and procured enough of Magda's phallus tonic to keep a battalion of Landsknechte stiff until Judgment Day.

Dismas tried to blot out the memory of Unks, unsheathed and throbbing. Reluctantly, he made his way to Paracelsus's surgery to bid farewell to Magda.

Magda was even more improved, up and helping with the other patients. Her memory had completely returned, as Paracelsus had predicted.

"Well," Dismas said with forced cheer, "what good hands you're in."

She looked at him curiously.

"So, we're off."

"I'll change. And I must thank Doctor."

"Magda. I am off. Not you."

"But I'm coming with you."

"No." He smiled. "You must stay. And heal. These injuries to the head. Serious business."

"I am well enough."

"You don't know where I'm going."

"What does that matter?"

"It should," Dismas said sternly. "If you did know, sure, you wouldn't argue with me."

"All right, then, tell me."

Dismas sighed. "It's not a trip for a girl, Magda."

"I'm no girl. Only a whore."

"Why should you say such a thing?"

"You know it's true."

"That wasn't your fault. It was . . . you are no whore."

"What difference? He took my virtue. Is that why you don't want me?"

"No," he said. He took her hand. "You have far more virtue than I."

"Then why won't you let me come with you?"

"Look, Magda—"

"Stop telling me to look. I can see as well as you can hear with your—goblin ears."

"If you knew how I came by these ears, you might listen better to me."

She looked away from him. "That was cruel of me. Forgive me."

Dismas pulled off his gloves and held out his hands to her, palms up.

She looked at them and gasped.

"This is why you must not come." He put the gloves back on. He smiled. "And you should see the feet."

"Who did this to you?"

"Do you remember in the forest, by the fire, when I told you that I am a sinful man?"

"Yes."

"Well, you see, now I must pay for my sins. I must do a penance. And well"—he chuckled—"it's not a small penance."

"Was it murder?"

"No."

"Rape?"

"Magda."

"Must we go through all the Ten Commandments?"

Dismas looked at the window into the courtyard.

"Let's go outside."

It was late afternoon. The stone bench was still warm from the sun. Paracelsus's parrot, Hector, a gift from a wealthy merchant who did business in the Indes, regarded them with aloofness from the crossbar of his perch.

"It's nice here," Dismas said. "Peaceful. Paracelsus is fond of you. I have watched him with you. He's like a father with you."

"Yes. I am fond of him, too."

"You could make a good life here. Learn from him. In time you could—"

"Dismas. Stop."

She took his hand. They sat in silence.

He said, "This thing that I must do. It will not end well."

"Then why must you do it?"

"It's a penance. If I don't, I will go to Hell."

"I could help you."

He shook his head. "It's not something for a woman. Even a clever woman like you. Who can shoot a crossbow."

"I owe you my life. Why won't you let me repay?"

"You repaid me when you tried to give yourself up to Lothar, in the forest. Anyway, it's I who owe you. Helping you was the only decent thing I have done in years."

"Then let me do something for you." She looked at him. "Not to repay. I have feelings for you, you see."

He wanted to kiss her. Instead he said sternly, "Are you so ungrateful that you would throw away the life that was saved?"

She took her hand away from his. Tears welled. "Now you are cruel."

He put his hand to her chin and turned her face back to his. He kissed her.

They sat beneath the tree, silent, pressed against each other. Birds twittered above them in the branches, exchanging the day's last gossip in the gathering twilight. Hector looked on condescendingly, majestically indifferent to the lesser creatures, so drab beside his sumptuous plumage.

Dismas said, "I'll come for you at dawn. Day after tomorrow."

"I will be ready."

They embraced. Dismas left quickly so she would not see the tears burning his eyes.

24

Gifts

Next morning at dawn, they assembled in front of the Edenhaus to make their departure.

The Landsknechte were wobbly and spent, having been unable to resist a valedictory night of libidinous mayhem. Dismas settled the bill. In the event there were inquiries, he told the proprietress a lie, that they were on their way north, to Freiberg.

They left by the St. Alban's gate, cleared their nostrils of the stench of paper mill, and rode west. In ten miles they reached the St. Gunther well, and took the southwest road that led over the Jura.

They were a glum party. The Landsknechte were so hungover from their debauch it was all they could do to stay upright in their saddles. Dismas and Dürer rode together in the cart, each silent within his own melancholy; Dürer asking himself why in God's name he was continuing on, Dismas miserable and self-loathing at deceiving Magda. It was no comfort to him that he'd done it for her own good. Even Dürer, sunk in his own gloom, noticed his friend's.

"What's eating at you, then?"

Dismas didn't answer. He had not shared with Dürer what had passed between him and Magda.

"There's a sight to cheer your cowherder heart," Dürer said, pointing over his left shoulder at the Alps, rising white and clean into the blue sky. Dismas barely glanced. It annoyed Dürer that Dismas's spirits should be lower than his own when he had made such a noble sacrifice. He said, "Oh, cheer up. I don't want to dance with death any more than you."

Dürer studied his friend's face, as he would if he were painting it. Painters read men's souls, and he saw this was neither dejection nor fear at the prospect of death.

"Ah. The girl."

Dismas sighed. Yes, the girl.

"Well, *I* miss her, too," Dürer said, shoehorning himself into Dismas's misery. "Splendid lass. And after everything she endured at the hands of that pig. Sure, *he's* squealing in Hell. I hope Hell does look like Bosch's vision." After a pause he said, "I'd have liked to do her portrait. What a beauty she is. What a wife she'll make some fellow. Maybe she and Paracelsus—"

"Nars. Please, shut up."

"Smitten! As I thought. Well, well, Dismas has a heart after all. Fine time to fall in love. But all right. Let's turn around and go back to Basel. I'll make a wedding portrait of the two of you. No charge. My present."

Dismas said nothing.

"Well, does she love *you*?"

"Can't you be quiet?"

"I think she must, the way she looks at you. Painters know these things."

"Am I to have no peace? She'd have looked that way at anyone who helped her. Look, Nars, I don't want to talk about this."

"If she does love you, why don't we—?"

"She does not love me! Gratitude is different from love. Love is . . ."

"Yes? Please, go on. Tell me about *love*."

Dismas groaned.

"What a fraud you are, Nars. You only want us to turn around so you won't end up on the fucking gallows with me in Chambéry. Gallows, if we're lucky. More likely, they'll break us on the wheel. From the bottom."

"All right. Very well. I confess. I confess, yes, that I would rather *not* die on the fucking gallows or be broken on the wheel—from the bottom. But don't lecture to me about love. If Cupid were a Swiss, he'd fire his arrows into mountain goats."

"What are you two squabbling about?" Cunrat said, from behind. "You sound like hens. Can't you be quiet? My head is coming off."

They made camp and ate a cold, joyless supper.

"I miss Little Sister," Cunrat said.

"And her cooking," Unks said.

"Why didn't she come with us?" Nutker asked.

Dismas said nothing.

Cunrat said, "What's the plan, then? How are we going to steal this rag? Everyone I spoke to in Basel said it can't be done."

Dismas stared.

"What can you mean by 'everyone I spoke to said it can't be done'? God in Heaven, Cunrat. Did you *tell* what we're up to?"

"Don't wet yourself, man. I made some inquiries, is all. It's only diligence."

Dismas shook his head. "God save us."

"I like to know what I'm walking into. And everyone I spoke to said it's locked tighter than convent cunny. So I am asking—what's our *plan*?"

"The plan," Dismas said. "Very well. Since you ask, the plan is to stop and ask everyone between here and Chambéry for their suggestions on how to steal it. Then we will take all the suggestions, from all the people we have asked, and select the most clever. For good measure, we will also ask the Duke of Savoy himself if *he* has a proposal for how we can steal his Shroud. There is the plan."

"There's no call for insults."

"That wasn't an insult. Here is an insult—you are an imbecile, Cunrat."

"Steady, *Reiselaufer*."

Dürer said, "Hey, hey, now. Everybody, cool down."

Dismas and Cunrat were on their feet.

"Say that again."

"You are an imbecile. Want it one more time? I'll say it slowly, so you can understand."

Dürer put himself between them. There was shoving. Cunrat threw the first punch, which glanced off Dürer's ear. Soon they were flailing and the three of them went down into the dirt, rolling in and out of the edge of the fire, Dürer wedged between the combatants. Nutker and Unks looked on amused, arms folded, happy to have entertainment on an otherwise sour evening.

The melee continued amidst snarls and curses and scattered embers.

Nutker and Unks deliberated whether it would be disloyal to Cunrat to wager on the *Reiselaufer*. Then at the edge of the fire emerged a rider on horseback. They reached for their weapons.

Nutker laughed and said to the three on the ground, "We have company."

Cunrat, Dismas, and the hapless Dürer paused and looked up blinkingly from their Laocoön-like entwinement.

Magda took in the scene before her. Nutker was already at her side, helping her off her mount. A second horse was tethered behind, laden.

Grunting and cursing, Dürer untangled himself from between Dismas's and Cunrat's grip. He stood covered with dirt and debris.

"Master Dürer," Magda said. "You are on fire."

The edge of his tunic was in flames. Dürer slapped at it with the flat of his hand.

Dismas and Cunrat remained frozen on the ground, staring at Magda, each still gripping some part of the other.

Dürer muttered, "Silk. Ruined!"

Later, when they were all bedded down for the night by the fire, Magda and Dismas lay next to each other, apart from the others.

"It's good I came when I did," she said. "Or all I would have found of you was ash."

Dismas said nothing.

"You shouldn't have, girl."

"Are we back to calling me 'girl'?"

"How did you know what road to take?"

Now she did sound like a girl, happily revealing what a clever thing she had been. "The first night in the forest, while you and Nars slept, I stayed awake, listening to the boys talking. About Chambéry. About the Shroud."

"All along, you knew? Then why did you ask me where I was going?"

"So I would know."

"But you already knew."

"Not that. If you cared for me. When you wouldn't tell me, then I knew that you did care. When you left the surgery last night, I saw your face. I knew that you were lying about when we would leave."

"Magda—"

She put a finger to his lips. "Shh." She took away her finger and put her lips to his.

They were quiet for a while, watching the stars.

"You came heavy," Dismas said, indicating her packhorse. "What's all that? Fancy dresses for the court of Duke Charles?"

"Gifts from Paracelsus."

"You told Paracelsus? God in Heaven, is there anyone in Basel who does not know our mission?"

"I didn't tell him it was Chambéry. Or about the Shroud."

"What did you tell him?"

"That you are on a quest."

"Is that what it is?"

"To free someone. Someone who is locked up and very closely guarded. Maybe what I told him is not completely the truth. But Jesus is 'someone,' yes? And you say that relics are living things. So he is alive, in the Shroud. And the Shroud is locked up. Which makes him a prisoner. So it's not such a lie. Is it?"

Dismas smiled. "Who taught you to reason in such a way? Was your tutor Satan?"

Magda continued, delighted.

"He was *so* curious, Paracelsus! He knew I was being mysterious. He kept asking, *who* are you going to free? I said to him I couldn't tell more. But still he kept asking. Finally he said, 'Aha! You are going to the château at Chillon!' On the Geneva lake. So I pretended. I made a face like this—*You know!* I said to him, 'Um . . . well . . . ,' so he would think that he had guessed correctly. He was so pleased. It's funny. Don't you think?"

"Magda. I don't find anything funny about any of this."

"Ah, yes. I forgot. You are Swiss."

"It's not that."

"Well, I think it is funny. Because, you see, it's in the castle at Chillon that the dukes of Savoy keep their special prisoners. So Paracelsus thinks that we are attempting to free a prisoner of the Duke of Savoy."

"This is amusing?"

"You *are* Swiss. Don't you see? We're freeing a prisoner in a different castle of the Duke of Savoy. So Paracelsus is clever even when he is wrong."

"Magda, I must tell you a story."

"Yes, if you like."

"It's not a nice story. But it's one you must hear."

"Very well."

"The Shroud is the most closely guarded relic in Europe."

"Yes, it will not be easy."

"We will be caught. I told you this in Basel. So now I must tell you what will happen after we are caught. They will want to make an example. Have you ever seen a man broken on the wheel?"

Magda said nothing.

"On the way to the scaffold, in the cart, the executioner takes nips of your flesh with red-hot pincers. For such a crime as this, there would be at least three nips. Perhaps four. So you are almost dead when they stake you to the ground."

"Dismas—"

"They put flat pieces of wood under your elbows and knees. Then the executioner lifts up the heavy wheel and he goes to work. If the judges have been merciful, they will decree that he start 'from the top.' One blow to the head and it's over. But if the offense is grave, as this would be considered, then the judges demand 'from the bottom.' First your feet. The ankles. The legs. The knees. And so on."

"Stop, Dismas."

"In Nuremberg once I saw such an execution. The victim was still alive, even after perhaps thirty blows. I can still hear his screams. It was monstrous. Because you are a woman, maybe they would commute your sentence to being burned alive. But maybe not."

Magda rolled away from him. He made a pillow of sacking and put it under her head and covered her with an extra blanket, then went to sleep by the others.

Dürer said, "What a fine bedtime story. You really are a swine. Now I will have nightmares."

"You earned yours."

Dismas closed his eyes and prayed to St. Catherine—she who had been broken on the wheel—that this girl whom he loved would be gone in the morning. But dawn found Magda still there, crouched over the fire, making a good breakfast for her men.

25

The Bauges

Three weeks after leaving Basel, Dismas and Cunrat stood on a mountain ridge high in the Bauges massif, looking down on Chambéry, capital of the Duchy of Savoy. They'd gone on ahead of the others to make a reconnaissance. Tomorrow they would enter the city.

It had been a tiring journey, by way of Neuchâtel, Fribourg, Lausanne, Geneva, Annecy, and the Bauges. Outside the Empire, they felt secure enough to lodge in towns. The Landsknechte happily took the occasion to sample every bawdy house along the way, fortified by their phallus tonic. Dismas wondered at the fortune this rampant venery must be costing them. But his mind was on other things.

"It seems we are not the only pilgrims coming to venerate the Shroud," Dismas observed.

"God in Heaven," Cunrat said, marveling at the sight below. "It's like two armies converging."

Chambéry stood at one of the great intersections of Europe, near a pass formed by the Bauges on the north and the Chartreuse massif on the south. The river Leysse bordered the city's eastern side.

Here was the crossroads for French armies bringing war into Italy and for Italian armies bringing war into France. At the moment, there was peace, but peace was always momentary. Dominating Chambéry's western side was the ancestral castle of the dukes of Savoy. Dismas imagined the present Duke Charles, awaking each morning and nervously looking out his bedchamber window, bowels in a knot, praying not to see an army marching toward him under the banner of François, King of France. It occurred to Dismas that four years before, François had walked all the way here from Lyon, dressed in the white tunic of a pilgrim, to give thanks at the Shroud for his victory at the Battle of Marignano. That he had done this must concern Charles, for it showed how greatly François esteemed the Shroud of Chambéry. And what kings esteem, they seek to possess.

From this height, Dismas and Cunrat had a clear view of the roads leading into Chambéry from the north and south. Both teemed with pilgrims and caravans. It was a spectacle, sure. The only time Dismas had seen such crowds was in Rome, where he chanced to be in the days after the death of Pope Julius II.

"The Duke must be happy," Dismas said. "All those coins, marching to his coffers."

Cunrat nodded. "That'll mean guards everywhere," Cunrat said. "On top of the regular chapel guard." He sighed. "Well, *Reiselaufer*, how are we going to do this thing?"

"We're monks. Pray for a miracle?"

"Who do you pray to, for this? Is there a patron saint of shroud-stealers?"

Dismas considered. "There's Saint Mark. He's not strictly speaking the patron of relic thieves. Seven hundred years ago, some fellows translated him from Alexandria to Venice. *There* was the greatest translation of all. So we could pray to him. Or to the clever lads who did it. Two merchants of Venice and two Greeks—one a priest, the other a monk. See, they feared that the Turks, who had taken Alexandria, would destroy the shrine of Saint Mark. So the priest and the monk switched Saint Mark's body with that of Saint Claudia."

"Why would they put another saint in his shrine?"

"Ah. The remains of a saint always give off a fragrant smell. In theory. They put Saint Claudia in so there would be a continuation of good aroma from the tomb."

Cunrat shook his head.

Dismas went on. "The two Venetians got Saint Mark aboard their ship. They put him in a chest and covered him over with pork. Clever, eh? When the Moors opened the trunk to inspect it, they saw all this pork and went *paugh!* For Moors, pig meat is an abomination. They closed the chest and told them to fuck off out of Alexandria. But I don't think pork will help us with this translation."

Dismas and Cunrat climbed back down to rejoin the others and told them what they had seen, the great crowds streaming into Chambéry.

They camped that night by a stream that descended a ravine to the outskirts of the town. There was not much talk around the fire. They were tired. Despite having finally arrived at Chambéry, Dismas was in a somber mood. A month of thinking had yet to produce a plan for the translation.

He kept up a show of confidence, not wanting to cause despair in his comrades. He had privately resolved this much: that if he failed to come up with a plan, he would spare them. Hurl himself alone at the Shroud when it went up on display, get it over with quickly, go down in a hail of arrows. Better that than breaking on the wheel. His penance would be done, Magda and Nars and the lads could escape. Dismas's secret plan made his gloom less.

It was a fine view from their camp. The sunset turned the sky purple. The fading light cast long shadows across the northern slopes of the Chartreuse range and lit fire to the gold-leafed spires of Chambéry.

Dismas looked over at Dürer. As usual he was sketching.

"Landscape?"

"Landscapes bore me."

Dismas got up to stretch his legs. He walked over and crouched behind Dürer to see what he was drawing. A portrait of Magda, done with colored chalk.

"Not bad."

"Of course it's 'not bad.' " Dürer had grown touchy the closer they got to Chambéry, perhaps contemplating his own dance with death. Dismas hoped that some of Nars's mood might stem from remorse at having caused this predicament.

His rendering of Magda's ginger ringlets was deft. Now Dismas had an insight that made him smile. Magda's hair was so similar to Dürer's that painting her was an excuse for yet another self-portrait.

"It's good, the way you've got the light on her hair. Gold, like."

"It's titian."

"What's that?"

"The color of her hair. But why should you know this?"

"Titian. It's an odd name for a color."

"He's a *painter*. In Venice. He's a friend."

"Magda," Dismas said, "did you know that your hair is the color of a painter in Venice?"

She was sitting across from them by the fire, doing needlework. She said without looking up, "My father used to call me Little Ginger."

"There's not much light left," Dürer said.

"Then you'd best work fast," Dismas said, sitting down. "Good practice, for down there."

The sun set behind the Chartreuse massif. Dürer continued to work by the light of the fire. When it was finished he handed it to Magda. She blushed.

"It's . . ."

"You may say. Beautiful."

"You have such talent, Master Dürer."

Dismas groaned. "Oh, don't tell him that. He'll be even more insufferable. Give it here. I will be the judge."

But it was beautiful. It seemed to Dismas unlike Dürer's own style, as if done by someone else.

"Well? We tremble to hear your artistic judgment," Dürer said.

"It's all right. I don't know about the nose."

Dürer snatched it out of Dismas's hand and gave it back to Magda.

"Wait . . ." He took it back, scribbled in the lower corner, and handed it to her. "There."

Magda looked at it. "What is 'TV'?"

"Tiziano Vecelli. Titian. It's done in his style. But Dismas would of course not understand that."

"To me it looks more like a Cranach," Dismas sniffed.

That night Magda had another of her nightmares. Every night she had one. Dismas woke her gently.

"It's all right. Go back to sleep. Dream good things."

She gripped his arm.

"Talk to me. Just for a little."

Because of her nightmares, Dismas had taken to putting his bed-roll on the ground near hers. A chaste arrangement. This way he could comfort her.

He looked up at the stars, abundant in the moonless night. She felt warm beside him, and gave off a smell sweeter than any saint's bones. How good it was to have an armful of warm girl on a cold night. He felt her finger gently tracing the edges of his mangled ear.

"Tell me about her," she said.

"Who?"

"Your wife."

"She died."

"Is that all?"

"I should have died with her. And the children. I was in Judea, looking for the lance of Longinus."

"I'm sorry."

They were quiet awhile.

"Who is Longinus?"

"The Roman soldier at the Crucifixion. He who pierced Jesus's chest with the lance."

"Ah. Did you find this lance?"

"Perhaps."

"How, perhaps?"

"With relics you can never really be sure. It's in Wittenberg. In Frederick's gallery. He was very pleased to have it. When he learned about my wife and children, he purchased indulgences for their souls. Generous indulgences. Sure, they are no longer in Purgatory now. Anyway, they died without sin. She was a good woman. Go to sleep, now. Tomorrow will be a long day."

"The Shroud of Chambéry, do you think it's truly the burial cloth of Christ?"

Dismas considered. "No. But it doesn't matter. The Cardinal gave me this penance. So here I am. And now here you are. Because"—he gave her nose a playful twist—"you are so stubborn."

"Was she pretty, your wife?"

"Yes."

"What was her name?"

"Hildegard. Go to sleep."

"Tell me something about her."

"What do you want to know?"

"Tell me why you loved her."

"Well, she was my wife."

"Dismas. What an answer."

"She was pretty. She loved our children. And she would make me laugh. I was never sad when she was with me. She was a good cook. She would sing while she . . ." He fell silent.

"Sure, they are in Heaven," Magda said. "You will be with them again. But not just yet."

26

Chambéry

After breakfast they put on their religious habits. Mindful of the embarrassing lack of crucifixes in the Black Forest when he performed the test of St. Boniface, Dismas had purchased a dozen in Basel.

"This wool scratches," Unks grumbled. "It's like wearing a cat. Are these hair shirts? What kind of fucking monks are we supposed to be?"

"Bonifacian," Dismas said. "And, Unks, please don't be saying such words in Chambéry. Monks do not curse."

"Ha. There was this friar in my village of Klotze. Every time he opened his mouth would come a stream of—"

"Yes, Unks, I'm sure. But *we* must be good monks. Why? Because if they discover that we are not monks, they will kill us. Is this sufficient incentive for you? Now, we must have names."

"Who gives a shit what our names are?" Cunrat said.

Dismas sighed. "All right. Be Brother Cunrat, if you prefer. If you want to use your real name so they can kill you later, fine."

Cunrat groaned loudly. "Give me a name, then."

"I will be Brother Lucas," Dismas said. He picked Cranach's first name to annoy Dürer. "Cunrat, you will be Brother Vilfred. Nutker, Brother Cuthbert. Unks—"

"Cuthbert?" Nutker said. "No. I don't want Cuthbert."

"What's wrong with it?"

"It's a sodomite name."

Dismas sighed. "He was a saint, Nutker, not a sodomite. But very well. What name do you wish?"

"I don't care. But not Cuthbert."

"Theobald, then. Is this satisfactory?" Nutker shrugged. Dismas pressed on. "Unks, Brother Sigmund. Dürer . . . hmm. You will be Brother Nars. For Saint Narcissus. Very suitable."

Dürer glared.

"Don't take offense. Narcissus was Bishop of Jerusalem in the second century. He changed water into oil. Perfect name for a painter."

"I have never heard of this supposed saint."

"Well, I would not expect a painter to know history. Now, Magda . . . you be Sister—"

"Hildegard."

Dismas stared.

"Hildegard of Bingen," Magda said. "Sibyl of the Rhine. She was very holy. She never said naughty words."

They descended the ravine and reached the road, where they joined the flow of pilgrims.

Dismas stressed the necessity of making note of everything they passed. Any detail might prove valuable, should they have to make a hasty departure, a possibility Dismas thought quite likely, should they get that far.

The road went through fields under cultivation by a monastery atop a hill. Dwellings became more numerous as they approached the river Leysse.

There was a single bridge across. Its abutments and cutwater were stone; the roadway across was of heavy wooden planks laid together. Curious design.

"Italian," Dismas observed. "See those holes on either end of the timbers. They can be pulled up in case of attack, to stop the enemy."

"A drawbridge that's not a drawbridge," Dürer observed.

"For monks who are not monks."

They came to the Porte Recluse, the city's main gate. Here was a proper drawbridge over the moat surrounding the city walls. A throng of pilgrims had bottled up traffic. The gate guards were demanding a "transit fee" to cross into the city, causing arguments and consternation. After their week in the sylvan Bauges, the din of the crowd was jarring and discordant. And what a smell!

Pilgrims had erected tents and lean-tos along the street by the moat. Little markets were doing brisk business, all manner of things for sale or barter: fowl, fish, game, wine, devotional articles, ointments, tonics, physics for every ailment.

Dismas viewed with professional disdain the abundance of relic-mongers hawking items of the most dubious provenance. He counted four separate *complete* Crowns of Thorns. Everywhere were replicas of the Shroud of Chambéry—in every size from napkin to bed linen. One was about actual size: fourteen by four feet, nailed upright between two poles. The image of Christ was atrociously done, in the most lurid and sanguinary way. The fellow standing beside it, presumably its author, was proudly pointing out various details to the crowd.

Dismas said to Dürer, "Let's hope you can do better."

Dürer sniffed. "Five guldens says he's a Spanisher."

"Why?"

"Look, all that blood. They're mad for gore, Iberians. A Spanisher is incapable of painting a still life of fruit or flowers without putting a decapitated head on the table, oozing. Take away a Spanisher's red paints—his massicot, sinopia, carmine, bole, cinnabar, lac, madder, solferino, vermilion, Pozzuoli, crimson—and he'll sink a knife into his veins and paint with his own blood. Never has there come a decent painter from that peninsula. They were ruled too long by the Moors. If the Moors caught you painting a portrait—*chuk*—off with your hand. Yet in every field—medicine, astronomy, mathematics—they were leagues ahead of us."

They came to the xenodochium, the charity hostel. They could afford better accommodations, but Dismas thought it congruent with their monkish imposture to lodge here. No one was delighted at the prospect. The building exuded a miasma of overflowing latrines, teeming lice, malaria, pustulating sores, stale wine, and wormy bread. Dürer flatly announced that under no circumstances would he inhabit such verminous quarters.

Dismas remonstrated with him. He pointed out to Brother Nars that he had taken not only a vow of poverty but also of obedience. Brother Nars replied that in this case, he would defrock himself and find his own "fucking" lodging. Dismas, in no mood for one of Dürer's tantrums, asked through gritted teeth: "Why don't you just knock on the Duke's door and demand rooms in his castle, commensurate with your dignity?"

Back and forth this went, escalating, until Magda intervened, lest the two friars come to blows in public. She proposed that they make temporary camp *al fresco* in the public gardens, around the corner of the city wall from the Porte Recluse. Everyone thought this an agreeable alternative to quartering with leprous pilgrims, however much God might love these most wretched of the earth.

They made a bivouac beneath the plane trees. It afforded a breeze and a pleasant view of the river. The Landsknechte took the cart and horses to find a livery and buy food and wine and learn whatever there was to be learned. Dürer, still fuming over the altercation at the xenodochium, stomped off to explore on his own.

Dismas and Magda sat beside each other on a blanket in the shade. But for being dressed as two religious, they might be two sweethearts enjoying a picnic.

"Dismas?"

"*Lucas*. Yes, Sister?"

"*Is* there a plan?"

"Yes. The Shroud will be displayed high up on the castle wall. From a balcony of the Holy Chapel. From the sixth hour to the ninth hour. Like the hours Christ spent on the cross. So. Brother Nars will get as close as he can, the better to observe the Shroud, and make his facsimile. On the linen we purchased in Basel."

"And then?"

"Then . . . then, we will switch his copy with the Shroud. Simple. See?"

"And how is that part to be accomplished?"

"Ah. Well. Once Brother Nars has finished making his copy—which he will have to do very quickly, and Brother Nars is not the quickest of painters—then on the day following, when the Shroud is again displayed . . . the six of us all together will rush at the castle wall and make a human ladder. Since the wall is seventy or eighty feet high, we will stand on each other's shoulders until the person at the top can reach the Shroud. This will be you, since you are the lightest of us. Then all you have to do is you just give a good yank—so—to pull it from the hands of the archbishop and deacons who are holding it. And give them the copy. Then . . . then we run like hell. Through the city, over the drawbridge, over the river bridge, and all the way up into the mountains. What do you think of my plan?"

Magda stared. "It's . . ."

"Yes," Dismas said. "It lacks something. Everything, really."

They sat in silence, fingering rosary beads for the sake of appearance.

Magda said, "You say if a relic wants to be translated, then nothing can prevent the translation?"

Dismas nodded. "This is the rule. But for *authentic* relics. The problem here is . . . well, there are many problems. The first problem is I do not believe this shroud is authentic. Second, even if it is, we have to ask, would Jesus desire for his shroud to be translated? From a duke who is called 'Charles the Good,' to a cardinal who should be called 'Albrecht the Not So Good'?"

Magda considered the problem. "If it's a fake, as you say, why does this Albrecht want it so badly?"

Dismas sighed. "Perhaps he has convinced himself that it is real. But mostly I think he sent me on this mission for another reason."

"What?"

"To get me killed, without causing a hoo-ha with Frederick."

Dismas wanted to tell Magda of his resolve to spare them, but it was too pleasant beneath the plane trees.

Presently the Landsknechte and Dürer returned, bearing an immensity of food and drink: wine, beer, sausages, bread, roasted capons. Dismas observed acerbically that such a display hardly made them resemble impoverished monks. But he was as hungry as the rest of them. They fell to their feast.

As they ate, a great procession hove into view from the south, crossing the bridge. Cavalry, foot soldiers, attendants, carriage upon carriage, banners.

"Is it a king?" Unks grunted, tearing off a bite of capon.

"No," Dürer said. "But a duke, sure. And from that direction, Italian. I can't make out the banners. Venetian, perhaps. Whoever it is, he doesn't travel light. I've seen smaller armies."

They watched as horse carriages rumbled over the bridge timbers.

"Might be Lorenzo, Duke of Urbino," Dürer said. "Not one to go without the basic comforts. Like his uncle."

"Who's his uncle?"

"The Pope."

"Ah."

"Do you know," Dürer said, "how he spends his time, this Pope?"

"I assume, interceding with God on behalf of mankind," Dismas said, "being the Pope."

Dürer snorted. "Hunting. It's all he does. Maybe if he spent a bit more time on church business, he and Luther would have come to an understanding. His other passion is his zoo."

"A zoo?"

"Did Our Lord not instruct the apostles to go forth and make zoos? Truly, Leo walks in the footsteps of the Fisherman. Even if he must step in enormous turds. His favorite is a white elephant named Hanno. Well, Leo's a de' Medici, isn't he? I've met him. Jolly, in his way. But . . ." Dürer made a face. "They are debauched, the Italians. It's their climate that makes them so."

"Titian and the Pope," Dismas said. "What famous friends you have, Nars."

Dürer cut a slice of apple. "If that is Leo's nephew Lorenzo, you peasants should feel honored. He's a very considerable personage."

"Just because he's a duke?" Nutker said.

"Dear Nutker, he's the ruler of Florence. And now his uncle-pope has paid for a war to procure for him the Duchy of Urbino. So you see, he's lord of maybe one quarter of all Italy. He is advised by Machiavelli."

"Who is Machiavelli?" Dismas asked.

Dürer shook his head. "What a scholar you are. Machiavelli is, well, he's a philosopher, isn't he? Among other things. He wrote a treatise for Lorenzo, about how a prince should rule."

"And how does one rule?" Dismas asked.

"I've not read it. I'm too busy trying to rule Agnes. For which purpose, you need a stick, not a treatise."

"Ha," Dismas said. "I'd like to see you try to rule Agnes with a stick."

"I think Machiavelli says to kill your enemies before they kill you."

Cunrat nodded. "Sound advice."

"Lorenzo is not well," Dürer said.

"Why?"

"He's Italian."

"Pox?"

"In Italy, they call it the French pox. In France, the Italian pox."

"I thought you liked Italians," Dismas said. "You are always running off to Italy."

"To learn, not to fornicate. Sure, I go to Italy. In art, the Italians are supreme. They have no equal. Except for one or two others."

Dismas grunted. "Anyone in mind?"

"As for morals, they have—none. *Nessuno*. The Pope himself is a well-known sodomite."

"Now you sound like Luther."

Dürer shrugged. "It's the truth. They say he has a . . ." Dürer glanced at Magda. "Well, it's hardly a topic for decent conversation. Suffice to say he is afflicted with an unpleasant consequence of unnatural venery."

"Yes," Cunrat said, "I have heard of this. A fistula in his ass, from being buggered."

"By the elephant!" Unks said.

The Landsknechte roared.

The lead carriage had now halted at the Porte Recluse. There came a fanfare blast of horns.

Dismas wiped capon grease from his chin and stood. "Let's have a look at your distinguished personage, whoever he is."

The soldiers cleared a space in the crowd. Dismas and the others shouldered their way through to get a closer view, the Landsknechte plowing a path with unmonkishly sharp elbows.

At the head of the procession they saw an attendant on horseback, holding a heraldic banner. A black eagle nesting in a ducal coronet, atop a black-and-gold battle helm. In its talons, a diamond ring. In the foreground, a gold shield adorned with a half dozen large red balls.

"De' Medici," Dürer said. "Lorenzo."

"The red balls," Cunrat asked, "what do they signify?"

"No one seems to know. Some say dents on the shield from great battles. Others say pawnbroker balls. Still others say pills. *De' Medici* is Italian for doctor. They were apothecaries, long ago."

"They did well, for apothecaries," Magda said.

The ducal carriage halted. From inside the Porte Recluse streamed a procession of Savoyard household attendants. The two entourages collided in a muffled crush of silk and velvet. Formalities were observed with much bowing and doffing of caps. A scrum formed by the door of the Duke's carriage. Another round of bows. The carriage door opened and out stepped Lorenzo, Duke of Urbino.

Magda recoiled. "Oh! Poor man!"

An attempt had been made to conceal with greasepaint the sores on his face. The Duke blinked in the sunlight and smiled at the crowd. He gave a feeble wave with his left hand. His right hand clutched at his chest.

The crowd gave him a cheer, which seemed to please him. Then he grimaced and clutched again at his chest. He withdrew into the carriage. The procession began to move forward, over the drawbridge and through the Porte Recluse into Chambéry.

"He will not live long," Magda said.

"How do you know this?" Dismas said.

"You saw the way he was holding his chest? In the last stages, it attacks the heart. The pain is very great. There is something that helps. A distillation from a flower. We passed many of them, up there, in the Bauges. Fingerhut. You saw."

"Yes, I know this flower," Dismas said.

"*Digitalis purpurea*. In England they discovered it. They call it glove of the fox."

Dismas considered. "A duke who rules one-quarter of Italy, sure, his doctors would know of it. With such an entourage, he must have twenty doctors."

"Perhaps. Still, you saw how he held his chest."

Indeed, Dismas had.

The next morning before dawn, Magda led Cunrat and Nutker and Unks back up into the Bauges to scour the meadows for fingerhut. They returned toward sundown, looking like flower merchants, sacks filled to bursting, trailing purple petals in their wake, Unks muttering that such a girlish errand was beneath the dignity of any self-respecting Landsknecht.

Dismas and Dürer spent the day in the city looking for quarters.

They shed their habits, since monks looking to rent rooms would only arouse suspicion. It came as no surprise that all the landlords were asking usurious, inflated rents.

"Pilgrimages always bring out the best in Christians," Dismas observed.

After lengthy searching, they found a usable space in a basement near the church of St. Anthony, not overly dank and only moderately infested with rats.

27

A Plan

Dismas sat watching Magda grind fingerhut petals in a mortar and drop them into a bubbling cook pot.

"It takes time," Magda said. "The liquid must reduce, to have potency."

Dismas took her wooden spoon and stirred so she could concentrate on her pestling. On the table were vials and bottles and boxes Magda had taken from her saddlebags—the gifts from Paracelsus. She finished with the petals and held up one of the vials, uncorked it, and sniffed.

"What's that?"

"He's always traveling, bringing back treasures. Especially from the East. He's a magus, like one of the three kings in the Bible. This truly is a gift."

Dismas took a sniff.

"Cistus ladanifer," Magda said. "He mixes it with twigs of rockrose. Also he puts in lavender."

"I think you *are* a witch."

"If a witch could stop pain as this can, there would be no more burnings. One day I watched Paracelsus remove the leg of a man. It had been crushed by a cart. The man was in great pain, crying out. Paracelsus put four drops in a cup of wine and gave it to the man. After drinking, he was quiet. Like he was asleep. Paracelsus took his saw and started. Not once did the man cry out. The only sound was the saw." Magda winced. "I don't like surgery. I prefer apothecary."

She held the vial over the cook pot and with her finger gently tapped out ten drops, counting silently as she did.

"You must be careful with *ladanum*. Too much and it stops the lungs."

Dismas had been leaning over the pot. He jerked back his head, not wanting his lungs to stop.

"What's in that box there?" he said.

"*Papaver*. Also from the East. They put it on embers and breathe the smoke."

"What does it do?"

"Makes dreams."

"Why would Paracelsus give you this?"

Magda smiled. "It brings sleep, with the dreams."

Dismas nodded. "Yes, that could be useful."

"Also . . ."

"What?"

"What you told me that night, when you tried to scare me to go away. About the execution."

"Yes?"

"If it should come to that, it would be good to have this."

Dismas left her to her cooking and went to the other side of the room where the others were. What a chorus of moaning and gnashing of teeth.

Dürer was complaining about the spiders. The Landsknechte were in a foul temper at being separated from their weapons. Dismas had ordered that the cart with the weapons be stabled outside the city gates. There was to be no killing. They'd come to Chambéry as translators, not assassins. He told them: if this *is* the burial cloth of Christ, and we commit murder to possess it—can you imagine who will greet us on the shores of the next world? Satan, with arms wide. Even if the Shroud is not real, and we arrive in the next life with innocent blood on our hands, do you suppose we will be greeted by angels?

A fine speech, but pointless. Homilies on the subject of virtue and the afterlife were wasted on Landsknechte. The lads listened impassively, then spat on the ground and said, "And who are you—Moses, with Ten Commandments? What was that we did, back in the Black Forest? What was that, but killing—killing good and hot?"

Dismas replied that surely even Landsknechte could distinguish between defending themselves from attack—for rescuing an innocent woman—and slitting throats in a chapel while trying to thieve the Shroud of Jesus. He threw up his hands.

He left the basement and walked the streets of Chambéry to cool his kidneys. Later he returned carrying a flagon of expensive wine as a peace offering.

Cunrat took from his satchel the soft leather pouch of boar scrotum that had been Lothar's purse. He emptied the contents onto the table. Jewelry, coins, and baubles tinkled onto the rough surface of the table, glinting in the candlelight. Cunrat picked idly through the remains of his loot, like someone at supper, picking out the choice bits.

Dismas spoke in a comradely tone.

"Ah, so that's how you scoundrels have been financing your nights of bliss."

Dismas reached and found a bauble. He held it to the candle. It was Lothar's signet ring. Dismas recoiled at the memory of Cunrat hacking it from the dead count's hand.

"Is this *all* that remains of your spoils?"

"Um," Cunrat said. "But it paid for some fucking good fucking. Didn't it, lads?"

"Did you sell some in Basel?" Dismas asked nervously. "To purchase your cock tonic?"

"Some in Basel. Some in Neuchâtel. Some in Fribourg. Lausanne. Geneva."

"It's a good thing no one's looking for us," Dismas said. "What a trail you'd have left."

But there had been no sign of pursuit. In every town, Dismas had discreetly inquired. No one knew anything about a vanished German count in the far-off Black Forest.

"Let's hope your trollops were clean," Dismas said. "So you don't end up like the Duke of Urbino." Dismas gave Cunrat a pat on his sternum.

Dismas said to Dürer, "Never mind how to rule. Your Machiavelli should have written Lorenzo a treatise on how to avoid the pox."

Cunrat held up a flask and regarded it mournfully. He turned it upside down. Empty. He called out to Magda across the basement, "Little Sister. Can't you cook us some?"

"Cunrat," Dismas scolded. "Don't you suppose she has more important work?"

"What could be more important than the rigidity of my cock?"

Dismas put Lothar's signet ring back on the table. "What else is left of your spoils? Wasn't there a sword?"

Cunrat said sulkily, "You said we couldn't *have* our swords inside the city."

"Yes. But didn't you take Lothar's sword? The gift from his godfather, the new Emperor. Or did you sell that along with the rest?"

"Of course not. That's special. Not for pussy-money. "It's in the cart. With our *other* weapons. Let's just pray we are not attacked." Cunrat held up the empty flask, smiling like a boy trying to wheedle sweets. "Little Sister. *Please?*"

28

Lothar Redux

"No," Dürer said. "Absolutely, no."

"Nars—"

"Are you deaf? No!"

"Don't you understand that—"

"I understand very well. I understand this is a lunatical proposal that will get me killed. I came with you—out of goodness of heart—to help you. Not to offer myself as a sacrificial lamb. Suicide is a mortal sin. So no. And don't ask me again."

"Don't you see the logic?"

"Logic you call this? Don't make me laugh."

"You're a melancholic. I gave up trying to make you laugh ten years ago."

"Well, you are making me laugh now. Ha-ha-ha. And go to Hell. *You* impersonate a dead count."

"If you would cease these hysterics and listen for one moment, you would understand why it is you—not me—that has to play the part of Lothar. If it works—"

"Ah! Did you hear?" Dürer appealed to the others. "Two sentences into his hortation and already he says, '*If* it works'!"

"Nars. There is no reason that the Duke of Savoy would not clasp to his bosom the godson of the Holy Roman Emperor. Duke Charles despises and fears the King of France. The Holy Roman Emperor also despises the King of France. Nothing would make the Duke of Savoy happier than to be host to the Emperor's godson. Why? Because the godson will go home and tell his godfather-emperor, What a wonderful fellow is the Duke of Savoy! Such a gracious host! I made a pilgrimage to Chambéry, to venerate the Shroud. Going as a simple pilgrim, of course I expected nothing from the Duke. But he learned I was there and treated me like his own son!"

Dürer's arms were tightly folded over his chest in a posture of defiance.

"If you think it's such a splendid idea, *you* play Lothar."

"Nars. Please to focus. It's not me who needs to get close to the Shroud in order to make a copy. You are the artist, not me."

Magda spoke. "There is wisdom in what Dismas proposes, Master Dürer."

"Logic and now wisdom?" Dürer snorted. "I think you are all deluded."

"Ach, show some spine, man," Cunrat said. "It's a good plan."

Dürer looked up at the ceiling, as if appealing for divine intervention.

"What if someone in the castle knows Lothar of Schramberg? Eh? What then?"

"Unlikely," Dismas said.

"Unlikely?" Dürer snorted. "You are blithe, Dismas, to gamble my life on 'unlikely.' "

"Nars. I'll be there with you, at your side. As your servant. It's my life, too. Don't play the solitary martyr with me."

"So we present ourselves at the castle? Knock on the door and say, 'Hallo! I am Lothar! Let me in!' "

"You wanted nice rooms, didn't you? But to repeat one more time—no. We do not, as you put it with such great drama, bang on the door and demand rooms. You present yourself to the castle guard. Give them them a letter, and leave. The letter will be from yourself, that is, Count Lothar of Schramberg. The letter will say that you are here in Chambéry, that you have come as a pilgrim, with a few retainers. You ask nothing. The letter is simply a formal courtesy, from one noble to another. The letter will say some nice things about how lovely is Chambéry, how wonderful that the Duke is displaying the Shroud for everyone to venerate. La, la, la. You wish him all health and God's blessing and bye-bye. That's it. If he takes the bait, then we're inside the castle. If not . . . then we must devise some other way to breach the ramparts of Chambéry. Perhaps a siege tower. But this would be easier."

Dürer fumed in silence, thinking of some way to avoid this unwanted role.

"A depraved oaf like Lothar, tell me this—why would he make a pilgrimage? Even if no one in the castle knows him personally, what if someone has heard of his appalling reputation?"

"Nars. Let me explain Christianity to you. Pilgrims make pilgrimages to atone. Do you think people walk hundreds of miles to grovel before relics because they feel wonderful about themselves? No. They do it because they think otherwise they will go to Hell. If someone says to you, 'Hey, are you the naughty Count of Schramberg of whom we have heard so much?' You give your breast a good *mea culpa* thump and say, 'Yes, I am this same naughty count. *What* a sinner I was! Then one day I was hunting in the Black Forest with my fellows—also naughty fellows—and suddenly I heard a voice in the sky. I looked up and—there was Jesus. He said to me, *Lothar, Lothar,* why *are you so naughty?* Like what he said to Saint Paul when he was on his way to Damascus to torment Christians. I fell down on the ground and rolled around.

It was then that I decided I must make a pilgrimage and walk all the way to fucking'—don't say 'fucking'—'Chambéry to worship at the Shroud and cleanse my filthy soul.' "

"No."

"Nars. I entreat. The Duke of Savoy craves the protection of the Holy Roman Emperor—your own godfather. The Duke is called Charles the Good. He is not going to eat you!"

"I'll consider it. That's all. I make no promises."

Dismas looked at his recalcitrant friend. Time to play his last card.

"There is another reason why you, Nars, are the only one among us who could do this."

"What?"

"Your sophistication. You are cosmopolitan. You've spent time at court."

"So have *you*," Dürer shot back.

"Yes, but in Germany. Mainz and Wittenberg are . . . I don't want to say second best, but how can they compare to the splendor of the courts you have seen, in Italy and other parts? You have met the Pope! You know Raphael and the other masters. Titian! This makes you a natural aristocrat yourself. You are on equal footing with dukes, kings, emperors. Me? As you say—often—I am only a Swiss peasant."

"I said I would consider it. For now, enough."

Dismas left Dürer to his ruminations and went out to take some air to clear his head. He returned to the basement an hour later. Only Dürer and Magda were present, the lads having gone out to whore.

Dürer snarled at Dismas, "Sure, you're a bastard." Dürer turned and huffed out of the basement.

Dismas went over to Magda's apothecary laboratory and sat.

"He's in a state," Dismas said.

Magda stirred her pot. "After you left, the lads had a little talk with him. I didn't hear everything. But enough."

"Ah?"

Magda smiled. "Inspiration takes many forms."

"I didn't tell them to threaten Nars. Inspiration shouldn't come at the point of a dagger."

"There was no dagger."

"Sweet reason, was it?"

"There was mention of a hammer. And fingers. And the effect of the first upon the second, with reference to the career of painting."

Dismas groaned. "He won't believe me when I tell him this was not my doing."

"I'll talk to him. He'll listen to me."

"He can be very stubborn. His people came from Bohemia."

"Why do you smile?"

"I should like to have seen his face."

29

Rostang

They sat, the six of them, under the plane trees in the public gardens, doing their best to look like pilgrims.

Dürer stood apart, facing away, leaning against one of the trees, striking a pose that Magda said reminded her of the depictions of Jesus in the garden of Gethsemane. Dismas said he had little doubt Nars was praying, *Lord, let this cup pass from me.*

Nars's expression was equal parts gloom, contempt, and fury. But these, Dismas thought, combined into a simulacrum of nobility. He looked quite plausible in his white pilgrim robe. The others were happy no longer to be wearing their scratchy monk habits. The white cotton pilgrim robes were greatly preferable to monk wool. Only Magda remained religiously garbed, as a nun.

Dismas rose and went over to Dürer and said, "If you want to hate me, fine. But if they come, for God's sake, play the part or we will all die."

Some hours earlier, Dürer had presented himself to the stony-faced guards at the castle gate to deliver his letter to the Duke of Savoy. As Dismas had instructed, he engaged the head guard in banter so that he would remember Dürer's face.

"They have to be able to find us," Dismas pointed out as a practical matter. Also per Dismas's instruction, Dürer had mentioned to the guard how pleasant he and his companions found the public gardens, where they were camped.

"How long must we wait like this?" Dürer grumbled. "It's been hours. It's obvious they're not coming. Let's go."

"Patience, your worship," Dismas said.

"If they were going to come, they'd have come by now. I say enough of this charade."

"What's the hurry? It's nicer here than in the basement, with your spiders."

"One more hour. One. Then to hell with this scheme of yours."

Dismas kept his eyes on the Porte Recluse.

Presently, he saw an older man with an air of authority emerge from the Porte, followed by a castle guard. They walked toward the public garden.

"Look alive, everyone," Dismas said. "And remember who you are. My lord? My lord *Lothar*?"

Dürer was still leaning against the tree, facing away. "What?"

"Why don't you turn around so they can see you."

Dürer turned and saw the guard approaching.

He said plaintively, "Dis!"

"Steady," Dismas said soothingly. "You make an excellent count. You've always been a terrible snob. Now finally you can greet yourself as an equal."

"Fuck you."

"Shh."

The guard was pointing at Dürer.

"All right," Dismas said, "here we go. Stations, everyone."

The older fellow approached and spoke to Dürer.

"Permit me, but are you by chance the Count Lothar of Schramberg?"

Dürer blenched, cleared his throat. "I? Er . . . well . . . er . . ."

The man bowed. "My *lord.*"

"Er?"

"Permit me. I am Rostang, chamberlain to his most royal highness Charles, Duke of Savoy. *Mm!*"

"Ah? Well . . . Hello."

Dismas mentally kicked Dürer in the shin. Whence this stage fright? Dürer regarded most monarchs as beneath him. Now he was tongue-tied speaking to a chamberlain. *Pull yourself together, man!*

"We received your letter. *Mm!*"

The little man appeared to have a vocal tic.

"The letter? Oh, yes. That. Well, it was just to say . . ."

Dismas interposed, nearly shouldering Dürer aside. He bowed deeply to Rostang.

"Permit me. I am Rufus. Chamberlain to the Count. As you can see, my master is quite overcome. He has been fasting and at prayer since we arrived in Chambéry. And we have had a long journey from Schramberg."

"Of course. Of course. *Mm!*"

Rostang was an older man, in his late fifties, tall, slender, and elegant with a perfectly trimmed beard, white as snow, inquisitive but not unfriendly eyes, and a nose so long that he tilted his head backward as if looking down a gunsight.

"But we were not expecting you!" he said with an air of mortification.

"No, we sent no word," Rufus/Dismas said. "My master the Count is here as a simple pilgrim. One pilgrim among many. His letter to your master was a formal courtesy. He wanted only to convey his most fraternal feelings. And of course, those of his godfather, he who is soon to become His Imperial Highness."

Rostang's gaze skipped from one to another in the entourage.

"And these?"

"Those three are servants. Sister Hildegard is of the Order of Cosmas and Damian."

"Cosmas and Damian."

"Patron saints of apothecary. German order."

"Ah. *Mm!*"

"She attends at my master's household in Schramberg. He thought it prudent to bring her on pilgrimage, the journey being long and taxing to the health."

"Yes. *Mm!* My master is most eager to greet your lord. Again, if only we had known, we would have prepared a worthy reception."

"Please." Dismas smiled. "You are too gracious. We are well content here in the gardens. The air is salubrious beneath the open sky. And his royal highness is surely busy with a thousand details in preparation for the Holy Exposition of the Shroud. And we see that you have a royal guest. The Duke of Urbino. We chanced to witness his progress into the city. Such splendor!"

Dismas caught the flicker of burden in the old man's face.

"Yes. Truly we are graced by his presence. *Mm!*" He smiled wryly. "As you observed, his equipage is, shall we say, slightly more elaborate than your own."

Dismas returned a knowing chuckle.

"A pilgrim is a pilgrim. We are all the same, before God. Well, more or less."

"I insist that you accompany me to the castle. My master will have my head if I return with empty hands. And I am fond of my head. *Mm!*"

Dismas turned to Dürer.

"My lord? What say you to this most gracious invitation?"

Dürer, ashen-faced, drew himself up straight.

"Well . . . don't want to be any trouble."

"Ah," Rostang exclaimed, "forgive me, my lord. In the excitement, I have forgotten my manners."

He knelt before Dürer and extended his hand in formal obeisance. *Yes*, Dismas thought. *He wants to see the ring.*

Dürer extended his hand, and sure enough, Dismas saw the old man examine Lothar's signet ring, to see if it matched the wax seal of the griffin and sword on the letter.

Dismas asked, "Should we accompany you?"

"Yes, yes. But for the audience with his grace, it will be only your master and yourself. The rest of you we shall endeavor to make comfortable with the other servants. We have had to put up tents in the courtyard. It resembles a bazaar. *Mm!* We burst at the seams! But always it is thus when his highness exposes the Holy Shroud."

"I marvel that you are able to cope," Dismas said sympathetically.

Rostang and Dismas walked ahead, enabling them to converse chamberlain to chamberlain.

"May I ask how it goes with your master's godfather, His Imperial Highness? *Mm!*" Rostang said.

Dismas had dictated the letter which Dürer wrote out in his own hand:

> *My beloved godfather, formerly King of Spain and now by the grace of God, soon to be Emperor of the Holy Roman Empire, commands me to extend his most Christian and fraternal love.*

If you're going to drop a name, Dismas thought, drop it good and hard.

"He is excellent well," Dismas replied, "considering the immense burdens that now rest upon his great shoulders."

Aware that courtiers enjoy nothing more than a bit of gossip, Dismas added, "I regret to tell you—between ourselves—that he is sorely beset by the gout. *What* a time for such an affliction to present itself."

"I grieve to hear it," Rostang said, shaking his head. *"Mm!"*

"His physicians—and our own Sister Hildegard—are of the opinion that it has resulted from his lifetime habit of eating only red meat. My master has scolded him—lovingly—about this. He tells him, 'Godfather, you must eat vegetables!' How gratifying, the intimacy between them. They are like . . . brothers."

It took only ten minutes to arrive at the entrance to the castle. They proceeded through the gate and up a steep cobbled ramp that brought them into the Court of Honor. As Rostang had said, it was so crowded with tents as to resemble a busy market.

On their right, they saw the Gothic-style Holy Chapel built by Duke Charles's ancestor Amadeus VIII. Since 1502, this had been the repository of the Holy Shroud. Dismas and the others genuflected and made the sign of the cross.

Rostang observed, "It was your master's godfather's predecessor, the Holy Roman Emperor Sigismund, who a century ago elevated my master's ancestor Amadeus to the title of Duke of Savoy. *Mm!* For this reason—and many others—the dukes of Savoy have always held the Holy Roman emperors in the greatest esteem and affection."

Dismas put his hand over his heart to show how touching was this sentiment.

They were swarmed by household attendants. Rostang instructed them to find a tent in which to install their new guests in comfort. This done, he bid Count Lothar and chamberlain Rufus to follow him up the steps into the royal apartments, across the courtyard from the Holy Chapel.

30

Charles the Good

Dismas paused at the threshold of the royal audience chamber as two footmen prepared to open the doors. He said pointedly to Dürer, "Your sword, my lord?"

Dürer stared, uncomprehendingly. Then said: "Ah. Yes. The sword."

They had rehearsed this, but in his nervousness, Dürer had forgotten that one does not enter armed into royal presence, even if one is also of the noblesse.

Dismas took the sword and presented it ceremoniously to Rostang, who handed it off to one of his men. This protocol would afford Rostang a second opportunity to confirm Lothar's identity, upon seeing the inscription on the blade from the King of Spain to his godson.

The great doors opened.

They followed Rostang into the chamber. Dismas reminded himself not to reveal by slip of tongue that he was a Swiss. Before declaring itself forever after neutral, the Confederation had invaded the Duchy of Savoy, on multiple occasions.

The room was crowded, but rather than browse, Dismas and Dürer kept their eyes fixed straight ahead, on the figure of the Duke of Savoy.

Duke Charles rose from his throne, opened his arms wide, and, forsaking all formality, descended the steps to greet his visitor. His smile was radiant, as if he had been long anticipating this joyous moment.

He was a pleasant-looking fellow: midthirties, large-boned, soft-faced. His most prominent feature was his beaky nose. Did *everyone* in Chambéry have one? Dismas wondered.

Charles was modestly dressed for a duke, neither extravagantly bejeweled nor upholstered in great quantities of brocade. He wore his hair in neat bangs, giving him a slightly feminine aspect. His eyes were brown and languid. This unprepossessing appearance was, Dismas thought, apposite in one who had grown to maturity with no expectation whatsoever of becoming ruler. By happenstance, both Charles and his father—Philip "the Landless"—acceded to the throne by dint of accident; what's more, legitimately, absent foul play. Very rare.

"My lord *Lothar*!" Duke Charles fairly bellowed, clasping the petrified Dürer to the ducal bosom.

Dismas held his breath and prayed that Dürer would not faint or wet himself. His prayers were answered. Count Lothar neatly bowed and in a steady voice rejoined, "Most *Illustrious* Grace."

They'd debated whether Dürer should greet him as "Cousin," but decided this might be presumptuous, given the disproportion in rank between duke and count.

"We are overwhelmed with joy at your presence," Duke Charles said. "But why did you not send *word*? We would have prepared the fatted calf!"

Pleasantries proceeded apace. Dürer warmed to his imposture, as Dismas had expected he would, given his inherently imperious temperament.

The Duke turned to his right and said, "Your grace, allow me to present my most welcome guest, Lothar Count Schramberg."

Dismas and Dürer had been so focused on Charles they only now saw that their audience was doubly ducal.

Lorenzo, Duke of Urbino, ruler of Florence, lay on his side on a gilded divan, propped up on pillows and elbow like a Roman emperor conducting his levee.

"Ecco," Dürer said, and performed an elaborate curtsy, arms extended forward, palms up. *"Serenissmo e maestoso duca."*

Dismas had never heard Dürer's Italian. It sounded quite good.

The Duke of Urbino gave a slight nod, either out of proportionate courtesy of duke to count, or because of his debility. The poor man did not look well. A fresh application of greasepaint had been made to his face; it was no longer caked. Dismas noted again that the duke's right hand was pressed tightly to his chest.

Duke Charles now turned to another personage, this one resplendent in the scarlet finery of his office, including *ferraiolo*, the cape worn over the princely shoulders. Scarlet, the color of blood, signified the wearer's readiness to die for the faith.

"Eminence, may I present . . ."

Luigi, Cardinal d'Aragona, was a Neapolitan grandee who in his youth had married the granddaughter of Pope Innocent VIII. Upon her death, he renounced his marquisate and entered into holy orders, at which career he had prospered, displaying a talent for administration and diplomacy. He was an intimate of the King of France.

Dismas had spent time at court, but this was heady stuff. He craved a fortifying drink. For his part, Dürer appeared quite at home.

The Cardinal of Aragon took in Count Lothar's plain white garment and nodded approvingly.

"You are on pilgrimage? King François—his grace the Duke of Urbino and myself were only just now speaking of him—also made pilgrimage to Chambéry some years ago, to give thanks for victory in a great battle. On foot, all the way from Lyon."

The Cardinal appeared to be waiting for Count Lothar to vouchsafe his own reason for trudging hundreds of miles here from Schramberg—wherever that was—dressed in a dirty white rag. A somewhat awkward question to be asked in public, in front of two dukes, no less. The Cardinal was in effect inquiring what dreadful sin had brought Lothar here in atonement.

But Dürer deftly seized the opportunity.

"I am giving thanks for my godfather's accession to the Holy Roman throne." He added with a hint of aloofness, "And what brings *your* eminence to Chambéry?"

"The Holy Shroud, of course. And, it goes without saying, the superb hospitality of his grace the Duke."

Charles smiled demurely at the compliment.

Aragon continued: "In addition to its charms, Chambéry is conveniently situated. His grace Lorenzo is himself on his way from Urbino to Paris, for the baptism of the dauphin. Myself, I progress back to Rome. From Paris."

Dürer plucked a cup of wine from a tray held by a footman. Dismas was about to reach for one himself until he remembered his place.

"Paris. Ah, *Paris*," Dürer said with an air of mild ennui. "And how was Paris?"

"Magnificent, as always."

"I'm pleased to hear it," Dürer said languidly. "On my own last visit, I found it . . . how to say it with delicacy? . . . filthy. One admires the French for their ability to coexist on such easy terms with vermin."

Aragon stared.

Dürer went on: "One hardly dares step foot out of bed in the morning, for fear of stepping on a rat." He gave an epicene shudder of revulsion. "Everywhere, rats. One I saw chasing a dog. And let me tell you—the dog was terrified. But then, it *was* a terrier."

The Duke of Urbino laughed, which made him cough. Dismas glanced furtively at Duke Charles, who was trying not to laugh.

The Cardinal of Aragon said stiffly, "I take it, then, you were not a guest at palace."

"Heavens, no!" Dürer replied. "I've learned, *quand à Paris*, to make my own arrangements. Fontainebleau I find drafty. On my last visit, I spent the entire time calling for more wood for my fire. Came away with a brutal catarrh. But I grant your eminence there are at least fewer rats at palace." He turned to Duke Charles and smiled. "Of one variety, that is."

The Duke of Urbino was now convulsing, making unpleasant pulmonic sounds. His retinue fluttered about him like swallows.

The Cardinal of Aragon excused himself. He glided, tight-lipped, from the chamber, *ferraiolo* trailing across the parquet, scurried after by monsignors.

Duke Charles's cheeks were dimpled from imploded mirth. His eyes were bright and twinkly. He said in a lowered voice with an air of delighted mischief, "I'll be sure to seat you and his eminence next to each other at the banquet tonight."

He waved over Rostang and instructed him to find rooms for Count Lothar. They huddled, murmuring. Dismas cocked an ear. Rostang was telling the Duke that there simply were no rooms. The Duke expressed horror. Rostang replied that much as he shared his master's horror—*mm!*—that the problem was nonetheless insurmountable. Urbino and Aragon's multitudinous equipages had filled every bed in the royal apartments, every nook and cranny.

Still the Duke remonstrated with his chamberlain. Rostang dug in his heels and said that if his grace insisted, then he would make room, but it would require an eviction. And his grace knew very well who must be evicted. Charles sighed airily as only nobles can and said, "Very well."

Presently Duke Charles turned to his guest Count Lothar and with pains explained the situation. It was intolerable. However, if his lordship Count Lothar would consent, a well-appointed apartment would be made available for him and his retinue. The apartment was, alas, not within the castle grounds proper, but it was close by, indeed, directly across from the Holy Chapel, opposite the wall on which the Shroud would be displayed.

Dismas thought, *Well.*

The Duke went on: From the apartment window, Lothar would have a splendid view. Was this acceptable? Count Lothar would of course be included in all the ceremonies and proceedings, starting with tonight's banquet.

Count Lothar replied that he was overwhelmed by such magnanimity. He accepted gratefully and humbly. His godfather would hear of this generosity, sure.

Dürer now turned to Dismas and with hauteur as flawless as his spoken Italian instructed him to accompany the chamberlain Rostang to see to the arrangements.

Dismas bowed and left him to his new friends.

Rostang kept up a show of cordiality, but Dismas saw that his shoulders were a bit slumped, indicating that he did not relish his present duty.

"These apartments," Dismas probed, "I gather they are occupied?"

"Alas, yes. *Mm!*" replied Rostang.

"Awkward."

"*Mm!* Most awkward."

"Might I ask whose apartments are they?"

"Quimper. Archdeacon of the Holy Chapel."

Dismas thought, *Hell.* So they were about to be the cause of the Shroud's guardian being thrown out of his own home. What goodwill that would engender.

"My master would be appalled to think he was inconveniencing an archdeacon," Dismas said with mock horror. "Have no further care, Master Rostang. We are well content to remain in the gardens."

Rostang looked at Dismas curiously.

"Why should you care about inconveniencing an archdeacon? *Mm!*" Rostang shrugged. "He's only a servant, like us. It's not the first time he's been rousted from his rooms to accommodate dignitaries."

"Perhaps I care because I *am* a servant."

"*Mm!* How long have you been in service, Master Rufus?"

"Well, not so long."

Rostang made another of his little high-pitched grunts. "*Mm!* It shows. Don't waste your pity on Quimper. These things happen. It's in the nature of things to happen. It's what things *do*."

"You're a philosopher, Master Rostang."

"I assure you, you will find me the most practical of men. *Mm!* I serve Charles the Good. Which means—as you shall shortly see—that on occasions I must be Rostang the Shit."

"That is philosophical."

"Does Heraclitus not teach us that the rule of the universe is flux? Embrace the flux, I say. Lest it embrace us. Well, here we are. Let us put on our aggrieved faces. *Mm!*"

31

Three Kings

Dürer threw open the shuttered windows of their new quarters. The lads and Sister Hildegard were exploring the various rooms, still warm from occupancy by Archdeacon Quimper and his household servants, all of whom seemed to consist of handsome and girlish young men.

"Yes, this will do," Dürer said.

The apartment was on the third floor, looking directly out at the castle wall where the Shroud would be displayed. Almost close enough to touch. Was God smiling on their enterprise? Dismas wondered why God would.

He said to Dürer, "Archdeacon Quimper was thrilled to be evicted. When you see him, better give him your best curtsy, like you did Urbino."

"It wasn't *my* idea to have the archdeacon evicted," Dürer sniffed. "As for my curtsy to the Italian, I only did it to avoid having to kiss his pustulating ring hand." He shuddered. "Uhh!"

"You made a good impression. But now we've made an enemy, who happens to be the Shroud's guardian."

"I'll invite him to come and visit me in Schramberg. At my *schloss*."

"I'm sure he'll be overwhelmed."

"Now," Dürer said, "what am I to wear to the banquet? I can't go in this revolting rag."

"What, am I your valet?"

"Yes, as a matter of fact. This being your idea. Nothing too elaborate, but appropriate to my station."

"Station?"

Dismas went over to the dining table, yanked off its cloth, and tossed it at Dürer.

"There. That's appropriate to your station. I don't give a billy goat's fart what you wear to the banquet."

"At it again, are we?" Magda said. "You two should be on your knees reciting hosannas at our good fortune, not hissing at each other like geese."

A knock on the door announced two of Rostang's people, bearing a trousseau of finery for Count Lothar, along with court attire for chamberlain Rufus. The timing of their arrival seemed an eerie validation of Magda's rebuke. Again Dismas wondered: *Was* God smiling on their enterprise? Did the Shroud of Chambéry want to be translated? To—Mainz? What was God thinking?

Duke Charles had diplomatically seated Count Lothar on his left, Urbino and Aragon on his right.

Dismas took up his servant's station, a few paces behind his master, where he could overhear the conversation; it was also close enough, alas, to make his mouth water at the procession of dishes.

Standing in his place behind Urbino was a man the Duke addressed as Signore Caraffa. Caraffa was about Dismas's age, elegantly attired, all in black: boots, hose, pleated breeches, and a tightly fitted doublet trimmed in sable. Dismas reflected that the Italians put their servants in finer livery than many northern nobles wore themselves. The Elector

Frederick cared so little for clothing that he often looked more like a shabby burgomaster than the ruler of Saxony.

On Caraffa's breast was an embroidered crest with the letter *M*, signifying "Medici"; the family had ruled Florence for nearly a century, since the time of Cosimo. Caraffa's complexion was dark and pitted from smallpox. He was handsome in a severe way, with a soldier's build and carriage, muscled and upright. His hair was cropped almost to the scalp, revealing what appeared to be sword-slash scars. Dangling from his left ear like a fat drop of blood was a ruby, a good one.

On noticing Dismas, Caraffa nodded collegially, managing a cursory smile. Dismas thought this gracious, considering the disproportion of their stations. He resolved to make a friend of this fellow, for he did not look the kind one wanted as an enemy.

A dish arrived, called a *tartiflette*, with a warm aroma of cheese, bacon, onions, and cream. Dismas nearly swooned. Food prompted the Cardinal of Aragon to launch into an epic account of papal banqueting.

"Sixty-*five* courses there were," he said. "Each consisting of three dishes. Small portions, superbly varied."

Dismas calculated in his head. Was it possible to consume that much food? But having seen a life portrait of the adipose Leo X, Dismas thought perhaps it was.

The Cardinal continued. "Then came a platter—enormous, requiring two servants to lift. Peacock tongues. Have you tasted this delicacy, your grace?"

Charles smiled demurely.

"Here, Eminence, we prefer to listen to our peacocks. They make very good guards. Tremendous screechings."

"Perhaps it is not for every palate. Myself, I found them sublime. Then, when we could eat no more, arrived the climax. A pastry of Homeric proportion. *Six* servants were required to carry it. Now you are anticipating that I will tell you his holiness cut into the crust and out flew a flock of blackbirds."

The Cardinal waggled a ringed forefinger to indicate—no, no.

"Nothing so prosaic. *How* many times have we seen the flock of birds flying out from pies? Instead, the Holy Father clapped his hands three times and said, 'Arise!' And from this pastry came—a naked child! Posing as Cupid! Such a dazzlement. The applause was like thunder.

"But I must tell you. Afterward, I found myself thinking, How did they accomplish such audacious gastronomy? Baking a pastry, with a child inside? I made inquiries. Well! I was informed that before this dish was perfected, there had been one or two, shall we say, misfortunes. But there can be no doubt"—the Cardinal turned to the Duke of Urbino—"that the hospitality of his holiness, your uncle, is without equal in Europe." The Cardinal added with solemnity, "And in this I include the King of France. Of course I should not be saying this, having only just come from his table."

Pivoting to his host, d'Aragona smiled beatifically and said, "And yet, my dear Charles, there is no one whose hospitality, whose table, whose company, gives me greater pleasure than your grace's own."

Charles mutely raised his hands and eyebrows to show how touching was this benediction.

Dismas thought he caught a flicker of disgust on the Duke of Savoy's face. Peacock tongues? Children baked alive in pastries? These seemed incongruent with the mild-faced and pious Charles.

Dismas glanced at Dürer, whose contempt for this sort of thing he well knew. Dürer's jaw muscles looked like he was cracking walnuts. Dismas uttered a silent prayer.

His prayer was answered in the form of a sharp gasp from the Duke of Urbino, clutching his chest.

Caraffa was at his master's side in an instant.

"Is your master unwell?" Charles asked.

"An indigestion only, your grace," Caraffa said. "It will pass."

Caraffa snapped his fingers at an attendant, who leapt forward with a vial. He tapped drops onto a lace handkerchief which Urbino held over his mouth, inhaling deeply. After a moment, some color—such as it was, beneath white greasepaint—returned.

"Forgive me," Urbino said. "The altitude . . . here, in the Alps . . . always it gets the better of me. I am well. Caraffa, stop *fussing*."

Altitude? Dismas thought. Chambéry was less than two thousand feet above sea level. He wondered what they'd given him. Urbino's hand remained clutched to his breast.

The conversation moved on from food orgies at the Vatican.

"The new Emperor," Urbino said to Count Lothar, "he is your godfather?"

Dürer nodded.

"How soon will he make war on France?"

"Your grace," Dürer said blushfully. "What a question!"

"But not an idle one. I journey to Paris, for the baptism of the dauphin."

Dürer downed a slug of wine.

"Intimate as we are, I am not a member of his imperial war council. I am not included in those discussions."

Urbino waited for more.

Dürer plunged ahead. "But it is no secret that there is little love between the Houses of Valois and Habsburg. I do not think that anyone will be surprised if it does come to war."

Urbino looked ready to fall asleep. Lothar was telling him nothing he did not already know.

"We hear," Dürer went on, "that King François desired to become Emperor. How he must chafe at not winning such a prize. Sure, he must be feeling a bit 'between the pincers,' situated between the Empire and my godfather's other domain, Spain."

Urbino perked up.

"Is there any message you would like me to convey from your godfather to his highness François?"

Dismas uttered another silent orison, asking the Almighty please to remind Nars that they had come to steal a relic, not to foment war between France and the Holy Roman Empire.

"Your grace is kind to offer. But I am here as a poor pilgrim, not an imperial emissary."

Thank you, Lord.

"However," Dürer added, "I think I speak for the Emperor when I say that he is vexed—oh, sorely vexed—by François's continued harassments of sovereign Savoy. It would sit excellently well with my godfather were these violations to cease." He added, "Forthwith."

Duke Charles was glowing. Dismas could almost hear him purr.

Urbino and Aragon looked at Lothar, perplexed.

"With all respect to our most gracious host," Urbino said, "is Savoy *truly* a concern of the Emperor?"

"Oh," Dürer said airily, "your grace can have no idea how it presses upon him. He looks on Savoy with fatherly concern."

Urbino stared. It was a stunning assertion—that the Holy Roman Emperor gave any thought at all to French scrimmaging in its own backyard with a quaint and—it must be said—somewhat pointless duchy.

Urbino's nonplussed expression now gave way to one betraying the suspicion that the Emperor's godson might be a dolt.

Urbino said blandly, "I will convey this to his most royal highness."

"Do please also convey my godfather's fervent wishes for the dauphin's health, longevity, and happiness."

Urbino nodded. He was done with this absurd Lothar.

The Cardinal of Aragon, a diplomatist equally conversant in geopolitics as the Duke of Urbino, also appeared flabbergasted at Count Lothar's proxy imperial hand-wringing over Savoy. He introduced an altogether different matter.

"Might I inquire of your lordship, what are the intentions of your esteemed godfather with respect to the heretic Luther?"

"Luther?" Dürer said. "Ah, Luther. *What* a business."

"Heresy is a terrible business. In his case, appalling."

"Um," Dürer said with emphatic ambiguity.

"His excoriations of the Holy Father continue unabated. I can tell you that it has become a great nuisance to his holiness. He is barely able to concentrate on his passions."

Dismas thought, *Please do not let Nars say, "What, buggery?"*

"Feasting?" Dürer said.

Aragon stared icily. "The rebuilding of the Saint Peter Basilica. His ardent support of the arts. His explorations in the field of zoology. What delight he derives from this. And his elephant. He is like a boy with Hanno. And the hunting. He is a man of diverse many passions, the Holy Father."

"Yes," Dürer said, "he seems quite relentless."

"As to the hunting, alas his infirmity in the saddle prevents him from the riding. But always it is he who delivers the coup de grâce with his spear. Like Saint George and the dragon. Bold. Firm. If Luther could see him, I think he would feel great fear."

Dürer nodded. "It must be something. Plunging the spear into an exhausted, wounded animal. What sport."

"You are German," Aragon said. "Pray educate me, for I have need. Why does the Elector of Saxony, Frederick, harbor and protect Luther? By all accounts, he himself has remained devotedly Catholic. I cannot fathom why, when his holiness is trying to silence Luther, Frederick continues to shield him. Elucidate this for me."

"Well, it's complicated, isn't it?"

"No. Not really."

"See, Luther's a Saxon. Frederick's the ruler of Saxony. Never mind the religious issues. The Elector is loyal to his subjects."

Aragon laughed derisively. "You say, 'Never mind the religious issues'? But Luther is an Augustinian monk. He is a subject, first and last, of Rome."

"Exactly," Dürer smiled. "As I said—complicated."

The Cardinal frowned. He tried again.

"Your godfather's predecessor, the late Emperor Maximilian, tried to get Frederick to allow the process of examining Luther to go forward. He did not succeed. I trust it will be your godfather's intention to support the Holy Father in his efforts to deliver Luther to account for his attacks on the Church."

"To account?" Dürer knotted his brow. "Ah. You mean *burn* him."

"How else root out heresy, except with the purifying fire?"

"Quite right." Dürer nodded. "Did Our Lord not say as much in his Sermon on the Mount?"

The Cardinal stared.

"What kind of world is it," he said in a plaintive tone, "when a monk—a single German monk—I mean no offense, of course; the obduracy of your people is among their many fine qualities—when one monk openly defies the authority of the Holy Roman Emperor and the Holy Father in Rome? What kind of world is this?"

"A new one?"

Aragon sighed, defeated, like Urbino, convinced that this Count Lothar of Wherever was an idiot.

For the first time all evening, Dismas relaxed. Better to be thought a fool than dangerous. Nars had played his hand well. Then:

Dürer said to the Cardinal, "Eminence, with respect to the Pope's passion for hunting . . ."

"Yes?" the Cardinal said, not looking up from his food, having no interest in further converse with an obtuse Teutonic minor noble.

"Am I mistaken, or does canon law not proscribe hunting by the clergy?"

Aragon stared. "Clergy?"

"Um. Priests and such."

Aragon laughed bitterly. "You consider the Supreme Pontiff in Rome clergy?"

"Ah," Dürer said. "Quite right. Leo wasn't even a priest when he was elected Pope, was he?"

"Under canon law, in which you appear to be a scholar, it is not required that a pope be a priest. But since becoming supreme pontiff, he has been ordained. What do you insinuate, if I may ask?"

"I only cite our beloved Church's own law. Which forbids the clergy, specifically the higher ranks, from indulging in such worldly pastimes as hunting. As well as certain, shall we say, *other* pleasures?"

Dismas's heart was pounding. He braced for Dürer to start enumerating the "other" pleasures. Sodomy, gluttony, simony . . .

Dürer smiled. "Eminence, you—not I—are the authority on such matters. Forgive my impertinent question." He added, "Tomorrow I will make a good confession!"

The Cardinal's face was flushing the color of his *ferraiolo*.

Duke Charles leapt in, clapping his hands together.

"How honored is Savoy to have such company at our humble table in Chambéry! Your grace, your eminence, your lordship, with your permission, I have arranged a small entertainment."

The Duke gave a signal. A curtain raised at the far end of the banquet room. The hundred guests gave a collective *ahh* of surprise at the scene before them.

Dismas had seen one or two tableaux vivants before. He found them a bit odd: still lifes, with humans instead of flowers and fruit and such.

This one's theme was the Adoration of the Magi, the visit to Bethlehem by the three kings, as related in the Gospel of Matthew. Considerable preparation had gone into it. In addition to the human characters, the kings sat atop three live camels. Touchingly, one of the kings had been made up to resemble the Duke of Urbino; another, the Cardinal of Aragon. The third king bore a kind of resemblance to Count Lothar.

The Duke of Savoy murmured to Dürer, "Because of your late arrival, we did not have time to properly prepare. Still, I hope you are pleased."

Dismas saw Dürer biting his cheek, trying not to laugh.

"It is *mm-arvelous*, your grace," he said.

Urbino and Aragon stared blankly.

"Extraordinary," Aragon managed. Urbino made a hand gesture to convey that yes, he, too, was overwhelmed.

The infant playing the role of the baby Jesus began to howl. Duke Charles stood and thanked the people in the tableau for playing their parts, and signaled for the music and dancing to begin.

32

Digitalis

"Was that necessary, about the Pope violating canon law?"

"Maybe not. But it was damned satisfying, after that grotesque recitation about papal gorging. Children, being baked in papal pastries! Next to such depravity, the outrages of the Caesars pale. *Suetonius* himself would be appalled. Truly, Rome is the new Babylon. Luther understates, if anything."

"Let me point out," Dismas said, "that the 'new Babylon' employs your friend Raphael. And many other artists."

They were sitting around the dining table in the archdeacon's apartment, all but Magda. The dancing and music had gone late. Urbino, fortified by his medicated hanky, had remained to watch the merriment, eyes lighting on various pretty young girls. Even dying, and in excruciating pain from his infirmity, his lust ran strong.

Seeing his chance, Dismas had approached his majordomo, Caraffa.

"I regret to see your master suffer so, signore."

"It is only a temporary affliction."

"I'm sure his grace's physicians are without equal. But if my master's apothecary, Sister Hildegard, can be of assistance, we are at your disposal, signore."

Caraffa regarded the offer without expression.

"We chanced to be present when you arrived at the city gate," Dismas said. "Sister saw his grace put his hand to his chest, as he did tonight. She mentioned that there is a medicine."

"For altitude?"

"I took her to mean for chest pain. She *is* skilled. Count Lothar values her greatly. He never travels without her. She studied with the great apothecary Paracelsus of Basel."

"Yes, we know of Paracelsus."

"The drops on the handkerchief. Might I ask, was it *ladanum*?"

Caraffa stared.

"What a mercy," Dismas went on. "Though I believe Sister had in mind some other medicine. Well, no doubt that your master is in excellent hands, and for that, I rejoice with all my heart. Pray accept my wishes for his swift recovery and robust health."

Dismas made a little bow and turned.

"Master Rufus."

"Signore?"

"Your nun. Send her to me."

It had been hours now since Magda had gone to the royal apartments, bringing digitalis. Dismas and the Landsknechte sat, fretful.

Noticing Dismas's nervousness, Dürer said, "Dis. She knows what she's doing. She's a capable girl."

"But a beauty," Cunrat said. "That's what worries me." Nutker and Unks made affirming grunts.

Dismas did not want to contemplate this. He was in torment. He'd sent Magda alone into a den of ravening Italian lechery.

"Come," Dürer said. "Do you suppose the Duke of Urbino would commit indecencies—on a nun? A nun in the retinue of a count who is godson to the Emperor? Under the roof of his own host? Stop *worrying*, all of you. You're like old women."

Dürer went off to bed. Naturally, he had commandeered the large one. He was, after all, the Count. How would it look, he said, if palace servants came and saw him in one of the lesser beds? It would give away the game.

The Landsknechte also went to sleep. It had been a long day, and it was very late.

Dismas stayed up, alone, his mind febrile with evil visions. What if Urbino forced himself on her?

Toward dawn, he heard the door open. He rushed to her and hugged her as if she'd been gone years.

"What's got into you?" she said.

"I'm glad you're safe."

"I'm all right. Tell you later. Too tired."

In bed she fell fast asleep in his arms.

When she awoke some hours later, Magda told them about the scene in Urbino's bedchamber.

The majordomo Caraffa made one of his servants taste her potion. When the servant did not die, she was permitted to administer it to the Duke. Almost immediately, his chest pains abated.

"He was very happy for that."

"Why were you there so long?" Dismas asked.

"I tried to leave, several times. The Duke would not let me go."

"He didn't . . . ?"

"No. No, he wanted only for me to hold his hand."

Dürer made a face. "You did?"

"I wore gloves, Master Dürer."

"Still."

"You cannot contract the pox just from touching. Unless it's an open wound. Or the contact is, well, intimate."

"You'd stake your life on it?"

"If Paracelsus tells me so, yes."

"Let her *speak*, Nars," Dismas said. "What else?"

"They are giving him *ladanum* for the pain. Drops, in the handkerchief. But too much weakens the brain. When I said this, the Duke's physician became angry. He called me a meddling fool. He was angry because I had helped his master. The Duke then became angry with him and ordered him from the bedchamber."

"There's another enemy we've made," Dismas said. "Not your fault, Magda. Just keeping tally of everyone here who hates us."

"I remained all the night. He was dreaming, with his eyes open. *Ladanum* does this. He talked. All night, he talked."

"Gibberish?"

"Perhaps. He spoke about people and things I do not know. But he knows that he is dying. And he does not want to die."

"There's a surprise," Dürer said.

"He talked about the Shroud," Magda said. She looked troubled.

"What is it?" Dismas asked.

"Caraffa, the majordomo. I don't like him."

"Did he . . . ?"

"No. It was just the three of us in the room. All night. Caraffa never once took his eyes off me. But it was not lust, or whatever you would call it."

"He's Italian," Dürer said. " 'Lust' is the word."

Magda considered. "I don't think he is capable of that."

"Ah, a eunuch," Nutker said.

"No. I don't think he cares for women."

"A sodomite."

"No. I don't think he cares either for women or men, in that way. He was watching me always. Like he thought I would any moment take out a knife and kill his duke. They could not search me, because I'm a nun. But every time the Duke would say something in his delirium, Caraffa became very nervous. His eyes, intense. It was . . ."

"Go on."

"Like he was afraid that the Duke would say something he did not want me to hear."

Dismas considered. "He is the ruler of Florence and Urbino. Sure, he's fat with secrets a chamberlain wouldn't want a stranger to hear."

Magda stared out the window, deep in thought.

"What is it?" Dismas said.

"It's nothing."

"Why do you look troubled?"

Cunrat said, "Come on, Little Sister. Let your tongue come out to play."

Magda hesitated. "Perhaps we are not the only ones who have come to Chambéry to steal the Shroud."

They stared.

"Did he . . . *say* something to suggest this?"

"No. It is only a feeling. Because of the way Caraffa became so nervous when his master spoke. Finally the Duke went to sleep. True sleep, not *ladanum* sleep. I left."

Cunrat clapped his hands on his knees. "Well, lads, competition!"

Nutker snorted. "From Italians?"

"Not at fighting, Nutker. Stealing. At thievery, the maccheronis excel."

"This is true," Unks said. "In the Bible, it says so. The maccheronis invented stealing."

"Where in the Bible does it say this?" Nutker demanded.

"No, no," Cunrat corrected. "The Jews invented stealing."

"No," Nutker said, "the Jews invented moneylending. The Italians invented stealing."

Dismas sought refuge from this torrent of Landsknechte babble in a quiet corner of the apartment.

He wondered: Could Magda be right? He examined the possibility from every angle, each time concluding that it made no sense. A duke—an important duke—stealing a relic, from another duke? Sure, not.

He said to Magda sternly, “It cannot be true.”

“I did not *say* it was true, Dismas. Why do you speak to me in this tone?”

“I am only trying to establish if it could be true.”

“But I told you that I don’t think it’s true.”

“Yes”—he wagged a forefinger at her—“but you *thought* it could be.”

Magda threw up her hands. “Yes. All right. I confess. This thought went through my head. Then it went out of my head.”

“Did Urbino say anything that could suggest—?”

“Dismas. If you continue, I will have to take digitalis. You are giving *me* chest pains.”

He pondered further and announced, “Perhaps it is the True Shroud after all.”

“Why?”

“Well, if two parties have come to Chambéry to steal it . . . you have to wonder.”

Magda groaned.

“Consider,” Dismas went on, thoughts racing ahead like a hound. “Let’s suppose that it is the True Shroud.”

“Very well. Suppose.”

“I have been sent to steal it—to translate it—by a corrupt cardinal. Yes?”

“Yes.”

“Now, if you were Jesus—”

“What a thing to suggest. I am not Jesus.”

“Yes, but—look, ask yourself: Would Jesus desire for his shroud to be translated for the benefit of a corrupt cardinal? *Or* would he prefer it to be translated by a . . . ?”

“Italian duke with pox? These are Jesus’s choices?”

“Or . . .”

“You are making me dizzy with these ‘ors.’ ”

“I am a professional relic hunter, Magda. This is my field. Here are the considerations that we must consider. If the Shroud does not desire to be translated to Mainz, then it might allow itself to be translated by Urbino. Don't you see? A preemptive translation, you could call it. True, Urbino has the pox. But he is also the nephew of the Pope of Rome."

"Why would Jesus want his shroud to be translated by anyone, when it is kept with reverence and care in a holy chapel by someone who is called Charles the Good?"

"This, too, we must consider." Dismas nodded.

"But you don't think it's real."

"Perhaps God wants me to think it's a fake. Hm?"

"You are spinning cobwebs in your head, Dismas. Any moment now, spiders will come out of your ears."

"I wish they would come out. So I could step on them."

33

Very Awkward

Later in that morning there was a knock on the door. Chamberlain Rostang, beaming.

"Your master made quite an impression on my master last night. *Mm!*"

"As did yours on mine," Dismas replied.

"Is Count Lothar in residence?"

"Yes, but still abed. After such a night, one needs rest."

In fact, Dürer was in his room, painting, with the door closed. Dismas thought it best not to apprise Rostang of his lordship's hobby.

"I bring an invitation. *Mm!* His grace invites Count Lothar to a private viewing of the Holy Shroud."

"Well, what an honor!" Dismas said.

"Today. Twelfth hour. After the viewing, his grace asks if the Count will join him for refreshment. *Mm!*" He added, "Just the two of them. Urbino and d'Aragona will participate in the viewing. But the

Duke would like some private time with the Count. He has some matters he would like to discuss. In confidence. *Mm!*"

"My master will be overwhelmed at such a delightful prospect."

Rostang looked over Dismas's shoulder into the apartment. "The arrangements are satisfactory?"

"Indeed, yes. But where are my manners? Won't you come in and take a glass of wine?"

Rostang wavered but then said he would be glad of a noontime restorative. *Mm!*

Dismas installed him in the dining room and scurried off to tell Magda to tell Dürer that they had a visitor and for God's sake not to emerge with titian all over his hands and reeking of terebinth.

He poured his guest a glass of *roussette de Savoie*.

"The tableau vivant," Dismas said. "It was very pleasant."

Rostang chuckled. "What can I tell you, Master Rufus? My master loves his tableaux. As a little boy, he would make them with little figures of carved wood. I have seen—*mm!*—many, many tableaux in my years of service here. They are good sources of revenue."

"Yes?"

"His grace sells—offers—roles in the tableaux to our prosperous citizens of Chambéry. And our Savoyard nobles. The girl in last night's tableau who played the Virgin Mary is the daughter of the mayor. *Mm!* Her husband, Joseph, is the owner of one of the vineyards here. This could be his wine we are drinking. It's very good, by the way. Thank you. The donation for each role is according to how big is the role. Joseph paid five florins to play the father of Jesus. The shepherds, two testons only. The magi each paid ten florins. *Mm!*"

Dismas smiled. "Very enterprising."

"Did I not tell you that I am a practical man? *Mm!*"

"The camels were a marvel."

Rostang rolled his eyes.

"They are not native to Savoy, camels. Procuring them was . . . a nightmare. And you must empty their bowels before the performance so they won't . . . And now we are left with three camels. Would your master like a camel to take home to Schramberg?"

"You are too kind."

"I would be happy if you took them all back to Schramberg. I tremble for the day when his grace will announce his desire to mount a tableau of Hannibal crossing the Alps. *Mm!*"

"Perhaps Pope Leo would lend you his white elephant. Hannibal, is it not called?"

"Hanno," Rostang corrected.

"That was quite a banquet at the Vatican the Cardinal of Aragon described."

"Yes," Rostang said with an air of exhaustion. "To be candid, Master Rufus, I find extravagance of that degree distasteful, anywhere. But in the Vatican! *Mm!* One must continually remind oneself that his holiness is a de' Medici. Do you know what he said when he assumed the mantle of Saint Peter?"

"No."

" 'God has given us the papacy. Let us enjoy it.' "

"He appears to be living up to his vow."

Rostang made another of his little high-pitched grunts. "Last night during the dancing I saw you conversing with Caraffa, Urbino's man. Tell me, what is your opinion of him?"

"I should not like to find myself in his disfavor. He's very severe."

"*Mm!* Be grateful he is not *your* guest. He treats our servants like his own, which is to say, very badly. His title may be Signore, but he is not a gentleman. No, I do not care for Signore Caraffa. *Mm!*"

"At his request," Dismas said, "I sent our apothecary, Sister Hildegard, to tend to the Duke. She, too, did not find Caraffa congenial."

"Congenial? *Mm!* The man is a viper in human form."

"In the event Sister continues to attend to Urbino . . . should I be concerned for her? Would Caraffa . . . take liberties?"

"Caraffa? No. He has no carnality. It would be better if he did.

Then at least he would *be* human. If I were you, it's Urbino who would concern me, for your Sister."

"But he's dying."

"He is not dead yet. *Mm!* Five of our girls so far, this visit he has attacked. Maidservants. Yet what can one do? It is awkward, let me tell you. Very awkward."

"Yes, I should think," Dismas said, reeling.

"I am like a father with our girls. They look to me to protect them. With the aristos, all right, you expect a bit of"—Rostang squeezed two imaginary breasts—"that sort of thing. But when you are oozing with the pox, it's not right to inflict it on an innocent girl."

Rostang smiled. "Do you know what I have done? I have changed their duties. *Mm!* Now the only maids who enter his bedchamber are old women without teeth." He laughed with delight. "His ardor is much quenched. As for your sister . . . take care, Master Rufus. She is a nun, but she is a lovely girl. *How* I count the hours until Urbino leaves for Paris. I should not say such things. *Mm!*"

"Did Urbino come to Chambéry in hopes of a miraculous cure by the Shroud?"

"I don't think he came for the tableaux vivants. *Mm!*"

They laughed. Rostang said, "Speaking of which, I will tell you a secret. His grace, my master, is arranging something very special for the night before the Shroud is exposed."

"Ah?"

"I must not ruin his surprise. But I will tell you that it will be a significant source of revenue. *Mm!* Now I must go. I thank you for your hospitality, Master Rufus."

"The viewing tonight. Might I attend, with my master?"

Rostang hesitated.

"*Mm!* Normally, these viewings are only for the principals. But since your master has made such a good impression, yes, all right. But hang back, yes?"

"Too kind."

"I think you will like our Shroud. It's—*mm!*—unusual."

34

Ecce Sindon

They convened in the Court of Honor at six o'clock in the evening.

"The Holy Chapel was constructed between the years 1408 and 1430 by Amadeus the Eighth. This Amadeus was the *first* Duke of Savoy, so of course I am very fond of *him*. He became also the Anti-Pope Felix V. But since the Cardinal of Aragon is with us, we will not talk about that, eh?"

Duke Charles chuckled. "Amadeus was my ancestor from eight generations ago—or is it six? I can never remember—but of course we are very grateful to him for making us such a beautiful chapel. As you can see, it was built in an ornate style . . ."

Dismas was charmed by the Duke's candid and boyish delight in playing the role of docent. Dürer found it a bit much. He kept looking at Dismas and crossing his eyes.

"Now, if you will follow me, we will proceed into the chapel proper. This way, please. Mind your step, Eminence. They can be slippery."

"The path to Heaven often is," Aragon quipped.

Dürer groaned.

Archdeacon Quimper—he whom Count Lothar had caused to be evicted from his home—awaited them at the front door. He was extravagantly vested under such a quantity of brocade that Dismas wondered he did not topple over. He was flanked on each side by three pikemen, also resplendently attired, wearing the conquistador-style helmets that were now all the rage. Their tunics bore the noble crest of Savoy, white cross on red shield beneath the banner of St. Maurice. They looked to Dismas like crusaders who'd spent all their spoils money on personal adornment. The Landsknechte would have been jealous. But for all the finery, Dismas saw these were hard men, not mere ornaments.

"Archdeacon Quimper."

"Most beloved grace."

Church and state bowed to each other and embraced. The Duke introduced his illustrious guests. Archdeacon Quimper knelt—with some difficulty underneath his vestments—and bussed the proffered hand of the Cardinal of Aragon. The Duke of Urbino received a bow but not a kissed hand. The formalities observed, they processed into the chapel as the Duke continued with his singsong monologue.

"In 1502, the Duchess of Savoy, Marguerite of Austria, daughter of the late Emperor Maximilian, and widow to my half brother Philibert—God rest their souls—decided that the Holy Shroud must have a permanent home, here in the Chapel Royal. And so it became the Holy Chapel. It has been thus for now almost two decades. And of course we are very pleased by this."

Dismas tuned out the Duke's narration to focus on more relevant details, such as the location of doors. The one that interested him most was to the left of the main altar as he faced it—it must lead to the balcony from which the Shroud would be displayed to the crowds.

"Of course, there are some who have suggested that the Holy Shroud is not genuine. That it is a fraudulency. But of course the

Shroud *is* real. How do we know this? Not only because it is unique. Not only because of the many miracles which it has caused. But we know this also because over the many years since it was first displayed by the knight Geoffrey, it has been tried. Yes. Tried by fire. Tried by being boiled in oil. Tried by being washed—many, many times. But it refuses to burn. It refuses to melt into the oil. And refuses to come out in the wash. The image of the crucified Jesus remains, as you will see shortly."

Dismas noted another door as he faced the altar—to the right. This one would lead to some room in the adjoining wing. As they moved closer to the altar, he examined the curtained, recessed area on his left. Behind the curtain would be the sacristy, where the vestments and altar vessels used in the mass were kept, and where the celebrants would robe.

"And now let us sit."

Chairs had been set out to accommodate the noble and eminent guests. Those who were neither could stand.

Dismas, Rostang, Caraffa, and the Cardinal's attending monsignor took their places at the rear. Dismas positioned himself at an angle behind Caraffa so that he could observe him. Caraffa was examining every inch of the chapel, as Dismas had.

"It is a bit warm," the Duke said, noting that the Cardinal was perspiring greatly under his carapace of brocade. Urbino's face was streaming with sweat, causing the white greasepaint to streak and cake, giving him a ghastly aspect.

"Air. Let us have some air, *please*!" the Duke commanded.

A subdeacon opened the door to the balcony, admitting a welcome breeze. Immediately nostrils began to twitch from the miasma of the thousands of pilgrims massed in the great square below.

"Umph." Duke Charles held his pomander to his nose and inhaled. "Incense. Quickly, please!"

Minions scurried and brought in two enormous braziers filled with glowing red coals. They set them at either end of the altar. A subdeacon appeared carrying a large silver and gold chest from which he scooped copious amounts of incense onto the coals. Billows of smoke wafted upward, filling the chapel with intense but pleasant aroma.

"*Much* better," Duke Charles said. "We love our pilgrims, but they are fragrant. I prefer the scent of myrrh. And now . . ."

The Duke reached inside his cloak and produced a large key. The archdeacon produced a second key. Two bishops wearing miters appeared from behind the curtain. Each in turn produced a key. Dismas eliminated any notion of obtaining four separate keys from four different people.

The archdeacon collected all four keys and walked to the altar. He genuflected before it, then walked around it, disappearing behind the tabernacle. Presently came the sound of locks opening, and the squeal of metal from the heavy iron grille protecting the Shroud.

The Duke resumed his narration:

"In 1509, the Duchess Marguerite commissioned a most beautiful reliquary for the Holy Shroud . . ."

As he spoke, the archdeacon emerged from behind the altar. In his hands was a silver casket, coruscating with jewels.

". . . made by the Flemish artist Levin van Latham. I don't like to say how much this cost because it would be vulgar. But since I am a vulgar man"—he smiled—"I cannot resist telling you that this was accomplished at a cost of twelve thousand gold ecus."

His guests nodded appreciatively. It was a princely sum that princes could appreciate. Dismas calculated it was about half what Albrecht had borrowed from Fugger in order to purchase his cardinalate.

"This was of course a very nice thing of Marguerite to do," the Duke continued. "Ah, but the Duchess was also a very shrewd lady. Why do I say this? Because she attached a condition to her gift. What was this condition? That every day, for all eternity, a mass would be said in the chapel for the repose of the soul of her husband, Philibert. And for her own. *What* a clever lady she was! I think I will myself make some nice gift to the chapel so that I will have masses said for all eternity for my soul. Surely I shall need them. And now . . ."

The Duke nodded. The archdeacon set the silver casket on the altar, opened it, and reached in.

The Shroud of Chambéry was folded to what appeared to Dismas three-by-one feet. He counted quickly, before the archdeacon and the bishops began the unfolding. Thirty-two layers of folds.

"And now let us pray in silence," said the Duke.

All bowed their heads, except Dismas, and—he noted—Caraffa.

"Ecce sindon," the archdeacon intoned. Behold the Shroud.

Apt, Dismas thought. After having Jesus scourged, Pilate presented him to the baying mob saying, *"Ecce homo."* Behold the man. Not "Behold the King of the Jews." Perhaps the mob would see that this pathetic, bleeding man was no king. The ploy failed. The mob demanded crucifixion. Out of petulance, Pilate ordered the *titulus* nailed to the cross over Jesus's head to be worded tauntingly "Jesus of Nazareth, King of the Jews"—in Latin, Greek, and Hebrew.

Dismas now remembered a detail from one of his shroud hunts. A fourth-century saint—was it St. Nino of Georgia?—said that Pilate's wife had kept the Shroud. There were so many versions. He tried to summon the name of Pilate's wife . . . Claudia? According to the legend, she converted and ended up a saint. In the Gospel of Matthew, she sends Pilate a message, telling him Jesus is innocent. She'd had a dream. Just as Caesar's wife Calpurnia did on the eve of his assassination. They were always having terrible dreams, these Roman wives of high officials. No wonder, the way they ate, at their interminable banquets.

Now there was a collective intake of breath in the chapel. Dismas's mind cleared like air after a thunderstorm.

35

That Was a Viewing, Eh?

"Fuck the Shroud. Twelve thousand gold ecus? I say we steal the casket."

Dismas sighed. "Cunrat, we may no longer be monks, but such language. Have you no care for your soul?"

"You said it's a fake."

"Well . . . I don't know anymore. Maybe it is. Maybe it's not. But all the same, don't say such things."

"Go on," Magda said.

They were all together in the apartment except for Dürer, who'd gone off with Duke Charles after the viewing for some "private time."

"I have seen many, many shrouds," Dismas said. "None like this. With the others, you could tell right away they were the work of human hands.

"The image is faint. At first, you don't even see it. Then you do. The linen is fine. It has the fishbone pattern, a tight weave. A good match with the linen Dürer and I purchased in Basel.

"The man is tall. His face is long. The nose is prominent. The eyelids are closed. Duke Charles told us that up close you can see the impression of the Roman coins they put on the eyes. But we were not close enough.

"The five wounds are indicated by the bloodstains. On the forehead, from the Crown of Thorns. The hands are folded across the groin, so. Here the blood has flowed from wounds in the wrists. Not the palms. This is accurate, for if the nails went into the palms, the weight of the body would cause the palms to tear and come out.

"The soles of the feet display the greatest concentration of blood. Also there is blood from the spear wound in the side, made by the lance of Longinus. This lance I procured some years ago for Frederick of Saxony. The lance wound is on the right side of the man's chest. This, too, is correct. Roman soldiers were trained to spear on that side, since their opponent would be holding his shield with the left hand, protecting his left side. The blood itself is not red, but light orange, like stains from old iron.

"It's all one piece. I estimate fourteen feet long and four feet wide. One side shows the front of the body, the other, the back, as if it was folded over the body at the head. And here is the problem. I learned—in the Holy Land, from rabbis, the Jewish priests—that the custom then was to use a separate cloth for the head. Indeed, the Gospel of John refers to a separate head cloth. But this is all *one* Shroud. What do we conclude? We don't.

"On the back of the man, there are hundreds of wounds. To be scourged was a most terrible cruelty. The Romans put pieces of lead and bone on their whips, to tear the flesh. You would think that this alone would be enough to cause death. Sure, in many cases, it must have been. But for Jesus there was much more to suffer. *Then . . .*" Dismas shook his head.

"What?"

"Well, then took place a most extraordinary thing.

"It was now very quiet in the chapel. Duke Charles, who had been talking without cessation, even *he* stopped talking. Everyone was thinking, *Here is the Shroud in which lay the crucified body of Jesus Christ.* It makes you quiet. So there we were, everyone having quiet thoughts. Then came this sound.

"From the Duke of Urbino. He was overcome. Completely. He was beating his chest with his fist. Not because he needed more of Magda's fingerhut. No, he was making *mea culpa, mea culpa, mea maxima culpa*. Then he commenced to weep. Sobbing. So now we are all looking at each other and it is, well, embarrassing. And then . . . God in heaven . . .

"Urbino is kneeling, like the rest of us. Suddenly he is on his feet and he *lurches* at the Shroud.

"The archdeacon and the two bishops who are holding the Shroud by the edge . . . their faces, when they saw what was happening. They did not know what to do. After all, here is the Duke of Urbino, nephew of the *Pope*, their master's honored guest. After today, I don't think there will be further private viewings for Italian dukes afflicted with the pox."

"What happened?"

"What happened is that the Duke of Urbino grabbed the Shroud with both hands and before the archdeacon and bishops could pull it away, he buried his face in it."

"Good God!"

"Yes. And *what* a face—with the awful makeup they put to cover his sores."

"Disgusting," Cunrat said.

"Yes, Cunrat, very disgusting. From the look on the face of poor Duke Charles, I think he, too, was thinking it was disgusting."

"Then what?"

"Now the archdeacon and bishops are trying to pull the Shroud away from the crazed Urbino. But Urbino is not letting go. Oh, no. He is seizing it, with both hands, weeping into it, copious weepings and moanings, begging Jesus to heal him. I thought, *My God, it's going to tear*. Can you imagine?"

Magda crossed herself.

"Now Caraffa is holding Urbino by his waist, trying to pull his master away. Finally he succeeds. Well, by now the atmosphere in the Holy Chapel is very different than before, let me tell you.

"Duke Charles is saying nothing. I think because he is about to faint. But you can see from his face that he is not happy. No.

"As for the guards, the myrmidons of the Holy Chapel . . . they did not know what to do. But I can tell you, from experience, that guards of holy places are . . . you don't want to make trouble with them. They are not like normal soldiers. They take special vows. They were now pointing their pikes. For one moment I thought they would impale Urbino in the chapel with the pikes.

"So now the archdeacon and bishops, who are very pale in the face, get back their shroud—and never mind folding it—they take it and *run* from the chapel. They are fleeing. So they can remove the"—Dismas winced—"*detritus* left on the Shroud by Urbino."

No one spoke.

Nutker said, "If this rag *is* real, then his pox'll be healed. Won't it?"

Dismas considered. "I had not thought of this, Nutker. Well, yes. Perhaps we will now find out if the Shroud is real. But even if he is not healed, that would not necessarily mean that it's a fake. Relics have discretion in healing. They heal only those they desire to heal."

"I'm not going to touch it now," Cunrat declared. "I don't want to get his pox. And, Little Sister, don't tell me you can't get it from dribble."

An hour later, the door opened. Dürer.

"That was a viewing, eh?"

He tossed his hat onto the table, sat, and poured himself a hefty slug of wine.

"How is his grace?" Dismas asked.

"Not bad, considering that a prince of Italy wiped his revolting face all over his most precious possession. He's a bit shaky. He drank three glasses of wine, one after another. Then the archdeacon arrived. I think he had been weeping. His face was like a raspberry. But he informed the Duke that they had managed to remove the ducal residue. When he heard this, Duke Charles almost wept with relief. He's a sweetie pie, Charles," Dürer said. "Here the Duke of Urbino had just defiled his Shroud, only days before it is to be displayed before thousands of people. Anyone but Charles 'The Good' would have been fulminating and cursing and chopping off heads.

"Instead he was very calm. He drank a fourth glass of wine. Then he said, 'Poor fellow!' I said, 'Poor fellow?' He said, 'Well, he was overcome.' He said this was not the first occasion when a guest has been overcome at seeing the Shroud. But he said normally they don't use it for a handkerchief.

"He said—his words exactly—'One's heart goes out to him.' Can you believe? If I was the Duke, if it was my shroud, I would be summoning my army to march on Urbino. *And* Florence." Dürer drained his glass.

Dismas considered. "He doesn't have that kind of army. But he's a Christian, sure, to have such compassion."

They fell silent.

Dismas was troubled. "How can we steal from such a fellow?"

"Agreed," Cunrat said. "We steal the casket and leave the rag."

"Cunrat, that is not what I meant."

"Ah. He'll commission a replacement casket," Cunrat said. "Then he can have masses said for himself every day for eternity."

The other Landsknechte agreed this was an excellent proposal.

Dismas suddenly felt queer and dizzy, as if a hurricane were rising in his brain. He stood and paced, holding his head.

"Dismas?" Magda said. "Are you not well?"

He didn't hear. He looked at Dürer. Dürer's lips moved but Dismas couldn't hear him. He heard something else. He couldn't make out what it was. But it was addressed to him. He closed his eyes.

Suddenly, there before him was the man in the Shroud. The coin-closed eyes, the long nose, the forehead trickled with thorn blood.

"What's wrong with him?"

"Dismas?"

Magda was on her feet.

"Dismas?" She took his head in her hands. "Dismas!"

This day you shall be with me in Paradise.

"Dismas!"

Dismas opened his eyes. Everyone was staring at him strangely.

"What's the matter?" he said.

"Give him some wine."

Dismas looked around the room.

"Why are you all staring?"

Dürer said, "You looked like Urbino, just before he hurled himself at the Shroud."

"I'm fine. What were we talking about?"

"I was about to say that I am a very clever fellow," Dürer said.

"You're always saying that."

"I know how to do it."

"Do what?"

"The *Shroud*, stupid man. What did you think? The Ghent altar-piece?"

Suddenly Dismas felt a great weariness. More tired than he had ever been. Why was he lying down on the floor? Everyone was now looking down at him. Strange.

"What's going on?" he said.

Magda crouched by him, her palm to his forehead.

"You're feverish," she said.

"Christ, the pox!" Unks said. "Stand back!"

"Unks," Magda said sharply. "Don't be foolish. He doesn't have the pox." She gave Dismas water. He gulped it down.

Dismas said, still lying on his back, "You know how to make the shroud?"

"Yes."

"That's good. But still there remains the problem of how to switch them."

"Wait," Magda said. "One moment ago you said it was not right we should steal it from such a sweetie pie as Duke Charles."

"No," Dismas said. "No, it *is* right that we steal it. It's very clear."

"I don't understand."

"The Shroud *wants* to be translated."

They stared at Dismas.

"It spoke to me."

Dürer whispered to Magda. "He needs rest."

"Nars," Dismas said, "don't talk like I'm a madman. The Shroud wants to be translated. I'm telling you."

They all looked at each other.

"To keep it from Urbino," Dismas explained.

"Well," Dürer said, "if I was Jesus, I would not want my shroud to be used as a hankie by a diseased Italian duke. Still . . ."

"We will translate the Shroud," Dismas said. "And after, we'll give it back to Duke Charles."

"Oh no. No, no. What sense does this make?" Cunrat said. "We're to risk our lives to steal it, only to give it back?"

"Is it not marvelous?" Dismas said. "It's not every day you witness the workings of Divine Grace."

Then everything went black as Dismas fainted.

He heard words. Female and male. Nearby. He felt something pleasant and cold on his forehead. He thought of opening his eyes but that took too much effort, so he left them closed and listened to the voices.

"Has this happened before?" the woman's voice said.

"Never," said the man's.

"Paracelsus speaks of this. He was a surgeon in the army. At first the mind cannot absorb what has happened. Later comes the shock. Sometimes in strange ways."

"Hearing a shroud speak to you is strange, sure."

"To be hung from hooks, by the ears and hands and feet, for a week . . ."

Dismas opened his eyes. "What's going on?"

"You fell," Magda said. "How do you feel?"

Dismas propped himself up on his elbows. "Fine. I had a dream. Where is everyone? What's the time?"

"It's the middle of the night. You slept a long time."

Dismas looked at Dürer. "What are you doing up?"

"What do you suppose? I was worried about you."

Magda said to Dismas, "What do you remember?"

"Nars was saying that he knows how to make the shroud."

"Do you remember anything else?"

Dismas shrugged. "No. Why?"

Magda smiled and caressed his head. "Nothing."

Dürer said, "While you were in the arms of Morpheus, *I* solved the problem of how to switch the shrouds."

Dismas looked at him groggily. "Well?"

"Duke Charles is planning another tableau vivant. The night before the Shroud is displayed."

"Yes?"

"What do you suppose is to be the theme of the tableau?"

"I don't know. The Apotheosis of the Painter Dürer?"

Dürer chortled. "Ah. You *shall* witness the apotheosis of the painter Dürer. The theme is to be the Last Supper. And who do you suppose has been cast in the role of the apostle whom Jesus loved?"

"Didn't get the lead? What a shame. You know it so well."

Dürer said to Magda. "The fever has passed. He is himself. Alas."

36

Did It Do the Trick?

Past midnight the following day, one of Rostang's men arrived at the apartment with a message for Sister Hildegard from Caraffa. It said, simply and commandingly, "Come."

Dismas told Rostang's man to wait outside. It was only himself and Magda in the apartment. Dürer and the Landsknechte had gone out to see about things he needed to make his shroud.

Magda sighed then nodded with resignation. "I must go."

"No."

"How can I refuse?"

"You weren't there in the chapel when he grabbed at the Shroud. He's mad. There's no telling what he might do."

"I'm a nun. How will it look if I don't go?"

"You're not *his* nun. You are under no obligation to an Italian duke."

But Magda was already gathering up her habit and apothecary things.

"He's sick," she said. "He may even be dying right now. If you're concerned he's going to rape me, don't fear. He wouldn't have the strength."

"He had strength enough in the chapel to play tug-of-war with an archdeacon and two bishops."

"Dismas. He wants a nurse, not a whore."

"Rostang says he's attacked five of the servant girls. Five."

"I can take care of myself." She pulled a short dagger from underneath her robe.

"Magda. Please."

"If you're so sure they're here to steal the Shroud, don't you want to find out what we can? Maybe he will say something in his delirium."

"And if Caraffa hears him tell you? Do you think he'd hesitate for one moment to cut your throat? The man was suckled by tarantulas."

Magda went to the window.

"What are you doing?"

"Looking for the time. It's half-midnight, by the clock. At half-one, come to Urbino's bedchamber. Ask to see Caraffa, outside the bedchamber. Keep him distracted for as long as you can. When I'm alone with Urbino, I'll give him extra *ladanum*. Maybe that will loosen his tongue."

It was pointless to protest. She was going.

Magda smoothed her scapular and slung the beaded rosary from her belt.

She took Dismas's face in her hands and kissed him. A long kiss that Dismas wanted to go on even longer.

"What a nun I am!" she said and was out the door.

Dismas went to the open window. He saw her emerge into the square below and follow Rostang's servant across it and then up the cobbled ramp to the castle.

He prayed for her safety.

And remember, Lord, that she is named Magda, for the Magdalene, she to whom you first appeared after you rose from the dead.

Dismas was overwhelmed by weariness. He tried to keep awake by sitting upright, but he kept nodding off. He lay on the hard floor. That would keep him awake, sure.

And fell asleep.

He dreamed.

Mary Magdalene was going to the tomb at dawn on the third day, carrying small pots of oils and spices to anoint the body. She arrived at the tomb and saw the large stone rolled back from the entrance. Saw the Roman soldiers standing guard over the tomb, slumbering. Went into the tomb and beheld the empty Shroud. She went to pick it up. It was blank. White as bone. No image of Jesus was on it.

Dismas awoke from his dream, gasping and upright, drenched in sweat. He ran to the window to see what the time was. A quarter past one o'clock. Thank Christ, he hadn't overslept.

He thought about his strange dream, about the blankness of the Shroud. Why would he dream such a thing? He tried to make sense of it.

There was a Bible in the archdeacon's study. It was on a stand, with four mirrored candleholders. He lit the candles. Their light fell on the vellum. It was a splendid Bible, exquisitely illuminated by monks now long dead.

As he turned the pages, Dismas rebuked himself for having gone so long without so much as a glance at holy scripture. He had no Greek, but his Latin was good enough to understand at least the straightforward stuff.

He thumbed through the thick, lushly illustrated pages and read, in one after another of the Gospels, the passages having to do with that morning in the tomb.

None—not one—had anything to say about the Shroud bearing the image of Jesus. How, then, could the Shroud of Chambéry be real? If Christ had left his image on his Shroud, surely Matthew or Mark or Luke or John would have found this worthy of mention. It was hardly a minor detail.

He blew out the four candles and went back to the other room and paced.

So the Shroud must be fake. Then he remembered the strange episode of the day before, when he fainted after hearing the voice say, *This day you shall be with me in Paradise*. Wasn't that the Shroud, communicating with him? How was he to make sense of this?

Now he was seized by great anxiety at the thought of Magda in the clutches of the lunatical and poxy Urbino. He went to the window. Almost a quarter to two. He must hasten. He rushed out the door, forgetting his gloves.

He ran so fast he was panting and out of breath by the time he reached the ducal bedchamber in the royal apartments.

The two guards standing outside the door regarded him with curiosity. A footman went into the bedchamber to inform the majordomo that a sweaty, wheezing German had arrived, craving an audience.

Dismas tried to peer inside but it was dark and the angle was wrong. But no female shrieks came from within.

A moment later the door opened and majordomo Caraffa emerged, looking surprised, and not especially pleased.

"Master Rufus."

"Signore." Dismas bowed. "Forgive . . . out of . . . breath . . . It's a . . . mountain, this castle."

"Is there an urgency?"

"No, no."

It only now occurred to Dismas that in his headlong dash to rescue Magda from these evil Italian clutches he had neglected to confect a pretext for presenting himself at the Duke's bedchamber at such an hour, and in such a deoxygenated state.

Think, he commanded his brain.

"It's only that my master is concerned," he said. "For your master."

Caraffa stared.

"He sent me to inquire. After your master's health. Your summons to Sister Hildegard was urgent."

"The needs of a duke are always urgent," Caraffa said. "Perhaps this is less so in your country, with your nobles."

"Ah." Dismas grinned. "Well, I wouldn't know about that. My master can be a Tatar when it comes to his needs, let me tell you. Oh, yes."

"Inform your count that his grace is better. Now I say to you good night." Caraffa turned to go.

"Ah?" Dismas said. "So he's all well, then?"

"As I said."

"God be praised. We were worried. After that business in the chapel."

Caraffa turned slowly, took a step closer to Dismas, putting his face right in his.

"What concern is that of yours?"

"Well, signore, I was there. I saw."

"And what did you see, Master Rufus?"

"Why, the power of the Shroud."

"Yes. It is something, this relic."

Dismas said in a tone both collegial and conspiratorial, "So? Did it do the trick?"

Caraffa frowned. "How do you mean?"

Dismas whispered, "Did it *cure* the old boy?"

Caraffa's eyes glazed with rage.

"Old boy? Do you speak of his grace, the Duke of Urbino, Lorenzo de'—"

"Ah," Dismas said jauntily, "you don't have to play the nose-up-the-arse with me. We're just the same, you and I. Lickspittles to a pair of nobs."

The veins on Caraffa's neck bulged, as if vipers were slithering up from under his collar. Dismas kept on. "Well? Did it cure the old boy's *pox*?"

"Stronza!"

"Stronza?" Dismas said. "Ah, yes—Dago for 'cunt'?" Dismas gave the outraged majordomo a thump on the shoulder. "Come, come, none of that. We're all friends here, sure. Sure, your master's got a dose, and no small one. No wonder he grabbed ahold of the Shroud. Still, a bit nasty. Let's hope it came out in the wash, eh? But don't be coy. Did it *cure* him?"

Caraffa's hand was on the hilt of his dagger. Dismas prepared to deflect the thrust. They were eyeball to eyeball.

Then suddenly Caraffa relaxed. He smiled. He was staring at Dismas's hands. Dismas realized they were gloveless, and silently cursed.

He said, "If your master's well, I'll escort Sister Hildegard back."

Caraffa disappeared into the ducal bedchambers. A moment later the doors opened and out came Magda.

Neither spoke until they were back in the apartment.

"Anything?" Dismas asked.

"When Caraffa left to speak with you, I gave Urbino three drops of the *ladanum*. I said to him how wonderful is the Shroud and wouldn't it be wonderful to own it? He said nothing."

"They're going for it."

"How do you know?"

"I tried to provoke Caraffa to attack me. He didn't. And he wanted to, sure. Oh, yes."

"What does that prove?"

"Killing the servant of a fellow guest would be bad manners. It would compromise their plan. If they had no designs on the Shroud, Caraffa would have struck. At the least, given me a slash on the face to teach me manners."

"A strange way to get information."

"It was all I could think of at the time." Dismas held out his gloveless hands. "I screwed up, Magda. He saw these." He smiled gamely. "Well, maybe he'll think I have the stigmata and be more respectful."

37

Consummatum Est

Dismas and Magda awoke the next morning to the sound of the apartment door banging open and the loud mutter of Landsknechte curses.

He wandered groggily into the foyer in his nightshirt. Nutker and Unks staggered in, holding armloads of firewood, which they dumped without ceremony onto the floor, making a great clatter. What must the archdeacon's neighbors be thinking?

"What's all this?"

"Ask his majesty Count fucking Lothar," Unks said sourly.

The two Landsknechte lumbered out. Shortly Dismas heard another clumping of feet on the stairs, and again came Nutker and Unks bearing another cargo of firewood, which they deposited with similar contempt.

"It's spring," Dismas said. "It's not that cold. Why do we need so much firewood?"

"Ask his royal highness."

The lads were perspiring heavily. They wiped their faces with a shared cloth, which seemed odd to Dismas.

Dürer appeared, roused from his lair by the commotion. He was wearing his painter apron.

"More," he said to Nutker and Unks. "At least three more loads. And don't forget the water. Four buckets."

This elicited such blistering profanities Dismas thought the framed Madonna on the wall might blush.

"Come," Dürer said to Dismas. "And bring some of that wood."

Dismas followed Dürer into the kitchen. Dürer had sealed it off, nailing curtains and bed linens over the doors.

Dismas looked. There were bowls and pots and vials, a fruit press, various instruments including a clyster syringe. What on earth was Dürer planning to do with that? He wasn't sure he wanted to know.

The archdeacon's copper bathing tub was there, in front of a full-sized mirror leaning against the wall. Nailed to the wall beside the mirror was a large sketch Dürer had made of the Shroud. Dismas marveled at its precision.

In the center of the room was a long narrow table on which lay the linen they had purchased in Basel; half of it overlapped the edge and lapped onto the floor in folds.

The stove was going, with two large pots of boiling water from which rose vapors with a familiar scent. Myrrh.

"It's going to get steamy in here," Dürer said. "Best strip down. But first go and tell Magda we are ready to begin. And find out where the hell is Cunrat. It's been over two hours. Landsknechte. All they care about is fornicating and drinking."

Dismas went to fetch Magda.

He told her, "He's turned the archdeacon's kitchen into I don't know what. An alchemist's den."

Presently there came another clumping of feet in the stairwell and a torrent of curses. Cunrat entered groaningly, carrying a large wooden bucket covered over with a damp cloth.

"What's that?"

"For Painter, him who can't be troubled to fetch his own fucking supplies," Cunrat growled, setting it down with a clatter. He stretched backward, massaging his lumbar area.

"I'm not a damned porter."

Dismas went to the bucket and pulled back the cloth. He recoiled.

"Jesus. Where did you get this? The slaughterhouse?"

Cunrat wiped sweat from his brow with the same cloth Dismas had seen the others use.

"Painter made some arrangement with a barber. A barber on the fucking outskirts of town." Cunrat grunted reflectively. "I've spilled a lot of blood. But till now I never had to carry it about like a damned milkmaid. Tell him if he wants more, he can fetch it himself."

Dürer appeared.

"*Finally*. What took you so long? Did you stop along the way to have a screw with some slut?"

"Don't start with me, Painter," Cunrat said. "Or you'll be painting with your own blood."

Dürer drew back the cloth on the bucket.

"As I thought. Half congealed. Well, hurry *up*, man. Bring it in, bring it in."

"Let me," Dismas said, lest Cunrat make good on his threat to spill Dürer's blood.

Nutker and Unks now grunted in through the door, each carrying two great buckets of water slopping over their brims. They set them down and leaned against the wall, gasping and wheezing.

"Fucking hell," said Nutker. "That's it. No more."

"Listen to you," Dürer said. "You'd think you'd never done an honest day's work."

"Call this honest?" Cunrat said.

Sensing mutiny aborning, Dismas went to his room and came back with a gold ducat. He gave it to Cunrat.

"Go on. Replenish your fluids."

Dürer said, "Give me the sweat rag."

The Landsknechte handed it over. Dürer held the dripping rag by the corner.

"All right, let's get started." He went off to the kitchen.

"What's he want with our sweat?" Cunrat asked Dismas.

"Artist." Dismas shrugged. "Go on, lads, before he gives you another job. See you later."

"Maybe you'll see us. But we may not see you, for sure, we won't be sober."

Dismas and Magda followed Dürer into the kitchen. Dürer had the sweat rag in the fruit press and was turning the vise handle. Landsknechte perspiration flowed from the spout into a small bowl. Dismas winced.

Dürer and Magda held a discussion over the bucket of blood.

Dürer said, "Look, how it's thickened, already. Good-for-nothing Landsknechte."

He ladled some blood into a bowl.

"The blue vial," he said to Magda.

Magda passed it to him.

Dürer uncorked it and poured an amount of yellowish, syrupy liquid into the bowl.

"Stir. Gently."

"What's that?" Dismas said.

"Viper venom. Two ducats, this cost. But nothing works better."

Magda said, "Paracelsus speaks of a leech whose saliva is also effective."

"What is the purpose?" Dismas asked.

"To arrest the congealing," Magda said.

Dismas shuddered.

"Blood. Viper venom," he said. "Landsknechte sweat. What else? Unicorn tears? Liver of raven? If anyone comes in here, we *will* be arrested as witches and burned. And who'd blame them?"

Dürer gave Dismas the menial job of keeping the stove going and the water pots boiling. He and Magda went about their business.

Dismas watched. Painter and apothecary spoke in a shared

vocabulary that mostly eluded him. But this was fine, since he found the whole business frankly disgusting.

There was a basket of eggs on one of the tables. Magda cracked them and carefully separated the yolks into a bowl. She whisked them, adding drops from another vial.

"If that's breakfast," Dismas said, "none for me. I have no appetite."

Dürer muttered, "You know nothing of art."

"If this is art, I am content to know nothing."

"It's called tempera."

Dürer added a quantity of Landsknechte sweat to the bowl containing the blood, then other liquids from more vials. Now he stripped off his clothes and stood naked.

"Nars," Dismas said. "Some decency, for Magda's sake."

"Ready?" Dürer said to Magda.

She nodded and handed him a paintbrush with short, stubby bristles, and held out the bowl with the yolk mixture.

Dürer positioned himself in front of the mirror.

Dismas said, "As I suspected. A self-portrait."

Dürer dipped a brush into the egg yolk and went to work. He started at the forehead, dabbing here and there. Using another, thicker brush, he traced a line on the right side of his chest, below the rib cage. Then dabbed at the wrists and feet.

"Clyster," he instructed Magda.

Magda dipped the tip of the syringe into the bowl of blood and drew back the plunger, filling the chamber.

Dürer stepped into the archdeacon's copper bathtub in front of the mirror. He took the syringe from Magda and began at the forehead, squirting the yolked areas with precise bursts of blood from the syringe. The blood adhered.

Next he squirted the line on his chest. Switching hands, he did his wrists and feet.

He regarded himself in the mirror. It was remarkable. Dürer eerily resembled Christ with his five wounds.

"Mister," Dürer instructed Magda.

It was the kind that ladies used to spray themselves with perfumes. Magda filled it from a second bowl containing Landsknechte sweat and a small amount of blood.

"Now," Dürer said, closing his eyes.

Magda misted his body entirely from head to foot, leaving an oily, reddish film.

He opened his eyes and examined himself in the mirror. "More on the face. And the beard," he instructed.

Satisfied, Dürer pointed to the table.

Magda picked up the two coins.

"Sesterci," Dürer said. "He was a good fellow, Joseph of Arimathea, but aurei or solidae would have been an extravagance."

"Where did you get those?" Dismas asked.

"Basel. Stop talking and help Magda."

He stepped out of the tub and went to the table. He lay down upon the linen on his back. He placed the two coins over his eyes and crossed his arms over his groin.

"Fold it over me. Don't pull. Let it settle naturally. Make sure it covers all the way to the toes."

Magda and Dismas each took a corner and together lifted the linen off the floor. They covered Dürer. The linen settled and clung to his moistened body.

"And now?" Dismas said. "Are we to wait three days for you to rise from the dead?"

"Dismas," Magda scolded. "Some respect."

From beneath the shroud, Dürer murmured, "Keep the pots boiling. The room must be filled with steam."

Dürer remained still for three hours. The linen saturated, clinging to his body. The bloody wounds began to show through. His face appeared: forehead, eyes, beard, nose. Neither Dismas nor Magda spoke.

At length Dürer said, "Well?"

"Yes," Magda said.

"All right, then. Peel it off me. *Slowly*."

When this was done, Dürer rose stiffly from the table.

"Christ, I'm stiff," he said.

He examined his work. He said to Magda, "Now the back."

Magda whisked a fresh batch of yolk while Dürer busied himself preparing another bowl of blood and viper venom and Landsknechte sweat. Dismas thought he might be sick from the smell and the vapors.

It took Magda over an hour to trace the scourge marks on his back where the flagrum had torn the flesh. How could a man have survived this? Toward the end, she broke down and wept, but quickly regained her composure.

When this was finished, Dürer did the soles of his feet, which he coated entirely with thick blood. Magda then sprayed him all over with the syringe, then with the mister. She and Dismas helped Dürer position himself on the linen.

Dismas tended his stove. Dürer remained so still that Dismas had the strange illusion of keeping vigil over a corpse.

After three hours Dürer said, "Enough."

They pulled back the linen and helped him to his feet. They stood, the three of them, and looked. No one spoke.

Dürer rubbed his neck. *"Consummatum est."*

It is finished. The last words he spoke on the cross.

Why not? Dismas thought. It was a bit late in the game to be fretting about blasphemy. Dürer said he wanted a bath and then a drink. Many drinks.

38

At the Bibulous Bishop

They all needed a drink, so together they went to a tavern in the southern quarter, away from the castle precinct. Its name, the Bibulous Bishop, struck Dismas as cheeky, Chambéry being a center of pilgrimage. But it was just what was needed after their hours of strange, grim toil—noise and bustle.

Dürer purred with self-satisfaction over his triumph of mimesis. Such preening was well familiar to Dismas, but tonight he inclined to let Nars have a wallow. He had created something unusual, extraordinary.

The three of them sat at a corner table and recounted moments of their day in the warm afterglow of labor well and truly done.

"Dismas! Good God, is it you?"

Dismas looked up.

Christ—Markus, whom he'd last seen in Mainz. It seemed a century ago. What was *he* doing here?

Dismas stood and embraced his old friend, trying frantically to think how to explain his own presence here.

Markus clapped Dismas on the shoulders and looked him up and down.

"You look like an old man. Where's your cane?"

"Within reach, if I need to crack you over the head with it."

"What are you doing in Chambéry? Ah, of course. On a bone hunt. Come to steal the Shroud of Chambéry?"

Dismas smiled thinly. "There's no fooling you. But shh, not so loud or everyone will know."

"My silence will cost you a drink. Or two."

Dismas turned to Magda and Dürer.

"These . . ." Magda was not wearing her nun's outfit, nor was Dürer dressed as the Count of Schramberg. Dismas's mind went blank. It had been a long day. Magda and Dürer would have to invent their own lies.

"Sorry, I'm not good with names." Dismas said to Markus, "We only just met."

Magda and Dürer stared.

Dismas said to them, "Here is my friend Markus. We were soldiers together. *Reiselaufers*. Long ago. He's a Swiss, like me. So. Well. How . . . jolly, yes? Good to meet you. Come, Markus. Let's not bore these two with lies about our bravery. Let's find a table where we can bore each other."

But Markus was going nowhere, having fixed his eyes on the lovely Magda.

"No," he said. "We will sit together. If the lady does not mind?"

"No." Magda shrugged. "Of course."

"Excellent. Well, you know my name. What is yours?"

He addressed himself exclusively to Magda, showing no interest in Dürer.

"Hildegard."

"A beautiful name! Hildegard of Bingen. Sibyl of the Rhine."

Dürer waited to be asked for his name. For once Dismas felt

sympathy for Nars. A moment ago he was in narcissist Eden, basking in plaudits for his artistic feat. Now he was demoted to mute bystander while a scruffy ex-*Reiselaufer* set about trying to hustle Magda into the nearest bed.

If only Magda *had* worn her nun's habit. But nuns did not frequent taverns. Dismas thought best to keep the conversation focused on Markus. What was he doing here?

"Now then," Dismas said, filling Markus's glass. "Last I saw you, you were headed back to the Valais to find yourself a nice milkmaid with big . . . What happened to all that?"

"It was all right for a time. But *so* dull. Hildegard, tell me, where are you from? What part of the world produces such beauty?"

"Too kind."

Dürer interjected, "It is true. Switzerland is dull. Nothing of interest has happened there since Hannibal crossed the Alps with his elephants. And he was not Swiss himself."

Dismas recognized the look on Markus's face. He had seen it many times. What usually followed was a lightning blow of his fist. Magda saw it coming, too, and put a protective arm on Dürer's shoulder.

"Here is my husband. Heinrich."

Markus did not hide his disappointment. "Ah. Well, what a lucky fellow you are, *Heinrich*."

Dürer now put his hand around Magda's waist and grinned triumphantly.

"Yes. Am I not?"

"Heinrich is a painter," Magda said. "Of houses."

"Houses?" Markus said. His expression was clear. Why would such a fetching woman settle for a laborer?

"Drink up, drink up," Dismas said, filling everyone's glass. "So, Markus. The cantons did not provide sufficient drama to contain you. No surprise. But what's here for you in Chambéry? And don't tell me you're here on pilgrimage. The last time we were together, you used a church for target practice."

"I'm on my way to Spain."

"Spain? I thought you hated Spanishers, after Cerignola."

"I abominate them. They stink of garlic and fish. And they lisp, which I find unpleasant. You cannot trust them. Always they are making the sign of the cross and then trying to cut your throat. You can predict that a Spanisher will cut your throat because always he will first make a sign of the cross. No, I don't like them. But they have made a path across the sea. Sure, you've heard of the discoveries? Gold. Mountains of it. Silver. Emeralds. Rubies. Pearls." Markus's voice lowered in wonder. "They have found a city made *entirely of gold*."

"Well. That is something."

"Dismas! A city made of gold? Are you so Swiss this does not excite you?"

"Oh, yes," Dismas said, summoning a show of enthusiasm. "Yes. A whole city, you say? Good heavens."

"The streets are cobbled in gold. Cobbles *this* size. So I will go to Spain and I will find a ship. I hate ships. I get sick. But a city made of gold is worth a few buckets of puke."

"What a pleasant image," Dürer said.

"Three or four cobblestones and I'll be rich. Perhaps I will stay there. To protect the savages—from the missionaries." Markus chuckled. "There's a noble calling. Maybe I will find a beautiful savage woman. They say the women are . . ." He smiled at Magda. "They say the women are beautiful. But sure, they could not be as beautiful as some women *here*."

"It's a good plan, Markus," Dismas said. "Let's drink to it. Drink up, drink up. When do you leave Chambéry? Soon, sure, with all that gold waiting for you." He made it sound as though Markus's gold cobblestones were being pried up by malodorous, lisping, throat-slitting Spanishers even as he spoke. Not a moment to lose!

"I will stay until Friday. They're displaying the Shroud from the castle walls. Might as well see it, since I am here. You're the expert on this crap. Is it real, or just another piece of nonsense?"

Dismas shrugged. "With relics, you never really know."

"What *are* you doing here, then?"

"Me? Like you. Passing through. Italy. Did you come over the Bauges, like we—like I did?"

"No. By way of Eggs."

"Eggs?"

"The spa town, on the lake, north of here."

"Ah, Aix. Yes. The mineral baths. Did you have a nice mineral bath?"

"Yes. I met some interesting fellows there. Hunters."

"Ah? Yes?" Dismas said, relieved that the conversation had taken a dull turn. "Hunters. Stag? Boar?"

"Man hunters. From your part of the world. Imperial irregulars. Pursuivants."

Dismas stared. "Oh?"

"Some noble—a count—got himself murdered in the Black Forest. Nephew or some such to the new Emperor, Charles."

Dismas's mouth went dry despite the quantity of wine he'd poured into it.

"Listen to this," Markus went on. "He goes missing. With his entire retinue. A dozen men. Search party goes out to find them. Nothing. It's like the earth has swallowed them up. God knows, things happen in the Black Forest. Still.

"So they're on their way back to Rottweil. They camp in the forest in this nice spot. Clearing, with a pond and so forth. So they're making a fire and gathering up wood. And they find this piece of paper, in a crease in the cliff. It's a drawing. A good drawing, of right where they are. But in this drawing there are crosses, like the ones on graves. They think, Fucking hell, what's this? Forgive my language, lady.

"They dig where the grave markers are. And what do you think? They find the bodies of the Count and his people. It's like the killers wanted them to find the graves."

Dismas swallowed. "Well," he said, "that *is* peculiar. Yes." He glanced at Dürer. Dürer had gone pale. Dismas went on: "But it's a long way from the Black Forest to Aix. How did these hunters know to . . . I mean, are they following a . . . trail of some kind?"

"A very long way," Markus snorted. "But it seems these killers are imbeciles. They left a trail blind Homer could follow. They looted the Count and his men. They've been hawking the spoils in every town they pass. Either they are stupid, or they want to be followed."

"Hm. Did they say where they were going? After Aix?"

"They think maybe they went through the Bauges. You said you came through the Bauges?"

The door to the tavern swung open. In stumbled Cunrat, Nutker, and Unks. They were so drunk they had to hold on to each other to remain upright. Dismas's gold ducat had purchased many drinks.

They looked about the tavern—clearly the latest in a series of taverns—and spotted their comrades. They waved and began to make their way toward them.

In an effort to head them off, Dismas announced, "*Oof*, I've got to piss!" and stood up. But rising so suddenly, combined with the amount of wine, made him light-headed. He flumped back into his seat.

"Masher Rufus!" Cunrat hailed, wobbling. "Masher *Roo-fuss*! Ash your *shervice*." He saluted, slapping himself on the forehead.

Markus regarded the three inebriates.

"Why does he call you Master Rufus?"

Dismas whispered into Markus's ear, "Just some drunks. Don't make a scene. They look a bit rough."

Markus snorted. "Rough? Let me handle this."

"Markus—"

"You there, Ignatz," Markus said to Cunrat. "Off with you. Quickly, if you know what's good for you."

Cunrat stared, hanging on to Nutker, whose head drooped.

"Who do you call Ignatz?" Cunrat said.

"You. Go on. And take these other two Ignatzes with you."

"Now, now," Dismas said merrily. "No need for names. No need for names. We're all good Germans here."

"You're Swiss, like me," Markus pointed out.

"Germanic."

Dismas addressed himself to the Landsknechte.

"Greetings, good fellows. We have not had the pleasure of meeting. *Have we?*"

The Landsknechte stared, pie-eyed, weaving. They looked at Markus, then at Dismas, then at each other.

"Ahhh," Cunrat said. He smiled and attempted to tap the tip of his forefinger against his nose, poked himself in the eye. *"Yesssh!* We have *not* met!" He turned to Nutker and Unks. "Ishn't that right, lads? *Shhhh!*"

"No," Nutker said, shaking his head like a St. Bernard trying to shed snow. "Never . . ."

Unks, incapable of speech, nodded and shook his head, to ensure every possibility was covered.

Dismas rummaged in his pockets and pulled out a demi-teston. He put it in Cunrat's palm.

"Allow us to buy you and your friends a drink. Why don't you take this over to the—"

"Noooo!" Cunrat said, knocking the coin out of Dismas's hand. "Nooo! *We* will buy *you* a drink!"

"Many drinks," Nutker affirmed, staggering sideways.

"Drinks for *you*, Masher Roofiss . . . Dishmuss. And for Shister Hiltuh-de-gart . . . And his imperial mashesty, Count Loothor of Schramp."

Cunrat attempted a ceremonious bow, but so doing, pitched forward onto the table, making a chaos of overturned mugs and candlesticks and such. He remained facedown upon the table, surrendering to unconsciousness long postponed.

39

Pursuivants

Markus listened in tranquility to Dismas's account of the events that had brought him to Chambéry. Dismas apologized for trying to deceive him, saying it was only a desire to spare an old and much-loved friend from becoming entangled in a machination whose success was very far from certain.

Markus accepted all this without protest. It was only when Dismas told him that the Shroud had spoken to him, asking him to translate it so that it wouldn't fall into the hands of Urbino, that Markus expressed an opinion.

"What a lot of shit."

"I'm only telling you what I heard and saw. I don't ask you to believe it."

"Those bastards in Mainz hung you from meat hooks in a dungeon. That scrambles a man's brain. You'll heal. Whether you live that long is another matter."

"It's perfectly straightforward. The saint—or in this case, Jesus himself—communicates through the relic. Not by words, but—"

"*Enough*, Dismas."

"You've become very cynical, I must say. You didn't used to be. You weren't cynical at Rocca d'Arazzo when you took that lance in your gut. As I recall, you were quite pious. Never heard such fervent paternosters. But then, blessed *are* the wounded."

Markus groaned. "What a sanctimonious fart you are. Don't give me the Sermon on the Mount. Something's been speaking to you, sure, but not Jesus. The moon, more like."

Dismas sniffed.

"There is no point in arguing if you are not susceptible to reason. Embrace your cynicism. Hug it."

The first glow of dawn lightened the sky over the Bauges. Dismas and Markus sat in the public gardens. They'd gone there after hauling the inebriated Landsknechte back to the archdeacon's apartment. Magda and Dürer stayed there with them so Dismas could have time alone with Markus to explain the strange situation into which he had wandered.

"Do you really want to be part of this?" Dismas said.

"Why not?"

"Well, because we will likely die."

"Better to die with a friend than stinking Spanishers."

"Why do you smile?"

"Well, if you're killed, and the rest of us make it, Magda will need protection."

Dismas chuckled. "You're a friend, sure."

Markus shrugged. "You'd do the same."

Dürer dipped a quill in the inkpot. Dismas dictated:

"To his most exalted honor Lothar, Count Schramberg . . . be advised, your worship, that a French courier has been intercepted by agents of His Imperial Highness Charles V, by the grace of God, Holy Roman Emperor, King of Castile, Leon—"

"Wait," Dürer said. "Why do we need all this? It's a dispatch, not his fucking pedigree going back to Charlemagne."

"Just write, Nars.

". . . *Defensor Fidei*, et cetera . . . at Württemberg. This dispatch was deciphered and found to contain information pertaining to a most heinous and insidious French plot . . ."

When Dismas finished his dictation, Dürer said, "How do I sign it? 'Kisses from Godpapa Charles'?"

"It's not *from* the Emperor, Nars. But how good that you find amusing the fact that an imperial force is on its way here to arrest us. Because you left a drawing of the graves. Will you also be amused when they put hot pincers to your flesh? On your way to be broken on the wheel? From the bottom?"

"Why must you be so peevish?"

"Sign it . . . 'Raven.' It's a good spymaster name. Let me see it."

Dürer handed Dismas the vellum scroll.

"We need a seal," Dismas said. "Magda, look for a seal in the drawers. He must have one. He's an archdeacon. Archdeacons are always sealing."

Dürer said, "Will they not wonder why a secret imperial dispatch from Württemberg bears the seal of the archdeacon of Chambéry?"

"There is no reason they would examine the seal, Nars. We just need a seal. Now go put on your Lothar clothes. Markus, get soot from the stove. Put it on your face. Look like you have been riding for days. And put some vinegar in your eyes, to make them red."

Magda found the archdeacon's seal. Dismas heated wax and sealed the dispatch.

"All right. Let's go."

"Dismas," Magda said. "Gloves."

Dismas shook his head in self-rebuke. He hadn't slept in over a day. He was tired. He was making more and more stupid mistakes. Magda gave him his gloves and kissed him.

Charles the Good, Duke of Savoy, listened aghast as Count Lothar read him the dispatch.

" '. . . Such are the lengths, nay, depths, to which François, duplicitous, scheming King of France, will descend in order to put the snake of enmity between Savoy and the Holy Roman Empire.' "

Dürer cleared his throat and continued:

" 'Without delay, pray inform his excellent and most beloved Christian grace Charles, Duke of Savoy, of this abominable Gallic machination. Assure him that the love and fraternity in which he and all Savoyards are held by his imperial majesty is stronger and more durable than the fiendish plottings of the whoreson French king.' "

Charles dabbed at his eyes with a kerchief. Rostang stood beside him, looking aggrieved on behalf of his master. Dismas felt a pang at having given the poor Duke such a start.

Dürer reached the end of his narration and put his hand over his heart to show how acute was his own misery at this odious news.

He rerolled the dispatch scroll and handed it off to Dismas, as if eager to be physically relieved of such a repugnant object.

"How can I express myself to your grace?" Dürer said. "My heart is more heavy than a millstone. Yet I thank God that word of this hateful . . . I have no words . . . this *French* scheme to cause mischief between Savoy and the Empire has reached us in time."

Rostang said, "These men posing as imperial irregulars, you say they are *German* mercenaries? *Mm!*"

Dürer nodded gravely. "Yes, though it rends my heart to say. To think that my own countrymen would sell their souls for French coin. Scum! Dregs! But the greatest scum of all is he who sits in Paris, on his throne of evil. Oh, perfidy, sure, thy name is François!"

Steady, Dismas thought.

Dürer went on:

"But diabolical though their plan is, your grace must admit its ingenuity. A band of fraudulent imperial troops arrives at Chambéry, on pretense of making pilgrimage, and makes mischief. Starts brawls. Makes blasphemies. Insults the dignity of Savoy. Insults . . . even yourself. Insults"—Dürer made a sign of the cross—"the Holy Shroud itself. To provoke conflict. What could your grace do, in the face of such provocations, but declare your grief and your wish no longer to have the friendship of the Emperor? *How* François would rejoice at this! How much easier would be the march of his armies, when he sends them south—to destroy you."

"Rostang!" the Duke said.

"Your grace? *Mm!*"

"Alert Villiers. Treble the guard at all gates. And when these fiends in human form show themselves . . ."

Charles turned to Dürer.

"Most dear Count Lothar—does the dispatch specify how *many* fiends there are?"

"May I?" Rostang held out his hand to Dismas.

Dismas squeezed the scroll, crumbling the seal into bits of undecipherable red wax that fell on the stone floor.

"Forgive me," Dismas said. "Such is my anger."

He handed the scroll to Rostang, who uncrumpled it and read it over.

"It does not specify how many. *Mm!*"

Markus, who had been keeping back, as befit his status as messenger, said, "Permission to speak, my lord?"

Dürer turned. "Yes?"

"In Württemberg, I heard mentioned the number fifteen."

"May I speak?" Dismas said.

"Yes, Master Rufus."

"Your grace, in my day I did a bit of soldiering. I know these mercenary types. They are called Landsknechte. Worse creatures do not walk the earth. Indeed, you would have to travel to Hell to meet their equal."

"Well," Charles said with a hint of miff, "I think my entire guard can handle fifteen mercenaries."

"I do not impugn your grace's troops. I have no doubt that they are superb both in mettle and in their devotion to yourself and to Savoy. That said, your grace, I most respectfully urge caution. These men are the very hounds of Satan. They will not go down without a fight. And in this fight they will, I fear, annihilate many a good Savoyard. But even more, I fear their guile. They are skilled in the arts of deception. In this, they are the true heirs to devious Ulysses, author of the Trojan horse. I should tremble if they gained entry to Chambéry."

Charles's brow furrowed. "What is it you propose that I *do*, Master Rufus?"

"Seize the upper hand, your grace. Attack them before they can attack you. Send your troops to surprise them on the Aix road. For sure, they will come from that direction. And send another troop to the foot of the Bauges, in case they come that way. Have your men greet them with artillery."

"Artillery? But they are only fifteen."

"Why take chances? When these hellhounds present themselves, welcome them to Chambéry with grapeshot. Let them turn tail like whipped dogs and run squealing to their frog-eating paymaster. You will not soon again be troubled by French on Savoy's soil. Let King François know that he deals not with Charles the Good, but Charles the Indomitable."

Duke Charles seemed a bit stunned by it all.

"Er, thank you for this counsel, Master Rufus."

Dismas bowed deeply.

"I heed what you say about the wiles of these scoundrels. But I repose confidence in our guard. We must make an example of the naughtiness of François. I should like to hear their confessions. And *publish* their confessions, so that all may hear of the perfidy of François." He looked at Dürer and smiled. "And of the unbreakable bond between Savoy and the Empire. Master Rostang, is there space in our cellars for fifteen guests?"

"Yes, your grace. *Mm!* Our dungeons are scarcely occupied. One or two debtors, only."

"Then let these impostors experience the hospitality of Savoy. We may have to examine them to obtain their confessions. Do we have someone who can . . . you know . . . do the necessary?"

"*Mm!* No, your grace. When need arises, we usually borrow the executioner of Lyon. Or Milan."

"Well, send for one. And alert Villiers straightaway. When these scoundrels present themselves at our gate, arrest them. Wrap them well in chains and put them in the cellar, where they may meditate upon their sins. And, Rostang?"

"*Mm?*"

"Keep this quiet. We don't want word getting out that there are infiltrators looking to stir up trouble. We will examine them after Friday's exposition of the Holy Shroud."

"Very good, your grace. *Mm!*"

"My dear Count Lothar. How can I express the gratitude of Savoy for your intervention? You have prevented a great wickedness from achieving fruition."

"Your grace is too generous. What are friends for?"

40

Rehearsal

"I thought Count Lothar was rather good," Dürer said, looking very pleased with himself.

Dismas was in no mood for hallelujahs. He was depressed over not persuading Duke Charles to chase off the pursuivants before they reached Chambéry. What if they arrived at the Porte Recluse and presented incontrovertible bona fides? An imperial warrant, say, with an actual imperial seal rather than the archdeacon of Chambéry's? Dismas's scheme would come crashing down on them like the ramparts of Troy. Then would come a knock on the apartment door. Savoyard guards, to drag Dismas and Dürer and the rest of them off to the underutilized castle dungeon for a session of *peine forte et dure* with the moonlighting executioner of Lyon or Milan.

Nor was that the only problem. What was Caraffa up to? How was *his* plotting to steal the Shroud coming? And Dismas still had not solved the minor detail of how to switch Dürer's shroud with the real one.

" 'Oh, perfidy, thy name is François'?" he said. "A bit rich. I'd say, Vanity, thy name is Dürer."

Dürer stared archly. "Being a Swiss, you are doubtless unfamiliar with theater, and the other higher arts. But then for drama, you have your avalanches. And of course the annual leading of the cows from the winter barn to the summer pasture. What are the plays of Sophocles and Aeschylus beside *those* theatricals?"

"Sure, we didn't lack for drama tonight. I thought you'd draw your sword, shout, 'Death to François!' and leap out the fucking window."

"*I* thought he was good," Markus said.

"Thank you, Markus," Dürer said. "How encouraging to know that artistic excellence is not wasted on everyone of Helvetian persuasion."

Dürer stomped off to the kitchen.

"Touchy sort, is he?" Markus asked.

"Artist." Dismas shrugged.

Toward noon there did come a knock on the door. Dismas held his breath, but it was only one of Rostang's men, with a note saying there would be a rehearsal in the Holy Chapel that afternoon at four o'clock.

"Rehearsal?"

"For tomorrow's tableau, Master Dismas. The Last Supper."

"Ah."

Amidst everything else, Dismas had forgotten.

He went and banged on Dürer's door. Dürer had closeted himself within to pout over Dismas's failure to appreciate properly his latest manifestation of genius. Dismas banged again. Dürer opened the door, greeting Dismas with a baleful look.

Dismas handed him the note. "Your encore is awaited."

Dismas, Dürer, and Magda presented themselves at the chapel at the appointed hour. Inside was all activity. Costumes were laid out on tables. Workers everywhere, hoisting by pulley a great painted scenic backdrop with what appeared to be a nightscape showing rooftops of ancient Jerusalem under a gaudy full moon.

Dürer muttered, "Appalling."

The Holy Chapel had been transformed into the Upper Room, where Jesus and his disciples partook of the Passover meal the night before his death. To make the high-ceilinged chapel more intimate, a lower roof had been improvised with tent cloth. A large wooden table was set in front of the chapel altar. Dismas counted the requisite thirteen chairs, for Jesus and the twelve disciples. By the end of the evening, one of the chairs would be empty, Judas having slunk off to do his betraying.

Rostang saw them and came over. He looked harried but was his ebullient self. He bowed to Count Lothar.

"Ah! The apostle whom Jesus loved is here! *Mm!*"

"Impressive," Dürer said of the staging.

"His grace is meticulous. Especially for Last Supper tableaux."

One of Rostang's minions came over. Dürer went off with him to the changing area, to be transformed into the Apostle John.

"Might I be of assistance?" Magda asked Rostang. Before he could answer, she volunteered, "I'll go see if they can use me in the kitchen."

"Such a lovely girl," Rostang said to Dismas. "What a shame. *Mm!*"

"Shame?"

"That she is a nun. *Mm!*"

Dismas smiled. "Ah. Yes."

Rostang turned serious and lowered his voice. "There is news, Master Rufus."

"Yes?"

"Which I must ask you to keep to yourself for now. His grace is most concerned that nothing should interfere with the tableau, or the exposition of the Shroud. It appears that the dispatch was accurate. *Mm!*"

Dismas tensed. "Ah?"

"*Mm!* Only one hour ago the provocateurs attempted to enter by the Porte Recluse. There were fifteen, just as we thought. But thanks to God and your warning, Villiers was ready for them."

"Did they . . . resist?"

"Not for long. *Mm!* When you find yourself surrounded by the cream of Savoyard soldiery, pointing crossbows at you—the situation soon clarifies."

"I suppose they pretended innocence?" Dismas ventured.

"Oh, yes. *Mm!* They had with them some document purporting to be a warrant. But such things are easily forged. The French are masters of this. Rest assured, Master Rufus, we will get to the bottom of it. But after the Shroud. For now, these scoundrels are out of sight in a very damp part of the castle. Let us hope they do not suffer from rheumatism. Ah, Signore Caraffa. How is his grace Urbino?"

"Resting," Caraffa said. "He asks me to convey to your master his compliments. I am confident he will be able to attend this"—Caraffa looked about the chapel, somewhat at a loss for words—"event."

"Assure his grace of our prayers that he will join us. Now, if you will excuse me, there is much to do. Much! *Mm!*" Rostang scurried off, leaving Dismas and Caraffa alone.

Caraffa's manner was rather friendlier than before. "Strange little man. All this is amusing, don't you find?"

"Indeed, impressive," Dismas said.

"The Duke has offered my master the role of the Fisherman."

"A great honor. It's the second-best part, after all. And how appropriate, as his grace is nephew to a descendant of Peter."

Caraffa smiled. "Peter was not at his best that night. Did he not deny that he knew Jesus, three times?"

Some local nobles had arrived and were being shown their costumes.

Caraffa's tone was collegial and gossipy: "Duke Charles makes good money from these tableaux. Rostang tells me that to be an apostle tomorrow night, it's a donation of twenty-five ducats. The money goes to the poor of Savoy. So he says. To play the role of the dubious apostle, Thomas, it's only fifteen ducats."

"A bargain."

"He says it's always a problem to find someone to play Judas."

"Yes, I should think."

"Who will play Judas tomorrow? I wonder. For Judas really you need a Jew."

"They were all Jews around the table," Dismas said. "Strange, isn't it, that we are exhorted to abominate Jews, yet Jesus was one?"

"My master's uncle, the Pope, has been very lenient with the Jews of Rome. He has even permitted them a printing press. What can they be printing? I wonder. But he has borrowed great sums from them, so he cannot afford to treat them as they should be treated. His successor will restore a more correct perspective, I think."

"I should attend to my master."

"Before you go, Master Rufus, I must tell you something."

"Yes?"

"I have not been as courteous with you as I should have. I regret this."

"I took no offense, signore."

"His grace's health has been a great concern to me. And as we all know, it is not from altitude that he suffers. Your Sister Hildegard has been most helpful. His grace is grateful."

"She did nothing more than her duty."

"Perhaps. Still, his grace would like to show his gratitude."

"That is kind, but not necessary, signore."

"We can discuss that later. For now I will leave you to the preparations." Caraffa took a few steps, then turned back and said with a wink, "Don't let them cast *you* as Judas, eh?"

Dismas was glad to be rid of Caraffa's company. He went to mingle among the others, memorizing every detail.

Presently Magda reappeared.

"So?"

"I made a friend in the kitchen. The wine steward."

"I, too, seem to have a new friend. Caraffa. It seems you have made a good impression on Urbino. He wants to give you a reward."

"Do you still think they will try to steal the Shroud?"

Dismas considered. "Yes. Why else would he suddenly want to be my friend?"

Magda said, "Look there. Rostang."

Rostang was directing attendants who were carrying two large incense braziers. They placed them at either end of the table.

"Was there incense at the Last Supper?" Magda asked.

"His grace has a sensitive nose for smelly pilgrims."

Dismas watched. Another servant carried in the silver chest containing the incense. He set it on a stand next to one of the braziers.

Magda walked over idly and, affecting curiosity, lifted its lid. Delicately, with two fingers, she removed what looked like a pebble and held it to her nose. Rostang saw her and came over.

"Can you tell?" he said.

"Myrrh."

"Of *course* you would know! *Mm!* And now we are almost ready to begin. Finally!" He grinned and whispered, "Thank God, I was able to convince his grace not to wash the feet of the apostles. *Mm!*"

Dismas smiled. "My master would have been honored to have his feet washed by the Duke of Savoy."

Rostang took Dismas by the arm and with an apologetic air said, "Forgive me, Master Rufus, but I fear I must ask you for a very great favor. *Mm!*"

"Of course."

"It appears that we are lacking one apostle."

Dismas grinned. "Would it by chance be Judas?"

Rostang sighed. "Every time this happens. His grace would be very grateful if—"

"I would be honored."

The old man sighed with gratitude. "Now you are the apostle whom I love. *Mm!*"

Rostang turned to Magda, for whom he appeared to have great fondness. "If only I could ask you to participate, Sister. But I regret I cannot. His grace is very particular. He insists that the Last Supper tableau must be a true re-creation. There were no women. Though some silly people insist that the Magdalene was present."

"I understand," Magda said. "But allow me to help beforehand. In the kitchen they said they would be happy to have an extra pair of hands. I'll leave before the tableau commences." She smiled girlishly. "So as not to compromise your *authenticity*."

"Bless you. *Mm!* His grace does not even permit spectators in the chapel for the Last Suppers."

"No audience?" Dismas said. "But isn't the purpose of a tableau to put on a spectacle?"

"Normally, yes. Not the Last Supper. He feels it is too sacred. After all, there was no audience at the Last Supper."

"No, I suppose. Will the Shroud be on display?"

"The reliquary will be present. On the table. But the Shroud will remain inside. What a centerpiece, eh? *Mm!*"

"Beyond compare." Dismas smiled.

It came to him. He remembered a detail from his perusal of the Gospels in the archdeacon's Bible.

"Master Rostang, are you familiar with the Gospel of John?"

Rostang feigned umbrage. "I should hope. *Mm!*"

"My master would like to show his gratitude. He would like to contribute something to the tableau. A detail from the Gospel of John, as a thank-you."

"Which detail?"

"Well, as you recall, in the Gospel of John, when the Magdalene arrived at the sepulcher the morning of the third day, she looked inside and beheld . . . remember?"

Rostang brightened. "Two angels. All in white. *Mm!*"

Dismas nodded. "Sitting on either side of the Shroud."

"Mm!"

41

What Would Jesus Want?

"Do we have enough of this shit?" Cunrat asked.

"Don't call it that," Magda said. "But yes. I think. Perhaps. Anyway, we will find out if it is enough."

"That's cutting it close, isn't it?"

"If it's not enough," Dismas said, "then when you and Nutker enter, I'll signal you, so." Dismas pulled at the tip of his nose twice. "If I do that, then come in, look beatific for a bit, and leave. Nothing more. It will be my signal to abort."

"What's 'beatific'?" Unks said.

"Like an angel," Magda said. "For those two"—she indicated Cunrat and Nutker—"it will come naturally."

"Those two? Pah."

Cunrat said, "It's not a bad plan, Dismas. Maybe even a good one. But it depends on many parts, which must all work. Why don't we just torch the fucking chapel? In the smoke and confusion, we go in, pry open the grille with iron bars, and *pfft*, we are gone."

"We have discussed this, Cunrat. Again and again. We are not going to burn down the Holy Chapel. And you should pray that God is not hearing you suggest such a thing. Let me remind you—all of you. We are translating the Shroud. In a just cause. To keep it from being stolen by Urbino and Caraffa."

Markus groaned. "And what is Jesus telling you now, Dismas? Have you been having more speaks with him?"

"Don't be impious, Markus. Sure, Urbino and Caraffa have intentions on the Shroud. I am confident of this."

"And if they don't?" Cunrat said.

"Then they will leave in peace and go to Paris for the baptism of the French brat. And if our plan is sound, we will translate the Shroud of Chambéry."

"And then?"

Dismas sighed. "Well, Cunrat, what do *you* think we should do with the Shroud?"

"I'll tell you what our orders are. To bring it back to Albrecht. After we kill you."

Magda gasped.

"Don't worry," Cunrat said, "those were our orders. But that was before. We are all comrades, now."

Magda gave Cunrat a kiss. Then kissed Nutker and Unks. "You are good boys, all."

The Landsknechte blushed.

Cunrat said, "But being comrades, we should all have a say in what to do with our prize. I say we sell it. In Basel, at Dismas's relic fair. How much would it fetch?"

Dismas considered. He imagined the scene. What a delight for Schenk.

"A fortune," he said. "But the sale would have to be private. You can't just go to Basel and announce, 'Here is the Shroud of Chambéry, freshly stolen from the Duke of Savoy.' You put out word, quietly, to a half dozen of the top brokers. And see what the market will fetch."

"What *would* it fetch?"

"A very great sum, Cunrat. Enough so that every one of us would never have to worry ever again about money."

Unks rubbed his hands together.

"But before we count our shekels," Dismas went on, "let us ask ourselves . . . what would Jesus want? Would he want us to steal his Shroud from Duke Charles and sell it to the highest bidder?"

"He said, 'Blessed are the poor,' didn't he?" Cunrat said. "Well, we're poor."

"Yes. Good point," observed Nutker.

"Well," Dismas said, "if we want to quote scripture, let's also remember, 'And they divided up his garments among them, and cast lots for them.' "

Nutker said to Cunrat, "What's he talking about?"

Magda said, "Shame, Nutker. It's from the Gospel, Nutker. Did you *never* go to church?"

"I was only—"

"Counting your shekels. Even before you have them. *Nutker*. Don't you see Dismas is concerned for our souls?"

The Landsknechte looked at each other. Souls?

Magda went on: "If we steal Jesus's shroud only to sell it for money, what will we say to him on the Day of Judgment?"

Unks spoke. "I will say, 'Thank you, Lord, for the money I made from your Shroud. What a fine time I had spending it.' "

Nutker nodded. "I will say, 'Because of this money, I could retire from being a Landsknecht. No longer did I have to kill people to earn my living.' "

"Yes," Cunrat affirmed. "By taking the Shroud, Jesus is leading us to live good lives. Yes. Now I am seeing the workings of . . . what did you call it?"

"Divine grace."

"Yes, that."

Dürer shook his head. "What supple theologians you fellows have become."

"Hold on," Dismas said. "I am not so sure this is what Jesus has in mind."

Markus groaned. "Everyone. Stop. You are giving me a headache. Not you, Magda. 'What would Jesus want?' Sure, Jesus is laughing through his asshole, listening to you. It's a fake, the Shroud. They're *all* fakes. Dismas himself was sure it was fake until his brain turned to porridge because of what that cocksucker cardinal in Mainz did to him. Now he thinks a bedsheet is speaking to him."

"Hold on, Markus," Dismas said.

"Shut up, Dismas. Which I say as your friend. You are not yourself. How long have I known you? We have gone through hellfire together how many times? Before they did this thing to you, you would never have had speaks with *linen*."

Magda spoke up. "I think what Markus is trying to say is—"

"That I have lost my reason," Dismas said.

"Look," Markus said, "I don't know, or care, what Jesus thinks. If we are going to do this, let's do it. And if we are still alive tomorrow, then we can decide what to do with it. We'll vote. And give Jesus a vote."

No one spoke.

Dürer said, "I don't know if it's real. But real or not, I don't like the idea of that reprobate Urbino stealing it from Duke Charles. He's a sweetie pie."

So it was decided first to proceed, and then to decide how to proceed from there.

The Landsknechte announced that they were parched and must go out for a drink. Dismas gave permission, but exacted a promise they would not get stinking, for tomorrow would require everyone's wits.

Markus went with them, not because he was thirsty but because Dismas asked him to keep an eye on them. Magda went to her room to do her sewing, leaving Dismas and Dürer alone.

"Come on, then," Dürer said. "Give me a hand."

Dürer's shroud was laid out on the archdeacon's dining room

table. It had to be folded identically as the one in the chapel: that is, twice lengthwise, then twice across the width, then again and again until there were thirty-two layers.

They finished and regarded it in silence.

"It's good, Nars."

"Um. Even better than the Duke's. Far too good to give to that pig Albrecht. If we do succeed, what then?"

"It seems we're to vote on it."

"And if the vote is to return it to the Duke? Are you confident the lads will abide by such a vote? We're not town council."

"We'll find out, I suppose."

"It does seem extravagant, Dismas. To risk our skins to steal something that we might give back."

"Yes. It makes little sense. As little as thinking that a piece of cotton is speaking to you. But what sense does it make to believe that fifteen hundred years ago a man who was dead for three days sat up in his tomb?"

Magda was sitting athwart the bed, her back upright against the wall, sewing a pile of white fabric bunched about her legs. Dismas crawled onto the bed next to her and put his head in her lap and fell asleep.

When he woke in the morning he was glad that the Shroud had not spoken to him again in his dreams.

42

What If They Drink the Wine?

The tableau of the Last Supper would begin—"Promptly, if you please!" Rostang asked—at six o'clock.

Shortly after midday, Dismas and Magda went to the Holy Chapel to make a show of helping with the final preparations. The chapel was conveniently still aswarm with servants and workers.

Magda disappeared into the kitchen. Dismas went around the table, adjusting chairs and folding napkins, seeing to this and that. The silver incense chest was there, near one of the braziers at the end of the table. He crouched over it, as if admiring its fine silversmithing, and opened the lid. He reached in and took out a bit of myrrh to sniff. So doing, he tugged on a drawstring inside his sleeve, releasing into the chest the contents of a tubular sack that Magda had sewn into the lining. He closed the lid and continued with his chair adjusting.

Magda emerged from the kitchen. She nodded. Together they left the chapel.

Descending the chapel steps to the Court of Honor, they heard a sound. A carriage rumbled up the cobbled ramp into the courtyard. Then came another, and another, and still more—a dozen or so. As the carriages passed, Dismas saw on each the de' Medici ducal insignia. One of the carriages, painted light blue, he recognized as Caraffa's. They turned in a wide circle and came to a halt in front of the Royal Apartments across the courtyard from the chapel.

"What's this?"

He and Magda watched as footmen emerged from the entrance carrying baggage and loading it onto the carriages.

"Urbino's leaving."

"Thank God," Magda said.

Still more carriages arrived. Rostang emerged from the door of the Royal Apartments and walked across the courtyard to the chapel. He saw them, waved, and came over.

"What's going on?" Dismas asked.

Rostang made no effort to conceal his delight.

"Our distinguished guest departs for Paris and the baptism of the French brat. *How* we will miss him. *Mm!*"

"Is he not staying for the tableau and the exposition?"

"Alas. Signore Caraffa informs me that his grace is feeling poorly. And as the journey to Paris is long, he has resolved to make an early start. *What* a lot of luggage Italians have. But always they look so pretty. Well, Master Rufus, Sister—six o'clock, yes? *Mm!*"

Rostang scurried off.

Dismas's elation at this double benison—no attempt by Urbino on the Shroud, and Magda no longer exposed to danger—was such that he wanted to hug Magda right then and there. But as they were in a public place and as she was dressed like a nun, he refrained.

"Come, hurry!" he said excitedly.

He felt like a bird that had been released from its cage. His feet hardly touched the cobblestones. They hurried from the castle grounds and ran up the three flights of stairs to the archdeacon's apartment, Magda having to lift her nun skirts. Dismas burst through the door, startling Dürer and the others.

"Wonderful news!" he announced, gasping. "Wonderful, glorious news! The Italians—they're leaving! As I speak, they are loading their carriages and fucking off to Paris!"

"So?" said Nutker.

"Don't you see? It means they're not after the Shroud. Which means, my friends—my good friends—that *we* no longer must translate it!" Dismas collapsed into a chair. "What a fine day. *What* a fine day."

Cunrat said, "I thought we agreed to steal it first and then decide?"

"I, too," Nutker said.

"Lads," Dismas said. "Duke Charles is a good fellow. Why would we steal his relic?"

The Landsknechte considered.

"What about your penance, then?" Cunrat said. "All this time you've been mewling about going to Hell if you didn't perform your penance."

Dismas nodded. "Yes, my penance. Well, Cunrat, I have been thinking about this. Asking myself, what kind of priest gives as penance to steal the burial Shroud of Jesus? Would Luther give such a penance?"

Cunrat frowned. "*That's* convenient."

Dismas laughed. "I'm touched that you are concerned for my soul. I call that convenient."

"You said we'd snatch it, and then vote whether to sell it."

"Cunrat. The Italians are *leaving*."

"I don't see that changes anything. A plan is a plan. I say we see it through. And then vote what to do with it."

Dürer interjected a rather more practical matter.

"What about the wine and the incense?"

Christ, Dismas thought. In his elation over the Italian exodus, he'd forgotten.

There came a knock on the door. Dismas answered it. One of Caraffa's men, breathless.

"Signore Rufus! Sister Hildegard!"

"What's the matter?"

"His grace Urbino is stricken. Dying. He asks for the Sister."

"But isn't he leaving?"

"We were preparing to leave when came the attack. His confessor has been summoned. *Please*, Sister. He asks most urgently for you. And to bring your heart potion."

Magda gathered her apothecary bag.

"I'll go with you," Dismas said.

Magda signaled Dismas to close the door so the servant wouldn't hear.

"A moment," Dismas said, closing it.

Magda said, "You must go to the chapel."

"But—"

"I don't know what to do about the incense. But the wine is in a large earthenware jug, on a table next to the door into the chapel. There's a cloth with a small red cross over the jug."

"I can't just go into the kitchen and make off with the wine!"

"The wine steward is a fat man with a red cap embroidered with the ducal crest. His name is Bertrand. He flirted with me. Go into the kitchen and find him. Tell him . . . no, better—whisper to him: 'Sister Hildegard asks you to meet her after the tableau. In the castle garden.' He will be very happy to hear this, I promise you. Then, when you are leaving, knock over the jug, like a clumsy accident."

"What if it's not there? If they've moved it? What if it's served at the tableau?"

"Then," Magda said, "Jesus and his apostles will have a very happy Last Supper. Look, Dismas, the wine is there. Just go in and knock it over. What can they do but call you an oaf?"

"All right. All right. But the *incense*. What am I to do about that? Kick the chest over? Never mind. I'll think of something. But I don't want you going to him alone."

"Don't worry, Dismas. All will be well. He's dying. It will all be over soon." She kissed him and smiled. "Now, go and be a good Judas."

She left with the servant.

43

Let Us Ambulate Together

Dismas rushed to the Holy Chapel in great anxiety. Reaching the courtyard, he saw the train of carriages outside the Royal Apartments, still being loaded by servants. He thought this strange, as the Duke was dying. He hurried on until he heard his name being called.

He turned and saw Signore Caraffa approaching from across the courtyard. Why was the Duke's chamberlain not at his bedside?

"Ah, there you are," Caraffa said with discrepant jauntiness.

"Signore. I— How is his grace?"

"At rest."

Dismas placed his hand over his heart and bowed. "Accept my most profound sympathy at this wretched hour."

"No, no. He's sleeping."

"Oh. Your summons had us most concerned. Is Sister Hildegard attending to his grace?"

"Come, Master Dismas," he said. "It's a pleasant day. Let us ambulate together."

Dismas stood his ground.

"Why do you call me that?"

Caraffa smiled. "It's your name. How appropriate. Dismas the Good Thief. What was the name of the Bad Thief? Gestas? One only remembers the Good Thief. Why, I wonder? No matter. Come."

"Where is Sister Hildegard?"

"Am I your sister's keeper? Ah. I make a jocosity. I don't, usually. I am not a jocose person. Come."

Dismas started toward the Royal Apartments. Caraffa said after him, "You will not find her, Master Dismas. Don't make a scene. What can you gain if they learn who you are? And your purpose here?"

Dismas hesitated.

"It would be better for you to listen to what I have to say."

Dismas fell in beside Caraffa, heart pounding.

"Now, shall we first agree not to waste such a fine day with denials? Good. What a relief, that finally we can speak to each other without masks. Your friend, the so-called Count Lothar—he's good. I cannot rid myself of thinking that I have seen him before. Has he been to Florence?

"What he said, that business about how his godfather is the great champion of Savoy—*most* amusing. But what a sour face you make, Dismas. Are you not in the mood for badinage? Very well. Neither do I like to waste time. We are both busy fellows. I as chamberlain to his grace. You as relic master to Frederick of Saxony. And to the Cardinal of Mainz. Having two masters, you are even more busy than I."

Caraffa's bodyguards fell in on either side of them as they walked.

"Now, is it necessary to explain what I require? Surely not. You will give me something, and in return I will give you something. Look, the clouds. It's pretty, Savoy. It will make a nice part of France. So, we will see each other after the Last Supper? What a silly man is Duke Charles, with his tableaux. But how fortunate for us, eh?"

"I say we grab him and carve him piece by piece, until he hands her over."

"Don't be foolish, Nutker," Dismas said. "You wouldn't get within ten yards of him. It would take a troop of cavalry to penetrate his bodyguard."

Markus said, "*I* don't need to get close."

"Killing him with a crossbow bolt won't get Magda back."

"Why not go to Rostang?" Dürer said.

"For Christ's sake, Nars. Do you suppose Rostang will be pleased to learn who we are? In the Chambéry castle dungeon at this moment are fifteen imperial pursuivants with a warrant for our heads. Do you want to be handed over to them? Do you know how they execute killers of nobles in Swabia? They wrap you in chains and lower you into a pit of starving dogs. Slowly. So you're eaten piece by piece. It's called Cerberus, after the dog who guards the entrance to Hell. Want to experience *that*? We've no choice. Either we give Caraffa the Shroud, or it will go very badly for Magda."

"I don't understand," Dürer said. "How did this swine know?"

"It doesn't matter, Nars. He knows. Perhaps it was these."

Dismas held up his hands.

"A few days ago I forgot to put on my gloves. A colossal stupidity. Caraffa saw them. Someone like him would know of the various regional techniques. Of the Little Marionette. He would logically conclude that I am *not* a servant of a German count. And by the way, he thinks he's met you before. In Florence. No matter. Either we procure the Shroud for him, or Magda will endure torments I would prefer not to imagine."

Dismas stood.

"This is all my fault," he said. "I've no right to ask any of you to risk your lives. Leave Chambéry. Now. I will surrender myself to Duke Charles. He will make them give Magda back. For the rest, it doesn't matter."

It was Unks—simple, stupid Unks—who spoke.

"She's our Little Sister." Which was all that needed to be said.

"Even if we succeed and give this asshole the Shroud," Cunrat said, "can we trust him to give her back?"

"What choice do we have?"

Dürer said, "It's not much to put our hopes on."

Dismas considered, pacing the room.

His eyes lit on a miniature portrait under glass, hanging on the wall of the archdeacon's apartment. He pulled it off the nail.

"Nars. How long would it take you to paint this?"

"You want a copy of *that*?"

"No. A miniature. *Like* this."

"Well . . ."

"You've got one hour."

"An hour?"

"I'm not asking for a masterpiece, Nars."

Dismas explained his idea. Dürer went off to his room, muttering. An hour later it was done. Dismas replaced the glass cover.

"It's good, Nars. Good. All right, now, get some paper. I'll dictate."

Dürer wrote what Dismas spoke, occasionally looking up with an arched eyebrow.

When it was done, Dismas said, "Now give me the ring."

Dürer licked his finger and unscrewed Lothar's signet ring. Dismas rummaged through the archdeacon's desk. He removed a small leather pouch and put the miniature and the ring inside.

"Wait," he said to himself. He took the miniature out of the pouch and scrawled three words on the back, then replaced it in the pouch.

"Sword."

Dürer gave Dismas Lothar's engraved sword.

Dismas gave the pouch and sword to Markus and Unks.

"The carriages are outside the Royal Apartments. Caraffa's is the light blue one. Hide these inside. If you're challenged, say you are Rostang's servants and these are farewell gifts from the Duke himself. When you've done that, go to the stables. Get the horses ready."

Markus and Unks nodded and left.

Dürer said, "Will Rostang go for it?"

"We'll find out. If Caraffa keeps his side of the bargain, then we won't need it. If not, it's our only hope."

"God save us, Dis."

"Let's hope he's in a good mood."

44

The Last Supper

Dismas and Dürer paused at the foot of the stairs to the Holy Chapel.

"Will you be all right, Nars?"

"No. Yes. I don't know. Christ, Dis. What are we doing?"

Dismas handed him two wadded balls of flax.

"Remember, breathe through your nose."

"Stop telling me this. Four times you've told me. What's in the fucking wine anyway? More *ladanum*?"

Dismas stuffed his own nostrils with the balls of flax. "Some extract of mushrooms."

"Mushrooms?" Dürer said with alarm. "God in Heaven. Are we *poisoning* them?"

"No, Nars. Magda says it produces visions. Don't worry. Just don't drink it. And concentrate on breathing through your nose."

Rostang was all aflutter. He directed them to the changing room.

At six o'clock all was in readiness. The room was cleared of everyone but participants.

"Exciting, is it not? *Mm!*" Rostang whispered to Dismas. Rostang was participating, in the role of the Apostle Philip. The Savoyard noble who'd purchased the role had fallen off his horse en route to Chambéry this afternoon. Or so he claimed.

His grace the Duke of Savoy emerged from behind a curtain. The twelve apostles applauded.

Great effort had gone into his grace's wardrobe and makeup. He looked a very plausible—if dashing—Galilean carpenter, dignified yet ethereal. Charles blushed at the applause and made a little bow.

"Dearly beloved. Come, let us take our places."

Dürer had not required much makeup. His ginger ringlets and beard and fine slender face made him a fine choice for the disciple whom Jesus loved. He took his appointed seat, to the right of the Savior.

Dismas took Judas's seat at the end of the table, to be near the silver incense chest. The woman who did his makeup applied putty to his nose, to give it an exaggerated Semitic aspect.

He noticed that the other disciples, most of them drawn from the *gratin* of Savoyard aristocracy and officialdom, looked at him with unconcealed distaste. His smile was returned with cold eyes and tight lips. No wonder Rostang had a difficult time finding people to play Judas. Dismas thought: *This is what it's like, to be a Jew among Christians.*

The large earthenware jug of wine had been set on the table. Dismas recognized the tiny red crucifix on the napkin. He picked up the jug and went around the table filling everyone's cup. The sole "thank you" came from Duke Charles. Fitting, Dismas thought, that Jesus should be the only one at the table with manners.

Dürer absentmindedly raised his cup to his lips. Dismas cleared his throat loudly. Dürer caught himself and only pretended to drink.

The coals in the incense braziers glowed bright red. Dismas went to the chest, scooped out a copious amount of myrrh mixed with

Paracelsus's *Papaver* balls, and heaped them onto the coals. Great clouds of smoke billowed forth, wafting upward.

"Ah, myrrh," the Duke purred. "Of all the gifts of the magi, my favorite. Who would not rather have myrrh than gold?"

His nose twitched.

"Must be an old batch. Well, brethren, let us commence."

He raised his cup. "To him who brought us to the Upper Room."

Everyone drained his cup. Dismas immediately got up and went around the table, pouring refills to the brim. Again, only Jesus thanked him.

Dismas scooped more *Papaver* onto the coals, causing more opiated cumulus clouds to billow forth. The air inside the Upper Room grew thick.

Presently Dismas noticed that everyone's eyes had gone glassy. Speech became slurred. Encouraged, he kept pouring the mushroom-laced wine and filling the braziers with opium.

The disciple James, son of Alphaeus, became transfixed by the candle in front of him. He inserted his fingertip into the flame, blackening it. Thaddeus was stroking the beard of the disciple next to him, mesmerized, remarking that it felt like his wife's privvy parts. Bartholomew tore his unleavened bread into little pieces, which he made into balls, which he then attempted to juggle. James, son of Zebedee, thumped the table with the heel of his hand and put his ear to the spot, shushing the disciples as he listened.

"There," he said to Bartholomew. "Hear it?"

Intrigued, Bartholomew himself began thumping the table. Simon the Zealot became engrossed trying to extract his tongue with his fingertips while ululating.

Duke Charles clapped his hands together to quiet everyone. But then instead of speaking, he stared into his palms with intense curiosity.

"Ev-ery-one," he said. "Every*yyy onnnnne*." He rose to address his disciples.

"Verrrily I sayyyy . . ."

No one paid attention, being preoccupied with their own explorations of tongue extraction, fingertip immolation, and table thumping.

Duke Charles slumped against the disciple whom Jesus loved. He looked strangely sad.

Matthew slammed his cup down on the table hard and bellowed, "Lord!"

"Jesus! *What?*" said Duke Charles with a start.

"Am *I* the fucker who shall *betrayyyyyy-y-y* . . . ?"

Charles stared. "I haven't the faintest idea. Why? Who are you?"

"Mmm-athewwww."

Several disciples had formed a choral group and were making sounds resembling a cross between Gregorian chant and a pack of baying hounds.

Dismas wondered what the guards outside must be making of it.

"Stop! *Stopppppppp!*" the disciple Thomas demanded. "*There* is himmm who is the betrayer."

He pointed at Dismas and hurled his cup. It struck Dismas on the forehead. The other disciples joined in. Dismas ducked a blizzard of cups, candlesticks, and bread bits. He put up his hands to protect himself.

Charles began to giggle. "Now, now, boys."

Simon the Zealot had picked up the silver shroud reliquary and held it over his head, preparing to crush in Dismas's skull.

"N-n-n-noooo," Charles commanded. Simon set it down on the table with a loud thunk.

Dismas looked. A bat flitted back and forth beneath the tenting. Acting rather oddly for a bat, due to the opiated smoke.

Several disciples shrieked and took cover beneath the table. Others hurled objects at the bat, which continued to flit erratically.

Duke Charles leaned against Dürer's shoulder and began to cry, saying that he didn't want any last supper after all.

Dürer looked at Dismas with panic. Dismas was holding a napkin against his forehead to stop the bleeding.

Dürer mouthed, *"Do something."*

Dismas got up and went to chapel door and tapped three times. The guards opened the door slightly.

"What's going on in there?" the chapel guard asked.

"Glossolalia."

"Eh?"

"Speaking in tongues. Ready?"

Dismas turned and signaled Dürer, who was now patting Charles on the back to comfort him. He pointed to the chapel door and bellowed at the top of his lungs, *"Behold!"*

Silence descended like a mud landslide.

Dismas whispered to Cunrat and Nutker, "All right, lads, you're on. Remember, *waft*."

Cunrat and Nutker squeezed through the partly opened door, dressed angelically in the white robes Magda had sewn.

The apparition had a calming effect on the Upper Room. Charles looked up from Dürer's moistened shoulder. Disciples stared and gasped. Andrew fainted.

Dismas concealed himself behind Cunrat and Nutker's bulk as they approached the table, chanting melodiously.

"And on the third day, the Magdalene went to the tomb and, finding it empty, looked inside—and beheld *two angels*!"

Cunrat and Nutker wafted angelically toward the reliquary.

Cunrat opened the lid of the reliquary and took out the Shroud of Chambéry. He held it up dramatically, still folded, for all to behold.

Dismas saw with alarm that Cunrat and Nutker were breathing through their mouths, as he had instructed them firmly *not* to do. Cunrat's eyes were already glassy. Nutker was fumbling with difficulty inside his angel robe, where Dürer's shroud was concealed.

Dismas cleared his throat loudly, nearly sundering his esophagus. His *ahem* jolted the two angels out of their drugged trance. Nutker still fumbled for his shroud.

Finally he got it out and was about to slip it into the reliquary when Cunrat turned toward him. His elbow caught the edge of the reliquary and knocked it off the table onto the floor. It landed with an expensive clang and clatter. Dismas shut his eyes.

Cunrat smiled beatifically, as if knocking the reliquary off the table were part of an age-old ritual, ordained from on high. He and Nutker disappeared from view below the edge of the table.

A moment later, they rose. Cunrat hefted the reliquary back into place atop the table. Its lid was closed, Dismas saw. Nutker was fumbling beneath his robe. The switch was made. Nutker nodded to Dismas.

The two angels now wafted backward to the chapel door. A moment later, they were gone. It was done. *Consummatum est.* And thank God.

Charles and those disciples who remained conscious stared mutely into space.

Dismas gestured to Dürer: *I'm off.* Time for Judas to go about his nasty business.

Dürer gave him a stricken look. *Don't leave me.* Charles had ceased sobbing and now rested his head on Dürer's shoulder, eyes vacant and drooping.

Dürer would have to see it through.

Dismas quietly made his exit, through the door to the balcony.

He said to the guard, "I'm Judas. Have to go betray him. Might want to leave this door open. Bit stuffy in there."

"His grace does love his incense. Could use some out here."

He wrinkled his nose in the direction of the thousands camped in the plaza below.

"Stinky lot, pilgrims."

45

We Are Finished, You and I

Dismas tried not to break into a run as he hurried to the apartment. His only thought was to get the Shroud from Cunrat and Nutker and bring it to Caraffa.

He raced up the stairs. The tableau that greeted him now stopped him cold.

Caraffa stood at the center of it, holding the folded Shroud. The room was filled with his men, weapons drawn.

Nutker was on his back on the floor in a pool of blood. Cunrat was beside him, cradling his head. Nutker's eyes were open, unseeing.

"He wouldn't give it to them," Cunrat said.

Caraffa spoke.

"As I told you in the courtyard, Master Dismas, I don't waste time. Certainly not arguing with scum."

Caraffa gestured to his men. They seized Dismas and bound his wrists behind his back, and shoved him to the ground.

"You've got what you came for," Dismas said. "Let the girl go. That was the arrangement."

"Yes. But I serve my master, and my master has grown fond of your sister. So our arrangement, as you put it, is no more. What a pity for you."

Caraffa ran his hand over his prize, stroking it, as he might a pet cat.

"I congratulate you, Master Dismas. *What* a surprise will greet Duke Charles tomorrow when he opens his reliquary and finds it empty. How I would love to be there. But Paris beckons."

Dismas realized, *He doesn't know about the switch.*

"Are you a man of honor, signore?"

"The ultimate honor is victory, Master Dismas. And this I have achieved."

Cunrat spat: "Dago pig."

One of Caraffa's men kicked Cunrat between his legs. Cunrat rolled onto his side, groaning.

"They lack culture, Landsknechte," Caraffa said. "And lacking culture, they have no manners. What a pity. But no matter."

He continued to stroke the folded Shroud.

"But they are good fighters. I have seen them in battle. I can see why your Cardinal Albrecht would send them with you on your mission."

Dismas stared.

"Myself," Caraffa went on, "I, too, have grown fond of Sister Hildegard. What is her real name? When one is taking one's pleasure with a woman, it's only decent to call her by her real name. But it might be amusing to call her 'Sister.' I think best I take my pleasure with her before my master takes his. I don't want to catch his altitude sickness."

Dismas lunged at Caraffa's legs, an impulsive and futile impulse. Caraffa's men kicked him until Caraffa raised a hand to signal enough. Dismas lay on his side, writhing.

"Ah, Count Lothar joins us! What an honor!"

Dismas looked up and saw them seize Dürer. They tied his hands and shoved him to the floor with the others.

Dismas sat upright. Dürer looked at him with panic.

"I have been complimenting Master Dismas on his translation," Caraffa said. "Now I must compliment you. No doubt you were very good in your role at the Last Supper. As you were in your previous performances."

Dürer stared at the Shroud in Caraffa's hands.

Caraffa continued: "Have we met? I feel sure."

Dürer glanced at Dismas.

"No."

"I have a very good memory. In Florence? Or was it Venice?"

"I would remember someone as memorable as yourself."

Caraffa handed the Shroud to his lieutenant and crouched, face close to Dürer's. He reached with a finger and twisted ringlets of Dürer's ginger hair.

"So pretty." With his other hand, he took out his dagger and sliced off a handful of the ringlets. "A keepsake." He put the tip of the dagger to Dürer's cheek.

"What a shame, to mar such a handsome face. So I ask one more time: Where was it?"

"Tell him," Dismas said.

"Venice."

Caraffa smiled. He tapped the blade of his dagger on the top of Dürer's head like a schoolmaster reproving a recalcitrant student. He stood.

"The occasion?"

"Urbino and the Doge were making a visit to the Basilica di Santa Maria Gloriosa dei Frari. To inspect the progress on the altarpiece being done by Tiziano. *The Assumption of the Virgin.*"

"I remember! And what was your place in that tableau?"

"I am friend of Tiziano."

"I am impressed. And what are you doing in Chambéry, with this rabble, playing a noble?"

"They, too, are my friends."

Caraffa crouched again and held the tip of his dagger beneath Dürer's right eye.

"What shall I do with you, Count Lothar? Shall I remove this eye? Or . . ." He moved the dagger tip at the other. "I cannot decide. You decide. Which do you prefer to lose first?"

Dismas spoke. "He's Albrecht Dürer, the painter. Of Nuremberg. Do you want to be famous as he who blinded the greatest of the German painters?"

Caraffa rose, tapping the dagger blade against his palm.

"Dürer. I have heard of Dürer. *Are* you the greatest of the German painters? I wonder—*is* there such a thing as a great German painter?"

"Yes," Dürer said. "But they're rare. Almost as rare as Italians with morals."

They heard from below the heavy sound of carriage wheels on cobblestones through the open window. Caraffa went and looked. More sounds followed. More carriages and clattering of hooves.

"His grace departs."

Caraffa said to the lieutenant holding the Shroud: "Convey this to his grace. He is anxious to have it. Inform him that I will join him shortly on the Aix road. First I must attend to some details."

The lieutenant bowed and took the Shroud.

"Take Rosano and Griffani with you," Caraffa said. "Fulco?"

"Signore?"

"What you hold in your hands is more important than your life. Which you will forfeit if you do not yourself place it in Urbino's hands."

Fulco bowed and departed, taking two of the men. Five of Caraffa's bodyguard remained.

"Now," Caraffa said, "we must make a tableau of our own. What shall we call it?"

He crouched in front of Cunrat, smiled, and sliced open his throat. Cunrat gurgled, head sagging.

"We will call it Landsknecht with Throat Cut."

Caraffa stood and wiped the blood from his dagger.

"We will proceed in order of rank, from lowest to the highest. So, now . . . Hmm . . ."

Caraffa pointed the dagger at Dismas, then at Dürer, then again at Dismas.

"The Good Thief? Or the greatest of the German painters?"

He crouched in front of Dismas and said in a mock-apologetic tone, "I think you must be next, Master Dismas. For surely a great painter outranks a thief."

Dürer spoke. "You've given your master a fake."

"What can you mean?"

"The shroud. It's a copy. I made it."

Caraffa tut-tutted. "You should not lie, right before meeting God."

"I wouldn't. It's the truth."

Caraffa stood, face clouding. "What nonsense are you saying?"

"It's why I'm here," Dürer said. "He needed someone to make a duplicate shroud. To switch with the real one. But we weren't able to make the switch after all. The one you gave your man is the one I made."

Caraffa stared. He shook his head. "I don't believe you."

"Very well. Then stay. And tomorrow at noon, through that window there, you can watch the real Shroud of Chambéry displayed."

Caraffa glanced through the window.

Dismas said, "What will your master say, Caraffa, when he learns you've deceived him?"

Caraffa crouched and put his blade against Dismas's throat.

Dismas went on: "Your master is half mad from pox. He thinks the Shroud will heal him. When he hears that the real Shroud is hanging from that balcony . . . when he hears of the miracles in the square, what will be his reaction?"

"What *miracles*?" Caraffa snarled.

"Oh, there *will* be miracles. I heard the Duke and Rostang discuss it. Always there are miracles when a shroud is displayed. Good for business. How then will it go for you when Urbino hears, and thinks you've tricked him? When he learns that the shroud he hugs to his diseased body in hopes of a miraculous cure is a forgery? And that his own chamberlain has played him for a fool?"

Caraffa's blade pressed against Dismas's throat.

Caraffa stood and went to the open window and looked out. The chapel balcony was directly across, no more than thirty yards.

"Suppose what you say is true. And they display a shroud from the balcony. Suppose even that there are miracles. And my master hears of them. What does it matter? I have only to tell him that Charles was so mortified to discover that his reliquary was empty, that his precious Shroud had been stolen, that he displayed a copy. To avoid the humiliation of everyone learning of the theft. Who in the crowd would be able to tell the difference between the real Shroud and a copy?"

"Will your master believe that a fake shroud caused miracles?"

"One more word, *Reiselaufer*, and I will remove your tongue."

Reiselaufer, Dismas thought. *He knows everything. How?*

"Listen to me, Caraffa. For your own sake. What will Urbino think when he hears that pilgrims with pox were healed by the Shroud of Chambéry? He *will* hear. News of such things travels faster than a duke's carriage."

Caraffa stuck the dagger through Dismas's cheek.

Dismas's mouth filled with blood.

Caraffa returned to the window and stared out again. He spoke as if to himself.

"A perfect vantage point."

Dismas spat out a mouthful of blood and gritted his teeth against the pain.

"Yes," Caraffa went on, murmuring to himself, "perfect."

His gaze turned from the balcony to the square below. "So many pilgrims." He sniffed. "They don't need miracles. They need a bath."

Caraffa turned and looked about the place.

"This is the apartment of the archdeacon. Rostang told me that he had to requisition it for their surprise visitor."

He looked at the corpses of Nutker and Cunrat.

"What a mess. It looks more like an abattoir than the residence of an archdeacon. I fear it will be an even worse mess before we are finished." He chuckled. "How appropriate, for the archdeacon to die from a bolt fired by a crossbow from his own window. What symmetry?"

Caraffa gave instructions to one of his men. He was to fetch Silvio and Pelucco with their crossbows. And to have Andino, Sinzo, and Paulo prepare bombs, a dozen.

The man left.

"What are you doing, Caraffa?" Dismas said.

"Making arrangements. Because you have been so persuasive, Master Dismas."

Caraffa leaned out the window to have another look at the balcony across.

"To display it, the archdeacon and the two bishops hold it by the edge over the balcony. From here, it will be an easy shot for Silvio and Pelucco. They can shoot falcons—in flight—at two hundred feet. I have seen them do it.

"The archdeacon is usually in the middle. So Silvio will kill the archbishop, Pelucco a deacon. The other deacon will I think quickly retreat, with the Shroud. So there will be only a glimpse of the Shroud. Not enough time for it to cause miracles.

"Then Andino and the two others here will throw bombs into the crowd of pilgrims. *Boom. Boom. Boom.* To create some chaos. As if this was part of the plan by the Shroud robbers. To facilitate the escape of the accomplice who would catch the Shroud below, when it fell. But alas it did not fall. What do you think of my plan so far, *Reiselaufer*? The best is yet to come."

"Killing bishops and pilgrims. What a lot you and Satan will have to talk about."

Caraffa laughed. "So says he who tried to steal the burial Shroud of Jesus! Satan and I made our peace long ago. Killing pilgrims is unfortunate. But necessary. Of course, the point isn't to kill pilgrims. The bombs in the square are only a pretext. A bigger bomb will explode here, in this room. An accident, by the careless plotters. Whose bodies—that is, yours—will be found. So unpredictable, gunpowder. After such a *fracasso*, I don't think that Duke Charles will again display his shroud for a very long time. Not during the lifetime remaining to my master. Which anyway will I fear not be long.

"So now I must leave you. I must attend to Sister Hildegard, to see if she still has air inside her trunk."

"Wait," Dismas said.

"No, Master Dismas. We are finished, you and I."

"How did you know?"

Caraffa hesitated. He shrugged.

"If it will make your last hours even more unpleasant, why not tell you?

"My master was tasked by his uncle the Pope, to whom he owes very much, to procure for him the Shroud of Chambéry. Since our plan was to pass through Chambéry on our way to Paris, the opportunity presented itself.

"Cardinal Albrecht learned of our plan. The Vatican is full of spies. But since my master's uncle is the Pope, *we* are the best informed of all.

"Albrecht sent Leo a letter, saying that he would be happy to procure the Shroud for the Pope, on the condition that the Pope release him from having to pay him half the indulgence money. Albrecht said he would send the best relic thief in all Europe. He said we would be able to recognize him by his hands.

"Leo did not answer the cardinal. Why give up half of Albrecht's indulgence money? And now we had this very useful piece of information. And here we are.

"And now I must go, or Sister Hildegard will, as you would say, suffocate, *sure*."

46

Places, Gentlemen

Dismas and Dürer sat, backs against the wall with the stiffening corpses of Nutker and Cunrat.

The wound in Dismas's cheek seeped blood into his mouth, causing him to spit gobs. Caraffa's men kept a relaxed vigil over their immobilized charges. The boss was gone. One of them found a bottle of wine. Another, searching for loot, returned with Dürer's sketchbook.

"You're a painter?"

The guards were impressed by his portrait of Magda.

"Is there one of her without clothes? I'd like to see *that*."

Laughter.

Dismas murmured, "Don't. They're trying to provoke you."

The soldiers were taken with Dürer's portfolio. They flipped through the leaves. Here was a landscape of the Bauges; a cityscape of Chambéry; Duke Charles on his throne; Urbino recumbent, pale with approaching death.

Dürer said to them, "You like my stuff?"

"Our painters are better."

"Have you ever had your portrait painted?"

"Why should I?"

"Who will remember you when you're gone?"

"All the girls I've fucked."

"And when they're dead? Who'll remember you then?"

"Who cares?"

"My portraits make people immortal."

"Listen to this asshole."

"Why do you think emperors and princes pay me good money to paint them? So they'll live forever."

"All right, then. Paint me."

"I don't work for nothing."

The guard held out the wine bottle.

"One drink, for my portrait."

"I get more than one drink for my work."

"All right. A drink—and I won't cut off your balls."

"How can I paint you, with my hands tied?"

The guards murmured. The one seeking immortality drew his dagger and crouched in front of Dürer. He sniffed.

"Any tricks, German, I'll peel you like an orange." He reached behind Dürer and cut the rope.

Dürer rubbed the circulation back into his hands.

"Bring me my case," he said. "The wooden box. In the room where you found the sketches."

The guard brought the case.

"I need more light. By the mirror, there."

Dürer slowly and painfully got to his feet. As he did, he swiveled toward Dismas and, concealed from the guards' view, slipped behind Dismas's back a palette knife.

Dismas began to saw.

Dürer arranged his sitter by the mirror. He called for more candles and began. He sketched leisurely with the charcoal, knowing very well how people are fascinated to watch as their likeness is conjured into existence. Soon the guards were absorbed watching as he drew their comrade. They stood intently over his shoulder.

"You're making him too handsome!"

"Shut up," said the sitter. "Keep at it, German. Make me beautiful and maybe I'll give you two drinks before I cut off your balls."

Dismas sawed with the palette knife. He saw Nutker's dagger, still sheathed.

One of the soldiers lost interest in the portrait and turned away. He went to get the wine bottle and resumed watching, a short distance from the others.

The rope parted. Dismas shifted the palette knife to his left hand. He filled his lungs and sprang, seizing Nutker's dagger with his free hand.

He plunged the palette knife into the side of the wine drinker's throat, and in the next motion buried Nutker's dagger between the shoulder blades of another man. Both went down. Now Dismas was unarmed.

Dürer lunged at one of the two guards, who gave him a blow to his face, knocking him down. He and his comrade turned their fury on Dismas, swords drawn.

Dismas knew it was over. They were young and strong. He was too old for hand-to-hand. He stepped backward over the body of the dead guard and tripped. He went down hard, air knocked out of him. He looked up and saw the two swords coming at him. But it wasn't over.

He heard a roar, a savage sound, Unks hurtling himself at Dismas's attackers with such fury the three of them flew through the air and crashed into the floor. Unks decapitated one man with a sword slice and, with its hilt, pounded the other man's face into a jam of gore. Unks's fury did not abate. He continued to pulp the man's skull until Markus pulled him off.

Unks sat panting. He crawled, murmuring and weeping, to the bodies of his comrades.

Cunrat was still alive, barely. Unks lifted Cunrat's head and pressed it to his chest.

Cunrat's eyes flickered. They looked at Dismas, lips moving.

Dismas put his ear to Cunrat's mouth.

"The rag . . ."

"It's all right, Cunrat," Dismas said. "We'll get it back for you. Promise."

Cunrat shook his head.

"No . . . Nutk . . ."

Cunrat died. Unks began to wail, hugging his lifeless friend, rocking back and forth.

There was no time for obsequies. Dismas told Markus and Unks of Caraffa's plan, the crossbowmen, the bombs.

"We must go," Dürer said, rubbing his jaw where he'd been struck.

Dismas looked at his friend.

"You did well, Nars."

"We have to *go*, Dis."

"No," Dismas said.

"Dismas. Five are coming back. With weapons. Bombs."

"Yes, Nars. Which we need. Markus, Unks, get ready. Nars, go to your room."

"Why?"

"I need you to live. To take the dispatch to Rostang. If I'm killed, you've got to see it through. Bolt the door to your room."

"But—"

"Bolt the door, Nars. Do it."

Dismas turned to the others.

Markus was assembling his crossbow. As he did he said, "And if they come back, all five of them together?"

Dismas sighed. "We have the advantage of surprise."

"At this range a bolt will go through two, even three men. Once I got four. But that was lucky."

Dismas said, "If I'm killed, see it through. Make sure Nars delivers the dispatch to Rostang. It's the only way."

"Will Rostang believe?"

"It's the only way. Caraffa has thirty men. We are four. Swear you'll see it through, Markus."

"Why did I stop in Chambéry? I would be walking now on gold cobblestones."

"You'd have been shipwrecked on the way. Or died from puking. Swear."

"Yes, all right."

47

He'd Better Be

Boots, coming up the stairs.

Dismas stood next to the door, back flattened against the wall, clutching sword and dagger. Unks was on the other side. Markus crouched behind an overturned table at the far end of the room facing the door.

"Don't shoot *us*," Dismas whispered.

The footsteps neared. From the sound, it was the five of them.

Dismas's heartbeat quickened. His cheek wound oozed blood.

On the landing now.

Caraffa's men threw open the door and entered the room. They froze.

Dismas and Unks attacked, pushing them together for Markus. Markus stood and fired. The bolt went through the throat of the first man and into the chest of the man behind him, through him, and into the wall. Unks quickly killed two; Dismas the one remaining. It was over in seconds. The archdeacon's apartment was a true abattoir now, strewn with eleven bodies.

Markus and Unks seized weapons from the dead. A good harvest: two crossbows and two boxes with the bottle bombs.

There were a dozen, packed with gunpowder, fuses protruding through the corks. One was larger than the others—probably the one they planned to detonate in the apartment, that would "accidentally" kill the Shroud stealers, thwarting their vile plot.

"Careful with those," Dismas said.

"This one," Unks said, holding the largest, "I will light and stuff up his Dago bunghole."

Dismas went to Dürer's room.

"Nars. Open up."

The door slowly opened a crack. Dürer peered at Dismas from within, palette knife clenched in his hand.

"Is it . . . ?"

"Yes, over."

Dürer exhaled and opened the door.

"Get dressed," Dismas said. He left Dürer to his wardrobing and went back to the others.

Markus said, "What if Rostang doesn't go for it?"

"Then, Markus, we will die."

Dismas's legs went out from under him. Markus caught him and put him in a chair.

"We have to stop the bleeding."

Markus went to the kitchen and shortly emerged with a red-hot poker. He summoned Unks.

"Hold him."

Unks gripped Dismas's head. Markus pushed the tip of the poker into the hole in Dismas's cheek. Dismas passed out and awoke to the smell of roasted flesh.

Markus held out an open palm with one of Paracelsus's *Papaver* balls.

"For the pain."

Dismas shook his head.

They heard a rumble of carriage wheels and hooves on cobblestone. Dismas peered cautiously from the window. Caraffa.

There came a second carriage behind his, with a large trunk strapped to the rear. Dismas counted the riders. Thirty. Caraffa's bodyguard, his *truppa elite*.

Dismas went to Dürer's room. Dürer was dressed now, sitting at his table, the dispatch before him. He looked miserable and pale.

"It's time, Nars. You know what to say."

"Yes," Dürer said. "And when Rostang has me thrown into the dungeon, what shall I say then?"

"Well, he's a decent old thing. And Charles is Charles the Good. You could appeal to their Christian sense of mercy. Offer to be his court painter. Who knows? You could become the greatest painter in all Savoy."

Dürer picked up the dispatch. It was sealed, like the other, with the archdeacon's seal of office.

The two men stared at each other awkwardly, knowing this was likely their last meeting.

"God be with you, Nars."

"He'd better be."

At the door, Dürer turned. "Dis."

"Yes?"

"Get her back."

48

The Bridge

Dismas, Markus, and Unks left by the Porte Recluse and turned north toward Aix.

They rode hard, spurring their mounts bloody. They kept to the Rue du Bois, the forest road that paralleled the main one. It was imperative they intercept Caraffa before he joined up with Urbino's train and its hundreds of cavalry and foot soldiers. After that, he would be unassailable. They had to reach the bridge before he did.

The forest road was rough, and tricky work by night, but being on horseback they had the advantage of speed over Caraffa's carriage. In every other way, the advantage was his.

They made the bridge in under two hours. The horses were nearly dead. Dismas guessed they were less than a half hour ahead of Caraffa.

They left Unks to examine the bridge while they searched for a perch for Markus and his crossbows. There was a group of boulders about fifty yards from the bridge. Beyond them was a dry riverbed and some bushes where they could conceal the horses.

"Is the range too far?"

Markus gave him a rebuking look.

"I wasn't trying to insult you."

They left their weapons at the boulders and went to assist Unks at the bridge.

He was grunting with exertion, trying to pull up one of the planks by himself. The bridge was of the kind they'd crossed the day they entered Chambéry: the Italian design, with the planks that could be pulled up to stall an advancing army.

They hitched a rope to one of the horses and pulled up enough planks to make the bridge impassable. With luck, if Caraffa and his train were moving fast in the dark, they might not see the gap in time. They toppled the planks into the waters of the Leysse and watched them flow downstream and washed up against a sandbar.

They returned to the boulders and took up their position. Markus assembled the three crossbows. He reviewed with Dismas and Unks the machinery of the cranequins and the loading, then laid out his bolts neatly on a flattened roll of leather.

"If they come before first light"—Markus shrugged—"I'm good, but I can't see in the dark."

Unks proposed that he conceal himself beneath the bridge with two "pomegranates," as he called the bombs. When Caraffa's carriage halted, he would toss them inside.

Dismas shook his head. "Magda might be in the carriage with him."

"I thought you said she was in the trunk."

"We don't know for sure, Unks. He might . . ." He didn't wish to complete the thought.

"Then I'll look inside first. And if she's not in there with him, in they go."

"You'll be surrounded. They'll cut you to pieces. There are thirty of them, Unks."

"I wish there were fifty."

"Too risky. And, if it's dark, how will you know who's in the carriage? We'll decide later. If he comes after first light . . . then maybe."

Unks nodded.

Dismas said, "Once Caraffa realizes what's happening, you know what he will do."

Dismas had a clear image of the scene: Caraffa holding Magda with a knife to her throat. What then? Pray Markus could kill him at this distance, without killing Magda? Pray he was the second coming of Wilhelm Tell?

"If she's in the trunk, and they move to get her," Markus said, "I'll make it cost them."

Dismas tried to imagine how it would play out. It was dark, pomegranates were unreliable, Caraffa's elite wouldn't just sit still while Markus leisurely porcupined them. Everything depended on Dürer.

And *that* was . . . Dismas slumped against a boulder, immensely weary.

"Once it starts," Markus said, "they'll organize themselves quickly. I'll get as many as I can. But they'll come at us, hard." He grinned. "Remember, at Cerignola? When d'Alègre called retreat, and the fucking *jinetes* still came at us?"

"Must we relive Cerignola now, Markus?"

"I'm only trying to cheer you up. We survived Cerignola."

"Thank you for this encouragement."

The three of them sat in silence. There was nothing left to say. It was cold. Dismas's cheek hurt very much. He thought of Magda, of what she must be enduring, bound, inside a trunk, bouncing along a rough road; or enduring a hell of a different kind, inside the carriage, prelude to a hell even worse. He forgot his own pain.

Dismas opened his eyes and looked up at the sky to say a prayer. He saw the first traces of the new day turning the sky pink over the Bauges. His last dawn? No matter. That would be settled before the sun, now casting warming rays on the soft hills above, sank tonight beneath the foothills of the Jura. Dismas watched as the sky lightened, feeling a strange calm. He wanted to sleep. Then came a thunder of hooves from the south, on the Aix road.

49

Suggestions, Gentlemen?

There was no need to whisper at such a distance. They did so out of soldiers' habit.

"In this light, they'll see the gap."

"Yes," Markus said. "But now there's light for me. Keep me loaded."

Unks lit his fuse. His pomegranates lay next to him in two rows.

Four horsemen preceded Caraffa's carriage, two and two. The light was faint. They didn't see the gap until too late. The two in front reined up sharply but the hooves skidded on the dew-slick wood and slid forward into the gap. They went through into the water.

The two horses behind stopped in time, but the four carriage horses behind them crashed into them, pushing them forward into the gap. The carriage driver braked to a halt. The four riders who'd gone into the river flailed as they made for the riverbank.

Markus murmured to his targets. Dismas had forgotten this habit of his.

"Come on . . . out of the carriage . . . Don't you want to see what's happening? Come on, signore."

But Caraffa did not emerge. The chaos in front of the carriage gave way to discipline in the rear, as two lines of riders advanced forward, forming a shield on both sides of the carriage.

"Neatly done," Markus said. "Sure they're Italian? All right, fellows. Want to be orderly? Let's be orderly."

Markus fired. A soldier dropped to the ground off his horse.

"Only twenty-nine to go. Weapon."

Dismas handed him the loaded crossbow and gave the spent one to Unks to reload. Unks rotated the cranequin deftly and quickly. The string drew back taut and snapped into the catch.

Markus fired. Another man fell.

"Twenty-eight."

Caraffa's men were pointing in various directions, trying to locate the attacker's position.

"It won't take them long," Markus murmured, aiming. "We must make the best of it." He fired. "Twenty-seven."

Caraffa's men were pointing now at the boulders.

"Unks, ready," Dismas said. "Wait till they're close."

Six riders charged. Markus dropped two. When the four others were in range, Unks stood and hurled his pomegranates. They sailed through the air, fuses leaving a cindery comet trail. The riders, intent on their charge, didn't see them.

After the blasts, there was a sickly silence and choking clouds of smoke. Then cries of wounded men and beasts. As always it was the cries of the horses that tugged at the heart. Why? Dismas wondered.

Taking advantage of the stunned confusion, Markus got off two more shots toward the carriage.

"Twenty-three."

Caraffa's men were now dismounting and scrambling for cover. A voice came from inside the carriage, livid and commanding. Caraffa. Dismas listened.

"Markus, the *trunk*!"

Two men were approaching it, covering their movement behind the carriages. Markus fired. A man went down on the ground, screaming and clutching at the bolt embedded in his shin. A remarkable shot.

Markus aimed again. The second man fell writhing, a bolt in his ankle.

"Twenty-one."

"Do you ever miss, Markus?"

"You asked me that on the Rhine."

Caraffa's voice again came from inside the carriage, more furious, shouting commands.

Six of his men remounted and rode directly away from their attackers, protected by the carriage.

"Cowards," Unks said. "Look how they flee!"

"No," Dismas said. "They're flanking us."

When the riders had put themselves beyond the range of Markus's crossbow, they turned ninety degrees to the right.

Another six now rode away in a similar maneuver. When they were out of range, they turned ninety degrees to the left.

Dismas looked behind toward the dry riverbed and bushes where the horses were tethered.

"They'll come at us from behind, there. Suggestions, gentlemen?"

Unks put his pomegranates into a sack and slung it—gently—over his shoulder, lit fuse in his other hand.

"Let them approach," he said. "Pretend to surrender. Like that day in the forest. Put up your hands. Then quick-quick, down."

Unks ran off.

"Well, let's not waste time," Markus said. He aimed at the carriage, searching for targets. "Now that we know she's in the trunk and not the carriage, let's see if we can make Signore Caraffa shit his fine breeches."

Markus fired. The rear window of the carriage shattered. From inside came a shriek, but one of surprise, not pain.

Markus mimicked an excretory sound.

Dismas looked behind. The first group of riders was approaching the riverbed in a wide circle, keeping out of crossbow range.

The attackers now emerged from the riverbed and made for the boulders, swords out, charging.

"Look scared. Put down the crossbow and stand, arms in the air."

Dismas and Markus held up their hands in surrender. The sight of charging cavalry made Dismas long for his halberd.

Markus saw it first: a small, round object with a bright little sizzling yellow tail, spinning. Up it went, then downward in a parabola.

"Down!"

Dismas and Markus hugged the earth.

The air ripped, as if torn. A blizzard of glass splinters *tinked* against the rocks behind them. They lifted their heads and looked out across the smoking field. Another piteous cacophony of beast and men. Four men lay dead. The other two rolled about, clutching their faces.

"Seventeen," Markus said.

The second group of riders halted a hundred yards away, deciding a course of action.

Had they spotted Unks in the bushes?

"Stay on the trunk," Dismas told Markus. "Caraffa will be in a rage by now. Sure, he'll try for it again."

The six horsemen had now formed a plan. They fanned out, keeping a distance from one another as they spurred their mounts toward the boulders. Unks wouldn't be able to get more than two with one bomb.

He emerged from his cover and hurled his pomegranate at the closest rider, sealing his fate. Three horsemen wheeled and charged him.

"Down!"

Dismas grabbed the back of Markus's coat and yanked him down.

The bomb exploded, killing rider and horse. Two riders charged at Dismas and Markus. The other three had reached Unks and were hacking at him with swords.

Markus fired from his hip, dropping one horse. Its rider pitched forward but expertly rolled and came up, sword in hand.

Dismas faced the other. He sidestepped and swung his sword, missing. The rider wheeled and charged again. His sword caught Dismas on the shoulder. But when he turned to finish him, Dismas swung with his blade and knocked him off the horse.

The other was now flailing away at Markus, who deflected blows with his crossbow. Dismas ran at Markus's attacker from the side, screaming to distract him. The man turned to confront Dismas. In the next instant he went down, a bolt in the side of his skull.

Fourteen.

Dismas looked toward the bushes. Two of the three horses were riderless. The third rider was slumped forward in his saddle, clutching his arm.

Unks?

"Stay on the trunk," Dismas said. He ran to the bushes.

He found Unks in the bushes, on his back, neck and chest sliced open. They were mortal wounds.

He knelt and put his hand on Unks's shoulder. Unks nodded.

Dismas picked up the still-lit fuse and ran back to Markus.

"Unks?"

Dismas shook his head.

Markus pointed. "See how the carriage is tilting? Caraffa's having a conference with his boys through the window. They don't want to expose their legs—for which I cannot blame them—so they're standing on the running board." Markus raised his crossbow and fired.

The bolt went through the center window. A body dropped to the ground on the other side of the carriage. Legs appeared, scampering and hopping madly like crickets, going for cover behind the rocks. The carriage wobbled and righted.

"Count?" Markus asked.

"Thirteen."

The rider Unks had wounded now reached the carriage. His comrades pulled him from the saddle.

"That's not good for us," Dismas said. "He'll tell them we are only two. They will make another charge, I think."

"I wonder if they're eager to charge."

"Caraffa will be giving them a choice. Charge, or be thrown into a pool of lampreys. Or whatever they do in Urbino to make an example of shirkers."

Markus cranked the two remaining crossbows. Dismas balanced two bombs in the crook of his arm, fuses in the other.

"Here they come."

Six, spread out in a wide semicircle.

Markus dropped one rider.

Dismas lit the fuses of both bombs. He tossed them, one after another. Two more riders went down in a vicious hail of glass splinters.

Ten.

Markus fired his last bolt.

Nine.

The two remaining attackers had now reached the boulders. Markus defended himself with his crossbow as before. Dismas threw himself under his attacker's horse, but as he tried to rise, became entangled in the horse's hind legs. The horse came down on him.

He felt all the air being squeezed out of him. His eyes bulged as if they might burst from his skull. The animal thrashed and kicked. Everything went black.

50

Why, Hammering?

Dismas opened his eyes.

He looked up at the sky. It was a fine, brilliant blue. Into his view above came Caraffa. He felt a sharp blow between his legs and gasped. He tried to cover his groin but his hands could not move.

He became aware of the sound of hammering. Why, hammering?

When he opened his eyes again, Caraffa was no longer there. He twisted his head to see. There was Markus, next to him. He was stripped to the waist, hands and feet tied to stakes. Ah, so this was why he could not move his own hands.

Now came a sound, a woman. Lamentation. Weeping. He lifted his head.

Magda. Alive, God be thanked. She was tied to the wheel of Caraffa's carriage.

"Magda!"

"Dismas!"

Caraffa appeared again and there came another painful blow to his groin. Dismas gasped.

More hammering. Were they making coffins?

Dismas craned to see in the direction of the hammering. He saw the two men who were making the noise. He craned some more. They were hammering at planks from the bridge. Were they repairing the bridge? But you had only to slip the planks back in. The whole idea was for the planks to be removable.

He was not thinking clearly. He understood this. He remembered now being crushed by the horse. Perhaps it had squeezed too much blood into his brain.

Again he heard Magda. She was pleading. For him.

Caraffa's face appeared above Dismas again. No longer scowling. Smiling. Not a warm smile, but a smile, still.

"Master Dismas. You are awake. That's good. You mustn't sleep through this. We cannot have that. No, no."

"Magda."

"She's over there. In a moment, you will have a much better view of her. Yes. What can I get you? Something to drink? Some vinegar and gall, perhaps?"

Vinegar and gall. Why did this sound familiar? Dismas could not think why.

The hammering ceased. One of Caraffa's men was saying something to him. Caraffa crouched, closer to Dismas's face.

"We are ready for you," he said. Caraffa poked at Dismas's palms. He laughed. "You already have holes in your hands. And your feet. We will make new ones. And afterward, you will have your *own* shroud."

Dismas felt the ropes around his wrists being untied. Hands lifted him by the shoulder, dragging him over the ground. He bent forward, to see. Markus was now also being gathered up.

On the ground nearby were two crosses, fashioned from the bridge planks.

"I thought to make a third," Caraffa said, "for Sister Hildegard. Then we would have three crosses, like in the Gospels. But my master is fond of her. And since my master will be very unhappy to hear that a shroud will be displayed today in Chambéry, we must not make him even more cross. Cross. I make another jocosity. What an effect you have on me, Master Dismas. So we will have only two crosses. One for the Good Thief, and one for the Bad."

Caraffa thrust his face in Dismas's. "But I don't think you will find yourself today in Paradise."

He gave the order. Dismas and Markus were laid on the crosses. Markus kicked and writhed and swore, calling out all manner of names.

Dismas did not, though he could not think why, for he understood what was about to happen.

He lifted his head to see Magda. Her namesake, the Magdalene, had been there at Golgotha. To give witness and comfort. She was weeping, poor Magda. He shouted to her.

"Magda. Close your eyes. I'll be waiting for you in Heaven."

He felt his arms being spread against the crossbeams, his wrists held fast against the wood. He felt the prick of something sharp in his palm.

One of the men said to the other, "If you hit me with that fucking hammer, I'll kill you."

"Look. He's smiling. What are you smiling for, piece-of-shit German? Don't you see we're going to crucify you?"

"Well," Dismas said, "you see, I've done this before. It's not so bad, once you get used to it."

"Ah? Then get used to this."

Dismas closed his eyes and waited for the pain.

Then came shouting and a great commotion. The clang of steel. Was this the sound of death, then? Dismas kept his eyes closed. Yes, better that way.

51

Vois. Ci. Loth.

One.

Caraffa. All his men were dead now.

They had tied him to a carriage wheel, as he had Magda.

He was screaming and shouting and cursing, indignant. With reason, for he was innocent of these absurd accusations that he was the killer of Count Lothar, a French agent, a provocateur who murdered the godson of the Holy Roman Emperor and made it look like the work of Savoyards, to drive a wedge between the Emperor and Savoy, so as to make Savoy vulnerable to France. Absurd! Preposterous! Insulting! Not only to himself, but to the dignity of His Grace Lorenzo, Duke of Urbino! When Urbino heard of this outrage, at the hands of German ruffians, their heads would be forfeit! He would—

Caraffa was silenced by a meaty cuff to the side of his head. His head hung limply.

The leader of the pursuivants was a severe-looking man, one Gruner. In one hand he held a miniature portrait of the late Count

Lothar; in the other, the same Lothar's signet ring. One of his men standing next to him held Lothar's inscribed sword, a gift from his exalted godfather. All these things they had found concealed in Caraffa's carriage.

Gruner examined the words on the back of the portrait: *Vois. Ci. Loth*. Here is Lothar. It was by this portrait that Lothar's killers identified him. Now, their leader was tied to the wheel of his carriage. How foolish of him to keep such pieces of evidence—and in his own carriage.

Gruner said to the man who stood in front of him: "Why would he do such a thing?"

The man whom Gruner addressed was an imperial agent. It was he who had secured their release from the Chambéry dungeon. A tall man, handsome, with abundant ginger-colored hair.

The imperial agent pointed to the bottom of the miniature, to a monogram: *AD*.

Gruner said he did not grasp its significance.

The imperial agent explained that this indicated that the portrait was the work of Albrecht Dürer, the greatest painter in all Germany. Some said, in the entire world. Therefore this painting, even though a small one, was valuable.

Gruner shrugged and said even so, it was foolish of Lothar's killer to have kept it. As it was foolish of him to have kept Lothar's signet ring and sword. But no matter.

He held a parley with his men. Caraffa had revived now and was able to hear what was said. As he spoke German, he could understand every word.

The pursuivants were in no good temper. They had been on the trail of Lothar's killers for six weeks. Then, on entering Chambéry, they'd been arrested, for mystifying reasons. They had spent days in a wet dungeon.

Gruner's lieutenant proposed summary execution. Their warrant allowed it. He proposed this be accomplished by leaving their prisoner tied to the wheel as they set off for home.

Hearing this, Caraffa became agitated and renewed his remonstrations, spitting fury at his captors and calling them unspeakable names.

Gruner himself now walked over and delivered him a blow to the side of his head that left him bleeding and unconscious.

Their conference resumed. At length Gruner announced his decision. They would bring Lothar's murderer back to Swabia, to have good German justice. For murdering the Emperor's godson, the sentence would be the Cerberus. So it was decided.

The company mounted. They were eager to be gone from Savoy.

Gruner said to the imperial agent, "Will you come with us?"

The agent shook his head. "No, Captain. My work keeps me here."

"We are in your debt."

"It was only my duty, Captain. It's I who thanks you for your help in rescuing these." He pointed to Dismas and Markus and Magda.

"God save the Emperor."

"God save the Emperor. Captain. A word of caution. If you go by way of Aix, best gag and hood your prisoner. He has friends there. Italians, like himself."

"No more towns for us. We go by the Bauges."

"Wise. God protect you."

Dürer and Dismas and Markus and Magda watched until they disappeared into the forest. Only then did they truly breathe.

The pursuivants had emptied Caraffa's baggage onto the ground in their search. His clothes were strewn on the ground. Markus picked up the pieces, squeezing them.

"Ah," he said, feeling. He cut into the seam of one of Caraffa's doublets. Jewels fell out. Markus grinned. By the time they had finished, diamonds, rubies, emeralds, and pearls filled Magda's two hands, cupped together.

They buried Unks where he fell. Magda gathered wildflowers and arranged them around the wooden cross they put over him. They said a prayer for him, and then one for Cunrat and another for Nutker.

They did not linger, eager to be out of Savoy. They went west, into the Jura, taking care to obscure their trail.

They made camp that night in a glade by a stream. The night was clear, the stars bright above.

By the fire Dürer told how he'd rousted poor old Rostang out of sleep to inform him about the urgent imperial dispatch that had arrived. A grievous error had been discovered. The men now languishing in the dungeon were imperial agents after all, not impostors. They had been sent to protect Count Lothar after an assassination plot against him had been discovered. The previous dispatch was lies, foul lies provided by a French spy, since unmasked.

Markus said, "He believed this?"

"Hard to know," Dürer said. "The old boy was logy. His eyelids kept closing as I spoke. He was still in a stupor from the incense and the wine. He gave the order to release them. I think he just wanted to go back to bed. He was too tired even to make his *'Mm!'* "

They laughed.

"I waited for them at the castle gate. Identified myself as an imperial agent. Told them it was I who'd got them released. They were grateful, after being in the dungeon with rats.

"I told them that I had identified Lothar's killer. Italian, working for the French, to make mischief for the Emperor. That he had now abducted a girl, a good *German* girl, who had come with her husband to Chambéry to make a pilgrimage. Her husband and a companion were giving chase."

Dürer smiled, looking very pleased with himself.

"Tell it again," Markus said.

"But I have told it twice."

"I know. But I want to hear it again."

Dürer told the story again, this time making his role sound even more heroic, which made Dismas smile.

Dismas said, "So Urbino has the Shroud of Chambéry. Too bad for Duke Charles. But at least the replacement is an authentic Dürer."

Dürer shook his head. "No."

"What do you mean?"

"The shroud Caraffa held in the apartment—it was *my* shroud."

Dismas stared. "But Cunrat and Nutker switched them."

"Cunrat knocked the reliquary off the table. Don't you remember? And they both disappeared from view? They were both in a fog from breathing the incense. They botched the switch. It was the real Shroud they put back in the reliquary."

"But how can you know this?"

"Don't you think I recognize my own work? Caraffa was this close to me in the apartment. I saw. That's what gave me the idea to tell him he'd given Urbino a fake. To buy time. It happened to be the truth."

Dismas sighed. "Christ."

"Yes. Christ."

They stared into the fire.

Magda said, "Will Urbino give your shroud to Pope Leo?"

"I suppose, yes. After he's slobbered all over it," Dürer said.

Dismas considered. "The Pope can't very well display it from the balcony of Saint Peter's. How would he explain it? 'Here is the Shroud of Chambéry. My nephew stole it for me'?"

Dismas smiled and pointed at Dürer.

"Look, how he smiles. Are you happy, Nars? Yes, you are happy, aren't you? Your shroud will take its place in Rome, in the private collection of the Vatican. A masterpiece, by the greatest painter in Germany."

Next morning at dawn Markus bid them farewell. He was off to Spain and his cities of gold.

"God be with you, Markus. Bring me back a cobblestone."

They took the long route, on foot, ten days through the Jura foothills, to avoid Savoyard patrols. The terrain steepened as they made their way into the high Jura. Then they turned northeast, toward Geneva, and one afternoon saw before them in the distance the great lake, shimmering. Here was the fork in their road.

Dürer and Magda hugged. Dismas saw the tears in Nars's eyes.

"Good-bye, Little Sister. Look for yourself in my work. I will make you immortal."

"Good-bye, Painter. God be with you."

Dismas walked with Nars some way so they could say their farewells alone.

They stood awkwardly, neither able to think of anything left to say.

"So. What will you do for art in Switzerland? Get some inbred half-wit to paint you a picture of cows?"

"I'm done with art. If I want to look at cows, I'll find real ones."

It was time.

"Well, Nars."

"Well, Dis."

They embraced and parted. They never saw each other again.

Vale

Charles III, Duke of Savoy, called "Charles the Good," cultivated an alliance with the Habsburg Holy Roman Emperor, but his duchy was finally overrun by foreign armies, mainly French, in 1536. He fled Chambéry and lived out the remainder of his life dependent on relatives, dying in exile in 1553. His great possession,

The Shroud of Chambéry was nearly destroyed in 1532 in a fire in the Holy Chapel. There being no time to assemble the four different keys required to unlock the iron grille protecting the reliquary, a blacksmith was summoned. He pried open the grille. The reliquary had melted from the heat, but strangely—some insist miraculously—the Shroud survived intact. When French troops invaded Savoy in 1535, the Shroud was moved to keep it from being plundered. In 1578, it was permanently installed in Turin, the relocated capital of Savoy, where it has since remained as the Shroud of Turin.

Giovanni di Lorenzo de' Medici, later Pope Leo X, died in 1521 of a violent chill following an operation on an anal fistula. His lavish spending left the Vatican bankrupt upon his death. His failure to deal conclusively with the growing demand for church reform in Germany, along with his arrangement with Albrecht over sales of indulgences, led to Luther's protest and all that followed. Not ordained into holy orders until after he became pope, Leo was the last nonpriest to be elected supreme pontiff of the Church.

Lorenzo di Piero de' Medici, Duke of Urbino, ruler of Florence, dedicatee of Machiavelli's tract *The Prince*, died in 1519 of tuberculosis aggravated by syphilis, less than a month after the birth of his daughter Catherine de' Medici. Unpopular and arrogant, Lorenzo's death went unmourned. His daughter became queen of France as the wife of Henry II. She produced ten children, three of whom became kings, and two, queens. Lorenzo's tomb in Florence's Church of San Lorenzo is often mistaken for the nearby tomb of his more famous namesake grandfather, Lorenzo the Magnificent.

Friar Martin Luther was finally excommunicated by Leo X for heresy in 1521. His indispensable patron, Frederick of Saxony, continued to protect him from Rome and the Holy Roman Emperor Charles. It is unlikely Luther would have survived without Frederick, who ironically remained a devout Catholic to his death, even as his protection of Luther deepened the cataclysmic schism from Rome. Shielded from powerful enemies, Luther continued aggressively to promulgate his Reformation. While in hiding in Frederick's castle at Wartburg, he translated the New Testament into the vernacular and later completed his translation of the entire Bible. Luther's Bible displays his genius for plain, emotionally charged narrative. It is regarded by many scholars as the basis of the modern German language. Lucas Cranach, court painter at Wittenberg, stood best man at Luther's wedding to a former nun in 1525. Luther died in 1546, married, fat, and happy. Centuries of religious warfare followed.

Frederick III, "the Wise," Elector of Saxony, gave up collecting his beloved relics in about 1520. The Reformation triggered by his university employee Martin Luther had undermined popular belief in their miraculous powers. Of his 19,013 relics, only one survives today: a beaker of cut glass, treasured not for any holy association, but because it belonged to Luther, who received it as a gift from Frederick's grandson. Frederick died in 1525. He is buried in the Wittenberg castle church, whose front door opened onto the Reformation.

Philippus Aureolus Theophrastus Bombastus von Hohenheim, called **Paracelsus,** was to medicine what Luther was to religion—an iconoclast and revolutionary. He rejected much if not all of conventional medical thought in favor of more natural remedies. He said that he learned more about healing from executioners, Gypsies, old wives, soldiers, and tavern keepers than from all the dry, classical scholastics under whom he had studied in the leading universities. He traveled extensively in the East, bringing opium to the West, which he refined into a distillate he called ladanum or laudanum (from the Latin *laudare,* to praise). Paracelsus's ladanum contained among other ingredients crushed pearls, musk, and amber. He can thus be considered the father of modern Western anesthesiology. He prescribed the first effective treatment of syphilis, using mercury; diagnosed silicosis in miners, which had previously been attributed to the evil influence of mountain spirits; and anticipated the modern practice of homeopathy and psychiatry. He died in Salzburg in 1541.

Albrecht of Brandenburg, Elector of the Holy Roman Empire, Archbishop of Magdeburg, and Cardinal Archbishop of Mainz, continued to sell indulgences even after the practice of hawking temporal forgiveness precipitated Luther's ninety-five theses and the Protestant Reformation. However, the market for indulgences soon collapsed as a result of Luther's reforms, along with the concomitant decline of Roman Catholicism in Germany and Northern Europe. He died in 1545, owing large sums to the banking house of Jacob Fugger.

Dominican friar Johann Tetzel, Albrecht's grand commissioner for indulgences, fell into disgrace, accused of fraud and embezzlement. He retired to a monastery in Leipzig, where he died in 1519, broken in spirit. Shortly before his death, he received a gracious letter from

Martin Luther, absolving him of responsibility for the scandal of indulgence selling, on the grounds that the practice had been ordained by higher ecclesiastical authority.

Albrecht Dürer, greatest of German painters, died in Nuremberg in 1528 at the age of fifty-six, possibly of complications from malaria. He left an estate valued at 6,874 florins, a considerable sum. Dürer painted one last portrait of the Cardinal of Mainz, in which Albrecht is said by some to bear a distinct resemblance to the subject in another of Dürer's works: Caiaphas, High Priest of the Sanhedrin, who condemned Christ to death.

No official records exist concerning the former relic master to Frederick of Saxony and Albrecht of Mainz, called **Dismas.** The only evidence that he existed consists of a simple gravestone in a Lutheran cemetery in the mountain village of Mürren, Switzerland, inscribed

DISMAS • MAGDA
MDXXXI • MDXXXIII
heute wirst du mit mir im paradiese

which, translated from Luther's New Testament, is

this day shalt thou be with me in paradise

Appendix

Extracts from the Report on the Findings of the Shroud of Pope Leo Investigation Commission (SPLIC)

- Characteristics of man in shroud image: height: 177.8 centimeters; weight (approx.) 79.3 kilograms; estimated age: 45 years. (Cf: estimated age of man in image on Turin Shroud: 33 years.)
- The blood on the shroud is human, consisting of five different types (O+, O–, A+, A–, and B+; negative traces bilirubin, indicating near-zero likelihood blood(s) came from person(s) undergoing severe stress, torture (e.g., beating, scourging, crucifixion, etc.).
- Wound areas (forehead, wrists, rib cage, feet) reveal 21 trace elements commonly found in egg yolk; also vinegar, white wine, and cinnabar.
- Traces of proteolytic venom present in the blood, of a type associated with common European viper (*Vipera berus*).
- Body image reveals traces of sodium, potassium, calcium, and magnesium consistent with eccrine sweat secretions, average pH level 5.2 to 5.4.

- VP-8 Image Analysis of eye socket area reveals contours consistent with Roman sesterce-type coins of 1st century AD.
- Linen is three-to-one twill "herringbone" weave, consistent with *tunica inconsutilis*–type seamless tunic; note: *identical* to Turin Shroud linen type; likely provenance: Palestine [see "Palynological Results," Section 14 (vii)].
- 47 distinct plant pollens present in shroud linen, including six halophytes prevalent in the Negev Desert. Note: outermost folds of Shroud indicate trace elements of *Papaver somniferum* (i.e., opium).
- X-ray, reflectance spectrometry, thermography, and photomicrographology tests consistent with blood- and sweat-permeated burial cloth.
- Radiocarbon-dating (carbon-14) on linen indicates age of shroud between 1100 and 1240 AD. (Note: carbon-14 testing on Turin Shroud estimated dates between 1260 and 1390 AD.) Leo Shroud would thus appear to predate Turin Shroud.

In the course of photographing the Leo Shroud, researchers noted a similarity between the image of the man in the shroud and a self-portrait (1500 AD) by the German artist Albrecht Dürer.

Research was unable to establish Dürer's whereabouts between February and June 1519. The Shroud of Chambéry (now Turin) was exhibited there on 4 May 1519. While the time frame is inconclusive, the coincidence is not absent interest.

The Commission emphasizes that it takes no position on this particular aspect of the Leo Shroud, whose provenance remains, even after thorough scientific and archival analysis, a mystery known only to God.

Respectfully submitted,
Silvestre Prang, S.J.
AMDG

Sources

Bainton, Roland H. *Here I Stand: A Life of Martin Luther*. New York: Abingdon-Cokesbury Press, 1950.

Bugler, Caroline. *Strange Beauty: German Paintings at the National Gallery*. London: National Gallery, 2014.

Cahill, Thomas. *Heretics and Heroes: How Renaissance Artists and Reformation Priests Created Our World*. New York: Nan A. Talese/ Doubleday, 2013.

Cohn, Norman. *Europe's Inner Demons: An Enquiry Inspired by the Great Witch-Hunt*. London: Chatto & Windus, 1975.

Craughwell, Thomas J. *Saints Preserved: An Encyclopedia of Relics*, New York: Image Books, 2011.

de Wesselow, Thomas. *The Sign: The Shroud of Turin and the Secret of the Resurrection*. New York: Dutton, 2012.

Freeman, Charles. *Holy Bones, Holy Dust: How Relics Shaped the History of Medieval Europe.* New Haven: Yale University Press, 2011.

Geary, Patrick J. *Furta Sacra: Thefts of Relics in the Central Middle Ages*. Princeton, NJ: Princeton University Press, 1978.

Guibert of Nogent. *Monodies and On the Relics of Saints: The Autobiography and a Manifesto of a French Monk from the Time of the Crusades*. Translated by Joseph McAlhany and Jay Rubenstein. New York: Penguin Books, 2011.

Hale, J. R. *Renaissance Europe: 1480–1520*. Oxford: Blackwell, 2000.

Harrington, Joel F. *The Faithful Executioner: Life and Death, Honor and Shame in the Turbulent Sixteenth Century*. New York: Farrar, Straus and Giroux, 2013.

Hibbert, Christopher. *The House of Medici: Its Rise and Fall*. New York: Morrow, 1974.

MacCullouch, Diarmaid. *Reformation: Europe's House Divided, 1490–1700*. London: Allen Lane, 2003.

McCrone, Walter. *Judgment Day for the Shroud of Turin*. Amherst, New York: Prometheus Books, 1999.

Ozment, Steven. *Magdalena and Balthasar: An Intimate Portrait of Life in 16th-Century Europe Revealed in the Letters of a Nuremberg Husband and Wife*. New York: Simon & Schuster, 1986.

———. *The Serpent and the Lamb: Cranach, Luther, and the Making of the Reformation*. New Haven: Yale University Press, 2011.

Strauss, Gerald. *Nuremberg in the Sixteenth Century*. New York: Wiley, 1966.

Vaughan, Herbert. *The Medici Popes: Leo X and Clement VII*. New York: G.P. Putnam's Sons, 1908.

Wellman, Sam. *Frederick the Wise: Seen and Unseen Lives of Martin Luther's Protector*. North Newton, KS: Wild Centuries Press, 2011.

Wilson, Ian. *The Shroud: The 2000-Year-Old Mystery Solved*. London: Bantam, 2010.

Winder, Simon. *Germania: A Wayward Pursuit of the Germans and Their History*. New York: Farrar, Straus and Giroux, 2010.

Zuffi, Stefano. *Dürer*. Munich: Prestel, 2012.

ACKNOWLEDGMENTS

John Tierney and Edmund and Sylvia Morris spent far more time on this than I had any right to ask, much less expect. Their help was invaluable. A plenary indulgence to each.

Thanks, too, to Anne Fadiman, Cullen Murphy, and Caitlin Buckley. At Simon & Schuster, Jonathan Karp and Trish Todd. At ICM, Amanda Urban.

My wife, Katherine Close, not only read every draft with patience and diligence, but drove the author from Wittenberg to Mainz at 115 miles per hour; then to Basel and Chambéry at a more sensible speed. This book would not have been possible without her, or worthwhile. *Gratias tibi ago.*

ABOUT THE AUTHOR

CHRISTOPHER BUCKLEY is the author of sixteen previous books (among them, *Thank You for Smoking* and *Losing Mum and Pup*), a number of them satires on contemporary American politics. During the most recent election cycle, he concluded that American politics were sufficiently self-satirizing, and decided to venture backward in time, to a more innocent, less cynical era and place, like, say, early sixteenth-century Holy Roman Empire, where he found abundant material and characters, some of whom actually existed.

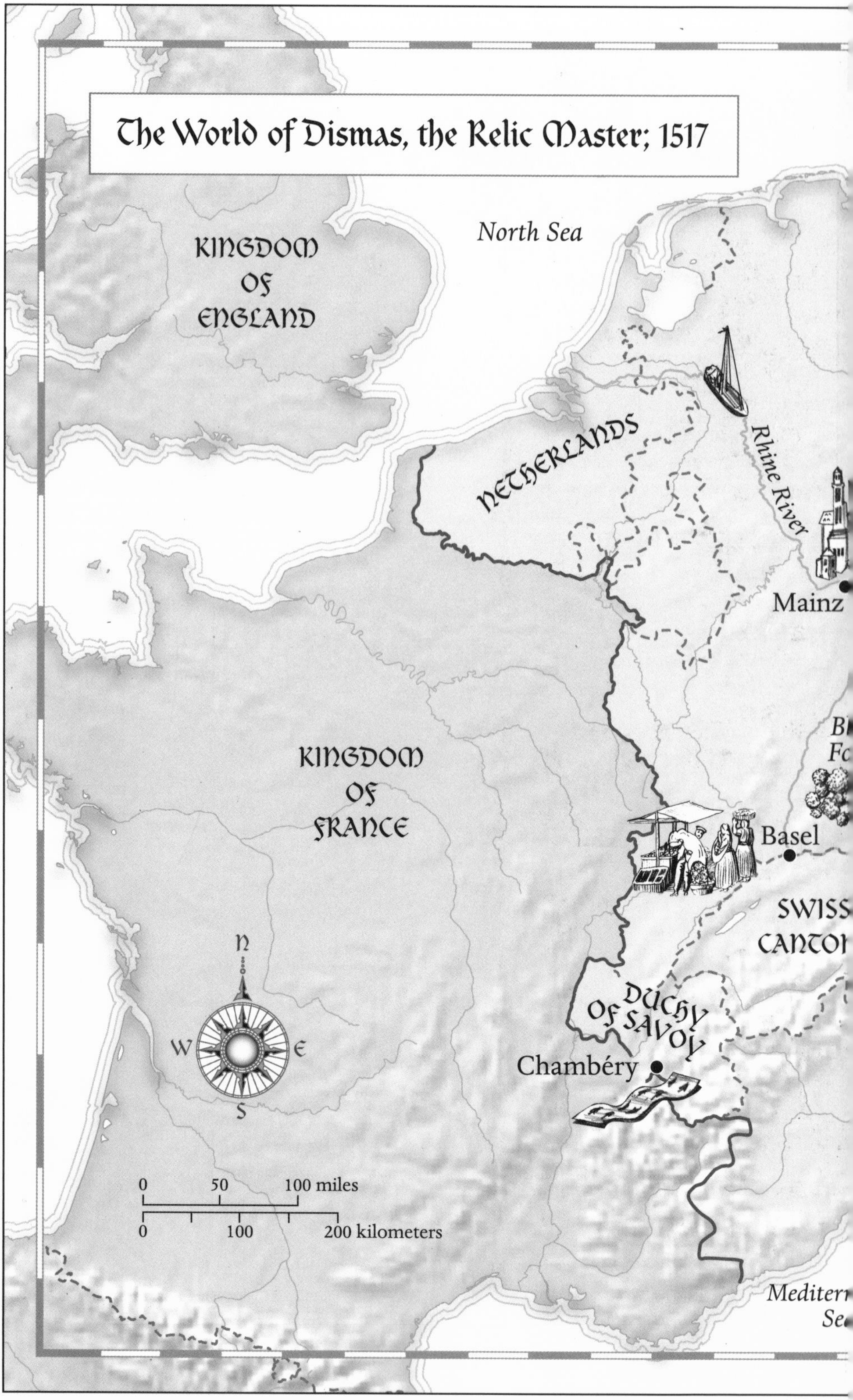

The World of Dismas, the Relic Master; 1517
North Sea
KINGDOM OF ENGLAND
NETHERLANDS
Rhine River
Mainz
KINGDOM OF FRANCE
Basel
SWISS CANTO
DUCHY OF SAVOY
Chambéry
N
W
E
S
0 50 100 miles
0 100 200 kilometers
Mediterr Se